CICI McNAIR was born in Mississippi, graduated from Briarcliff College in New York, and had many jobs before becoming a journalist. In Toronto, she worked as a researcher for CBC-TV's award-winning documentary on organized crime, *Connections*. In Rome, she was a news writer, newscaster, and producer of documentaries for Vatican Radio. She was also the weekend news anchor for WROM-TV. In Los Angeles, she worked in film.

McNair has published several novels, a memoir, and has written about true crime. Her firm, Green Star Investigations, handles all sorts of cases including missing persons, intellectual property, stolen art recovery and homicide.

Cici McNair is a private detective living in Paris.

Books by Cici McNair

Detectives Don't Wear Seat Belts
Never Flirt with a Femme Fatale

Books by Clarissa McNair

Garden of Tigers
A Flash of Diamonds
Dancing With Thieves
The Hole in the Edge

Detectives Don't Wear Seat Belts:

"A wonderful, wonderful read, an amazing true story told in the voice of a born storyteller . . . she's funny, she's honest and completely fascinating . . . This is a memoir written by someone who made her own life into an adventure story, and who knows exactly how to grab your hand and pull you along."
—Perri Klass, author of The Mercy Rule

"This improper Southern belle's memoir as a private detective combines the immediate impact of a newspaper column with the ironic detachment of a fine novel. McNair's crafted vignettes of low-rent detectives are like chocolate truffles: dark, bittersweet and addictive."
—Bruce Schimmel, founder and columnist, Philadelphia City Paper

"Detectives may not wear seat belts, but you definitely should hang on to your seat when you read Cici McNair's saucy, smart memoir about a hot female P.I. from the South. I always knew Cici was a pistol, but she really blew me away with this one!"
—Lewis Burke Frumkes,
author of How to Raise Your I.Q. by Eating Gifted Children

"Cici McNair is the most glammapuss lady detective since Nora Charles . . ."
—Phoebe Eaton, novelist and screenwriter

Never Flirt with a Femme Fatale:

"A classic from the hands of a pro . . . what makes this book work so well is that the author is part of the drama. Besides being a fine and skilled writer, she is a Private Investigator."
—John W. Bowers, associate professor, Columbia University,
and author of Love in Tennessee

"Real life drama told with a master storyteller's touch. If you like Dominick Dunne then you will love *Never Flirt with a Femme Fatale*."
—Donna Huston Murray,
author of The Ginger Barnes Main Line Murder mysteries

Kiss *the* Risk

Cici McNair

FEDORA PRESS

First edition March 2013

Library of Congress Cataloging-in-Publication Data
McNair, Cici
KISS THE RISK

ISBN: 978-0-9661087-2-9

I wish to thank Stephen Altschul, David M. Anderson, James C. Esposito, Dorothea Halliday, Charles A. Intriago, Lisa Romanello Johnson, Renwick Matthews, Judith Natalucci, Jan and Tad Ogden, and Michael McDonald for expert advice and inspiration.

CONTENTS

AUTUMN, 2007

Life is being on the wire, everything else is just waiting.
—Karl Wallenda

MANHATTAN

The door of the sleek, black limousine was opened by the chauffeur and a tall, handsome man stepped out. His driver, his communications director in the back seat, his security detail in the nearby black SUV all watched him stride away. He ambled through the lunchtime crowds, crossing the sidewalk towards the nearest office building. Several people smiled in recognition. "Great job!" called a man in a sweat suit. He nodded, kept walking. Clutching his cell phone, he positioned himself near the revolving doors, head down, far enough away from the nearest smoker so as not to be noticed or overheard. He knew the number by heart. Two rings. "Imperial Club, V.I.P."

"It's John Wolf. Did you get the money?" He listened. "Good. I want one hour today."

His voice conveyed tension. "Seven o'clock. With Caroline." He listened. "Yes, I'll hold." He turned to look back at his little entourage. They were waiting for him but he felt they were watching him. The silence on the line. Limbo. Waiting. He glanced at his watch, took a deep breath. Waited another long minute. Finally. He listened. "Well, I wanted Caroline." He switched the phone to the other ear. "Okay. Tell Savannah it's the Waldorf. Room 208. Thanks."

He snapped the phone closed and walked quickly back to the car. The door was opened by his driver and he slid in. Todd was reading *The New York Times*. He folded the paper closed and shook his head. "It's Brown. And it's every Republican in Albany. They're on the warpath."

"So what else is new?" said the governor.

"They're out to get you," Todd was saying as the limousine pulled away from the curb and slid, like a giant fish, into the surging river of midtown traffic.

MIAMI —THE FONTAINEBLEAU

The girls were lying on their backs, naked, amid tangled pink sheets. One brunette, one blonde, both in their twenties, they seemed to be all sleek arms and legs splayed out over the enormous bed. Clothes, his, hers and hers, were draped over the white brocade armchair, and three empty bottles of Veuve Clicquot were on the floor.

The Fontainebleau bedroom was a shambles. Stumbling in after a long dinner and too many mojitos, they'd opened the curtains for some reason then forgotten to close them and the fierce Florida sun was streaming in. A ray of it glinted on the glass table top; the magazines had been swept to the floor and the table was bare except for a lace-trimmed Perla bra and traces of a fine white powder.

Caroline rolled onto her side and looked at Alyssa. "Well, that was easy, wasn't it?" she said in a whisper. The huge, hairy back was between them. Massive shoulders, black hair, red face with black stubble, open mouth.

Alyssa scowled and whispered back. "He's drooling. You're lucky you don't have to see this." She fumbled for her watch, looked at the time and said, "It's eight o'clock and we're technically free." She was already thinking of her desk, the phone calls, the condo deal with the Venezuelan that was on the cusp of closing.

Caroline sighed. Her flight back to LaGuardia left at eleven. She could be at the auction house in plenty of time before tonight's sale. "Should we wake him for breakfast and tips or flee the scene of the crime?"

Miami airport was always a study in chaos. Too many people starting or ending vacations, too many people speaking Spanish, thought Cate. Horns honked, taxis broke rank and spat sunburned people out of back seats who then fumbled for luggage and change. In minutes, they'd realize they looked silly and regret those straw hats. The glass revolving doors glittered as they spun one person after another from Technicolor Miami to the neutrality of the airport. Lines snaked along past other lines within little roped-off corrals crowded with suitcases and future passengers. A plump woman in a flowered dress was shouting in Spanish at a little boy and several people wondered if they should intervene. Airport security appeared in the form of a beefy Hispanic male with a large moustache that seemed to droop with the burden of his job and a heated conversation ensued. Minutes later, whatever was wrong had been righted and mother and child were silent, holding hands, back in line, staring straight ahead as if daring anyone to make a remark.

Cate looked at her fellow travelers and decided it should be illegal for some of these people to wear shorts. Reaching down to move her carry-on bag a few inches forward, she saw the sandaled foot of the man behind her. She winced at the yellow toenails and hair sprouting like black grass on each enormous stump of a toe.

Two hours later, she was sleepily gazing out the window as the sweep of turquoise ocean disappeared. She leaned back and closed her eyes. Thirty-one thousand divided by two was fifteen thousand dollars five hundred minus fifteen fifty for Lori. Client pays for this ticket and my airport taxis back and forth so that means that $13,950 is mine. Travel time is billed and divided the same way: half for me and ten percent of it for Lori. Divine. I am very tired but nothing a little makeup and a twenty-minute nap won't fix. It's really easy, she thought. Everyone assumes I have this massive trust fund from my stepfather and I do have this very good job at Christeby's. I dress the way I should dress, go to the right parties, live in the right sort of building and meanwhile, I'm socking away money. Thousands at a time.

She thought of the last year. Her mother had come down to New York and, during lunch, she dropped the bomb. Holtie had made a bad investment. Actually it was the same bad investment for the past twelve years. He put millions of dollars in a Wall Street fund run by the friend of a friend and suddenly the friend of a friend was exposed as a fraud. The whole thing was nothing more than a giant, international, fortune-rocking, Ponzi scheme. "It won't change everything," said Catherine calmly. "It's just that I'm afraid we'll have to put Sunswept on the market and—"

"What!" erupted Cate. The house on the Cape! "That's incredible! How can you even think of selling it?" She stopped, seeing her mother's face. "Is it that bad?"

Catherine took a sip of wine and nodded. "That bad."

The two women sat in silence. They'd had thousands of lunches and dinners across from each other. In Rome, in Paris, in London. Now they were at a little Italian bistro on Lexington Avenue. Cate wondered why her mother had suggested it instead of Nosidam or La Galoue on Madison. Those restaurants were familiar, reasonable, every day choices to the Burroughs. And definitely pricey. Cate never thought about money but neither would she describe herself as extravagant. A Chanel bag or a pair of thousand dollar shoes was basic. Basic was what she was used to and her basic was expensive. She was so used to expensive that she never looked at price tags. Whether it was toothpaste at Duane Reade or a gold bracelet at Tiffany's she'd noticed in the window, she never looked at the numbers.

Now it hit her. That bad. Two minutes passed. The waiter started to approach and then backed away. The two women were both blue-eyed brunettes, slender, well-dressed. The older one had chin-length hair parted on the side and clipped back from her oval face; the younger one had the same nearly black hair that fanned out below her shoulders. From ten feet they could have passed for sisters. Cate spoke. "What can I do?"

"If you could live on your salary, that would help. Just see if you can. Of course, if you need extra, I'm here. Holtie, too. We'll try to pitch in." Catherine Burroughs looked wan. Her pear-shaped diamond earrings sparkled just as always because diamonds are forever but her face seemed to sag with the very weight of delivering the news.

So Cate's life had changed with one lunch. In the span of a glass of wine, her world had been shaken, her sense of security snatched away like Linus's blanket.

Cate actually canceled magazine subscriptions and cashed the refund checks which were always less than twenty dollars; she did her own nails. Most difficult of all was stopping the monthly highlights. She noted their absence every time she looked in the mirror. Cate compared prices and hated it. It made her feel weak to not have all of what she wanted, exactly what she wanted. Then it became a point of pride to live on her salary and Cate became so determined that, those first few months after lunch with her mother, she'd given up pedicures. Pedicures! Then she'd gotten placed one notch higher at Christeby's and been broke in a new way. Broke on a higher plateau. It meant that she could never complain about being poverty-stricken though anyone who knew anything knew she was poorly paid. The difference between being poorly paid at a travel agency and poorly paid at an auction house was that it was assumed she could *afford* to be poorly paid. Like all the other sleek, well educated, history of art majors with trust funds who worked there.

The ad changed that. It leapt out at her and she e-mailed immediately. A one-hour interview at the Grand Hyatt, a contract and her life was forever different. Gone were the economy measures. Now she'd get a call for 'Caroline,' be asked if she were available and usually she said yes. Cate was always impeccably groomed with standing appointments everywhere so there was never a last minute panic of 'can't go.' She had facials and manicures, pedicures and waxing sessions. Of course, haircuts and those highlights. Hair, she sighed. I spend most of my life either getting rid of it or getting it the right length. She yawned, closed her eyes, and slept.

Cate Burroughs dreamed of a sailboat knifing through cobalt blue water.

She was pulling down the spinnaker as Ned shouted something at her. He was always shouting something at her on his boat; it was in the nature of being the crew. She moved quickly across the bow in sneakers, doing what came naturally after so many summers on Cape Cod. It was an afternoon of bright, white sun reflecting on the sparkling bay and there was a strong, clean breeze. They were rounding the first buoy. Then she felt it; something was wrong. There was something wet on her leg. Something sticky. Cate looked down and saw a viscous syrup on the inside of her thighs coming from her white shorts. It was black and smelled. Horrified, desperate for Ned not to see, she grabbed the yellow nylon spinnaker bag and tried to wipe herself clean but it only spread. Ned was shouting at her from the stern. "What's wrong?" She didn't answer him and wiped her legs with big swipes. He couldn't see. She couldn't let him ever see. It was a substance like motor oil, the odor was disgusting and there was more and more of it coming from underneath her shorts.

"Ah!" she snapped awake with a gasp, wondering where she was.

"I'm so sorry! The pilot has asked that all seat belts be fastened. We'll be landing in fifteen minutes."

Cate looked blankly into the flight attendant's face, then nodded. She crossed her legs and thought, there's nothing there. It's okay. Then she pulled on the seat belt and thought, Paging Dr. Freud.

KEY BISCAYNE

Usually by half past seven, Annie had done thirty laps in the pool and was stripping off her bikini bottoms, stepping out of them on the Mexican tile floor of her bathroom. Today she came in, straight from the tryst at the Fontainebleau, tore off her clothes and headed for the shower. Her condo was modern, brand new, with every possible 'featured feature,' she smiled to herself. From the outrageous European shower head to walk-in closet to stainless steel appliances and granite counter tops.

She washed her short blonde hair and then stepped out to face herself in the twelve-foot long, mirrored back splash behind the twin sinks. Her freckles were usually covered by makeup and she was lean not lush when naked. However, her full lips were sensual and something in her deep blue eyes dispelled any idea of innocence. "Not bad," she thought. Her body was taunt, tan; her stomach was so flat that the top of the bikini bottom actually stretched between her pelvic bones without touching flesh in between. "I'm strong," she said flexing one slender arm in the mirror and grinning at herself.

In twenty minutes, she was mascara-ed and dressed, perfumed and perfect, behind the wheel of the yellow Mini Cooper speeding down Ponce de Leon Boulevard to the office.

"Annie! Can you come and see me for a minute?" called Marta.

Haven't even sat down and she is *on* me, thought Annie. "Absolutely," she said walking past the dozen other desks to the glass cubicle.

"Sit," said Marta. Her black hair was coiled in a messy bun on the nape of her neck. She looked very tired and much older than forty-five. One of the young brokers, dying of curiosity, had managed to get a look at her Florida driver's license. Did she not sleep well or did she not go home and even try? wondered Annie.

"Can you go to the Tides Hotel tonight? It's a reception for stock brokers who are in Miami for a convention. Just mix. Give out our business card, talk to all the people you can. Just be there." Marta spoke with a deep voice and still had her Argentine accent.

Annie didn't care for her but she respected her, knew she worked hard.

"Sure, what time should I be there?"

"Seven o'clock, seven-thirty. A lot of these people will go on to dinner. If you can meet someone, in a group, and join them for the evening . . ." She stopped. "It would be good. Give out our card."

Annie was surprised she hadn't picked Maria or Elvira for this. One of the Spanish-speaking realtors. Then again, since they were married, maybe she hated asking them to spend even more time away from home and family.

"I'll give out our card to everyone within twenty feet," she said. "You can count on me to be charmingly aggressive. I'm feeling pretty fierce."

Marta smiled very slightly. It was close to a grimace. The two women had never taken to each other. Annie was too American for Marta and Annie thought Marta was a bitch, had witnessed her tirades to the cleaning woman. Annie thought Marta had been used to having servants in another life and never gotten over it.

One perk of doing anything for Marta was getting to leave early, decided Annie. At five p.m. she was steering into the river of traffic pouring off the ramp and onto I-95. At home on her balcony, she snapped open a diet soda and stared out at Biscayne Bay. Actually, she decided, Marta is doing me a favor because anyone at this party who wants to buy or sell property will be meeting me *first*. That means the listing will be mine unless they come to the office and specifically ask for someone else. Maybe I should try to like Marta a little bit.

Her cell rang on the table beside her. Seeing the familiar number, she answered with a smile. "Are you calling to save me from the Miami real estate bust?" It was Becky and she felt they were friends since Becky had lived in Miami up until a few years ago. "We're going down the tubes here. It's bad. I'm going to a reception in an hour. Business men. Both wannabe tycoons and has-beens on the way out. Probably mixed in with men who are just about to lose it all. They're going to serve peanut butter and call it pâté." They chatted. "Tomorrow at eight. Right. Four hours? I'll try for five and hint how great I am when I spend the night." She listened and laughed. "Thanks, Becky."

MANHATTAN

It was one of those typical long Sunday afternoons in the car. A stocky man with black hair going gray at the temples was driving. The slender young woman beside him wore her dark hair pulled back in a ponytail; she looked like his daughter, might have even been his granddaughter, but her hand rested lightly on his thigh. The black Honda slowed then stopped in front of the Upper East Side building. She'd wanted a Corvette but he had gotten his way and the Honda Odyssey.

A uniformed doorman trotted out and leaned towards the window; Bree pushed the button to lower it. "We called her. She knows we're here," she said and he nodded, touched his hat with one finger in an abbreviated salute and walked back under the awning.

Five minutes went by. "She's a flake," Jake said. "I know she's in demand but she better have all the money this time." He was tense about being double parked.

"I know," sighed the girl. "She told me she's having problems with someone she's dating. He's distracting her." She looked at her watch then pulled her jacket up and around her shoulders. She wasn't wearing it but had it bunched behind her.

Suddenly the back door opened and with a breath of perfume and a giggle, the girl was in the back seat. "Sorry. Sorry. I was locking the door and the phone rang and I had to go back." She handed Bree a brown envelope with 'Lehman Brothers' printed in the top left hand corner. "Ignore that return address," she said. "How are you?"

"Everything's good," said Bree. "Okay with you?" She passed the envelope to Jake and twisted around in the front seat to look at her. A Ford model, she was even-featured, pouty-lipped. The type in demand this year. Bree hated these little exchanges, wanted to go home. She couldn't persuade Jake that there had to be another way to get the money. Bree did not want to hear about a boyfriend, a problem at the gym or a co-op meeting. Talk about the clients was strictly forbidden.

"I have to tell you that Wednesday night was *not* what I thought it would be. I went to the Plaza. Up in the elevator, he opened the door. So far okay. After two flutes of champagne, he took off his jacket and told me that he wanted me to—"

Jake interrupted. "Stop!" he barked. "There's a clause in our contract that says no talk of that nature. Not acceptable."

The girl blinked and Bree gave her a 'that's the way it is' look. "Okay, okay! I'm in town all week if you want me and then I have a shoot on Long Island for *Bazaar* on Sunday. Ciao!" She was out of the car and gone in a flash of skinny jeans, blue suede boots and long straight, blond hair.

This was repeated, seven times, until after dark. One girl after another slipped into the back seat, handed over an envelope then hopped out of the car and, like a rabbit, disappeared into yet another doorman building. "Okay, just Sabrina and Anika on the West Side," said Bree.

At nine o'clock they were back in New Jersey, the car was parked underground and they were home. Five minutes later they were in their penthouse aerie, opening the white cardboard boxes of Chinese take-out. The glass dining room table faced a wall of glass so that anyone seeing them from the exterior would think that the couple sat in magical midair splendor, suspended above the Hudson with the glittering towers of Manhattan within arm's reach. They appeared to be royalty of a high-flying realm surveying their empire.

Cate Burroughs had been born Cathy Ann Baker in Akron, Ohio. She didn't really remember her father. Snippets, like nearly-forgotten dreams, jumped through her mind but these might have been memories of other fathers, of movie fathers or TV fathers and not her own real one who was actually less real. A laugh, but no face, a vague idea of being tucked into bed and kissed good night. Funny but she did remember her own voice calling out and crying for her Poppy. So she remembered the ache of missing him but not him. She wanted to remember things she thought she *should* remember. Like being pushed in the swing by him or being carried on his shoulders. There were photographs, of course, and she had stared at the figure on glossy paper and tried to imagine it as *her father* in three dimensions. Warm and breathing. She simply could not.

Her mother was entirely different. Cate's mother was her first memory. She was always beautiful, always admired for being beautiful. Whether it was in the post office, dropping her off at school or at the dentist, everyone, both male and female, stared at her mother. Catherine Baker was a slender brunette with wide-set eyes and white skin. Sometimes people said she reminded them of Elizabeth Taylor. Silly, thought her daughter. It was just the eye color that was nearly violet and the black hair and the perfect features. When little Cathy Ann was three, her mother told her she was getting married again. "This is your new father." She'd only seen him a few times when he had come to pick her mother up. Her mother always hugged her goodbye in a cloud of perfume and the tall man was nothing more than a large figure in an overcoat who patted her head as she sat in her high chair with the babysitter wiping her face. But he seemed nice enough. He was always calm and smiling, had a soft voice and a different way of speaking.

Soon after the wedding, which Cathy Ann did not remember, the three of them moved to Boston. Her mother began to talk differently. Cathy Ann could hear the frustration in her mother's voice when she would repeat something as if correcting herself. At first it was just in front of her new father and then it was all the time and gradually her very voice changed and she never stuttered or repeated a word again. Other things changed. Her mother stopped working and stayed home. Home was quite a big house and it overlooked a huge park that was bright green most of the year and absolutely white at Christmastime. In first grade, she learned to write her address which was Louisburg Square. It isn't pronounced the way it looks, her mother told her. It was 'Louie' like one of Donald Duck's nephews in the comics.

The biggest change was that little Cathy Ann Baker became Cate Baker Burroughs. The old name was left behind exactly like all the clothes in the closets of the rented apartment in Akron.

Cate was a scrawny, pig-tailed little girl with braces on her buck teeth. In fourth grade, she realized that her stepfather, John Holt Burroughs, was not only wealthy but powerful. "I think he owns some newspaper," she told a friend when asked. She was shocked when that same friend called her stepfather "sexy." The girl said her mother thought he looked like Cary Grant. Neither little girl knew who that was. Cate saw him only as Holtie: tall, broad-shouldered, with dark hair and a kind face.

In ninth grade, at Choate Rosemary Hall, the hated orthodontic hardware came off and people began to remark that she looked like her mother.

Ned Bartlett was Harvard, Cate was Barnard. "It was just one of those things," as Cole Porter wrote. First real kiss. First real frisson of attraction.

"Ned, we can't," she was sighing as she kissed him back and pushed him away at the same time. "Why not?" he asked when he could take a breath. He was putting his fingers in the waistband of her jeans.

Cate didn't want to fall in love with him and something she'd read, or heard, had convinced her that the first time was so special that you never forgot that first person. She wasn't sure she wanted it to be Ned but he was the only boy she was attracted to. Would he always be the only one? Was this good? Should there be choices and comparisons or should the attraction to him rule all others out? This was confusing.

Boys invited her for a beer, bought her a glass of wine, there were the dreaded football games which bored her stiff, there was Jason who wrote poetry and read it downtown in some squalid book store. She always felt like taking a shower after one of his readings. My God, had anyone dusted the poetry section since Sylvia Plath's suicide?

Ned took her sailing. Ned took her away from shore, out into the waves. Ned was the best-looking boy she'd ever seen in her life. He was stroke of the Harvard crew with that long, lean, anvil-shaped build. His face was high cheekbones and bright, dark eyes under straight black brows. He had a wide smile that was slow in coming. "But," said one freshman with a crush on him, "when Ned Bartlett does smile at you then *you have been smiled at.*"

Cate's college roommate didn't believe she could possibly be a virgin. First of all, she was so hot, even in a sweatshirt and jeans, that any male actually stopped whatever they were doing and stared at her as she walked past. Dressed up, with a touch of lipstick, Cate Burroughs was lethal.

Now Sarah was insisting, "It's just not possible, Catie! Are you mentally ill? Just do it and get it over with! I did it the first time when I was fifteen and—well, it's not a big deal." Sarah sat down on the edge of the bed and pulled on her knee-high boots. "You want pizza? I'll bring back a few slices."

"No thanks. Ned is coming at five."

Sarah sighed. "Ned is only Brad Pitt and George Clooney rolled into one and you—" She threw a pillow at her. "You're making *this god* wait?" Cate tossed it back at her and she ducked and then turned in the doorway. "You're making this too big a deal!"

Maybe I am, she decided that night in his room at the Carlyle. His parents kept a suite there; the elegant hotel on Madison Avenue was his home away from home. Cate had heard that President Kennedy had also had a suite there. For his mistress of the moment.

Cate was sitting on his lap in a big chintz-covered chair and she wondered if she'd always remember the green leaves and the yellow birds in the pattern. He began kissing her and this time when he scooped her up in his arms and carried her to the bed and undressed her, she cooperated. No virgin was he, thank God, she thought later.

On Sunday morning, we did it again, she told Sarah. She would say nothing more though her roommate wheedled for details. Cate wasn't the sort of young woman who told anyone her every thought. She had been that way as a little girl. Holtie had joked about it, hugged her and called her his Sphinx. She'd been conscious, as a four-year-old, of being in a new house because of this new man in her mother's life and she wanted him to like her, didn't want to disappoint him. The idea was that the tiniest thing might change her and her mother's bright and shining new reality. A reality of new clothes, a kitten of her own, birthdays with more than one present. So Cate's reticence to confide in anyone was all wrapped up in being well behaved, making the perfect presentation to the world, and never complaining.

So it was her secret, tinged with amazement, at how much she liked sex with Ned. All these years of riding horses and skiing, tennis and swimming and suddenly her body seemed aglow, alive in an entirely different way. The physiology made no sense. How could she feel so strong as her muscles seemed to melt? How was it possible to be so keenly aware of every cell as she weakly floated away? So this was *ecstasy*, she thought.

Cate stopped seeing anyone else. Ned's trips to Manhattan were nearly every weekend and on the others she flew to Boston and stayed in his apartment. They had dinner, made love, slept, waked up and made love again. The nights passed in a haze of warmth in his arms, his mouth on hers, his body over hers, inside hers. It was skin like silk and muscles and laughing and she loved its sheer athletic nature. So did he. Neither one of them could get enough.

Sunday morning was more of it and then a time of lying in bed, talking softly. Ned always wanted to talk about the future. He's like a six-year-old who always wants to hear the same bedtime story one more time, thought Cate.

Edward Horton Bartlett II was two years older, a senior, and had just been accepted at Harvard Business School. It was set. Maybe that was what provoked little pings of unease inside this thoroughly satisfied body of hers. All set. She had been programmed all her life and now it was assumed that she was joining her life with someone else's and *they* were all set. *We* are a set, she thought. Salt and pepper, a pair of candlesticks or matching end tables.

Two years passed. It was sailing in the summers which she loved, in between the trips to Europe that Cate took with her mother. Her stepfather remained in Boston and worked as his "two girls" toured every European capital and every museum. Cate and her mother knew them all, from the grandest like the Louvre and the Prado to the smallest one boasting one Munch or a few Rembrandt drawings. Catherine Burroughs had the same thirst to see them, had the same sensitivity towards art as her daughter.

The two women, sixteen years apart in age, were a strikingly beautiful pair as they sauntered arm in arm up a hilly street in Montmartre or crossed Brompton Road in Knightsbridge. They stayed at the Ritz in Paris, the Dorchester in London, the Beau Rivage in Geneva. When they were out for dinner, often an elegantly dressed man would send over champagne or a liqueur. Catherine would listen as the maître d' bowed his head and explained in a soft voice, then she would cast a glance across the room and decide if he were a worthy companion to join them for crème brûlée or the soufflé that would be another half hour in coming.

Catherine Burroughs was dazzling. She knew how to be charming, adorable and married all at once. There was usually a little curl of flirtation in her voice, in the way she ended a sentence with a blink of her amazingly violet blue, carefully made-up eyes; it was practiced, calculated and highly effective.

"Mother," laughed Cate in the lift at the Dorchester after one such dinner. "I felt sorry for him! The Marquis was ready to fall on the floor beside your chair and ask you to marry him! Or at least to run away with him! To someplace like Rio!"

"I'm married," shrugged Catherine as the doors opened. "I don't want anyone to ever forget that I'm married."

"Well, they *do*!" said Cate vehemently, wondering if she had the key card and opening her little silver evening bag to search for it.

They walked down the wide carpeted hallway to their suite. Catherine started to slide her card into the door, hesitated and turned to her daughter. "But Cate, no matter what . . . married or not . . . I still want to have fun."

When they entered the suite, the phone was ringing with Holtie on the line from Boston so Cate never had the chance to ask exactly what she meant. Her mother's words would resound in her ears for a long time.

DELAFIELD, WISCONSIN

Annie's mother and father married two days after high school graduation and before Christmas of that same year, Annie was born. Of course, people did the math but college had not been in anyone's plan so getting married and having a child was looked upon as inevitable. To everyone but Ingrid's father who was furious, it was simply sooner. The seventeen-year-old Richard Larsson was doing odd jobs around town until, as he put it, "Something I really want to do comes along." Athletic, a star hockey player in his very recent past, he often said he could not sit at a desk all day. He worked as a carpenter, sometimes he'd unload a truck for thirty dollars cash. In the winter months, he'd chop firewood and bundle it with kindling and sell it at Harmon's Nursery next door to Wal-Mart.

The couple rented a small house, more like a cabin, from Richard's parents. It had been used for storage until the newlyweds moved in with all their belongings in cheap suitcases and open cardboard boxes from the grocery store down the block. Richard's father was strict and if they couldn't pay the rent, they were out. They couldn't keep up so the young couple and their infant daughter had to leave before summer. Then it was the trailer that was free in return for fixing it up. It was a mess with torn linoleum that Ingrid could never get clean enough so the babies were never allowed on the floor. The bathroom was unspeakably primitive, the kitchen which was really a galley had no oven. Richard tried to fix the broken floor boards but he wasn't a very good carpenter. At twenty-three, he had three daughters and a wife, no steady job which meant no steady income and he had a gambling problem. Richard hung on, he really tried, insisted Ingrid who never stopped loving him.

The roof leaked over Annie's crib, there was the odor of mold in what was audaciously called the living room, the walls were thin and the Wisconsin winters were very cold.

Annie's first memories were of shouting voices and slamming doors. It was a merry-go-round of arguments, mostly about money, and making up.

At age five, Annie knew how to make a peanut butter sandwich, how to heat a bottle on the stove, and how to change a diaper. There was one thing she couldn't do and that was to go deaf to the fighting. At night, unable to sleep, she put wet pieces of toilet paper in her ears.

Richard Larsson disappeared on his oldest daughter's twelfth birthday.

That first week without him passed minute by minute. The second week the girls still ran to answer the phone but they stopped asking their mother when he was coming home. The third week the phone was disconnected because of an unpaid bill. "He's gone away," Ingrid said one night at supper. Nothing else. The police checked all hospitals within a hundred miles, did all they could. The tension and the fear Annie felt in those first few months became a raw ache of disappointment. His red truck was still parked in the driveway so he had simply walked out of their lives.

Early on, Anne Larsson learned to live with chaos. In Delafield, her friends' parents, her Sunday school teacher, her teachers from first grade all the way through high school graduation, thought her to be well taken care of, with shining blonde hair and clean clothes and a new parka every winter as she grew out of her old one. There was the hint of an imperfect life as she did live with her mother and her two younger sisters in her mother's parents' house. It was white, two-story, with an attic playroom, a back yard, a huge kitchen. The street in front was lined with trees that created a golden tunnel of autumn leaves every October. For four months of the year, the bare branches were sugared with snow and then bloomed into such a luxuriant green that Haddon Lane was often photographed for calendars and was featured in a "Visit Wisconsin" film produced by the state's Tourism Board.

That first week, one of the deans at the university recognized the address and said, "Very Norman Rockwell." Annie looked at him and thought, if you only knew.

Annie was sitting on her French grammar in the snow on a hill above the campus, watching the sun set on a day in late January. She was twenty-one; it was the start of her second semester, senior year, and last night she had turned down a third proposal of marriage. And for the third time, a man she liked to go to bed with but couldn't imagine being married to, had proclaimed her to be "too independent." She sighed and her breath came out like smoke. Not independent *enough*. My grandfather has paid for my boots, my sweater, even my underwear, she was thinking. I've got the scholarship and the job in the library for four afternoons a week and I'm making straight As but it's not enough.

Annie visualized her grandmother, always bent over, washing something, straightening something, cleaning something. Dishes, the floor, something. She saw her mother's tired face, still very pretty at thirty-eight, and thought, no. I won't be anything like you. I won't get pregnant. I won't go near a man who is more brute than human. Men for protection? Men for security? Or did all that boil down to men for money?

Mom works but even with overtime it would never be enough to take care of herself and me and two teenaged girls. There had been a check for a hundred dollars in today's mail. Written in Grandma's spidery handwriting, but signed by him, of course. It was for this next semester, for books, for toothpaste and shampoo at the co-op and I feel both grateful and uncomfortable. I will force myself to call tonight and thank him. It will be a chance to have a quick word with Mom and my sisters. Very quick for it was long distance and therefore an extravagance. No one could get through to him that times had changed and so had the price of a phone call.

Annie had felt guilty leaving for college, leaving her mother, grandmother and sisters to cope with all that went on in that white house on Haddon Lane. Behind the windows which were washed eight times a year, lived the women with their secret bruises.

Annie sat with bent knees drawn up under her chin staring out at the last rays of the glaring, orange sun. She thought, Grandpa, always respectfully called 'your grandfather,' can do what he wants because he has the money and we have to deal with him because he has the money. Next year I can take care of myself. In six months, actually. Suddenly she felt the cold and realized it was dark. Annie squeezed powdered snow tightly in her hands, shaping it. Then she stood up and swinging her arm in a wide arc threw the snowball straight ahead into the black sky, aiming right at the fingernail moon. I will have my own money.

BOSTON

Cate graduated in June. Ned was there. At the graduation and at the family dinner afterwards at some Italian restaurant on the West Side. Sarah and her parents were invited. Also included were Sarah's three kid brothers, triplets, who "should be on leashes," she warned the Burroughs. They all laughed at the time but it turned out to be a fairly accurate assessment.

The following week, Cate and her mother flew to Paris. Ned drove them to the airport, kissed them both goodbye. He was there when they flew back three weeks later. He is always there, thought Cate.

They sailed, they made love on his sailboat, in his Cambridge apartment, even dared to do it in her bedroom at the Burroughs house in Beacon Hill. The lovemaking was always intense, satisfying. The summer flew and on the last evening in August, Ned took her to dinner at a new restaurant on the water. The maître d' led them to an outside table; flowers seemed to be everywhere, candles flickered in hurricane lanterns and the air was faintly scented with salt.

"You're different tonight," she said watching him absent-mindedly skim the wine list.

He sat across from her wearing a navy blazer with silver buttons. The antique buttons from some great-great-uncle's admiral's uniform. Ned was windburned, tanned, looking serious. "Everything's different," he said. The waiter stood over them waiting for their drink order.

"Appletini," said Cate and Ned asked for a double vodka.

This is new, she thought. What's he steeling himself for?

"I really had no idea," she would tell her mother and stepfather the next morning at breakfast.

"Well, surely you did!" said Holtie.

"No." Cate shook her head. "I thought that we would just go on the way we are." She stared down at her fried egg and the yolk stared right back. "Or were."

'It's time,' said Holtie, folding *The Wall Street Journal* in that careful, narrow, one-column way of his. He was a man of few words, seeming to sit on the edge of any conversation involving his wife or daughter.

Catherine was talking to the maid about lunch, then leaned across the table, took Cate's hand and admired the ring again. "What about next spring?" she asked. "We could have a wedding at the club if we book it now."

"I don't know," said Cate slowly. She stabbed the yolk and it ran like yellow paint and she began to eat.

Upstairs, she stood in front of her bedroom mirror and imagined herself as Mrs. Edward Horton Bartlett the Second. She pulled her dark hair back and squinted, imagining some kind of veil. She turned to the side and imagined herself, big-bellied and pregnant. She said, aloud, to no one, "I'm Mrs. Bartlett. I'm Cate Bartlett. I'm Ned Bartlett's wife."

She didn't hear the phone ring but she did hear the maid calling, "Miss Cate, it's for you! It's Mr. Ned for you!"

Cate wore the emerald-cut diamond engagement ring exactly one week then gave it back. "I can't," she said, tears slurring her words. Ned was putting ketchup on his hamburger and looked up at her as if she had just shot him. She pulled off the ring and the big diamond blinked as it was dropped on the red checked tablecloth and then she was gone. 'Free' was the word that came into her mind as she blindly rushed between tables and out into the street. Free. Free. On her own again. It was sadness mixed with relief. This was the way she'd felt after the two abortions she'd had and not told anyone about. Cate was someone who could keep secrets.

MANHATTAN—GRAND HYATT NEW YORK

Bree watched as the small, slender girl threaded her way through the low tables and sofas in the lobby. She stood over Bree and Jake with a questioning look. "Bree?" she said softly.

"Sit down," said Jake and she obeyed. She started to cross her legs, then changed her mind, leaned back on the settee and then leaned forward. Dressed all in black, very New York. Very short skirt, very nice legs. Black silk sleeveless blouse, toned arms. One small chain necklace, gold hoop earrings. Her hair was light brown, quite short; her eyes were hazel, almond-shaped. She reminds me of Jean Seberg in *Breathless*, thought Bree. Jake had a thing for French films and they'd seen it the week before.

He was tough on these girls and made them nervous. Bree was closer to them in age and knew she came off as more of a friend. "Kelsey, hi! This is Jake." He nodded, she nodded then looked back at Bree.

"Tell us about yourself," said Bree.

"I'm twenty-four and live in Manhattan. The Village." She tried to be light about it. "The apartment's too expensive and too small." She smiled nervously. "Just like everyone else's here."

Bree thought, what a voice. What a great voice. It was rich, rather deep, very sultry. She wanted her to relax. "What about a glass of wine? White? Or red?"

A waiter took the order and was gone.

"Your application was well written and you seem to be the sort of person we might be interested in," said Bree phrasing it carefully. She could usually read someone in two minutes but it annoyed Jake when she made up her mind quickly. He liked the girl to go through the entire appointment wondering if she would be picked. "Do you have a job right now?"

"I'm getting my doctorate at Yale. I take the train to New Haven when I have to do research, meet with my professors. On the weekends, I work part at an art gallery in Soho." She stopped. "The gallery doesn't pay much."

Bree had heard this so many times that she had joked to Jake that the Manhattan art world was actually pushing girls into prostitution. The waiter placed the wine and the two club sodas on the table. Bree said, "Could you bring some hors d'oeuvres, please? Cheese? Something?" With a nod, the waiter was gone.

Bree watched her grasp the stem and sip. Slender hands, freshly manicured, nails painted a pale pink. Probably the standard Ballet Slippers. So far, okay. Jake was lousy with small talk so it was Bree who asked her how long she'd been in New York, what she liked about living in the city, how far along was she with her thesis. The cheese plate came and Bree watched how she grasped the knife, noted how she chewed. She was relaxing a bit, she would be okay.

Jake looked at his watch and at Bree who nodded. "We have a contract if you are interested in working for our dating service. It's called, as you know from the website, the Imperial Club V.I.P.. We have strict rules and regulations."

Kelsey thought, whatever. I am so desperate for money that I would happily sell you a kidney.

"It is not complicated," he said. Even if Bree loved Jake passionately, could not imagine life without him, she hated his rough accent. To anyone meeting him for the first time, not knowing his background, he probably came off as Gestapo with some Dracula tossed in. "It's pretty standard. It's for your protection, too."

Jake opened his brown leather briefcase, grasped a stack of pages and pushed them across the table at her.

She flinched. They always did. Jake looked to his right to ensure that the couple nearby were not paying attention and then began in a low voice. "We will set the price which will start at one thousand dollars per hour. We will split that with you and each give ten percent to the booker. You give fifty of your five hundred and so do we. So, you will make four hundred fifty dollars cash per hour. In the beginning. When you are ready, we will charge more for you and you will make more. You will always receive fifty percent of what the client pays. This will not change." His voice was "zees veel not change." Bree interjected, "Your only expense are the photographs. We will send you to our man."

"If a client wants you to meet him out of town, then all expenses and transportation will be paid for."

Kelsey was quickly reading, listening. "What about these photographs?"

"Don't worry about the price. They'll be very good and will bring you clients. Our photographer works with professional fashion models. These photos will make your money back in a week." Bree handed her a business card. "Tell him it's for Imperial. Justin knows what we want and he wouldn't dare overcharge you."

Kelsey sighed. "I wasn't thinking of the cost. I don't want anyone to ever recognize me. That's what I'm most afraid of."

"Understood. Everyone who works for us has another life," said Bree. "The pictures will show you from the nose down or from the chin down. You will be holding a scarf across your face or turned away from the camera." She picked up her pen. "Now, you have to choose another name. A sort of stage name. What would you like to be called from now on?"

This was the moment that she and Jake always laughed about on the way home. These girls all wanted exotic, ridiculous names. Someone named Linda wanted to be Lucrezia. One Ann wanted to be Anastasia. Pronounced the Russian way: Anna Stass Ee Uh. Every Jennifer wanted drama. Every Sarah wanted sizzle. This time there was no hesitation. "I always wanted to be called Karen."

The first blank was filled in with Bree's heavy black felt-tipped pen.

The new Karen stammered, began again. "I just—I don't know how to ask this but—what if someone wants me to do something sexual that I don't want to do?"

Jake answered immediately. He was dogmatic. "We have nothing to do with sex. This is a dating service. Whatever you do or do not do with a client has nothing to do with the Imperial Club."

Karen blinked in surprise and opened her mouth to speak but Jake continued, "You will be called to meet with a date and then it is up to you. Whatever you do is your affair." Bree almost laughed at the word 'affair.' "This is not to be discussed with me or Bree or with anyone else. Not the booker who calls you and arranges dates or with any other person. This will be a direct violation of our contract and we will terminate the agreement we have just made." His accent gave more force to his monologue.

Karen looked at him and blinked again. Bree gave her a conspiratorial "it's okay" look and Karen reached for the pages and continued reading.

Ten minutes later, they were standing in front of the hotel, shaking hands. Bree was telling Karen she'd call her when she received the photographs from Justin. They'd be on the website within a day.

Jake and Bree started towards the parking lot on the West Side. "Karen! That was a surprise!" They were in agreement about her rich, warm voice. "She'll be more than okay. We'll sell her on the site as fresh-faced girl next door."

The men were fast and gasped with surprise or slow and took forever to come, rocking back and forth and panting as the girl lay under them and thought, oh, for heaven's sake, you're going to miss your Monday night flight to Zurich.

A week after the interview, Kelsey stood in the middle of her studio apartment staring at her little white toy poodle. "Oh, Tinker, it's nearly six o'clock and how am I ever going to get a taxi when it's the changeover when they all scurry back to garages in Queens?" She walked into the bathroom. "If you are in your apartment worried about finding a taxi, how do you imagine you'll get through *the rest of it*!" She stared into the mirror over the sink, fussed with the suit collar and then abruptly yanked off the jacket. "Shit! I look like I'm going into a board meeting!'

She grabbed her cell phone and punched in the number. "Hi, Lori! It's Kels—I mean Karen! It's Karen and I don't know what to weaaaaar!"

Lori used her soothing voice. She could give this pep talk in her sleep. These girls were always nervous the first time. "Karen! Take a deep breath, sit down."

"Okay." She plopped onto the sofa but was taut as a wire. Tinker looked at her from his special red cushion with big, concerned golden eyes. Kelsey leaned over and kissed the top of his head.

"You've still got plenty of time. What's wrong with what you'd wear to the office?"

"I haven't been to an office in two years so I can hardly remember. But should I be wearing some kind of —what my mother would call a cocktail dress?" Oh, God, she thought, *do not* think of Mother *now*! "I mean, does he expect something backless, frontless, topless, with slits at the side?" She was nearly wailing, she could hear the whine in her voice.

35

"Absolutely not. He wants a ladylike gorgeous woman and that's what you are. That's why Jake and Bree picked you. Have you done your makeup?"

"Yes, I'm just sitting here with ten outfits draped everywhere."

"A simple black dress. Do you have one?"

"Yes. I wore it to the opera last week." She thought of James then told herself not to think of James. He knew the New York art world but he was gay and he was boring. "It's just back from the cleaners, but is it the right thing for *this*?"

"It's exactly right for this. You are going to be getting out of a cab in front of the Waldorf and walking through the lobby and going to the elevator. You want to look like any sophisticated New Yorker, dressed appropriately." Lori was on automatic pilot. She realized she needed a manicure. She studied a little chip on her thumbnail and kept talking. "None of these men want anything flash. Except maybe your underwear."

Kelsey swallowed thickly at the thought of a stranger seeing her that way. Her underwear was new. Very lacy. Bought especially for this. But was it lacy *enough*? As if she could read her mind, Lori said, "You'll be fine. Relax. Have a nice dinner but don't drink too much." She added, "If it helps, pretend you're in love. You might be, after champagne and caviar."

ALBANY, NEW YORK

Everyone in Albany, including security, especially security, knew that Todd Wyman had 24/7 access. He strode through the lobby with a nod to the guards, went up in the elevator and directly into the governor's office. It was grand, with a high ceiling, a large chandelier, lots of mahogany, a large desk in front of a large window. Everything in it was oversized and Teddy Cantor hated it. He much preferred to be in his home office on Fifth Avenue.

Todd flopped into a chair, shook out *The Wall Street Journal* and began to read. Cantor hung up the phone, glanced at his Rolex and said, "I don't usually see you before eight o'clock so where's the fire?"

"I'm looking at it," said Todd. "You're on fire."

Teddy laughed. "Yes, I am. Using the Martin Act for prosecutions is genius."

"They are calling you The Sheriff of Wall Street."

"Has a nice ring. I like it. Maybe I'll buy a Stetson."

"You're page one again," said Todd, tossing the paper at him.

"As long as they spell my name right," Teddy said as he tossed the paper back.

"You're an arrogant bastard, you know? Listen. Just stop grinning long enough to listen." He found his place and began to read. "Cantor's weapons are shame, embarrassment, and concern for reputation. Blah blah blah. Then they quote Danielson who says 'Cantor should be skewered for bullying Wall Street firms into enormous settlements without trials. These firms never had the chance to prove in court that they did anything wrong.'"

Teddy swung his feet up on his desk, leaned back in his chair with his hands locked behind his neck. "Cry me a river. Those cock-sucking pieces of shit with their after-hours trading, with their pimping out stocks they knew were worthless to gin up their investment banking. I'm nailing them to the wall."

Todd shook his head. "You know, just because you went to Harvard doesn't mean you can get away with—"

Cantor gave a bark of a laugh and swung his long legs down from the desk. "Oh, you Yalies! Insecure forever."

Todd stood up, dropped the newspaper on the coffee table and sighed. "I was going to say that you can't eviscerate the most powerful men in the country and not expect to be number one on everyone's hit list."

"It's a compliment," said Cantor. "I'm after them and they know it."

Todd was in the doorway; he called over his shoulder, "Go get'em, cowboy." He was frowning when he said it.

HYANNIS PORT, CAPE COD

"What are your plans?" Holtie asked Cate a week after she'd given the ring back. She sat on the porch of Sunswept with a glass of wine staring past the ocean, staring into space. He'd been reading and she was surprised when he spoke.

"I think I'll go back to New York and get a job, get an apartment." She'd worked it out in her head, confiding in no one. With one finger, she lightly stroked the white wicker of the chair arm, back and forth. She and her stepfather sat at one end of the long porch; half a dozen identical chairs with blue striped cushions were placed to the right of them towards the garden which was lush, verdant most of the year. On this summer day it was bright with Catherine's pink, white, and coral roses.

"New York? Not Boston?" he asked.

"I'd rather be in New York."

"Your mother and I would love to have you home again. I know you're all grown up but your room is—"

"Thanks, Holtie. I know. But I think I'll go back to New York."

It was comforting, she would think later. Holtie was so good to her. A soft pillow to fall on.

KEY BISCAYNE

Annie kicked off her shoes and poured herself a glass of white wine. Nice to be home at six. She plopped down in a chair out on the balcony and began to thumb through her mail. Poor Maria. Today at the office, she'd shown up wearing dark glasses in a failed attempt to hide another black eye. She told Annie, Elvira and Marta she was now living with her sister and looking for a one bedroom to rent. No one had to ask why. Her husband, handsome and urbane, beat her. Finally, she had had enough.

Annie gazed out at the sweep of Biscayne Bay. Like crushed, liquid sapphires, she decided. The sky was white as snow. She remembered the first time. After Christmas vacation. Grandpa had shoveled the walk and was taking off his jacket in the front hall. Annie had put her backpack for school there on the floor right under the hooks where their coats and scarves hung. She was at the kitchen table, her mother and grandmother were at the stove.

"Goddammit!" The two women turned as one when he appeared in the doorway, red-faced from the cold or from anger, and began shouting. Grandma said, "Sven! Stop all that excitement! Your oatmeal's ready. Annie didn't mean for it to be in your way!" To the little girl's horror, Grandpa knocked her down. Annie saw a blur of red gingham apron and the elderly woman lying like a pile of clothes on the kitchen floor. The only noise was the clatter made by the metal ladle as if flew from her hand. Ingrid bent over her mother holding a damp dishcloth to her face, crying. Grandpa stormed out, calling them "brainless bitches."

Evidently this had happened all through her grandparents' marriage, all through her mother's growing up years but it was the first time Annie had seen it. The fear made her feel that her small, skinny little body had turned to water. She didn't feel thirteen, she felt as if she didn't exist.

A phrase that rang in Annie's ears long after she'd left that house was "decent, God-fearing people." Some politician running for Mayor had called the good citizens of Delafield that during a campaign speech on television.

Lutheran, Bible-reading, conservative and yes, probably God-fearing but let's waffle on the "decent," Annie thought. Was it decent that all five females lived in fear of the patriarch of the household? The brawny Swede who was her grandfather often punched his wife, his daughter and granddaughters for the smallest transgression. Too much salt on the fish at dinner, an overheard piano practice with too many wrong notes, a too-long phone call, a lost glove. Bam! The fist never came out of nowhere as Sven Karlson was a large man of six foot three but it was always sudden, always caught its target between the shoulder blades, at the top of a thin arm or under the chin as a horrible surprise. "He has the knack," said Kristin to her older sister, "to hit us where it won't show."

BOSTON

Holtie was disappointed by the broken engagement. He didn't understand his daughter at all sometimes. Or most of the time. He turned his attention back to the editorial on global warming and thought he'd run it past legal since they'd named several corporate entities. His mind wandered. Cate was just as complicated as her mother. He didn't understand Catherine either but it didn't matter as they got along perfectly.

There were really no arguments. Not ever. If he were provoked or disagreed, he would clear his throat, push back his chair and simply leave the room. No drama, no door slamming. He was a room leaver.

John Holt Burroughs was happy with his life and with the two women who ran it on smooth, parallel tracks. He existed in an orderly professional world with a very bright secretary who now insisted on being called an administrative assistant. His agenda as a publisher was Leona's agenda. She had been precise, loyal and utterly reliable for eighteen years.

At home, Catherine always had fresh flowers in the living room and on the dining room table, made sure all was flawless, that meals were on time and that she looked gorgeous. John knew she was very beautiful and told her often. He basked with her at his side. Her clothes, her makeup, her elegance. She was a universe away from the women his friends had married. Some of them so blue-blooded that they actually seemed anemic. Lots of navy blue, he remembered Catherine saying dryly after a lunch at his club. Whereas Catherine herself was more likely to wear turquoise or lavender.

John Holt Burroughs was not alone in finding his wife difficult to categorize. "She's hard to describe," said Wendy Trent, one of Catherine's Cape Cod acquaintances. She was talking to her sister who was visiting from Vermont. "She's John's first wife but she arrived with the daughter. They never had children together. She is most definitely not Boston born, not New England educated." Wendy suddenly wondered where Catherine had gone to college. Not around here, she was sure. She was not the only matron who wished that John Holt Burroughs had married someone from Boston. He was a very handsome man, with all that inherited money, an Ivy League background, and that incredible house on Louisburg Square. But, even in his thirties, he'd taken his time about commitment. Then, somehow, after all the deb parties and dating "appropriate" girls up and down the Eastern seaboard, he met Catherine and brought her home as his wife. Wendy added, "She picked up the mannerisms of Boston on her own."

Mitzi Belton joined in, "But there's an edge there. It's sort of like the time she was wearing that high-necked, long-sleeved black sheath and then, remember? When she turned around, the whole back was bare! Right down to the waist!"

"Do I ever remember!" laughed Alice Rainer. "At the symphony. And my husband still remembers!" She tried to keep smiling but his obvious delight at seeing the other woman's toned, silky back still annoyed her.

"She is sort of a mix of first and second wife but without the blatant sexuality of some of these young, blonde second ones," mused Mitzi.

Catherine Burroughs put on no airs, was friendly and generous. Generous to someone shy at a dinner party which was her innate gracious nature. She was also generous on a quiet, personal level as in paying for the maid's daughter to go to a specialist for lupus. As for charity work, she did the absolute minimum. It bored her senseless as did bridge and tennis but she was a presence at a cocktail party or a dinner. The women wanted to see what she was wearing and the men just wanted to get near enough to say a few words, kiss her hello and imagine that she might be attracted to them. Husbands tried not to stare into those eyes too long. Wives liked her but were a little afraid of her. After all, she was spectacular to look at *and* charming to talk to. She had panache and brains. This made Catherine Burroughs a force; she had power and she was a threat.

Lots of people in Boston talked about Catherine Burroughs. She knew it and didn't care. Her husband knew it and thought it was super.

BROOKLYN/CORAL GABLES

Annie reached for her ringing cell phone. It was under the glossy brochure of the new condo on Navarre Avenue. "Alyssa?" The voice was familiar but Annie paused to process the name. She couldn't get used to it. "Yes, this is she."

"Hi, it's Lori. I know it's short notice but are you available for dinner tonight?"

Annie looked at her desk piled with papers. She had that showing at the Miami Beach high-rise at six and the client was South American and unmarried. It should be easy but the bachelors often brought their entire family to wander through and give opinions. Little kids of seven and eight deciding if they liked the place well enough to come and visit their uncle there. The mother overly concerned about cupboard space in the kitchen as the father assessed the view from the terrace and decided whether or not a future new building would interfere. The brother's wife worried about the number of closets. The sister saying the washer and dryer should be replaced. Sometimes they'd stay so long she'd think the entire tribe was going to ask to spend the night. It drove her crazy.

"What time? Where do I have to be?"

"Seven-thirty. The Ritz Carlton. Client is Brazilian."

Silence from Annie who was wondering about traffic, thinking she really should get a helicopter for personal use. "Which Ritz Carlton?"

"The one in Coconut Grove. It's four hours. What do you think?" asked Lori.

Annie could practically hear the booker thinking, take it take it! As Alyssa she brought in thirty-one hundred dollars an hour and would keep half. The other half would go to Bree and Jake. Then Lori would get ten percent from Alyssa which was $155 times the hours. Four hours meant that $620 would be hers. Plus the ten percent from Bree: another $620. That was $1,240 for answering the phone and making a call to Miami.

"I'll be there," said Annie. She wrote 'RC-CG7:30' in her date book under 'Juan Martinez 6 pm' and then took a deep breath. "Where am I meeting him? Is there a room number? A name?"

There usually wasn't a name for the girls to know but they might see it later on the credit card. Or if the client said, "Call me Bart" or "Clint" or whatever, at some point in the evening, they might laugh and say, "My name is Harvey."

"His name is Joao. Rhymes with 'wow.'"

Or 'ow,' thought Annie.

Lori looked at her laptop screen. "He's in the Bay View suite. If there is any problem, of course, you can always call me."

Annie was visualizing what to wear and how to drape it on the back seat of her Mini Cooper without it getting wrinkled and how she could change between cars in the underground parking garage of the hotel. "Right. Good. Thanks."

"He's paid for four hours so Becky'll be calling you at eleven-thirty to see if he wants you to stay. Don't forget to keep your cell on."

"Okay and thanks." Annie was already imagining herself taking a quick shower at home and wondering what shoes to wear, hoping he wasn't a midget. Doesn't matter, she thought. Think Tom Cruise and Katie Holmes. Maybe it was first okay with Jackie Kennedy and Aristotle Onassis. She made short men 'in.' But only if their income made them seem tall. This is good, this is good, she told herself. I need this money. This is good. The landline on her desk began to ring.

"Have a good time," said Lori as the line was disconnected. She pushed the laptop away, fluffed up her pillows, grabbed the remote, took a big bite of the Mars bar and prepared to watch *Oprah*.

The men were tall, short, thin, husky, or downright fat. They were well-muscled or flabby and usually thrilled to be naked. Their skin was pale and freckled, pink, olive-complexioned or golden tan; they were North American, South American, Italian, German, French, Spanish, English, Middle Eastern or Nordic. They were covered with hair like apes or as sleek as seals.

PARIS

George Forrester had never done anything like this in his life. He took risks in business, with markets, but this was *personal*. Oh, sure, he'd thought of it plenty of times but never acted on any . . . was there such a thing as Internet impulse? Truth was, there was Sylvia. After the past four years, after what he'd gone through, he didn't feel a bit disloyal. Sometimes, he thought if he ever heard the words anorexia nervosa again he would drive his new Mercedes off a cliff. Not that there were any cliffs in Nebraska. And yes, he would hear those words again because he'd keep on keeping on. Seeing the doctors, keeping the food diary, talking about her progress with the psychiatrists, holding her hand, telling her how well she was doing and how proud he was. But not tonight. Tonight he was far away and he was doing something for *himself.* For a change.

The money was there, he'd made it and by God, he could spend it. Any way I want, he said to himself. Then he stopped, thinking back to twelfth grade. He remembered Joey, Danny, and Steve badgering him, taunting him to go across town where there was this woman who would do *it* for ten dollars. He would never go.

He stared into the bathroom mirror at his blonde hair going gray, turned sideways and thought, maybe I should have gone to the gym more than once a month.

George brushed his teeth again, gargled with Scope, shaved for the second time that day. Patting his face dry, he walked out of the massive marble bathroom into the ornately furnished sitting room. He stood at the window and stared out at the Eiffel Tower, majestic, bright, actually sparkling. Suddenly he turned and walked into the bedroom, grabbed a spanking white shirt from his open suitcase, shook it out and started to fumble with the buttons.

An hour later, fortified by just one scotch, he waited for the knock on the door.

Meanwhile, Véronique was getting into a cab at Place des Vosges. "Plaza Athénée, s'il vous plaît." Ten minutes later, a doorman helped her out, admiring the tailored black coat, her grace. Véronique was sleek, elegant as a greyhound, with dark hair pinned in a chignon, thick bangs and bright red lipstick.

She ascended in the elevator, feeling really hungry, hoping the concierge had directed him to make reservations at an excellent restaurant. Maybe it would be room service. Food, glorious food. Véronique had been so busy in the shop that she hadn't eaten all day.

All she knew was that he was an American, in Suite 500.

BROOKLYN

Lori put the Diet Coke can down on the bedside table as the Pink Panther theme sounded. She quickly pushed 'answer' on her cell. It never stopped ringing, never left her hand. She was eight to eight and felt overworked. This was her week to handle the all-nighters. "Imperial Club V.I.P.," she said sweetly.

The laptop was on her knees, the cursor blinking. The duvet was folded at the foot of her bed. She was barefoot, wearing a T-shirt and jeans that had suddenly gotten too tight. "Oh, Mr. X, how are you? Good. Okay, next Wednesday the fifth at the Waldorf. Dominique is unavailable but what about Maya? Are you online now?" She waited. "She's beautiful. And she's got a great personality." Silence as he presumably took a look at Maya's photograph. At last, he spoke again. "Maybe someone more sporty this time."

"Okay. Do you see Karen? She's on the fourth page." Lori was thinking it was great the summer was over since most of the girls were back from the Hamptons. She could hear the call waiting beep and knew that call after call was bouncing into her voicemail. Make up your mind!

She remembered Karen's panic the week before. Since then she'd had three clients and no complaints. Though she and Becky had never met any of the girls, Lori knew they had to be well-groomed and extremely attractive. Hot. But not hot in a blatant, cheap way. Those photos on the Imperial website were stunning. Playboy-centerfold gorgeous but no beaver shots. A lot more class. Both she and Becky fantasized about what the girls and the clients must be like. Lori talked to Becky and Becky talked to Jennie, her gay partner.

Silence on the line. She wondered if he were reading measurements. Most of the girls had these amazing twenty-two inch waists. She thought of Scarlet holding onto the bedpost while Mammy laced her into a too-tight corset. The call waiting beep sounded again. Lori told herself not to sigh. At last his voice, the Danish accent. "Yes, I like her looks. Karen. You have my credit card. Four hours. For dinner. Have her come at eight." Lori was tapping all this into the laptop. "Is she two thousand an hour like Dominique?"

Lori did not hesitate. "Yes. Call me when you've checked in and have the room number and I'll make sure she arrives."

Click! "Imperial V.I.P.," she said in a low, smooth voice.

She looked at her chart. It was nearly ten o'clock and time to start checking on who was having a good time, who wasn't. Damn. *Law & Order* was coming on with Jeff Goldblum. Oh, he was so good-looking. She grabbed the remote and pushed the 'mute' button staring at the screen as she began to dial.

The only problem, she decided at two a.m. was that she ate all night. She always meant to ask Becky if she did the same when she was on the graveyard shift. Lori thought, I have no self-control. Ice cream at midnight, the salsa at three, the grilled cheese sandwiches I like to make at four. She told herself the sandwiches were just an early breakfast and weren't such a bad thing. She looked down at her round belly. Between midnight ice cream and the next foray to the fridge, she managed to send her e-mails to Bree. Who was where, how many hours at how much per hour.

Karen better be good. She'd just been promoted, had been doubled in price. Mr. X was a repeat customer. Ha! Mr. X! Did these men really think she didn't know their real names? They had to give the name on their credit card when making the reservation. Even with a corporate account, all she usually had to do was Google and find them. Mr. X, my ass!

Lori dozed off at 4:30 a.m. clutching the cell. At five of eight, it woke her with "da duh, da duh, da da da da da da—" She never even sat up but snapped open the phone and said, "Imperial," in her fake awake voice.

"Hey, I'm on! How'd it go last night?" Becky was always annoyingly chirpy in the morning.

Lori started to rub her eyes then realized she was still wearing her contacts. "All okay. A few extensions. Thirty-one overnights. No problems. I'll forward tonight's new appointments to you right now in an attachment." She struggled to sit up and tapped 'attach file,' 'send' and yawned. They patched in Bree.

"All okay?" Bree asked. She was wearing a T-shirt and sat at her desk in the New Jersey apartment. A mug of tea was beside the keyboard, Jake slept behind her. She ran the day to day operations of it all. It was typical for her to answer a hundred e-mails and then move on to confirm the bank deposits before lunch. She would later say "I ran the whole operation in my panties." Now she woke up Jake to make the switch on Vonage so that all calls would be forwarded to Becky's cell for the next twelve hours. He stood behind her, groggy and silent, until she relinquished the chair.

Lori yawned. "I'm hanging up and sleeping til *General Hospital*. Talk to you tonight." She turned off her phone, closed the laptop, pushed it away and within seconds was snoring softly.

There were men who said they weren't married and were and men who said they were divorced and weren't. There were men who took out photos of their children and that Internet tycoon from Seattle who kept talking about his dog. A Jack Russell who could load and turn on the dishwasher. "But he always forgets the soap."

MANHATTAN

Oh, boy, am I sick and tired of these women! He waved goodbye in general and pushed open the glass door. Out on the sidewalk, he breathed deeply. Delicious Manhattan air. Traffic fumes as opposed to conditioner and tints and that new hair spray that made him want to gag. He started east towards Lexington and the subway. I want to go to a spa. I want to drink martinis until I don't know who I am anymore. I want to buy that silk shirt I saw in GQ in all twelve colors. Mark was fed up with everything in his life.

The train was jammed as usual. It was an unseasonably warm day for the fall and nobody knew what to wear. His leather jacket was too hot, his turtleneck alone not warm enough. I'm like a woman with hot flashes, he thought with annoyance as he clutched the metal bar over his head and tried not to think about how sticky and uncomfortable he felt.

Forty minutes later, walking across the street to his building, he was talking to himself. Someday I'm going to move. He turned the lock on the front door and pushed it open. To a doorman building on Park Avenue. I am not made for Brooklyn. I am a Manhattan, Park Avenue, Fifth Avenue sort of person, he told himself.

His mailbox was jammed; he stood in front of it and flipped through the flyers, the ads, the envelopes. "Lori Stevens?" he muttered. The address sticker said she was in 3B.

The doorbell sounded so he knew it worked. He could hear music so someone was home. A female voice called out, "Who is it?"

"It's Mark. I live on the fifth floor and I have some mail addressed to you. I can't push it under the door. There's a carpet there." Silence. "Do you want me to just leave it out here?"

The locks started to click. One, two , three. "Fort Knox," she smiled when she finally opened the door and saw his face. He was trim, good-looking. He was cute actually, with dark hair, dark eyes.

She had a great voice and a good smile but she was decidedly overweight and looked rumpled. "Strict security," she said. "Buckingham Palace." He handed her the mail. Something about her was so likable that he put on his gayest accent and said, "And *I* am the queen!"

She laughed a contagious, sincerely amused laugh, thanked him and closed the door.

Mark went upstairs and in three minutes was in the shower wondering who he should call for take-out. The kitchen cabinets held a cereal bowl, some stainless steel cutlery and six wine glasses. Furnished by Ikea, the apartment had bare white walls and bare wooden floors. It was clean, no-nonsense orderly. At least once a week he thought he'd get some sort of flowering plant but he kept forgetting or else just felt too tired to deal with picking anything out and carrying it home. The only signs of life were bookshelves filled with magazines. *Vanity Fair*, every issue in the past eleven years. He couldn't throw them away. The white lacquered coffee table was loaded down with *Vogue*, the *New York Observer*, fashion magazines for both sexes. He devoured them. Tonight he plopped down on the couch wearing a white terry cloth bathrobe and tried to decide which was least repellant: Chinese, sushi, or pizza.

"My God," he said aloud. "I can't cook, can't decorate an apartment, can't take care of flowers. What kind of a gay am I, anyway?"

Lori tossed the unopened mail on the kitchen counter and moaned. "Even if he's gay, he saw me and I look revolting!" She looked down at the stained T-shirt, the too tight jeans, the flip flops. "I have to change my life," she swore.

MANHATTAN

"Mrs. Cortland, good morning!" said Mark. She looked up and smiled faintly. "Follow me and we'll get started. How are you today?"

She put the magazine on the Lucite table and followed him past a dozen other stylists wielding dryers and scissors to his chair which was in its own exalted cubicle. This had happened last year and was a sign that he was special, that he rated a private space. The chocolate brown plastic cape was draped around her with all the swish of a toreador's and snapped into place at the neck.

Mark stood behind her and they both stared at her reflection in the Lucite framed mirror. Mrs. Cortland was one of about a dozen customers Mark actually liked. She had good manners, she never complained and though she was married to one of the richest men in the country, she never acted like it. She had an account at the salon but unlike nearly every one of the other women who did, she never forgot to tip him in cash.

He gently drew his spread fingers through her hair and then said, "So we're doing color today? We trimmed it last time. Do we want to keep these streaks?"

Her eyes filled with tears. "Sorry," she gulped. "Would you mind getting me a glass of water?"

Mark darted away immediately and came back with a Kleenex and a crystal goblet of Perrier. Poor thing. She didn't look at all well today. Sixty, he guessed, and feeling it. She'd done the Botox, he could see. Once they'd talked about Pilates but other than saying she was going away and needed to time the color or get a haircut before such and such a charity event, she said nothing about her life.

The other women went on and on and on. They'd caught the maid stealing lipstick. Their driver was drinking. The country house needed a new gazebo. Plane tickets to St. Bart's were so difficult to get even when one booked a whole year before.

But Mrs. Cortland confined any talk to her hair situation, always thanked him and tipped him generously. She made him remember why he had wanted to become a hairdresser.

"A little headache," she said vaguely, took a sip and put the water down on the marble counter beneath the mirror. Fully in control again, she said she liked the streaks so "Why don't we do them again?"

Today, with the tears in front of Mark, was a turning point for Brooke. She was forced to admit that she was unhappy.

Nothing has changed, she told herself. From last week, last month or last year so I don't know why I'm all weepy today. He still shouts at me, I still get dressed up and stand beside him and smile. I still have meetings with other wives about raising money to help stamp out cancer or illiteracy. There are the organizations to save rain forests, sequoias, AIDS orphans in Africa, oceans, whales, sea turtles, African elephants, Indian tigers. My public persona. She sighed as the towel was wrapped around her neck and the color was mixed on the little tray. I guess I miss being valued. I miss affection. I miss imagining that my husband takes me seriously or even cares that I live or die.

An hour and a half later, Mark had blown her hair out, and she was staring into the mirror again. The tears were back. Mark had this happen before but always with a more gregarious woman, a woman who confided in him long and hard for weeks preceding the appearance of tears. Tears were nothing. He'd had women sobbing in his chair. Complete with those big shoulder-moving gasps. This time he didn't know what to do. He only knew her first name from reading it in the Sunday *New York Times*. She'd been standing beside her husband in an evening dress at something to do with the Museum of Modern Art. Had she found a lump in her breast? Was her husband about to lose all his money in a deal gone south? No, that couldn't be it. Stanford J. Cortland had more money than God. *Vanity Fair* had done a huge interview piece on him three years before and Mark knew the man's life story.

He kept twirling this strand and that one with little whoooooo's of the dryer as the tears slipped down her face. He couldn't ignore it any longer. "Mrs. Cortland?" He put the dryer down and handed her another Kleenex. Wordlessly, she dabbed at the tears and then said, "Mark, do you ever make house calls? I mean, could you come and do my hair before the Red Cross Ball on Friday? It's 993 Fifth Avenue. Come at six."

She stood, unsnapped the cape and pressed bills into his hand before he could speak. He nodded, staring at her. Tears still glistened in her blue eyes. "Thank you." He held her suit jacket for her and she slipped her arms in and buttoned the top button. With great dignity she put on her sunglasses and with head held high, walked through the salon and out into the bright sunshine of Madison Avenue.

BOSTON

Holtie read *The New York Review of Books* slowly and thoroughly whereas Catherine glanced at the titles, turned the pages as quickly as possible, skimming from top to bottom and then put it right into the basket by the fireplace for recycling.

The second time she saw the ad, she tore it out and stuffed it into the back pocket of her corduroy trousers. She told herself to tear it in half and throw it away before she tossed her clothes in the laundry hamper. She thought about doing this so many times on Saturday afternoon that she finally went to her desk in the little room off the upstairs hall, took the ad out and prepared to rip it to confetti and never think of it again. But she didn't. She put it in her wallet.

The next morning after Holtie left for the office she drove to an Internet café on Tetlow Street, parked across from it and paid three dollars to use a computer. Catherine asked for an e-mail address and was given one scrawled on a piece of notebook paper. "Take number three," the young man directed her. She sat down at computer number three, tapped a few words on the keyboard and pushed 'send.'

This e-mail was to change everything.

LONDON

Gabrielle, she whispered to herself. I am somebody named Gabrielle. She was massaging her entire naked body with lotion in front of the full-length mirror in the bathroom. Somewhere, a million years ago, she'd read that Jerry Hall did this hour after hour when she was bored. More and more body lotion, she'd been quoted as saying, "like polishing a saddle." Could living with Mick Jagger have been *that* dull?

Manicure, pedicure. Yesterday. Fine. She stood upright and looked at herself critically. What she saw was a tall, slender woman who'd been a fashion model for a few years before her marriage. The cheekbones, the ribcage, the impeccable posture. "It's all pretty much still here," she said aloud.

Her husband said that she was more beautiful now than when he'd married her. He swore that she was far more lovely at twenty-seven than at twenty-four and that living with him was the reason. They bickered about it; he teased her and she did feel she had flowered under his touch. It's being loved, she decided. It changed me. I am actually a little bit unselfish and a little bit giving. I actually want to please someone. She frowned. The old me was the brittle taker of anything I wanted. A bitch. Cool or cold only depending upon how little I cared. Consequences and hurt feelings be damned. Lawrence changed all that.

She turned to the closet which had once been a fourth bedroom and walked in. A black and white silk dress, black peau de soie shoes, the red silk evening bag. The periwinkle blue Chanel suit, the black alligator pumps, the Chanel handbag. All very silly, really, as I would never dare to leave the room. It was like being in a play. Dressed to be undressed. Dressed for dinner in a hotel suite awaiting the room service cart. Her little suitcase was open on the bed. Beside it were Jackie-O dark glasses and a black cloche. That's fine. With my hair stuffed under it no one can tell if I'm blonde or brunette.

Stella, the cook, has gone off to be with her daughter on the Wandsworth Road. Taking the Lab with her. Her grandkids are all crazy about that dog. She thinks I'm in Surrey. Lawrence is in Bonn for the next four days and I am Gabrielle. Maybe for the last time. She tossed in two nightgowns, one for each night, the usual white lace underclothes. He'd told her he preferred white. Snow white, like a virgin. Men were so easy. The opposite sex had been easy for her since seventh grade. She'd been a skinny girl with big eyes but she knew early on how to get her way. Even if, at that age, getting her way only meant dancing with the best-looking boy at Miss Hatley's dance class.

She stood over the open suitcase, computing what was there, what might be missing. No toys. No massage crèmes. Not necessary. He didn't like them. Then she flipped the lid closed and pulled the zipper around on three sides. She walked to her bureau and opened the second drawer, grabbed panty hose then put them back. In seconds she was hooking a little garter belt around her waist and pulling on silk stockings. "I am Gabrielle until Thursday," she said aloud this time. "Doing what must be done."

PARIS

George Forrester had asked for the same suite at the Plaza Athénée thinking it would be good luck. He checked his tie in the rococo mirror over the bureau for the fourth time, looked at his watch and walked out to the living room where he turned around in a circle making sure all was in order. He plumped a pale blue velvet pillow on the loveseat then backed away staring at it as if expecting it to move. "I am nervous," he said under his breath. "She is so elegant, so sophisticated." He sighed, touched his tie again and jumped when he heard the knock at the door.

MANHATTAN-THE FOUR SEASONS

"I married her because it was easy," he was saying. "She was just fine. Good-looking enough in that horsey, Long Island way that is just fine." She could sail, she was an excellent equestrian, had gone to the best prep schools. Her family was old money. Not a lot of it but what there was of it was old. What he didn't come out and say was that her looks were adequate not mind-blowing. What he didn't say was he wanted her to be faithful and he thought she would be. When she was twenty years old and he was forty, it was important to him that he not lose face. That sort of age gap always had people wondering and he couldn't stomach the idea of that. Not at thirty and fifty or forty and sixty. Not ever.

Stanford Cortland had lunch at the Four Seasons, in the Grill Room, three times a week. He liked to be recognized by the maître d' and ushered to his table with a very slight flourish, he liked his waiter and he liked the attention that was his due.

"I met her at some debutante ball." He remembered it well. "I was thirty-nine and much too old to be going to those things." What he didn't have to say was that he was a catch. A good WASP family, an Ivy League pedigree and an inheritance that he was already multiplying on the stock market. No wonder he had been invited to "those things."

At six foot two, with a shock of thick white hair, he was a ruggedly handsome man, even at seventy-five. He was known as a first-class sailor, a terrific skier, and a shrewd tactician in board rooms. Behind his back, he was often described as one tough son of a bitch though hearing it would have pleased him.

Bill Frankel was his lawyer. Estates and trusts. He did not appreciate Stanford's description of Brooke. He knew her well, had known her for years, and she was much more than the cold, rather cruel summation. She was a good person, a good mother, a good friend to his wife when she'd had breast cancer. Brooke Cortland was unselfish and kind. Their oysters on the half shell arrived and he squeezed lemon juice over the platter. He knew enough to never interrupt Stanford.

"So now I have the four sons. That's fine. They turned out pretty well," the older man seemed to be assessing his life. This might take the entire lunch. Frankel thought it was the sort of conversation that they should be having at his club over brandy and cigars. The Grill Room seemed curiously, what? Somehow it was too *bright* for this. Too *daytime*. He glanced up at the two-story windows, at the French walnut paneled walls.

Stanford rambled on, in between bites of rare sirloin. It seemed he would never get to the point though Frankel had enough experience to know what he wanted without his coming right out with it. He never asked one personal question of Frankel. They'd known each other for twenty years and his daughter was graduating from med school, his son was getting married in June, the new wing on the Vineyard house was ready for the summer. But Stanford was a self-involved blowhard. Frankel comforted himself over crème brûlée thinking that if he *had* asked, it would have been insincere anyway.

"Shit, Bill," said Stanford leaning forward, "What I want to know is—can you get me out of that damn pre-nup post-nup whatever the hell it was I signed?"

There were men who never took off their shirts. There were men who never took off their socks. There were men who wore boxers and men who wore tighty whities. There were men who wore women's frilly underwear under their pinstriped suits.

MANHATTAN

The doorman lightly touched his hat and said, "May I help you, sir?" Mark stood under the gray awning with his little suitcase and said that Mrs. Cortland was expecting him. Pretty vigilant, he thought. They didn't even let me inside before asking what I was doing here.

"Oh, yes," Bobby nodded, turning to open the big double door of glass and wrought iron. "It's the eleventh floor. Harry will take you up." Harry wore a gray uniform like Bobby's, the same color as the awning. He nodded as they stepped into an elevator lined with rosewood; a small banquette on one side held a forest green velvet cushion. Mark resisted the urge to try it out because he'd never ascended in an elevator sitting down before. His parents had a co-op on Park Avenue but sold it soon after he'd been born. Mark had grown up with an easy sense of his family's being well-off which meant that the excesses of Manhattan rarely surprised him and never intimidated him. When a client talked about spending a million dollars for a bar mitzvah it amused him more than anything and never incited envy.

"Here you are, sir." The door slid open into a foyer larger than Mark's kitchen. A William Merritt Chase hung on the wall over the little console table. There were white flowers he couldn't identify in a vase, the same flowers in the painting, he realized, and a silver tray with keys on it. "Come in," said a maid in a black uniform with a white apron. She had a slight Spanish accent. "Shall I take this for you?"

"No, no, that's alright. No thank you. I need it," he said.

"Mrs. Cortland is waiting for you. Come this way."

He followed her through a main hall, under a dazzling chandelier, past paintings, past open doors to a large living room, down a hallway of closed doors to a room at the end.

"Mark! So good of you to come!" She seemed quite recovered from the other day and was wearing a bright blue terrycloth robe. "I'm just out of the shower, just washed my hair."

He tried to smile, feeling slightly ill at ease. The room was tremendous. All one wall were closets; many of the doors were open and it seemed that clothes were arranged by color.

"Azura," she directed the maid. "Would you bring in some wine or—what would you like? I know it's been a long day. Champagne? Would that suit you?"

She didn't wait for him to answer but said, "Champagne, please, Azura. Bring the bottle in an ice bucket. Thank you."

Their flutes sat untouched as Mark blew dry her hair. She didn't bother sitting at the dressing table facing the mirror but sat on a velvet-covered stool in the middle of the room and stared straight ahead as if deep in thought.

Afterwards, she turned, looked at herself for a good two seconds and stated, "Good. Can always count on you." She retrieved her champagne.

Two glasses later they were face to face on the loveseat. "I want to look better than I've ever looked tonight." She glanced at her little wrist watch. "I know it's not possible as I'm—I'm fifty-four and won't ever look younger than I look right now."

"Yes, you can," Mark said. The champagne had lowered the barriers. "You really can."

"If you mean face lifts and losing five pounds . . . yes, yes, I *know* I could do all that but—"

"I don't mean that. Don't lose five pounds. You have a great figure but your clothes—" He stopped, horrified. What was he doing? This was Mrs. Stanford Cortland!

"Go ahead! Tell me—what about my clothes?"

"They are too old for you." Mark winced. It was out.

"Too old? What do you mean?"

Mark thought, okay, I'm in it now. There's no turning back. "I mean that you have a terrific figure and you don't show it off." He stood up and walked over to the closet.

Half an hour later, she was dressed in a long scarlet silk dress, wearing bright red lipstick and he was clicking closed the suitcase of dryers and brushes. "You look really great," he said sincerely.

"I feel really great," she said with surprise in her voice. "I can't believe this dress. It was always a favorite of my husband's and I haven't worn it for years. I always thought it was a bit tight but if you say it's not..."

Out on Fifth Avenue, Mark walked an entire block before daring to unfold the check he still clutched in his left hand. He looked at the numbers and levitated right off the sidewalk.

Things changed. Mrs. Cortland canceled her standing appointments at the salon and asked that Mark come to the apartment on a Friday or Saturday afternoon or early in the evening before an event. Sometimes he did a comb-out, other times he blew her hair dry and then she asked if he could do the streaks and coloring right there in her dressing room that was bigger than his living room. Azura would bring in a big piece of plastic that may have been a shower curtain and lay it over the carpet. Mark mixed the color in a tin tray and applied it to Mrs. Cortland as she sat on the stool in the middle of that little island.

Azura always arrived, at some point in the proceedings, bearing a silver bucket with a bottle of Veuve Clicquot and a tray of sandwiches cut into triangles without the crusts. The formality slipped away. Mrs. Cortland had a dignity, a reticence that Mark liked but now she was more relaxed, actually smiled more. He was happy when he could make her laugh.

It soon followed, quite naturally, that she asked his advice about makeup and he gave it. He thought it would be good if she let her hair grow longer, used a lighter foundation and a smoky eye shadow and everything he gently suggested, she did. Mrs. Stanford Cortland began to look younger and she began to get the occasional complimentary glance.

This reliance made Mark a permanent fixture in her life. He cut back his time at the salon to two days a week; the owner knew why and actually used it to his advantage. Gossip was rife anyway but he let it be known that Mrs. Stanford Cortland's hairdresser was only available at *his* salon on Tuesdays and Wednesdays. Mark was immediately booked solid for those two days right up until August.

BROOKLYN

It was on a Tuesday afternoon that Lori was in the lobby with the UPS man. "Do you know a Mark Cameron?" he asked, juggling a clipboard and a large box.

"Is he on the fifth floor? That's the only Mark I know and I don't really know him."

"Sign here. I'm running late." She did, the package was thrust into her arms and the door slammed.

"Well, thank you, too," she said to nobody and went up to her apartment.

Okay, this time I'll be ready, she decided. I don't have to be at the phone until eight o'clock and he rang my doorbell at six-thirty before. Lori washed her hair, actually stuck in hot curlers, put on lipstick, found a pair of jeans that she could still zip and high-heeled boots that made her look thinner. Or just less chunky, she decided in front of the full length mirror. Then she moaned at her reflection, "He's *GAY*. I am doing this for a gay guy! This is what's happening in New York! It's the end of the world and no one is telling us!"

She rang his doorbell at six, went downstairs and then went up again at seven. "Hey!" the elevator doors opened behind her and he stepped out, looking tired but smiling. "Hey, yourself!" she grinned. "It's my turn. This came today."

"Thanks! Oh, it's the sweater I ordered." He took the box and fumbled with his key. She turned to step into the elevator as he said, "Do you—do you want a glass of wine?" He pushed his front door open and she saw a sleek, pristine, white apartment. "I'm not dangerous. I promise. Of course, all the psychopaths say that."

Lori was right behind him. "If they don't then they should. It's such a good line."

BOSTON

Catherine Burroughs never panicked. She never had heart palpitations or sweaty palms or trouble sleeping. She was a woman who faced situations directly, who could probably look a tiger in the eye without blinking and have it reconsider eating her. But this afternoon, she was nervous. Holtie had gone to New York to see someone about the Wall Street mess and Cate was in Manhattan at the auction house. Fine.

Tea. How nice. Nice? It wasn't nice actually but it was harmless, she told herself. The Copley Plaza was the sort of place where she was comfortable. She leaned back in the armchair. It was sparkling chandeliers, brocade and velvet, and heavy carpets in rich autumnal colors; it harked back to another era, felt European. One of the oldest hotels in Boston. Anyone she knew would think it an appropriate setting for Mrs. John Holt Burroughs to be having tea.

She had taken off her wedding ring and the big diamond and sapphire engagement ring, greeted Bree and Jake using no name at all, answered questions, lied about her age. Impetuously she had become thirty-two and that seemed to be fine. Since Cate was now twenty-four, it would have taken some sort of Biblical miracle to have gone into labor at age eight but these two didn't know that. They'd ordered another pot of tea as she'd read the contract keeping it flat on the table so as not to appear to be doing anything businesslike were she to be noticed by a friend.

"I have a few stipulations," she said before signing. Bree was a sharp girl, probably close to her daughter's age but lifetimes older in experience, Catherine decided. Jake was a tough guy. Eastern European or Russian. To Catherine he was very foreign. The black leather jacket over the white turtleneck she didn't care for. She noted his boots, decided his sideburns were too long and seemed to be going gray. Catherine thought he might be dyeing his hair. Still, there was an animal magnetism between the two of them. It was palpable. Bree appeared to be taking the reins in the interview but she deferred to him. The young woman, though dressed in black leather which Catherine thought very unappealing, had education, knew how to handle a pot of tea. What was she doing with him?

They listened to her and they promised. Jake and Bree were taken aback by her elegance, her unstudied sophistication and would have done nearly anything she'd asked. She said she wanted to be called Claudia, she signed the contract with her new name, no last name, and that was that. On the way home, she bought a throwaway phone at a drugstore with cash then programmed it from a phone booth on Boylston Street. Looking over her shoulder, she punched in Bree's number, dictated her new number to an answering machine and hung up. She has been assured that only the bookers named Lori or Becky would ever call her. Catherine Burroughs went up the front steps of her house in Beacon Hill and told herself she was ready.

"Okay," Catherine said softly as she paid the driver and got out of the cab. Eight dollars away from my real life, she thought. Three days after her interview, she'd gotten that first call. She'd had two days of thinking about it, memorizing the address, wondering if she'd actually go through with it. Or would she put the new phone in a trash bin on the street somewhere and laugh at what a crazy adventure it had been to have tea with a pimp and a madam at the Copley Plaza?

Catherine slammed the taxi door and looked at the modern apartment building which overlooked the Charles. The doorman, in navy blue livery, gave the revolving door a push for her and she walked, as she'd been instructed, directly through the lobby under a too ornate chandelier to the bank of elevators and pressed the button.

One thing at a time, she thought. Doors opened, she stepped in, doors closed, doors opened. Sixth floor. She walked slowly down the navy blue carpeted hallway. Sconces lined the walls. It was okay, actually quite okay, she thought. It was comforting to think that whoever she was about to meet could afford to pay three thousand dollars for three hours of her company. So he won't have dirty fingernails, she decided.

She stopped in front of a mirror framed in silver above a marble table and stared at herself. One deep breath, she advised and took it. Okay. I have to trust them. I trust her more than him. I have to think that they want me to keep doing this so they won't betray me. They won't betray me because it's money. It's just for the money. Fifteen hundred of it for me minus one hundred and fifty for the booker. I'm just going to do this one time. I made them promise that it won't be anyone who lives in Boston, it won't be in any hotel and I won't go to any restaurant, ever meet anyone in public. It won't be with two men or another woman. I am going to knock on the door and a stranger will open it and we will do whatever he wants for three hours and then I will get dressed and go home. I want to know what it's like and then I will never do it again.

There were men who called out for God at the moment of climax, men who screamed for Jesus and an Italian who always shouted, "Mama!"

PARIS

Véronique looked down and smiled as he attempted to order champagne in stunningly bad French. He saw her expression and actually blushed. The waiter said, "Oui, Monsieur," and retreated. Dimly lit, the restaurant was crowded, expensive; George Forrester had read about it in a travel magazine and actually made the reservation before he'd booked Air France. Now he wondered if it had been a mistake.

The Dom Pérignon came and was poured. The ice bucket was set up with a bit too much fanfare and George thought, we're alone again. I'm looking across this white tablecloth at the most beautiful woman I've ever seen in my life and I'm actually speechless.

The tables are so close, he worried, that anything I say I might as well say to the next couple. If I could think of anything to say other than you smell so good and then I could ask how can your skin actually be as smooth as marble and yet be so warm to the touch? This was dinner before bed. The first time to have dinner outside of the suite but the third time he'd seen her. Seen her? Ordered her? Requested her? *Had* her? He wanted to know her, wanted to talk without the distraction of flesh and fingers and her mouth. Don't think of that now, he warned himself. As he glanced just a few degrees to his right, he saw that Véronique was looking at the couple at the next table. The woman's face was white with rage and the man's jaw was clenched, his eyes glaring. Their plates were untouched between them. They were so close that George could have helped himself to their bread basket.

In a whisper, Véronique began to translate. George stared at her lush mouth bright red with lipstick and her perfect teeth as she leaned towards him. Actually one front tooth was slightly crooked. This small imperfection thrilled him. She was unbelievably beautiful, he decided yet again.

"She just told him she hates him, has hated him ever since he began sleeping with—" Véronique hesitated and then continued, "that little whore called Pierrette." George moved closer, leaning across the table. "He says he had to sleep with someone as his own wife appears to prefer some idiot called Gaston." George was intrigued. The woman was actually hissing like a snake. Véronique went on, "She says Gaston is gay but if he weren't, she would go to bed with him twelve times a day to avoid tu, or you or—" she laughed. "Or him!"

George smiled broadly as Véronique continued, "She just called him a dog and he called her a cow." At this point, George exploded with laughter and Véronique joined in. When the couple turned to look at them, they tried to stop and couldn't. Véronique held her napkin over most of her face as her brown eyes filled with tears. George began to cough in an attempt to mask his laughter and a waiter rushed over with a glass of water. Nothing helped; the two of them had entirely lost control. In unison, they rose to leave and then, weak with hilarity, stumbled, as quickly as they could, through an obstacle course of upturned faces at crowded little tables and out of the restaurant.

WINTER, 2007-2008

If you'll regret it in the morning then sleep until noon.
—Anonymous

BROOKLYN

Lori was wakened at seven by the Pink Panther theme, punched to answer the phone and recognized the voice right away. That wasn't difficult. He was always imperious bordering on rude. Some of the men called twice a week, spent money like water on overnights, trips, dinners. All in pursuit of what made their willies happy. She knew many of their voices.

"I'll be in London on the fourteenth and fifteenth of the month. Same girl as last time. Gabrielle? Yes, that was her name. I think." He paused though he knew very well.

"Yes. Gabrielle. And you were at Claridge's." Lori could see his account on the screen of her laptop.

"Well, I'd like her again. Both nights. All night."

"That will be thirty-one thousand per night," said Lori. She said it crisply, rather pleased to repeat such a high number. He'd done this before but the first time, in October, she had wondered if he would gasp, change to a dinner instead of one night or hang up entirely. He'd opted for one night but been so satisfied that now he always asked for two.

"Right. Sixty-two thousand. I will arrange for the wire today. Same coordinates?"

Coordinates? At first, Lori didn't know what he meant but managed to say, "Yes, same account, same name," and that seemed to be what coordinates were.

"I'll call on the thirteenth with my suite number," he said. His usual suite was unavailable. Lori thought he sounded displeased.

They hung up then Lori looked at her watch and added five hours and called Gabrielle. Twelve noon. She'd been an escort for the first year Lori had been a booker and then stopped for nearly three years. Now, just in the past few months, she was back. Lori heard she'd gotten married but didn't know for sure. Maybe her marriage hadn't worked out.

"Hi, it's Lori. Are you available on the fourteenth and fifteenth for Mr. Brown?" They both knew very well who Mr. Brown *really* was and both smiled when they said or heard the name. Lori hoped she'd say yes because she'd turned down two other appointments the week before.

"Fourteenth and fifteenth?" Lori could hear pages turning and pictured Gabrielle flipping through a date book. "That works."

Lori said, "It's same time, same place but different suite number. I'll call you when Mr. Brown tells me."

"Perfect," said Gabrielle. She circled the dates in black ink, closed the Filofax and hung up the phone. Just perfect.

ALBANY/MANHATTAN

"We'll finish him off one way or the other," Joe Burton was saying on the phone. His office door was closed and everyone was at lunch. "With the special investigation into campaign finance money. With the investigation into using his security detail for personal errands. With the ethics investigation." He listened. "Right. It's only a matter of time. Let me know if you turn up anything I haven't covered. I don't care if it's day or night. Call me at 2 a.m." He felt he should redeem himself slightly in the eyes of the private eye. "Look, Winters, I hope you understand. I hate his guts but this is not personal. It's politics. And I've got dozens of Republicans up here who would say the same thing I'm gonna say to you: Bring the fucker down."

MANHATTAN

"Stanford, there is not a thing to be done about it. You asked for a post-nup and I made it solid. Dynamite-proof, rock solid." Bill Frankel stared out at skyscrapers as he drew little cubes on a legal pad. He was glad to be on the phone and not in for an entire lunch of discussing this.

"Oh, come on, Bill! There must be some loophole, some little—"

"There isn't. I had Stewart look it over and he and I agree: it stands. You can't get out of it."

There was silence on the line. "I can't complain that you did a good job, I guess."

"If you hadn't had me draw this up, Brooke would have left you eleven years ago. Look at it that way." She had actually packed her bags and moved to a hotel. It had been a close call and the post-nup had saved the marriage. Stanford had been desperate to not lose her. At that point, there had been a grandchild and one more on the way. There had been the new property in Bermuda and Brooke held it all together, managed everything. Stanford had seemed genuinely sorry for his transgression and claimed it was "only once." He had been despondent and Brooke had believed his promises that it would never happen again. She was long-suffering. Too much so, he and his wife agreed.

"Read it to me again, will you? Do you have it in front of you? Torture me."

"I can get it and read it to you later or fax it to your office later or I can tell you what it says now," said Bill.

"Tell me now."

"It says that if you are unfaithful," he paused and then added, "Again." He could almost see Stanford's face and he was surprised to realize that he was actually enjoying the older man's annoyance. "That the marriage will end without dispute and that Brooke will be awarded ten million dollars for every year of marriage beginning with the initial year. The year of your wedding." He stopped. "When was that? How long ago? Thirty years ago?"

There was a sigh like air being let out of a bicycle tire. "Thirty-five years ago come this June twelfth." The voice was somber.

Bill suddenly felt like laughing. Stanford was a shit. Even his oldest friends thought so but at least he was a husband who remembered anniversaries.

BROOKLYN

The two of them were destined to become close friends. It was inevitable. "You *get* me," said Mark a few weeks later. And Lori felt that Mark *got* her. She told him about growing up as an only child in Winnetka, having both her parents die before she graduated from college. "One day I had a feeling of complete trust in the world. Nothing could harm me. And then with one phone call everything I'd taken for granted exploded. No. That wasn't it. Not exactly. It all just collapsed. Evaporated. There was no warning, no bedside good-bye, no moment to brace myself. Suddenly I was on my own." She took a sip of wine. "It was like waking up in a pitch-black room and wondering where you are." She continued. "There's been an accident. That's what Dean Draper told me. She called me into her office and said, "Please sit down. Lori, there's been an accident.""

Lori told herself not to get teary and swallowed with difficulty. "Small plane crash over the Rockies. They were on the way to Aspen. A friend's plane. No survivors."

"Horrible," said Mark. He looked at her and thought, not for the first time, that she had really beautiful eyes, long dark eyelashes, a flawless complexion.

"Could have been worse. I was nineteen and not an orphan of six but I had no grandparents, no aunts, no uncles. One cousin in Nebraska. I've never met him. He wrote me a beautiful letter when my parents died and sometimes he calls on Christmas. He sounds extremely nice but we don't know each other so it was really no one."

"You mean that both your mother and father had outlived their entire families?" asked Mark.

"My grandparents had all died by the time I was in high school. My mother had one sister who was a widow and then she died of Parkinson's and my father was an only child and they had me. That was it."

Lori graduated from the University of Chicago, married briefly and divorced. "I floated through job after job. I always quit. I know I'm competent—magna cum laude must mean I have half a brain—but actually, until now, I never really liked my jobs."

Lori told Mark all about the Imperial Club. It was liberating to confide in him. They agreed that prostitution wasn't such a bad thing unless it involved minors and drugs and sex slaves. "And pimps who beat up women," added Mark pouring her another glass of wine.

So he knew all about it. Pretty much how it worked and he knew there was someone named Bree and there was Jake and another booker like Lori named Becky. He knew that Jake and Bree and Becky could be contacted via e-mail or cell. Everyone was only a cell phone away. Mark understood what Lori did all night or all day and thought she deserved her ten percent. He knew about the meetings every two weeks at the Starbucks on Broadway when she'd be given her cut. For all credit card charges and wire transfers, Bree would write Lori a check for her percentage. The rest would be hundreds, twenties and tens in cash in a blue envelope lined with flowered paper. The kind of envelope that came in a box of flowered note paper that Lori couldn't imagine Bree ever using. Bree was a tough, little, tech-savvy texter.

Sometimes Lori brought her laptop up to Mark's apartment and took calls in his living room until midnight when he really had to get to bed unless there was a reason to stay up later. *Casablanca* was that sort of reason. So was *Gone with the Wind*, *The Postman Rings Twice* and anything by Alfred Hitchcock.

One typical evening, they curled on the couch, popcorn in a salad bowl between them and a wine bottle in a wine bucket Lori had brought from her apartment. The flat screen on one wall was as enormous as a movie screen; it had cost about an hour and a half of a Mrs. Cortland comb-out.

The popcorn was nearly gone and *Some Like it Hot* was ending. Jack Lemmon had confessed to Joe E. Brown that he couldn't marry him because he was a man and Joe E. Brown was saying, "Nobody's perfect."

Lori turned to Mark and said, quite seriously, "If only you weren't gay." Mark responded instantly, "If only you weren't a woman."

NEW JERSEY

"Wow," said Bree to Jake as she tapped on the laptop. They were in the living room which was bright with sun streaming in the floor-to-ceiling glass windows overlooking the Hudson. "Remember Claudia up in Boston? She's raking it in!" She waved him to come over. "Take a look."

Jake stood behind her; she was sitting cross-legged on the white sofa. "Too bright in here. Can't really see so tell me," he said, squinting down at the screen. He needed glasses but he didn't want Bree to know he needed glasses. Bree pointed to line after line with Claudia written beside it. "We're putting her out at $3,100 an hour and she's been with eleven clients so far and every one of them want to see her again." Bree shook her head. "Who knew? When she would not agree to a photograph, I thought that would be the end of it. I really did not think that anyone would request a blank square on the website even if the description I wrote was pretty fantastic."

"It helped that we put her at seven diamonds that first week," said Jake. The diamonds were a ranking and seven diamonds under a photograph made the 'date' more desirable. And more expensive.

"Incredible looking and elegant but I worried she might be cold."

"I didn't," said Jake. "There was some little . . . I don't know . . . something a little bit dangerous about her."

Bree turned to look at him. "Dangerous?"

"Maybe not dangerous exactly," amended Jake. "She's a risk taker. She was daring herself to do it."

Bree tapped 'Enter' and then went into the Accounts file. "Claudia is amazing. She must be divorced and with no job. Or a job with free afternoons."

"What about overnights? That's thirty-one, right there. Or fifteen and a half for her. Does she realize that?"

"Lori said she refuses all overnights. So maybe she's married. Or lives with someone. But, look, if she's doing four hours four times a week then that's nearly fifty thousand or twenty-five for her . . ." Her voice trailed off as she did the math. "Minus ten percent. She's raking in over $22,000. That's over $100,000 every five weeks. Not bad."

"Especially if they want her back," agreed Jake. "And who knows what the tips are." They had discussed what to bill her out as and decided to start at one which was usual and then when the first client called the next day to ask for an overnight, Bree told Lori and Becky, "What the hell, go for it!" Obviously the men thought she was worth $3,100 an hour. Now they decided to have her billed out at five thousand an hour. Bree texted Lori then Becky of the rate change. "Let's see how that goes," she said to Jake. "Let's see if any of her clients cut back on hours or if anyone falls away."

Bree was going over the e-mails from the bookers. Sabrina was being requested more times than she could accept, Chloe was late for the last two appointments, Anika had changed her hair color and, as a brunette, was not getting as many requests. The L.A. girls were all doing what they were supposed to be doing. Eight out there on the West coast. Neither Jake nor Bree mentioned Serena who had looked like a winner during the previous week's interview. She had her first client for a dinner the evening before last, a three hour appointment, and then called Becky sobbing at midnight.

Becky told Bree that she seemed to be shocked. He didn't get out whips or chains, pee on her or tie her to the headboard. She had gone through with it, with clenched teeth, and then thrown up in the taxi on the way home.

Bree was focused on the deposits. "Remember Gabrielle in London?"

"Gorgeous but a bitch. A model for French *Vogue*, for Valentino, for Versace. How could I not remember?"

"Well, she's back. Sort of back. She turns down nearly every call but there are one or two clients she will take." She scanned the columns. "Actually, it looks like it's only one client. Claridge's once a month." She looked again. Bree was watching for a love affair or for a girl to defect to a man who offered to pay her the full fee directly.

Jake laughed. "You!" He rumpled her hair. "Are you looking for patterns here? Will this be some sort of sociological study? The Claridge Syndrome," he teased.

Bree laughed, closed the laptop and pulled him down on the couch beside her. "All this talk about clients . . ." She murmured as she began to kiss him. Jake supported himself above her on one elbow and with the other hand quickly unzipped his fly.

MIAMI

"No, Mother," I'm not walking on a beach. Not exactly." Cate was lolling on the big coral striped sofa with her shoes off. She was an hour early but expected the door to open any minute. "It's business." She listened. "Even with the lousy economy, it's good for me to come down here and check in with dealers and collectors. Even if no one is buying this minute, they will start to again and when they do then—" She listened. "Yes. Exactly. Holtie's right. When the stock market goes up a bit and the housing market begins to recover—"

There was the noise of the door opening and Annie's blonde head popped around it. She grinned and came in with a suitcase and a garment bag as Cate put her finger to her lips. "Mother, there's someone at the door. I think that I'd better hang up. Call you when I'm back in New York." She listened. "Ummm. Tomorrow afternoon. Yes. Okay. Bye."

"Oh, I'm so glad it's you!" she laughed as Annie came over and gave her a hug.

"I'm so glad it's YOU!" said Annie with relief. "Lori didn't say. My second line was ringing like mad and I could hear call-waiting on her end and she just said 'he wants two of you' and gave me the suite number. I was tense in traffic all the way over here."

"Oh, you don't even know? He specifically asked for us again. Wanted me to come all the way down here. It's the Argentine. Señor Rubber Lips!" Cate made a face.

"Oh, God, no! Caroline!" shrieked Annie.

"Shhhhhh!" Cate shushed her and then they both exploded in laughter.

'I have to hurry," Annie said as she put her suitcase on one of the little racks in the walk-in closet. "I have to get out of these clothes. I came right from the office for this."

"Alyssa, what are you wearing for dinner?"

"It's a white linen sheath with a little gold thingamajig on the belt . . ."

"White? Sooooo pure, so virginal," said Cate.

"Yeah, yeah, yeah," came the voice from the closet. "What are you wearing?"

"It's pink. Sleeveless, A-line. Simple. With a fuchsia and white flowered shawl as a defense against the air-conditioning. I get so tired of wearing black in New York that it's kind of nice to come down here and wear colors, to have a change."

"Is Lips from Buenos Aires coming here or are we meeting him at the restaurant?"

"He's coming here so we should cool it. What if he hears us?" said Cate, bent over and peering into the mini bar.

"It would destroy his ego and you know what that means."

"It means we'd be forced to work very hard—no pun intended—to get this over with." She grabbed a can of tomato juice, stood up, gave the little can a shake and snapped it open.

The banter went on as they took showers, got dressed, sprayed on perfume, compared shoes. They'd done this before, it was more fun with a friend and it was lots of fun to think they'd each have $15,500 by breakfast time.

Alyssa and Caroline never knew the other's real name or that one worked in real estate and that the other specialized in 20th Century American art. All they knew was that they were in this together.

COCONUT GROVE/PHILADELPHIA

My office phone was ringing. It was under about 103 files but I found it before the caller hung up. "Hey, Charlie!"

"Oh, it's you again," I said feigning great boredom. My favorite money laundering expert. "I left Miami and still can't shake you. You just keep finding me."

A bark of a laugh. "How is the City of Brotherly Love?"

"I am not feeling the love." I sighed. "My life is full of killers."

"Please enlighten me."

"I was contacted by a lawyer who does only capital cases. He's court-appointed so I submitted all the paperwork and am now a court-appointed private detective for the County of Philadelphia. Up to my neck in killers."

"What's this guy like?" Intriago was immediately protective. "Is he okay?"

"He's okay but I told him I would not work only for him which is what he wanted. I'm working for other lawyers, too. Mostly I'm doing the death penalty cases and it's rather depressing."

"You watch out, Charlie. I bet you're going into really scary neighborhoods."

"Is a crack house scary?" I asked innocently.

"Shit! Watch yourself!" He sighed. "Changing the subject, do you want to fly down here and I'll tell you what I need over dinner?"

"What's the weather like?" I asked, staring out the window at the rooftops across the street laden with snow.

"It's eighty-two and I had a swim before breakfast."

"You're a sadist. Tell me what you need." I missed my daily swim at the Biltmore Hotel. Philadelphia did not have a Biltmore with the biggest swimming pool on the continental United States.

"The name's Solito. He's Colombian and a really, really bad guy. Drugs, mostly. But toss in the torture of anyone who crosses him, kidnapping, underage kids working for him in the meth labs, mules dying the white death, and murder when anyone annoys him."

"Isn't he in Miami?"

"Yes. But he has property in Manhattan. It's a little thing, Charlie. Bill me whatever you want but find out everything in his name and shoot me an e-mail."

"Hey, you're not a federal prosecutor anymore so what's going on?"

"I know. But Solito is my Moby Dick. I've been on his tail for years and things are heating up for him. I'm hoping he can be snared on money laundering charges."

"Do you mean the Feds are after him more than they used to be or usually are?"

"It's not the Feds scaring him these days. It's other Colombians. A power struggle. Solito has been on top for a long time. There are at least three very strong contenders for his position in the drug trade."

"I'd love to help you get him. I'm going out to see my new client this afternoon but—"

"Watch out, Charlie. I know you and—"

I laughed. "I couldn't be safer! He's in the slammer."

A huge sigh of resignation from Coconut Grove. "Take care of the killers first and take a week for this if you need it. I'll e-mail with the details when we hang up."

"Super. You'll have what you need by Friday morning at the latest."

"Remember, you have an open invitation for dinner down here..."

I laughed and we hung up. Intriago was wise and funny and I liked him and was glad he called. A good man. He could get that information from at least three people in his office so I knew his request was just an excuse to touch base. Unless he didn't want anyone to know what he was doing.

I smiled. I wanted Intriago to get his great white whale.

My name is Charlotte McCall. I'm usually called Charlie and I'm a private detective.

Let's get the looks out of the way. I'm five foot nine with shoulder length brown hair and brown eyes. Being brunette has always been good for undercover especially when I've dealt with Middle Easterners or Hispanics and had to blend in. I couldn't hack it as a blonde. I just don't feel *blonde*.

I'm slender not just for vanity but as an economy measure. Everything in my closet fits me. Saves time and prevents last minute hysteria. I can still wear that blue jean miniskirt I wore in college. I think it's twelve inches from waistband to hem. Not that I would ever wear it outside of my bedroom but I pull it on and zip it up once a year and decide I'm okay. If I'm gaining weight I have a can of tuna fish with lemon juice and black pepper and a glass of white wine for dinner. This might be necessary three evenings in a row but it works.

I've been told I have a good smile and my mud brown eyes are fine. Better than fine by dint of great effort. I would not go to an all-night drugstore at one a.m. or open the door to the UPS man without mascara, eye shadow, the works. I have my mother's nose which is straight in profile. It's an entirely reasonable nose; I've never given it a second thought.

I'd like to think that I could unblinkingly disorient any male over the age of ten but I don't think it. If men imagine me as sexy it's probably in a sporty kind of way though I can wear high heels and something strapless and dispel any semblance of tomboy with one flash of a bare shoulder.

I live in Philadelphia, in a neighborhood called Fishtown. If one wants to be romantic, one could say it was once the site of a fishing village on the shores of the Delaware. Charles Dickens was in town visiting Edgar Allen Poe in 1842, and supposedly saw the fishermen hauling their nets in, filled with shad, and named it that. If one does not want to be romantic, one could describe it as an old neighborhood of Polish and Italian families, with row houses originally constructed for the sailors and factory workers. A few very large houses, like mine, were said to have been owned by the ship owners and sea captains. Mine was built in 1888, as was Tom's on one side; Betty's house, on the other side, was built before the Civil War.

My office is on the third floor of this house. It's a good commute for anyone who prefers to work barefoot, likes to be at home with her beagles. I can watch *Oprah* while I do billing, can stop for lunch and a soap opera in the library on the second floor or work at my desk all night.

In between cases, I write novels under the name Cordelia Blake.

BOSTON

Catherine left the house at noon and walked a few blocks before getting a cab. She felt a frisson of excitement as she slid into the back seat and gave the driver the address. It was a new condominium overlooking the river. Twenty-fourth floor.

As the cab nosed through traffic, she realized how much she liked what she was doing. A few months and she felt . . . what? Certainly no guilt.

The appointments were always afternoon, usually began with champagne or anything she wanted to drink. Armagnac, Grand Marnier, Port, whatever. There might be an entire lunch waiting for her but usually it was some arrangement of caviar, pâté, smoked salmon and toast points. There was always chocolate. It might be an open box of Godiva or chocolate mousse in a cut glass goblet. There might be strawberries, grapes, sliced pineapple in a silver bowl. Catherine always appreciated that this was to make her feel comfortable but she actually ate almost nothing.

These men are successful, they must have manners and education to rise professionally to the point of being able to afford me, she told herself. She repeated this a thousand times between the call from Lori and knocking on the door of a first-time client.

As for the client, when they opened that door, their first impression was of a startlingly beautiful, confident, impeccably dressed woman who expected to be treated well. She let the man talk and whether it were about his business, his delayed flight or his tennis lessons, she listened. Catherine could talk about politics, history, art, the latest best seller, a play she'd seen the week before or a popular movie. Every client was enchanted and every single one called Imperial the following day and said they wanted to see Claudia the next time they came to Boston.

Catherine decided, in the back of the cab on this Tuesday, that she felt *alive*. She had a happy marriage. It was companionship and trust and that light banter of two people who are fond of one another. Sex with Holtie was always good. These 'dates' were usually not great sex but were excitement at the unknown of a new man's body, of the way he would touch her, even the new mouth at the first kiss. Catherine felt quite bold, curiously detached and very strong. Even if the sex were not so great, even if the man did not have a flat belly as Holtie did, she liked not knowing what would happen next.

Catherine's body was taut, milk white; she always weighed the same. She had her daughter at age sixteen and showed not one sign of ever having borne a child. Long legs, tapered waist, small, firm breasts. These men stood over her as she lay naked on the bed and she felt admired and even adored for the span of an afternoon.

So, though she would have heatedly denied it, this became what motivated Catherine. After ten minutes with the first client that first afternoon, the money had receded into the background. But the money was there and she did it for the money, she told herself.

Catherine Burroughs pulled the fat brown envelopes out of the post office box, made her way home and then put the cash in a safe place. There were more and more brown envelopes and she was running out of what she hoped were safe places. Bree had offered to write her a check but she had demanded cash. A check seemed dangerous and a bank, any bank, even one across town, was not a good idea. She naively wondered if she were supposed to pay taxes on the money and then how would she explain how she earned it? Consulting fees? From Pliameri Consulting? Catherine was bright enough to know she knew nothing about money. She held minimum wage jobs, never had a savings account and then she became the wife of a man who took care of her. The best Catherine could do was find a hiding place for the money. The legal-size brown envelope was so packed, she'd had to get a second one then a third and she had money in her lingerie drawer, too. These afternoons had netted Catherine Burroughs over two hundred thousand dollars.

Friday night dinner was over. All the plates had been cleared, the dessert dishes taken away. Catherine and John Holt Burroughs remained at the big dining room table with the last of the Bordeaux. Snow was predicted before morning.

"Remember when my aunt died?" she was saying.

Holtie looked at her over the centerpiece of African violets and dark green leaves. At least, dinner hadn't changed. He still had his wine cellar, they'd let one of the maids go, but all was pretty much the same as far as day to day living conditions went. "Eight years ago? Ten years ago?"

"In 1999," said Catherine. "Well, I didn't go on and on about it but she left me some money. It was such a nice thing to arrive out of the blue."

She'd thought about making deposits into their joint account but didn't dare. Holtie never looked at the statements but their accountant did and even a thousand dollars once in awhile would be noticed. Catherine took a deep breath. Would he believe her? "I was thinking today that fifty thousand dollars would help pay the property taxes on this house."

"Yes, it would help," he nodded. "But—"

"Well, let's use Aunt Lillian's money for it. Simple. Done. I'll put it in our joint checking account tomorrow."

Holtie blinked in surprise. "Catherine, I had no idea it was so much! But wait a minute, it's your money. She left it to *you*."

"Me, you, what's the difference? We need it now so it's settled."

She stood up, left her place at the long dining room table and walked over to where he sat at the opposite end of it. She kissed him on the top of his head and then he put one arm around her waist and looked up. "You never stop surprising me."

Catherine said, "Good thing."

"Love you madly," he whispered.

On Wednesday afternoon, Catherine dressed with care, told the maid she'd be home in time for dinner and left the house. In the cab, she pushed her hair under the big black felt hat and put on the dark glasses. It was the first time she'd consented to go to a hotel and she hated the chance she was taking.

Twelve seconds max, she told herself, to get out of the cab, go through the door and stride through the lobby. She knew very well where the elevators were and had been in the Grand Plaza lobby and the ballroom dozens of times for charity events, dinner dances, lunches with friends, receptions with Holtie. It was a new hotel, modern, what her husband jokingly called "swanky." Catherine was in the elevator. Easy.

Top floor. The button lit and the elevator doors slid closed with a whisper. Alone. Sigh of relief as the elevator rose. The doors slid open and she started down the hall to the penthouse. Catherine looked at her watch, then took off the sunglasses and the hat and shook out her hair. She tapped on the massive, carved wooden double doors and waited.

There were footsteps crossing a stone floor and then the door was opened. A tall, very attractive man with black hair going gray stared at her. He appeared stunned then his face broke into a smile. "My God! " he said. "Kitty!" He gathered her into his arms, pulled her into the room and kicked the door closed behind him.

Catherine struggled to free herself and then drew away and stared. "You don't recognize me?" he grinned.

Catherine thought she might faint. She didn't speak, just stared wide-eyed.

He took her hand but she shook herself away and backed the few steps into the living room of the suite. It was all white and chrome and mirrors. Catherine noticed the paper whites on the glass table and thought it was all other-worldly. This was a dream.

"Brandy? Champagne? Water?" he was asking as she sat down heavily, eyes never leaving his face. "Smelling salts?"

A moment later, she extended her hand for the snifter, never blinking. "I thought you were dead."

He laughed. "Why would you think that?"

She took a gulp of brandy which burned like fire in her throat. "Because the year after we signed the papers, no, not even a year later, someone—it was your friend, Martin— told me that you'd been killed in a car accident in San Diego."

He was plainly enjoying all this. He poured himself a flute of champagne and sat down across from her on the facing sofa. "Oh, that! Nobody thought I'd make it. Touch and go for weeks, I heard later. Coma, whole deal. I guess somebody jumped the gun and said I'd croaked but hey, I was only sleeping."

She shook her head and took another swallow of brandy. "You're still the same."

"I know. I know. I don't take anything as seriously as you think I should. I would say you're still the same but you—Kitty—you look sensational."

She put down the snifter. "What are you doing here?"

"I might ask you the same thing," he said.

"You first. What are you doing in the penthouse of the Grand Plaza in Boston?"

"I like penthouses. I always ask for the penthouse. As for being in Boston, I'm doing a deal, just signing contracts tomorrow morning and I wanted some companionship."

"What kind of deal?"

"I am buying a television station and the two radio stations that are part of the package. Just for fun."

Catherine felt as if she were sitting, breathing, talking, listening in a dream sequence. This was not happening.

"And you? What is it called? Imperial? Not *you*?"

"May I have some champagne now? Please." Playing for time. Please have trouble getting the bottle open, please spill it, please not be able to find a glass. She was frantically thinking of how to handle this. Brad only knows my first name. Doesn't know my last name, where I live, where our daughter is. My wedding ring is in my top desk drawer at home. I'm okay.

She suddenly felt a bit stronger. Maybe it was the warmth of the brandy or maybe it was because her brain was working again. "I'm here for fun, too," she smiled and took a deep breath.

Brad Baker still had the look of the football hero he'd been back in Ohio. There was the same roguish appeal of the bad boy who'd gotten her pregnant at the drive-in and then married her in front of a justice of the peace on a Saturday afternoon. The face she had loved, the face she looked for every day in the hall between classes, the broad shoulders she had clung to when the baby came too soon to get her to the hospital. The pompadour was tamed, swept back, and wrinkles fanned out from the dark eyes but that mouth was the same, the quick flash of grin exactly as she remembered.

"What shall we do?" he said and she was surprised he used the word 'shall.'

I can't give him his money back and leave. It would have been wired anyway. Bree told me anything over ten thousand is wired. She felt panicked. Four hours here since I have to be home for dinner with Holtie, she thought in confusion. I can't leave. I will be a courtesan, she decided. I will be a concubine. "Tell me where you've been, what you've done. I want to hear everything," she said, trying to make her voice light.

His brown eyes never left her face. He took a sip of champagne, put the flute down and then he moved across the room and kissed her. It was the longest kiss in the history of the world, she would think later. But when it was happening, she couldn't think at all. He picked her up, the way he used to, and carried her into the bedroom and there was no time for thinking, no time to remember, no time for anything but his mouth, his hands, his body on top of hers. Then his body was inside hers and she ached with the sweet familiarity of the man she had loved so many years ago.

Catherine Burroughs took a shower afterwards, got dressed, even though all the silly towel flicking, kissing and teasing lengthened the process, and then she carefully did her makeup, left the suite and the hotel, walked three blocks for a cab and arrived in time for dinner with Holtie at home in Beacon Hill.

The next morning the little throwaway phone was vibrating like an angry snake as she discussed grocery shopping with Angie. Half an hour later, up in her bedroom she called Lori back.

"He wants overnights. He wants you in Chicago tonight. He wants you next week in Boston." Lori sighed. "Claudia, what did you do to this man? He's obsessed with you!"

"I really don't know. I thought we got along." Her voice was even, her manner crisp but she was thrilled and terrified. Suddenly very glad Lori did not know her name was Catherine, had no idea of her last name or where she lived. She was Claudia on this phone that only rang from Imperial.

"If you do an overnight, we'll bill you out at forty-five thousand and he will pay for first-class airfare, every single expense to get you there, travel time and your return. You understand that an overnight is what most of the girls want?" Lori kept thinking, Do it! Do it! So that I'll get my ten percent. Then she was trying to do the math and thinking that she should call Bree and see if it should be forty-five. Then she wondered if forty-five was *enough*. No one else was getting so many calls for overnights. And turning them down! "Listen, I should really ask Bree what to charge. I shouldn't say anything yet."

"Don't bother Bree with this. No overnights."

"Are you sure?" asked Lori. She made a face to keep from making a noise. "Positive."

Silence on the line. "Okay. I'll get back to you to sort out next week's schedule. I think you have two already and then there is this Mr. B who is out of his mind over you."

"Mr. B!" She laughed.

Lori laughed, too. "I know it sounds silly but don't forget—these clients have as much to lose as you do."

More laughter from Boston. "Oh, Lori, I don't think so!"

MANHATTAN

Men liked Karen. They liked her voice. Someone once said it was Lauren Bacall-ish. She wasn't dazzling but was very pretty with fine features and that exquisite profile; this meant she could dare to wear her light brown hair as short as a boy's. She had an olive complexion and always looked as if she'd been skiing or swimming or sailing, though she was, in fact, not remotely athletic.

More appealing than her looks was her manner. She was graceful as a fawn, had a delicate quality that was very feminine. What men liked most of all but probably wouldn't have been able to define was that Karen was a very good listener. Her eyes focused on the face before her as if that person were the only person in the world. She appeared to viscerally absorb whatever they were saying and to deeply appreciate it. Men liked a woman who realized that their conversation was brilliant, their ideas unique. All it took was undivided attention, to resist that urge to ever notice another face or someone moving in the distance. This worked for Pamela Harriman and it worked for Jacqueline Kennedy. It worked just as well for Karen.

At the end of the evening, when she might have endured bad breath or stifled her repugnance at a hideously ugly birth mark, her client was usually delighted with her. Karen was in demand. Bree raised her hourly fee within a week and the girl from Cincinnati left the studio in Greenwich Village for a large one bedroom on West 74th Street. A doorman building. The next month, Bree raised her fee again. To $3,100 an hour. When Karen was kissing a man she really didn't care for, she simply did the math and decided she could kiss a walrus for $23.25 a minute. She needed money. Lots of it. Kissing walruses was fine. Nothing would ever pay her this well and allow her the flexible hours.

Kelsey wore boots and jeans, studied hard, did the round trip to New Haven every week and worked in the Soho gallery on weekends. Karen was taken to dinner in expensive restaurants, to the occasional play or concert. Later she took off lacy lingerie in expensive hotel suites and counted the minutes until she could put it on again. Often she lay on her back and wished there were a way she could spend that horizontal time answering her e-mails.

STATEN ISLAND

Becky punched in the number and waited; it rang and rang. Kelsey fumbled for the mobile which was at the bottom of her bag under several pounds of art books and then gasped, "Hello!"

"Karen, it's Becky! I almost hung up!"

"Sorry. I'm on the train to New Haven and couldn't find the phone." She pulled the red scarf from around her neck and draped it on the seat beside her backpack.

"I have something fabulous for you. *Unbelievably* fabulous! Remember the Spaniard from two weeks ago?"

"Yes. He was nice." Kelsey remembered feeling she was on a date, she actually forgot that she was being paid. "And fairly good-looking."

"Well, he's more than that," said Becky. "He's some kind of count, according to Bree, and he wants you to be with him for three days of parties in Barcelona!"

"Wow," breathed Kelsey. "He wants me to fly to Spain?"

"Yes! Three days of parties and then a few days on his sailboat. Hold on. I want to look at what he paid for you before. Oh, never mind!" Becky was euphoric. "We were going to bill you out at thirty-one thousand a night but before Bree could negotiate that he offered two hundred and fifty thousand dollars for the week. He has paid that for other girls in the past. He asked specifically for you."

"I don't know what to say!"

The man across the aisle put his book down and gave her a long stare. Kelsey glanced away in embarrassment, resolving to lower her voice. All she wanted was to dance in the aisle.

"Okay, do you have a pen? Or do you want me to text you? It's the week of the fourteenth. Some kind of wedding and the celebration goes on and on . . ."

Kelsey opened her diary, thumbed to the page then felt a physical blow of disappointment." I can't," she said. Her voice was flat, leaden with disappointment. She suddenly felt drained. "I have my oral presentation and defense." She'd picked the date and time three months before so that Professor Ramsey could be there. It was only one of two dates her thesis committee could meet and Ramsey was on the committee and it was the only date he had confirmed. He was flying in from Seattle. It was impossible to change.

"Can't you cancel it?" wailed Becky. "Or postpone it?" She saw her commission disappearing. She imagined hundreds of dollar bills blowing out an open window. He'd specified Karen. Would he accept another girl?

Kelsey stared at the appointment book in disbelief. "No. It's for my doctorate. I have to show up even if I'm in a body cast." Regret was palpable, she could taste it. So much money. And how she'd love to go to Spain! "Oh, Becky, I just can't do it. Will you tell him how sorry I am? Please tell him the reason. We talked about art, he knows I'm going for my Ph.d."

It was a long day. New Haven was gloomy. She walked through Jonathan Edwards College and wanted to feel uplifted by the architecture as she usually did but everything seemed to depress her. The students in jeans and parkas looked disheveled even unbathed, the streets were dirty and the sky was gunmetal gray. Kelsey noticed, for the first time, that her favorite professor needed to trim his nose hair. She fell asleep on the train at Stamford and waked up in Grand Central with a cramp in her foot. Home at midnight, she got her mail from her box in the lobby, went up in the elevator then opened and closed the front door carefully in the canyon lined with shoe boxes. Three white envelopes fell out of the latest issue of *New York* magazine: invoices from Visa, MasterCard and American Express. Kelsey frowned, picked them up and tossed them on the living room table. Tomorrow, she thought.

MIAMI

Every once in awhile, Annie thought how much she loved her life now. Miami was *not* Delafield. "Wisconsin is fine if you are crazy about cheese—and cows," she said to the good-looking man in front of her sipping champagne. "And are you?" he grinned.

"Not so much that I want to *be* with them," she said.

"Sounds very x-rated," he said. "Maybe Wisconsin is not as conservative as I've heard." A waiter took his glass and he smoothly took two glasses from the silver tray at his elbow. It was another real estate function on a hotel rooftop. "Okay, fair maiden of the north, tell me your name." He handed her a flute. "I'm Charles Intriago. Lots of my friends call me Carlito."

"Annie. Annie Larsson." He took her hand. "Sister of the fabulous Steig?" She shook her head, laughing. "You are probably the only natural blonde on this entire enormous terrace. Swedish, of course?"

"Absolutely." She did not add Lutheran, conservative, Bible-reading and God-fearing. She was reminded of her grandfather's fist. "And you?"

"Ecuadorian. My father died and my mother came here when I was five years old. To start over. She worked hard, in a factory. We were up in New York for awhile and then came to Miami where there were some relatives. I grew up here in south Florida."

"You are the face of this city," she said. "Miami. The capital of Latin America."

They chatted. About real estate. About the stock market. Two more flutes of champagne replaced their empty ones. He made her laugh. He was bright. He was charming. He was married.

CARACAS, VENEZUELA

Somebody once told Rafael Solito that his Columbian-accented Spanish was as rapid fire as an AK-47. It had been a long time since anyone had dared to make a comment like that to his face as any attempt at humor could be misinterpreted with dangerous repercussions to follow.

Solito was surrounded by men who were afraid of him because he believed it was better to be feared than loved. With a third-grade education, it was unlikely he'd ever read it; his knowledge came from the street, from older men he'd watched carefully. Solito was also an advocate of keeping your friends close and your enemies closer.

He was very angry this morning and when he was in this state, his voice became softer and softer. Solito paced back and forth in the enormous living room which overlooked the Olympic-size swimming pool and, beyond that, the greenhouse filled with orchids. The focus of his wrath was Pedro, his aide de camp, who stood before him, sweating, as he strained to hear every word. "Find out who is talking! Find out who they are talking to and why. We leave for Miami in two hours—" he leaned forward, face red, "and I don't want to be handcuffed in the fucking airport!" Solito was emphatic, enraged and whispering.

The drug business breeds paranoia. If you attain any success at all, the panic is always with you. Awake or sleeping, you are always alert, always vigilant for betrayal. If you start to sample your product the fear goes away and then you are in the sort of trouble that leads to addiction, incarceration or death. Sometimes all three.

Rafael Solito had been an undernourished kid of nine in the slums of Cali when he became a runner. He was quick, reliable, kept his mouth closed and progressed to being a dealer in a few years. At the age of twenty he bought his peasant mother a house and a Cadillac. He had wanted to buy her a Jaguar or a Mercedes but she had seen Cadillacs in American movies of the 1950s and she was adamant. Doris Day and Marilyn Monroe would always be in a Cadillac and that was the car she wanted. Cherry red. Solito paid for a driver to ferry her back and forth to the Saturday market in the village of two hundred people. Though they might want to laugh when they saw the squat, round woman being helped into the tremendous red car as her driver held the door and her little shopping basket, they did not dare. Everyone knew she was the mother of Solito and that Solito would kill if he sensed a breath of disrespect. And no matter where he was, Solito would know.

Miami was yearned for in the early days. It was an obvious dream; the very skyline symbolized success. The moment he arrived, Rafael Solito told everyone he was Venezuelan. "They hear Colombian," he said, "and they think one thing: drugs."

Solito had private planes, yachts on two continents, a cigarette boat in Florida and four hundred and twenty-four suits made by his tailor in New York. He owned a three thousand square foot penthouse there and bemoaned the fact that business kept him away for long periods of time. He also owned a mansion outside Cali where peacocks strode imperiously through the manicured gardens. Hundreds of acres of farmland surrounded it. There was the house on Star Island in Miami, the house in Ibiza and the Caracas house where he was now.

His houses and his toys did not make him as happy as they once had. Rafael was forty-nine and he had let himself get fat. It was disgusting, he thought, looking in the mirror as he buttoned the new white shirt with his initials embroidered on the pocket. No one meeting him today would recognize him as the handsome, slender young man of twenty he had been. He hated how paunchy he was but he liked his food and he only liked one kind of exercise.

Alyssa and Caroline were paid well to make him feel good. He would take them to dinner and they would all drink too much, the girls would do a little coke and then he would watch them make love to each other until he was aroused enough to be able to join them.

LONDON-CLARIDGE'S

It was always the same and for that she was grateful. Strictly missionary. He was a big man, not fat, but tall and athletic even at his age. He was actually handsome, she had to admit. For his age. Gabrielle had read somewhere that he was seventy-four. He had a big appetite: for her, for pâté, for lobster, for steaks. So American, she thought. All washed down with scotch. He said he didn't have to pretend to like wine with her and he could drink the single malt he preferred. Gabrielle wondered if that meant he was comfortable enough to be himself with me or does it mean he doesn't care what I think of his Philistine tastes?

She actually thought of him as a rutting animal with money she didn't care about. This made her feel superior. No, she *knew* she was superior. She wasn't in it for money. Let him imagine she was a model making cash on the side. But she knew all about him. The wife, the four sons, all healthy and high achievers, his business background. She knew he'd gone to Yale and to St. Paul's before that and who his parents had been. She had even found an article on CEOs that mentioned him, linking testosterone, ambition and high IQs.

Gabrielle had researched him carefully.

"Gabrielle," he said, across the dining room table. The suite was big enough for a large dining room table. His companion was not impressed. She was thinking that her dining room table in Knightsbridge seated fourteen. "Tell me what you are going to do to me after dinner."

She smiled at him and twirled her wine glass, admiring her own manicure and her beautiful hands. Everyone admires my hands, she thought. Just like Mother's. A pang of guilt distracted her for just one second. "Oh, Mr. Brown," she said seductively. "Just you wait. I prefer to surprise you."

He gave a satisfied little grunt of a laugh and she smiled and thought, what a pig.

PARIS

"Oui, oui," she nodded. "Yes. Friday evening is fine." She hung up the phone and grinned with delight. "George, George Forrester," she said to the mirror as she brushed her long, dark hair back into a ponytail. She knew his full name because he'd told her. She'd tried to stop him but he had introduced himself immediately and seemed to have no qualms about it. Véronique saw it as a sort of American openness and thought it was naïve, but adorable all the same. In the same breath, he'd also announced that he was married. Keen to be honest, what? Like a Boy Scout, she had responded as he handed her the flute of champagne.

Oh! Stop thinking about him! She put down the hairbrush, grabbed a jacket and her keys and, in minutes, she was out on her bike. The Thursday morning market was a few blocks away and she found the fruit , the fresh fish, the tomatoes, nearly everything irresistible. "Un kilo, oui," she said to the vendor. "Merci. Je voudrais les pommes aussi, s'il vous plaît. Deux kilos." Véronique then went to the boulangerie on the corner, bought a baguette then to the cheese shop for some chèvre. But underneath all the chat about how many grams and kilos and counting her change and loading the basket on her bike, she was thinking, George. George Forrester. She could not get him out of her mind.

MIAMI

Art Basel. There were parties at hotels, at penthouses, on terraces, on yachts, in clubs. Alyssa, Madison and Donatella each went to nineteen parties in two days. The town was full of rich men looking at paintings, looking for a good time. They had lots of money to spend on both.

MANHATTAN

The private detective got the same voice mail at his downtown office about every four days. Burton's gruff voice. "Winters, keep at it." The dial tone. He leaned forward and deleted the message then opened a desk drawer and took out the fat file. At this point, it was all numbers. Expenses. Winters sighed. This was not the kind of case that turned him on.

Kelsey sat in her living room on the big red sofa and thought, what now? She threw *The New York Times* Sunday magazine on the floor and told herself not to bite her fingernails.

She groaned, remembering. Disgusting, she decided. Her cell phone rang and she saw the familiar number. The follow-up call after a new client. "Karen, it's Becky. Hi! How are you?"

You are much too cheerful, thought Kelsey. "I'm okay," she said. "Actually I'm not okay."

"What happened?"

Kelsey knew she wasn't supposed to say anything specific about these meetings; it was forbidden to talk about anything except appointment times and the hours and fees. This was the "how did it go" call after a first time client. If a client had been violent or unpleasant it should be reported. Nothing more. Becky's voice was insistent. "Tell me."

The ultimatum about details from Bree and Jake went through Kelsey's mind but hell, she thought, I have to tell *somebody*. "I got all dressed up. The black dress, the black suede pumps, everything. I looked pretty good."

"I'm sure you looked much better than pretty good," said Becky.

"I got a taxi, went to the Waldorf and straight up to the suite. You know, Becky, I'm not afraid any more. I used to have this pounding heart thing but I'm over it. The men are always so nice. But—oh! This time was different."

"Did he hurt you?" Becky demanded.

"No, but he opened the door in this huge sort of Hawaiian muumuu thing. Blue and white. That's okay. But honestly, the fabric in that thing—it was like a king-size bedspread! Mr. K was *huge*. He took up more space sideways than upright. I made up my mind to smile, to pretend everything was fine and that I was happy to see him. We had a glass of champagne and then we had dinner. The room service carts started rolling in. My Lord. There was so much food. Those waiters must have thought ten people were in that suite. He had three huge sirloin steaks and about six baked potatoes and gobs of sour cream and butter and two entire platters of fried shrimp—"

Becky was fascinated. She actually stopped staring at her laptop screen.

Kelsey continued. "There was this huge serving dish of fried onion rings—it must have been four orders put together—and don't even talk about dessert!"

"What was it?" insisted Becky.

"It was four servings of chocolate cheesecake and about a gallon of ice cream. He ordered six bowls." Kelsey stopped to take a breath. "I was sitting there poking at my sole amandine, sipping white wine, thinking what if he has a heart attack? What if the chair disintegrates into splinters after the next bite?"

"Ohmygod! Did he? Did it?"

"No. Worse."

"What happened? Did he get drunk?"

"Drunk? On ten Diet Pepsis?" She had worried about that in the beginning. The thought of being alone in a hotel room with a strange man drunk or on drugs had terrified her but she always made sure the man was not between her and the door. Unless, of course, he was on top of her and then she had other things to worry about. "Maybe it would have been better if he'd been drunk and just fallen asleep."

"What happened?"

"We pushed all the room service carts—it looked like an amusement park with about eight bumper cars in there—out of the way or sort of out of the way and then he starting pulling off the muumuu thing."

Becky was making a face.

"I nearly died. His breasts were like watermelons but flat, like they'd been ironed. They were hanging down to his waist. But he didn't have a waist. I guess he was eight feet around. I'm not kidding. He was like two sumo wrestlers morphed into one." Kelsey made a noise. "Oh, it was so awful! And I couldn't even see his penis. *Could not see it!* And I was terrified I would be crushed if he got on top of me! Becky, I wanted to run screaming out of there!"

"What did you do? What did he want you to do?"

"He wanted a blow job. I guess he thought the bed would not hold him so we went through this—" She started to laugh. "We had to—" She couldn't stop laughing. "We had to make this sort of pallet for him in the living room to lie down on, with blankets and the sheets from the bed and the pillows—"

Becky started laughing, too.

"I never even took off my clothes. When I saw him lying there—" She started laughing again. "All I—I kept thinking—this is like some whale that has gotten off course and beached itself and I was kneeling beside him—" She exploded with laughter. "I thought, this is when all these volunteers run up with buckets of water to save it!"

Neither of them could talk. They were giggling, shrieking, couldn't stop.

When she caught her breath, Kelsey began again. "I was nice to him. Really I was. I stroked him all over and then did what I had to do." She felt like gagging at the thought. "Becky, the most horrible thing of all was the smell."

"What smell?" Becky's face was screwed up in disgust.

"With all those folds of fat, I guess he can't wash and it was like the worst body odor in the history of mankind. I nearly vomited about six times."

"Oh! Oh! Oh!" Becky entirely forgot about playing the calm, older sister.

"So—afterwards, I was a really good actress and I covered him up and thanked him for dinner and I left. Now I'm going to the dry cleaners with my dress and I've taken three showers and—what I'm saying is—I don't know if I want to do this anymore."

"Well, of course, you don't! He will never be a client again! You will never have to go through such a repulsive experience again! Forget it. Put it out of your mind. You handled it beautifully."

"No. What I mean is—I don't want to be with Imperial anymore. I don't think I can do it. It's been leading up to this. I don't feel good anymore." She was thinking that she had never felt good about it. She'd only felt good about the money. Kelsey suddenly realized she was weeping.

Becky waited until she could speak. "You or Lori, I guess, are the only ones I can talk to about it," she said reaching for a Kleenex. "Stop me if you have to take call waiting. I mean, of course, you have to take it."

"Talk to me," said Becky.

"It's been the strangest experience of my life. I was pretty desperate for some money and dared myself to do it. I met Bree and thought she was okay and I thought that it was so much money that the men would have to be okay."

"And weren't they? Haven't they been okay?" interrupted Becky. "Except for Mr. Beluga?"

Kelsey laughed, tears on her cheeks, holding a Kleenex under her nose. "Yes, they have been okay. The dinner part is fine. I am not overly shy about meeting someone and talking over a glass of wine. I always have a nervous breakdown *before*—I try on half my closet and think I look like shit so I run around in hysterics—but once I'm there, I'm okay. The restaurants, the clubs—fantastic. The men I date would be able to afford these places in a few years but not now, not at their age, not as they are working their way up to what they want to be in New York." She paused. "I actually like the dinners. The men, except for maybe one or two, have treated me like a date; it's been like meeting the friend of a friend. It's actually been romantic sometimes. Even though I see the wedding ring or hear about the kids, the client and I are in some kind of play." She stopped, thinking. She'd wanted to talk about it ever since she'd started doing it. "That's what it's been like. A performance. I get dressed up, put on makeup and I walk into the restaurant, into the hotel room and I'm on stage." She dabbed at her eyes. "The part that still shocks me is—" She stopped.

"Go ahead. This is between us," said Becky though she would be tempted to report every word to Bree within hours. But she wouldn't. Unless Karen really did quit. Becky knew that Bree and Jake feared the bookers getting too close to the girls and then cheating on hours and any cash transactions.

"It's . . . it's not taking off my clothes. I know I look pretty good. It's not even seeing him without clothes though that *can* be a jolt. Kissing is okay, oral sex, being touched, touching him, faking passion, all of that is okay. It's —it's when they come inside me." Kelsey suddenly felt herself go limp with tears splashing like rain down the front of her green sweatshirt. It was as if she had been straining to hold her shoulders back for her entire life and then someone had told her to relax. She felt herself melting as she talked and cried. "Maybe it shouldn't mean so much, maybe it doesn't mean anything to anyone else but, at that moment, I feel it isn't right." She swiped her arm across her wet face.

"You think it's wrong," said Becky.

"No! Well, yes! It's not their *right* to do that, to come inside my most secret place. It's wrong for it to happen. They don't have the right!" Tears were coming in torrents. "It's when I think I've given away too much. And it's then that I think they don't deserve me." She gasped. "It doesn't matter how much money they've paid—it's wrong somehow for me to let it happen!" Kelsey remembered losing her virginity in college to someone she loved at the time. The lovemaking with Phillip, the lovemaking with Peter. That was real and this was play acting but flesh and skin, hair and scent were real. She was being mauled, being *assaulted*. By strangers.

Becky didn't know what to say. All she could hear was the person she knew as Karen crying. Her call waiting began to beep. "Karen, hang up the phone and get yourself a big glass of vodka. A very big glass. Call me later if you want to. I have to go."

Kelsey didn't even hear the click but sat in the chair weeping until she ran out of Kleenex and had to go into the kitchen and blow her nose on paper towels. Tinker stood up in his basket, very slowly on arthritic legs, and stared at her in unblinking sympathy.

There were men who cried when they came. With relief, with sadness or with joy? There were men with medical conditions; the worst of which was a man without a penis. Lori was told the next day, "He only had a tube there. I just held him in my arms. That's all he wanted."

BOSTON

I won't let Brad change my life, vowed Catherine as Holtie pulled her into his arms that night. He was a skilled lover. After these afternoons, if anything, she was even more receptive to her husband. She was constantly ready for sex. She'd always liked it. It was fun, it could be playful or serious with no talking. Just skin and muscles and tongues. It was also something that pleased Holtie more than anything else. Why didn't women understand that?

The next morning, when Holtie kissed her before he left for the paper he let his hand linger on her breast until she smiled and pulled it away from the red cashmere sweater. He laughed and kissed her again. Hard. She helped him with his overcoat and then he was out the door. Both of them smiling, in good spirits for the day.

A few hours later, she was in a taxi and at one o'clock she was in Brad's arms.

Catherine Baker Burroughs felt a tremendous sense of power once she left the hotel room with Brad or an apartment with someone else. The door closed and she went down in the elevator, out into the early dusk that was the gray winter of Boston, and took a taxi to within a few blocks of her true life. Home in time for dinner.

Catherine watched Holtie pour the wine and wondered if she were more like a man about sex.

"Don't you find it ironic that I'm paying you to sleep with me? My ex-wife?" Brad turned to her and shook his head. "How absurd is that?"

Catherine laughed merrily. "Maybe it should be part of everyone's divorce settlement. That the couple would do this twenty-three years later and that the ex-husband would pay a fee commensurate with whatever his income was at that future time."

"If only we'd been able to see ourselves as we would be now," he said. "Remember the drive-in? The back seat? We were contortionists! Remember our place behind the stadium after all the football field lights had been turned out?" Brad shook his head. "Bed is definitely better or maybe I'm just not seventeen anymore."

"I remember trying to explain away the grass stains on the back of a certain white blouse. My mother was furious with me."

It seemed like yesterday. Catherine felt the way she had as a teenager. She felt *like* a teenager. Brad's gray hair was black again, the wrinkles around his eyes, the laugh lines didn't exist. And she was sixteen and . . . in love? She didn't know and she refused to think about it.

They were sitting in bed, after lovemaking, leaning on pillows against the ornate headboard. Billie Holiday was singing in a smoky voice on a CD in the living room and snow was falling outside the window. "And you're so damn expensive!" he grinned and handed her a newly-filled glass of champagne.

"But I'm worth it," she said, taking the glass and sipping.

"If we're going to talk in commercials, then let me say 'you've come a long way, baby.'"

She waited. This part was the most difficult and she knew it was coming.

"Kitty, my Kitty, my beautiful Kitty," he sighed, putting a hand on her thigh under the sheet. "Why won't you tell me anything about the last twenty-something years?"

"It's better if I don't," she said.

"Better for you? Better for me?"

"For everybody."

"And who's everybody? Are you married? Is that why you won't ever spend the night with me?"

She looked at him and said, "I don't think I like you enough to spend the night with you."

He laughed then became serious again. "Why don't you tell me if you are? Married, I mean. Your skin has always been so white that there's no tan line so I can't tell if you leave a wedding ring at home while you take taxis to our little assignations."

She felt a little dart of panic. "Taxis? Who says I take taxis?"

"No one does. But I bet you take taxis."

They stared at each other for a long moment.

"You know that I've been married three times, divorced three times and have no children. Except Cathy Ann. You know about my business—"

"Tell me more about that. I know you ended up at getting an MBA, went to work in investment banking in Chicago. I know that the other day you mentioned vultures." She grinned and he laughed.

"Vulture funds! I look around, do research, have researchers working for me, find businesses that are in trouble, about to go bust. They might be in the hands of a Receiver or Administrator. Anyway, then I move in with vulture funds and buy them for as low a price as possible."

"Then you break them up and sell the parts separately. And the parts are worth more than the sum of those parts." She took a sip of champagne. "I know that because I'm thinking of how you used to take apart that red Thunderbird convertible all the time. In your driveway on Saturdays." She paused, remembering. "With your shirt off."

He pulled her to him and kissed her. They put the glasses down and the lovemaking began again.

The hotel suite of shining glass and chrome was another universe for her. For those four hours. Catherine left a city of dirty snow in the gutters, walked through the hotel lobby quickly and was transported far away from anything at all familiar. The elevator might as well have been a space ship. Her own house was filled with English and Italian antiques, with velvet, chintz, leather, gesso and Oriental rugs. But when she entered the suite, the sun would usually be streaming in, making it all whiter and shinier than seemed possible. Every chrome, glass and mirrored surface reflected light.

Brad, at six foot two, took up space, dominated any room he entered. His broad shoulders, his eyes that always glinted with amusement and his smile when he saw her all made Catherine feel embraced before he ever touched her.

They played. They joked about high school, about people they'd known, about teachers. About who they used to be, what they used to think, all that time ago in Ohio. The years fell away. Catherine felt the same sweet intensity in his kiss, in his lovemaking as she had as a teenager. They knew each other's bodies. His was the first male body she'd ever touched and they had taught each other how to stroke and how to respond. They'd stared in each other's faces, as kids, trying to keep their eyes open at the moment of climax. They'd explored with fingers and tongues and were sure that they were the first and only ones to ever do such things.

One afternoon, they fought, they shouted, and he took her by her shoulders and shook her to make her listen to him. "You!" she shouted at him in the heat of it. "You and your parents! Making a decision like that! Taking control of something that was an accident. Your parents couldn't stand *an accident*." Her eyes were bright with anger. "So they decided to erase it! As if it had never happened! As if we had never happened!"

"Kitty! They told me it was for the best! I did it for you, too!"

She reached up to slap his face but he grabbed her hand and forced it down.

"Won't help to hit me!" he said pushing her away. She fell backwards onto the couch. She was wearing bikini underpants and a teddy, he was bare-chested, wearing boxers.

"To annul . . . annul!" she whispered, freshly enraged at the memory. "That is to erase everything! Me and the baby! To erase us! We never existed! Your Catholic family!"

"Yeah, my Catholic family," he agreed. He had drifted far away from any church and his family had a great deal to do with that.

"I could have dealt with a divorce but an annulment?"

He sighed and sat down across from her. He put his elbows on his knees, his face in his hands. "Okay. I'm sorry. I'm sorry it wasn't a divorce. I'm sorry I left town."

"Left town? You disappeared," she corrected him. "God, I needed you," she said in a level voice. She sounded sad and tired, remembering. "My parents treated me like a whore. They were certainly no help and you . . . you vanished. No. You ran away."

"I'm sorry for everything." He stopped. "Except for loving you, except for our little girl." She waited. He swallowed loudly. "I am so sorry, Kitty. If I'd been older I think I would have done things very differently."

She moved to sit next to him then and kissed his cheek tenderly. She was surprised to realize that his face was wet with tears.

NEW ORLEANS

"Karen?" said the man in the trench coat coming towards her across the hotel lobby. It was crowded with people milling around the front desk. He was tall, thin, with glasses, in his forties. He was wearing a dark suit under the tan raincoat and a red bow tie.

"Hi, there," she said smiling. Impetuously, he embraced her and then drew away to take a good look. Obviously pleased at the young woman, perfumed, dressed in a simple black dress with crystal earrings, he beamed. "Did someone pick you up at the airport? I told the concierge to take good care of you. Are you settled upstairs? Is everything alright?"

"Perfect," she answered. "I'm unpacked, had a long, hot bath." This was going to be okay, she thought. I can do this. Becky had called and talked her into trying again. No more Mr. Beluga. This will be okay.

He was taking her arm, guiding her out the front door. "I thought we'd walk around the French Quarter, find a nice place for a drink and then I have reservations for dinner at a place that I'm told is fantastic." He looked down.

"Is that shawl going to be warm enough? If it's not I'll give you my raincoat. Are you okay to walk in those shoes? Just say the word and we'll hire one of those horse-drawn carriages."

Karen assured him she was very comfortable then allowed herself to be led outside and fell into step beside him. Sometimes these men were *so* very nice. Sometimes she actually wondered why they ever had to pay. Mr. Z turned to her and said, "I love this town. Have you ever been here before?" As he took her hand, she felt the metal of his wedding ring.

There were men who drank too much and made the girl work very hard as they lay back on pillows and watched Larry King. Sometimes the girl labored diligently all through *The Jon Stewart Show*, too.

BOSTON

Yet another Friday and Catherine and Brad were in bed. "So, you're here in Boston to sign papers? As usual?" she asked, pulling the sheet up to cover her breasts.

"No, I'm meeting with people to talk, to see if it's feasible to buy a certain company. The company isn't here but the man I want to see is here so I met with him this morning. It went very well." Sometimes he told her who he was meeting with or what the meeting was about but it was only in passing; she never asked questions, was entirely disinterested in business.

"How did this happen?" she teased.

"How did what happen?" he asked, putting his hand on her shoulder, absentmindedly rubbing his thumb back and forth, thinking that every inch of her body was like silk.

"How did the football hero who barely got Cs in anything, suddenly become this entrepreneur?"

He grinned then mocked her in a falsetto, "Entrepreneur! Oooh, that sounds so French! Oooh! That turns me on!"

She lunged at him, pretending to be angry. He grabbed her by the wrists, pushed her on her back then put his face gently against her neck as if inhaling her scent, her very self. Catherine thought she could barely breathe so great was the rush of wanting him. In a blur of minutes, he was on top of her, touching her, his mouth and tongue were teasing her, and the lovemaking began again.

MANHATTAN

Brooke Cortland told Allen Bernstein that she'd have everything in order for him before the end of February but she liked getting it out of the way. The sooner the better. She'd intended to do it all while Stanford was in Los Angeles but he'd come back yesterday and she still hadn't had time to sit down and concentrate. Brooke was very organized and the household accounts were easy. It would take her one morning, a few hours before lunch, to make sure all the checks and the bank statements were there to forward on to him.

She was at her little desk in her office. It was all French, maybe a bit too ornate for the way I feel these days, she thought, looking at the pale blue, watered silk wall covering. Maybe I'll get Lewis to come in to make some changes. Then she thought, no, I won't. He'll push me into doing it the way he did it ten years ago. She flipped open her leather-bound date book and wrote: ask Mark for decorator.

The phone rang, the cook wanted to discuss taking the weekend off, this and that interfered until it was nearly noon when Brooke actually started with last year's January bank statements.

After lunch, she went back to her desk and by four o'clock she'd progressed to October and noted every cent that had gone in or out of the joint checking accounts, the household accounts and all her credit cards.

"That is odd," she said aloud. On October 12th, there'd been a debit of thirty-one thousand dollars. She went back and forth looking for details and finally called the bank. "Yes, Mrs. Cortland, I see it. It was a wire transfer."

"But—"

"Your husband authorized it via telephone on the twelfth of October."

Brooke was trying to remember if there'd been some large repair to the cottage in Bermuda, some special Christmas present he'd paid for in advance, something that he'd bought, maybe the January trip to St. Bart's? "Thirty-one thousand dollars even," she said trying to sound businesslike, as if it were nothing. Why didn't she know about this? Brooke thought that there had to be a reasonable explanation. Or maybe she'd found a rather expensive mistake.

"Where was the wire sent?"

"It went to another bank in New York, HSBC, to a company called Pliameri Consulting."

"Would you spell that for me, please? Thank you so much," said Brooke writing down the name on the pad and hanging up. Pliameri, Pliameri, Pliameri. She turned to her date book for 2007, and flipped to October, hoping to see something that would make sense of this. A loan to one of their sons that he didn't want her to know about? But all four were doing so well. Turning the pages quickly, she was in mid-October. Dinner invitations, lunches, teeth cleaning with Esther at Dr. Lowenburg's, the flood in the hall powder room. The usual flower delivery every week. The twelfth. They'd had the Stephensons for dinner that evening. The luncheon to raise money for the preservation of the Everglades had been the next day. Brooke's finger went down the page. The fourteenth and fifteenth were circled. In the margin was written: S in London. Claridge's.

"Brooke!" came Stanford's voice from the front hall. "Guess who I picked up crossing Fifth Avenue! A notorious reprobate! Who looked thirsty! I've invited him for a drink! Come out and join us!"

Male laughter. "Don't tell her who or she might not come!"

Placing her 2007 diary on top of the bank statements, she closed the little drop-front desk and forced herself to sound enthusiastic. "Coming! Two minutes. Don't start the martinis without me!"

It had been fun, she was thinking. Stanford's old roommate from St. Paul's had stayed for dinner. Amazing to think that anyone could have a friend for over sixty years but he did. Sometimes Brooke felt much younger than her husband. Younger than the twenty years that separated them. Yesterday evening was one of those times. She squinted over her brandy snifter and thought the two men laughing across the living room looked like grandfathers. And they were, she said to herself. And she was a grandmother. Though she didn't *feel* it.

Now, she said to herself, as she sat down at the little desk. It's a new day. I'm going to figure this out. Pliameri! Sounds Italian. Not the sort of thing Stanford would dabble in. Consulting! Consulting for what? What new sailboat to buy? A decorating firm? No. That was her territory. What house to buy in the Caribbean? Stock market stuff?

Well, whatever it is, Pliameri Consulting is not going to be a secret from me much longer.

Something made her wonder if this were a one-time wire transfer. Nothing in November or December so October was the only one in 2007. The January statement wouldn't be mailed until the first week of February but she wondered if the bank could check for any wires sent before the middle of January or for any check written for that amount.

"Yes, of course, Mrs. Cortland. Would you mind holding on for one second? I have your account numbers, the computer is just taking its sweet time."

"Okay. I see a wire transfer of—it's not thirty—it's sixty-two thousand dollars on the 14th of November, again on the 12th of December and another for sixty-two thousand on the 11th of January this year. Is that what you're looking for?"

Sixty-two thousand! Three more times? Brooke blinked and tried to keep the surprise out of her voice. "Right. That wire—those wires—were they sent to a New York bank?"

"Yes, to HSBC. To Pliameri Consulting."

"That is a bit odd because I'm looking at our joint account and I have one wire transfer in October 2007 for Pliameri but nothing showing up in the November or December 2007 statements." Sixty-two thousand! She wanted to scream.

"Oh, I'm sorry! I assumed you wanted me to look at the account in your husband's name, too." Suddenly the voice sounded a bit uncertain.

Brooke tried not to breathe. Sixty-two! Sixty-two! was echoing in her mind. "Oh, yes. I did. Don't be concerned. I'm looking at everything to get it ready for the accountant. Would you mind sending me those three statements? November, December and January? Do they usually go to his office?" She paused, listened. "Send copies here to Fifth Avenue. Wonderful."

The young associate on the line exhaled with relief and said everything would go out that afternoon. Brooke thanked her and hung up the phone. Sitting motionless for several minutes, staring at nothing, her mind raced with questions. What in heaven's name is Pliameri Consulting?

Brooke kept it to herself. She wanted to tell someone, just about anyone. She wanted to go into the kitchen and ask the cook to have a drink with her. A very strong drink. She wanted to ring for Harry or one of the doormen, any one on duty would do, and say 'Let's open a bottle of anything. I'm going out of my mind.'

Stanford James Cortland was doing something that he didn't want her to know about. Something rather expensive.

Brooke decided that he'd made a mistake on the October transaction. The wire had been sent from the wrong account. The other wires—all in the amount of $62,000—had come from his personal account. The one she had never seen or had anything to do with. The one that was between him and his accountant. Brooke wasn't even sure she'd ever known the accountant's name.

Mixed with the surprise and the shock that Stanford might be breaking the law, was the tickle of excitement that made her giddy. The man who criticized her every move, who thought he was infallible—had made a *mistake*.

The next afternoon, Brooke tore open the envelope from Citibank and stared at the proof. Stanford, you screwed up, went through her mind. Furthermore, she thought, grinning, *I caught you*.

BROOKLYN/BOSTON

"Hey, you're popular!" said Lori when she called on Monday morning to go over the schedule. "I've got you down for Tuesday, Thursday and Friday. Tomorrow is San Francisco, Thursday is Cowboy from Houston and Friday is Mr. B." All were repeats. She'd been with everyone except Brad at least nine times.

"Fine." Catherine spoke softly into the trakfone. She was at her desk in the little room she resisted referring to as her office, just off the upstairs hall. Catherine refused to have an office and this helped when she turned down all invitations to spearhead fund raisers or charity events. She did not want to see herself at a desk talking on a phone.

"Do you have every address or should I read them out again?"

"I have them, thanks. Is every one starting at one?"

"Yes. All end at five. As usual." Lori knew from Becky there was no way Claudia would ever accept an overnight or an evening. Five o'clock was the end. No dinners, no weekends either. Nothing would change her mind. The men had offered more money for her to come to them, more money for weekends. The Cowboy from Houston had wanted her to go to London with him for a week. No, said Claudia. The money—an amazing three hundred thousand dollars offered—didn't change her mind. Lori knew that Mr. B was the only client Claudia would consent to see in a hotel. All the others had a pied-à-terre or the use of an apartment; San Francisco rented a large Back Bay townhouse for his stays in Boston. Whatever Claudia did, the men adored her. There were a few she didn't want to see again and now she had her own little stable of clients she liked. None of whom could get enough of her.

Catherine clicked the phone closed and slipped it into her trouser pocket. She opened the bottom drawer of the desk and stared at the brown, bulging, legal-size envelope and then closed the drawer with a sigh. There was another envelope, just as packed with fifty and hundred dollar bills, in the false bottom of her bureau in the bedroom and four others in a hat box on the top shelf of her closet. I suppose I should get a safety deposit box, she thought. But not today. It was Monday and she decided to go shopping for lingerie.

It's expected, she thought an hour later as she fingered the lacy brassiere for two hundred dollars. "I'll take it in peach. And in the aqua. Why not?" she smiled. She looked forward to handing over the cash. Half an hour later, the nightgowns, panties, teddies, peignoirs, were layered in tissue paper and then slipped into a glossy taupe bag as shiny as patent leather. The sales clerk thanked her profusely for "stopping in."

Mrs. John Holt Burroughs crossed the street, humming, "Monday, Monday, can't trust that day." Vaguely she wondered what had ever happened to the Mamas and the Papas. Brad would know. She looked down at the little bag with the ribbon handle. All that silk and lace was as light as air. Catherine had a rule about this: Holtie got to see everything first.

MANHATTAN

"So why don't we cut it just a little bit shorter and angle it so that your neck shows?" suggested Mark. "I don't mean a crazy wedge cut but something more like the Vidal Sassoon idea of the sixties. But updated. Very now."

Brooke Cortland studied the photograph on her lap. "It's dramatic. I've never had any cut like it before. But do you really think it's okay for my face shape? And this model . . . come on, Mark, let's be realistic! She's probably twenty years old."

"Yes, she is, Mrs. C." He held up an index finger, "But you happen to have been blessed with a perfect oval face and this would be terrific on you. At the risk of sounding like some sleazy used car salesman . . . trust me!"

She shook her head in resignation. "Do your worst. I'm bracing myself."

They chatted about Mayor Bloomberg. Mrs. C had actually had dinner at his townhouse. Mark knew the Mayor's companion, Diane Taylor, from a friend who cut her hair. They chatted about George Bush and what his marriage was probably like. Then they talked about what Mrs. C should wear to a black-tie patrons' dinner for the Whitney. She looked at Mark in the mirror, his handsome face, that cowlick that he fought with, and thought, Mark is like the best friend I haven't had since college.

Mark thought, Mrs. C is like the coolly competent, always elegant aunt I fantasized about having ever since I saw my first Rosalind Russell movie.

Brooke Cortland had not told him anything about Pliameri Consulting but she wanted to. She wanted to ask him to help her. She felt that telling him what she'd found out would propel her into actually doing something about Stanford and she wasn't sure she was quite ready so she held back. Mark was the ace up her sleeve for she thought that he would supply her with the energy to take action. He might even, with his contacts, know what Pliameri was. She was sure that it would not be good news. She also thought that, if Mark knew about the wires, she would be too embarrassed to not confront Stanford and she wasn't sure it was the right time.

Mark was snipping away and chatting along with the click click click of the scissors. "So I told him to just go to Paris! Just go and live on wine and croissants forever but to write me a postcard before he overdosed on crème brûlée . . ." Click click. "And he had the shocking, the absolutely mind-blowing audacity to say . . ."

BOSTON/MANHATTAN

"Holtie is away for a few days," she told Cate. "He's in San Francisco for a conference. He's the keynote speaker actually."

"And you didn't go?" asked her daughter who was staring at her e-mails, resisting the impulse to answer at least one while she talked. Her mother would have a fit at the rudeness if she heard the faintest click from her. Cell phones ringing at dinner, texting, that sort of thing could unleash a diatribe on bad manners.

"No, which is why, if you want to come for the weekend and do some shopping, go to the movies, go to a play, whatever, then do it. It'd be fun. My treat. Take the shuttle. My treat entirely. Let's go on a big shopping spree."

Cate was puzzled. "I thought we were selling Sunswept and cutting back," she said.

"Things are getting better which reminds me, I've put a little something in your Boston account at First Federal. It's just-in-case money. Just between us."

"Mo-ther! Really? That is so nice. And so unexpected." Cate was doing very well, actually felt quite guilty spending money on clothes when she thought of her stepfather and that bad investment. It was on the news all the time. He wasn't the only savvy businessman who had been duped and robbed.

"Well, I have it and I don't want you to worry about anything."

"What happened? Have you been going behind our backs and playing the market?" teased Cate.

That's it. "Don't tell your father," she said sternly. "I want to surprise him. I've actually—well, I've done rather well."

"Well, brava, Mother! That is great! And you know what—yes! I will come up for the weekend. Definitely."

"Let me know what shuttle you're taking or just arrive in time for dinner on Friday."

Cate was thinking: my last client is Thursday night and I can leave Christeby's at two on Friday so I'll be free.

Catherine was thinking: I'll be with Brad until five and then I'm free.

Friday around dinner time is just perfect, they decided in unison.

BOSTON

After breakfast the next day, Catherine kissed Holtie goodbye and then picked up *The Wall Street Journal* from beside his plate. He always started it at breakfast and then left it behind to finish in front of the news before dinner.

Catherine stared at the stock page like the Rosetta stone and then sighed. All the rows of tiny initials meant nothing to her. She went back and forth trying to find what the abbreviations stood for and couldn't decipher much of anything.

So much for my successful foray into the stock market, she decided and put the paper down. Then she thought of Holtie's cousin, Douglas. He would know how to do this.

"Doug, it's Catherine. Catherine Burroughs. How are you? Yes, it has been a long time. That cocktail party before Thanksgiving last year?" She listened, smiling. "Is there any chance I could stop by your office today? No, I can't have lunch but I can come just before lunch." She nodded. "Yes, that would be perfect. I would like some advice. And I have a favor to ask of you."

Minutes later she was in the shower thinking, first it's Douglas for the stock and then it's Cowboy from Houston. I'll spend some money and I'll make some money. What shall I wear that would be appropriate for both men?

Doug had been so nice and this was so easy, she thought later that afternoon. They'd had the kiss kiss thing in the reception area and he'd been very pleased to see her. Doug had motioned her down a long hallway and into a bright, sun-filled office, twenty floors above Boston. Though he was Holtie's second cousin they never socialized. Not really. It was at big cocktail parties or maybe at a fund raiser when she'd see him and his wife. Holtie wasn't fond of him though he never said why. "I . . . well, this is awkward," she began.

"Sit. Please, sit." He waved her to a club chair in navy blue leather.

"Your office is just beautiful," she said sincerely. "The view. The sailing prints . . ."

"Rosenfeld," he said then specified, "Stanley Rosenfeld. The son, not the father."

He sat across from her, behind his big desk, waiting. He was a small man, impeccably dressed, maybe a bit insecure around Holtie who'd gone to Harvard whereas he was a graduate of a liberal arts college in the Midwest. Doug and Emily had always been very nice to Catherine and she wondered why Holtie gave him a wide berth. But, at this moment, that was a good thing. Maybe his silk tie is a bit too bright, thought Catherine.

"I want to do something to help," she began. "Very awkward as I don't really want Holtie to know about it." She stopped but he was nodding so she went on. "You know that—"

"Catherine, I know. Don't worry that I don't know. It was a terrible blow to lots of people, bright people, all up and down the East Coast. You don't have to explain. I understand."

"Good," she sighed then squared her shoulders to begin. "Now, I have some money and I want to buy some stock and I don't know how to do it. I know a few company names like Coca Cola and Ford but maybe you can guide me, buy the stock and maybe it'll go up in value."

"That's the idea!"

Doug mentioned some company names, many she'd heard of, none that appealed to her. "What about Quire?" she asked. She spelled it.

"New to me." He tapped a few keys on his computer and stared at the screen. "Its stock has gone way down in the past year. It's twelve dollars a share after a high of twenty-three two years ago. Some problem, obviously." He turned back to her. "How'd you hear of it? How do you know about it?"

Brad. He talked about companies all the time but this one she'd asked him to spell. But she couldn't mention Brad. Smoothly, she explained, "I heard a woman mention it over lunch the other day. She was telling a friend that her husband had bought shares." Catherine faced him unflinchingly. She was a facile liar and knew it. "Quire makes a chemical they put in fabric to make it stretch. For instance, in denim for jeans."

Silence.

Doug reached for a pad and scrawled 'Quire' and then looked up at her. "So do you want to buy some of Quire and a few others? Some tried and true, solid but slow earners? I can suggest—"

"No, I think I want to buy all Quire stock. Just keep it simple."

"I really don't recommend that," he said. "I always push to diversify. Keep your losses reasonable, don't get wiped out if the market swings against you."

"No, I have a good feeling about Quire." She reached down for her tan Hermès Kelly bag beside the chair leg. "I will get this one stock, see how it goes and then I'll come back next month and buy some more. Maybe more Quire, maybe something else."

Doug was tapping into the computer. Name. Catherine Burroughs. He knew the address by heart, too. He was glad she'd come to him, very pleased that she trusted him. "Social Security number?"

She rattled it off. The bag was in her lap and open. She looked down at the soft gray-green bills and thought it would be good to get rid of them, to put them out in the real world, to make them legitimate.

He pushed the computer aside and looked down at the calculator. "It closed yesterday at twelve-ten but right now it's at twelve even. How many shares?" Doug was thinking that Catherine probably had three hundred bucks; he was telling himself not to change his expression no matter how pathetic the amount was. John Holt Burroughs had taken a beating. Everybody knew it and here was his wife with the money from her piggy bank. Rather touching actually. Catherine had not come from money, she didn't work so it was bound to amount to a really paltry commission. But the nice thing was that she has come to *me*. "So how much money do you want to invest?"

"A hundred thousand dollars," she said as she handed over the bricks of bills with rubber bands around them. "Each one is ten thousand," she said as she put them on his desk as if she were putting sandwiches on a picnic table.

Doug was home, having a martini, staring at CNN without seeing it. Je-sus! Catherine Burroughs and all that money. Just pulling it out of that expensive handbag as cool as could be. He yanked at his tie. Hermès. Doug liked expensive ties. His wife liked expensive handbags which is why he knew Catherine's cost over seven thousand dollars. He saw her again, in his mind's eye, pulling the money out of the Hermès bag.

I explained it to her, he told himself. I told her about the Patriot Act which Congress passed in record time after the 9/11 attacks. I told her that I couldn't take all that cash. I explained about having to account for that amount with receipts and bank statements and she just sat there and stared at me. He could see her beautiful face across from him, framed by those bricks of hundred dollar bills. She was a bright woman but not about this! She'd just shrugged, as if to say, Count it. It's all there so what are we talking about? She had actually said, "I don't get it. I have money. It's not counterfeit and I want to buy stock with it."

Doug had finally said, "Look, I have to tell you that I should not be taking all this cash. It's not quite legal." He waited for her to say, I sold my diamond tiara. I won the lottery in Nigeria. *Anything.* But she was silent as if it were somehow *his* problem. Doug took another sip of the martini.

Emily came in and slammed the front door. She was laden down with shopping bags, cheerful as she always was after a successful binge at Neiman Marcus. He thought of his credit card debt as she kissed him.

Then he put Quire out of his mind. Let her have her fun. She'll watch it go up ten cents and go down twelve cents and it'll keep her occupied. Emily said that Catherine wasn't big on committees or fund raisers and turned down all kinds of invitations to chair anything. Maybe Quire would give Catherine Burroughs a little something to do in the afternoon.

The very next day, on the Internet, Catherine found out about e-trading and was excited until she realized that she couldn't use cash which was a great disappointment. She sighed, then shrugged and knew that this meant she would just go back to see Doug again. She tapped into Quire every morning to see how the market had closed the day before; it wasn't leaping up or down, it was not doing much of anything but she didn't care. The money was reachable now. Actually, it had stopped being money. She thought of it as belonging to both her and Holtie now, and not her secret anymore. It was no longer dollar bills stuffed in a manila envelope and it had ceased to have anything to do with her afternoons of taking off her clothes and going to bed with men who weren't Holtie.

ALBANY/MANHATTAN

Winters was having a pastrami sandwich at his desk. He'd just taken too big a bite when his cell phone rang. He fumbled in the paper bag for napkins and smeared mustard on his face and then on his cell phone. "Fuck! Fuck!" he swore and then grabbed the ringing phone. "Winters!" he barked.

"It's Joe Burton. You busy?"

Shit! Yes, I'm busy! Winters was wiping mustard off his sleeve and noticed that somehow he had mayonnaise on his watch. Those idiots at the deli. Who puts mayonnaise on pastrami? He flung the wad of paper napkins into the wastebasket. "I just had a pastrami sandwich explode right in front of me. I think I've got mustard on the goddammed ceiling. It's on my jacket, it's— "

"You oughtta wear a bib," said Burton. "Listen, I'm calling because I want to know about progress." Silence. "Have you found anything? Anything we can use?"

Winters wondered if he could fish an ice cube out of the paper cup of Diet Pepsi, let it melt on the corner of his desk then use it to mop up the grease stain on his lapel. He didn't want to make the trip to the men's room. "Nothing. I'm getting more bank records from my guy in three days."

Burton sighed and looked down at his stack of phone messages. Three from the hedge fund guy in Greenwich who was paying for half of this and two more calls from a powerful Republican whose office was down the street. Cantor had enemies jockeying to crucify him. Standing in line with nails and hammers. "Okay. Just breathing down your neck because I've got forty-five guys breathing down mine."

"Understood. I've delved into the wife's past and she's squeaky clean. If somebody gave her an extra dime in change she'd walk five blocks to give it back."

"Yeah, you won't get anything on her but keep at him."

"There's bound to be something and I'll find it," said Winters. He wiped a little dollop of mayonnaise off the edge of his desk drawer and licked his index finger. Both men hung up.

MANHATTAN

Cate walked into her apartment, kicking off one Christian Louboutin shoe at a time, pulling at the scarf, the gloves, the coat and dropping them in her wake. She was very tired. Preparing for the next sale was exhausting her. Problems with the provenance of that Rothko, problems with five entries that had to be rewritten. Lot 37 had not been photographed yet and another lot had been mistakenly assigned a half page in the catalogue instead of the cover as planned. The seller had been on the phone this morning and *not* pleased. Not pleased as in enraged, thought Cate. The reserves listed for Lots 51 and 52 had been reversed. Bettina had caught that yesterday but the final okay for every word and figure in the catalogue ultimately rested on Cate's shoulders. And of course, looming always looming was the deadline for the printer.

She sighed. Tonight she had four hours with the man from Rome. Cate clicked on the kitchen light, opened the refrigerator and peered in. A bottle of white wine lay on its side next to a carton of apricot yoghurt. Cate closed the refrigerator and left the kitchen. At least, it's dinner, she thought as she flopped onto her bed face down to sleep for half an hour.

She waked at six-thirty, took a shower, put on a black dress then fiddled with the clasp on her grandmother Burroughs's pearls. Black suede pumps, Judith Leiber evening bag in the shape of a strawberry. She blotted the bright red lipstick and surveyed herself in her bedroom mirror critically, turning sideways and then back. It was really very much like going out with Larry or Justin, she decided. I still have to pull myself together though I wouldn't get so dressed up and I might not sleep with them. A stockbroker and a lawyer and neither have any idea that I have another life; they assume family money keeps me afloat since a hamster couldn't survive in Manhattan on the Christeby's salary.

It was all a game with the men she dated. Plus there was Nick who was a friend with benefits. Cate was phasing him out. He had no idea how much sex she had in her life. These men wondered how much she liked them, should they take her to New Canaan to be introduced to their parents or was it too soon? Would she go to Jamaica or Eleuthera or St. Bart's with them after Christmas? Should they risk asking her and being rejected? But with anyone sent to me by Imperial, she thought, the game is all in making it fun at dinner. The outcome is a known factor.

It suited Cate. She liked her body, liked sex. It was easy. It was the same feeling she had serving on a tennis court. And she liked being admired. The more unattractive the man, the easier it was. It's Beauty and the Beast, she decided that first time. He was so astoundingly hairy. Hirsute. The word 'primate' went through her mind when he took off his shirt. But he'd been so goggle-eyed and admiring when she pulled her dress over her head and he'd seen that she wasn't wearing a bra. She had felt like a sex goddess, she had felt so powerful in the face of his awe. He had tipped her outrageously: five thousand dollars in hundreds had been pushed into her coat pocket as she kissed him goodbye in the doorway of his room at the Waldorf. Such a fat wad of bills that they'd both laughed and he'd had to put some in her other coat pocket.

Oh, yes, she sighed, looking in the mirror. I'm okay. She spritzed Chanel's Chance on her wrists and then into the air and walked quickly through the mist. And I'll be more okay when I have another few thousand to put into my Ming. The Ming was on the mantle; it was a blue and white porcelain pot that cost two dollars on Canal Street with 'Made in China' stamped on the bottom. A real one dating back to the 18th century would have fetched millions at a

Christeby's sale but Cate liked putting what she called her "fuck money" or her "hooker loot" into her two dollar Ming. It made her smile.

At quarter of twelve, Cate was home again. As she undid the pearls, she thought how odd it had been to be in the same restaurant where Ned had first mentioned marriage to her. Marriage, in general. Two years ago. Primavera. That same banquette. Had the maître d' recognized her? Doesn't matter, she told herself. The Italian had been urbane, attractive enough, and could have been a Christeby's client or a friend of her parents in town not knowing anyone. Ned had crossed her mind several times in the course of the dinner. Giovanni had ordered white chocolate mousse, just as Ned had.

In minutes, Cate was naked, in bed thinking it was nice to be paid to have dinner with someone like that sophisticated Roman. She turned over and pulled the duvet up around her shoulders. I could be married now and going to that same restaurant with Ned. She stared into the darkness, heard a siren wailing in the distance, and thought of Ned's face, the way he laughed. She remembered all those lunches, dinners and what he looked like across the table from her. He was amazingly good-looking. He had those ruddy cheeks the ways some little boys did. All English school boys had them. All the ones in movies, anyway.

But he never listened to me. He always had other things on his mind. Like the next race, the next exam or even the menu. Maybe that's why I liked sailing with him better than anything, better than any other time of being with him. Being on the boat, rounding a buoy, pulling down a jib and then pulling up a spinnaker was all in the here and now. I was doing something with him and I existed. He was aware of what I was doing, of how well I was doing it.

Ned. You never made me feel charming or funny. It was all about *love*. He loved to say he loved me. And I never felt like saying it back. Oh, ugh, it was like Tom Cruise saying to Renée Zellweger, 'you complete me.' That line makes me feel like throwing up. *You complete me*. That is how Ned thinks of me. Like salt and pepper or bread and butter. Husband and wife. It makes me want to grind my teeth. Her thoughts floated to the restaurant, to the Italian.

Lovemaking, passion, desire. Giovanni and she talked about it at dinner. Ned would never talk that way. He would not have opinions like that. Cate told Giovanni that she thought that one automatically fell in love with the first person who wanted you, who made love to you and that you were forever comparing everyone to that person, always wanting to be with that person. She likened it to being imprinted, marked, for life by that first time. Like those ducks and that experiment. How he had laughed! He asked her how old she was and then he told her that he had lived exactly twice the number of years on earth as she. The talk went from serious to flirtatious to foreplay and then the sex—Giovanni told her to stop being a silly schoolgirl and to call it what it was—had been fantastic.

Yes, she decided. *I could have been there in Primavera with Ned tonight and it would be every night for the rest of my life and how does that sound?* She frowned. And then she thought of the Ming vase. *Things are definitely better this way. Ned wouldn't give me thousands of dollars every time we went to dinner and fucked afterwards.*

BOSTON

"Why won't you tell me where she is? I won't interfere with her life. That is a promise. I'd like to see her. Just see her. Just see what she looks like."

"No." She was putting on lipstick, ready to leave. "I've thought about it ever since you brought it up, weeks ago, and the answer is 'no.'"

"But, Kitty! Doesn't she have a right to know her father? Forget about my right to know my daughter—don't even think of that!" He was angry, frustrated. "What if she would like to have a father?"

Catherine started to say 'she does like it.' Instead she gave a quick brush to her black hair and turned to put the lipstick and the hairbrush in her pocketbook.

"Where is she?" he demanded. He held her by the shoulders and looked down at her. Those big violet eyes stared back. "She's twenty-four, is she married? Do I have grandchildren somewhere?"

"I have to go," she said, trying to break away. She never said the time is up but this time she felt like saying it.

Silently, his hands dropped away from her. She heard the click click click of her high-heeled boots on the marble foyer floor. He didn't come after her, he didn't kiss her goodbye in the doorway, he wasn't even there to open the door for her. Out the door, down the hall, in the elevator, pushing her hair under the hat, she repeated to herself, I have to go. Walking on the icy sidewalks, feeling the sting of cold on her face, she said aloud, "Back to my life." A taxi slowed beside her and she stepped over the pile of slush at the curb, opened the door with a gloved hand and got in.

Becky called Catherine the next day. This was the only time that Mr. B. had not called to immediately set up another appointment. When Becky asked, as she was supposed to, if all had been okay, if there'd been any problems, Catherine said, "It went well," as was her habit. Becky confirmed Monday, Wednesday and Thursday for the next week. Afternoons, of course, four hours each at five thousand an hour and tips. The tips could be a few thousand, were never less than one. They were hundred dollar bills usually slipped into her handbag during the goodbye.

So there were three appointments the next week and none were with him. Catherine told herself it was for the best. They'd had fun, she thought. And she knew he was alive and prospering. All good, she decided. Divorced, with no children by anyone else and wanting to see their daughter. Not good.

On Monday, Catherine dressed and left the house, walked for awhile, got into a cab and was with someone else. Someone new. And on Wednesday, she was with San Francisco.

The men were usually interesting, at least interesting enough to spend the afternoon with; sometimes they were quite attractive looking, sometimes very witty. Claudia was raking in the money and Catherine was always home in time for dinner with Holtie.

MANHATTAN

Cate hurried through Penn Station, glanced at the big board then, without slowing down, headed straight for Track 12E. The conductor was already checking tickets at the top of the escalator. Her little suitcase on wheels felt light, her shoulder bag much heavier. "Business class?" she asked. "Second car," he said admiring the young woman's shining black hair, wide forehead, and surprisingly blue eyes.

111

She found two empty seats and spread out on the two drop-down trays. All the information on the paintings from the Luber estate was in her shoulder strap bag; she pulled the pages out and began to read. Five Roy Lichtensteins, twelve Andy Warhols were the most known. Cate found the images on her laptop, arranged the photos by painter and date, started a file she called Luber Collection 2008 and made notes. An hour and forty-five minutes later as Amtrak pulled out of 30th Street Station in Philadelphia, she decided to take a break and leaned back and closed her eyes.

Usually she was with him at the Waldorf. Dozens of times she'd walked through that very grand lobby and made her way to the elevators. This trek down to Washington to do exactly what they did in New York was crazy. Every time she got on the train she thought that and then asked herself why it mattered because the hours were paid for. She had to pretend she didn't know who he was but the minute he'd walked into the suite at the Waldorf a year ago and taken off his sunglasses and the Yankees baseball cap, she knew. He lived in New York, of course, so she guessed he had meetings in Washington which would make sense. He'd even flown her to the Caribbean a few times. Once Cate had seen a photograph of him on the beach with his wife who'd arrived the day after she'd been paid to be with him.

He was good-looking enough and in good shape in spite of his complaints that he'd pulled his Achilles tendon and hadn't been able to play tennis for weeks.

Cate liked to talk to him. That first time when he'd been prepared to get down to business immediately, she had been firm and refused to take off her clothes until they'd had a drink and some conversation. He'd been surprised then amused and then he seemed genuinely pleased that she knew about art, the auction world, the market. Later she'd gotten him to talk about politics and Cate thought that he had enjoyed it. They'd sat with drinks across from each other, she in a wingchair and he, with his tie undone, in the straight-backed desk chair, and really talked. He was married, of course, and under great pressure because of his position and she imagined that he liked the pocket of time with her. She thought he needed it as a release. They never spent the night together and when it was over, it was over and she would dress and leave and spend the night alone in another room he paid for and then she would return to New York the following day.

Cate knew from Lori, who was not supposed to tell her, that sometimes he had three girls in three nights and even three girls in Manhattan in one day but Lori also told her that she, Caroline, was his favorite and always his first choice.

"Union Station!" called the conductor hurrying down the aisle. "Union Station!"

Minutes later, Cate was outside and in a cab. "Mayflower Hotel," she said as she slammed the door. Tomorrow, she thought, I'll be more than $13,950 richer. Plus travel time. But the news of who I'm fucking tonight: priceless.

BOSTON

The woman pulled the padded envelopes out of the box, dropped them into her canvas tote bag, then clicked closed the little steel door and turned the key. She was surprised to hear him speaking to her. Usually she could get in and out of the little office without a word. "Ms. Sweeney, it's been three months," said the man behind the counter. He was fat and balding, always needed to shave, had watery pale eyes and clenched a thick unlit cigar between yellow teeth.

"What do I owe you?" she asked. She was wearing dark glasses, a shapeless khaki raincoat and a hat which covered all her hair.

"Another three or ya wanna go fer six or ya wanna commit to a year?"

She hesitated. Six months or a year would mean one less exchange like this but, no. She wouldn't need the box much longer. She told herself every week that it was the last one, the last time, that she would not do it anymore. "Three, please." She tried to keep her voice low, to say the minimum.

"Ninety dollars and with tax that's gonna run ya . . . oh, hell, make it ninety even."

The woman fumbled in the bottom of her bag, not giving him a chance to even see her wallet. She handed over exact change with a ten and four twenties and took the scrawled receipt saying "Thanks," under her breath. In ten seconds she was out on the sidewalk walking quickly past the hair-braiding salon blaring with rap music and the check-cashing bureau which was crowded with men in windbreakers and hooded sweat shirts. Walking east, as if towards the bus stop, she looked neither to the right nor to the left. The big intersection, the traffic lights were a one-minute walk away. A taxi, she thought. Please, a taxi. She hated this trip but she had to come at least every two weeks or the box would be jammed and once he had kept an envelope behind the counter. It had terrified her and she never wanted that to happen again.

A taxi, please. Away from this area she could never explain being in. And then a second taxi to Chestnut Street and a leisurely walk the rest of the way home. Sometimes she felt like a murderer fleeing the scene of the crime.

At last. Catherine opened the door and slid in. "Thanks. Get on the Fenway," she said. "I'll get out at the Gardner Museum."

MANHATTAN

Google. Yahoo. Brooke was all over the Internet. She could find nothing called Pliameri Consulting. There were a few people named that on FaceBook. One lived in Rhode Island and was fifteen years old. She kept tapping away on the keys. No Pliamieri Consulting. No business. Not anywhere. Not even a restaurant.

Mark was a whiz on the Internet. He knew about search engines and things called URLs and how to set up e-mail accounts and blogs. Maybe she would ask him to check on this for her. No. She wouldn't. Not yet.

Brooke dreamed of riding through a green field. She was on her first horse, her first real horse after Pebbles the pony. She was little and the horse was huge and she was looking out over a great expanse of emerald green. The vastness of the land was like an ocean and she and the horse were alone in the landscape.

When she woke, it was with surprise that she was in her bed, in the pale green bedroom. She glanced up at the chandelier from France then across the room to the bureau crowded with her perfume bottle collection. At last her gaze went to the closed door to the hall. It had been Stanford's idea to have separate bedrooms. Right from the start. She knew that some of her women friends in Europe had them, thought it was normal. She hadn't objected. How could she really? The privacy was nice. She didn't have to hear him get up in the night or blow his nose or cough in the morning. Her friend in Paris, Françoise, said it was very typical among a certain class without spelling out that it was those with enough money for lots of bedrooms.

Brooke had thought it breathtakingly exciting when, years ago, Stanford had opened the door and a triangle of light from the hall had wakened her just enough to anticipate his pulling back the covers and slipping into bed beside her. His strength, his warmth. The hardness of his body against hers. She loved turning in the dark and putting her mouth against a wide expanse of his tanned chest or placing her check against his shoulder.

Four sons later and that was over. We mated, I produced. Like a brood mare. Was that what I was? So I've done what I was asked to do, required to do, recruited at a long ago deb party to do. More than enough. All the boys educated at the best schools, all married well, all settled, with attractive children and houses and summer places. Our youngest is on the fast track to become the youngest partner in a law firm in Washington.

Brooke closed her eyes and thought of how good she'd felt in the dream. An empty landscape.

She turned to look at the clock on the bedside table and saw that it was nearly seven. She got out of bed to begin her day which was across the dining room table from Stanford.

Kelsey thought that it was important to buy clothes that were good quality and to make them last. She had identical cashmere cardigans in twenty colors and cashmere turtlenecks in sixteen colors. Three of each cardigan in those twenty colors and three of each cashmere turtleneck in those sixteen colors. They were classics and besides, what if one got a stain or a moth hole? She would need a need a replacement; Kelsey wanted to be prepared.

There was one drawer in her bureau that held fifty-four pairs of sunglasses. The underwear she kept in bags on a closet shelf. Dozens of never-worn bras and panties and nightgowns. She had fourteen winter coats; ten still had the tags on. Then there were the shoes.

Sometimes she actually thought it was silly to have so many clothes that she never wore but it didn't stop her from those afternoons at what she called her Three B's: Bendel's, Bergdorf's and Bloomingdale's. Picking things out and handing over her credit card made her feel good. She experienced a bit of a high with the smiling sales clerk. Seeing something she wanted and saying "I'll take it" affirmed that she was entitled.

Today, standing on the escalator with all the bags bumping her shins, she suddenly missed her mother. She remembered how achingly careful they had been after her father died. Kelsey stepped off the escalator and made her way through the gauntlet of young salesgirls hawking makeup and perfume. A few minutes later Kelsey was opening the door of a cab and thanking the driver for stopping. As she loaded the five shopping bags into the back seat, for a moment she had no idea what was in them.

BOSTON

Catherine's life proceeded smoothly. Her two lives moved forward, day by day, seamlessly without complications. There was her carefully tended existence within the territory of Beacon Hill and there was the life of Claudia in the afternoons, very *Belle du Jour*, at least two appointments a week but never more than four, when she knocked on a door and slipped out of her designer clothes and into a stranger's bed. But the men were no longer strangers. She knew them now, their habits, their little complaints about their wives or business partners, what made them laugh, what pleased them. Lori referred to them as her 'regulars' but Catherine could never regard these men as that mundane. Once in awhile, in a taxi, she thought of the things that could go wrong and discounted them the same way she never worried about a weekend of rain or catching the flu.

If Catherine could control what she did, she couldn't control her dreams. She lay beside John Holt Burroughs and dreamt of Brad Taylor Baker. Every night. In the morning, she waked in the big, pale blue bedroom with her husband beside her and, with a jolt, wondered where she was. Then she would wonder where *he* was. All she had to do was 'Google' him but she resisted. She did not want him to exist in any way outside of the hotel suite. She did not want his name to be printed for her to read. He was only real for those hours she was actually with him. Smelling him, touching him, tasting him and seeing all the colors that he was.

After a week of this, she wondered if she would ever be with him again. Though she knew it was best if she never were, she hated admitting that she wanted to be.

BROOKLYN/BOSTON

Lori said, "Yes, yes, I will." She listened. "I'll try but she never does overnights—yes, yes, I know, but—" Jesus, he was persistent.

She hung up and dialed the number. All she knew was that Claudia was in Boston. "It's Lori. Can you talk?"

"Yes, I'm actually outside. How are you?"

"I'm great. Listen, I just had a call from Mr. B in Chicago. He wants you to fly there for the weekend."

"No."

"That's what he thought you'd say so his second choice is to have you for three nights—from Friday to Monday morning—in Boston."

"No."

Lori was thinking, oh, do it! So I can get my gorgeous fat fee! Just do it! Okay, here we go, she thought. I'll plunge in again. "Third choice was to have you on Friday afternoon for five hours. In Boston, same place as usual." Lori waited for about ten seconds and then asked, "Are you there?" Claudia usually did four hours.

"Yes," said Catherine. "What else do I have this week? A Tuesday and a Wednesday, yes?"

"Right. Tuesday is San Francisco. Mr. Smith. I looked him up and it's your fourteenth time with him. And Wednesday is Cowboy from Houston again."

How Catherine had laughed that first time they'd met! He was a rancher with "enough head a cattle to populate Detroit!" His bragging made her smile when it would have irritated her under different circumstances. He spoke in a soft voice with a heavy southern accent; he had courtly manners and suits made in London. The only visual affectation that made his appearance blatantly Texan was the big, silver belt buckle in the shape of a Texas longhorn. She'd fumbled with that and they'd both laughed. And, of course, the boots that showed that first time when he'd crossed his legs. Under the elegant suit. Catherine told him she'd never known a grown man to wear cowboy boots and he had immediately invited her to Texas.

"Okay, Friday with Mr. B is fine. Grand Plaza, same penthouse suite?"

"Yes, I think, because he didn't say otherwise but I'll check with him to confirm that. If it's another place, I'll call and let you know. Otherwise, it's an hour earlier, at noon, until five. Is that alright with you?" Please, Lori was thinking, don't make me go back to him with bad news and have to get into another discussion about alternatives.

"Yes," said Catherine. She was gazing out at the snow melting in patches on the common. Someone with a collie dog on a leash rushed past her and a couple holding hands talked twenty yards away. The girl was wearing a red coat and the young man was leaning against her as she leaned against a tree. It was like a pen and ink drawing except for the splash of scarlet. "Just call me if anything changes. And thanks," she added and clicked the phone closed.

A part of Catherine was elated at the idea of being in his arms again, at the thought of seeing his face. Another part of her felt hollow and full of dread. She sensed that this time with him would be different. She wasn't afraid of him as much as she was afraid of herself. Would she be able to say 'no' again? To not let him know where Cate was? To resist the demand that he had a right to know? To walk away from the suite without telling him and return to her real life in time for dinner?

MANHATTAN

"Mrs. C," Mark was saying. "You can wear that tomato red. It rocks! Ditch anything maroon or wine-colored but that particular red is perfect."

The two of them were in Bendel's. Angora sweaters were on sale and Mark was at her side, as usual, picking out things she probably wouldn't have.

"Yes, I feel good in that red. And you're right. It has to have some yellow in it and not blue. Maroon or wine is death for me."

"But get it one size smaller." He held it out for her.

"What? But I've always been a size—"

"Not anymore," he said firmly. "Your sweaters are too baggy." He wanted to say "If you've got it, flaunt it!" but he censored himself and said, "You've been wearing your clothes too big for too long!"

She shook her head, faintly smiling, and watched him finger through the stack for the smaller size.

An hour later, they were at a little café on Madison Avenue, had checked all the shopping bags and the waiter had brought them Bloody Marys.

"I wonder what I'm doing this for," she said suddenly.

"What do you mean?"

"Buying the clothes, cutting my hair differently." She took the celery stalk out of the goblet then sipped.

"You're doing it for *yourself*," said Mark.

"Really?" she said. "I do wonder why I'm doing it."

Mark glimpsed the unhappiness in Mrs. Cortland very rarely. There'd been that day at the salon with the appearance of the tears but she so seldom let her mask slip. After they'd both ordered pasta and green salads, she spoke again.

"I guess I have everything. Four children, a successful husband, a cottage in Bermuda, and I live on Fifth Avenue. I have grandchildren and a husband . . ."

"You said 'husband' twice," said Mark.

"Did I?" She looked vague. "Funny." She sighed and took another sip of the tomato juice. "Because he is what I most definitely do not have."

"Do you want him?" asked Mark.

She drew back, away from the table, in surprise. "What an astounding question!"

"Sorry! I—I just blurted it out." Mark worried that he'd gone too far. He had never met Stanford J. Cortland but he'd seen his photograph and his name in *The New York Times*, in *Town & Country* and there'd been that huge interview in *Vanity Fair*. The couple were oh-so-social and he was always giving money to the Met or to some museum. He was a titan, a billionaire. Mark's only experience with him was hearing Mrs. C's side of the conversation with him on the phone. He shouted at her. Mark hated him because he imagined that he was terrible to his wife and Mark adored Mrs. Cortland.

She ignored his apology. "I don't know! But it is so funny that you would ask that because lately—just in the past month—I've been wondering what my life would be like without him."

Mark leaned forward over the white tablecloth. "Then let me tell you."

Brooke Cortland would think, as she got into bed that night, alone in her bedroom down the hall from her husband of thirty-five years, that it was so simple. All she had to do was pick up the phone and call a lawyer. Her lawyer. This wasn't Victorian England or present-day Yemen. She fluffed the pillow and slept. Deeply, with no dreams.

BROOKLYN

Mark was saving money. For the first time in his life he was doing better than scraping by. It was because of Mrs. C. She had changed his life. Previous impossibilities seemed less impossible. "You know what I want more than anything?" he said to Lori one evening as he poured her a glass of their favorite sauvignon blanc. Lori was feeling very relaxed and had actually left her cell phone downstairs. She did not have to even think until 8 o'clock in the morning. They were in Mark's kitchen, all white and stainless steel.

"What? To find a lover who looks like John Barrymore? Who has a chateau in France and a villa in Italy—

"No. Seriously."

Lori was silent for a moment. "Tell me."

"I want my own salon. I want it in Manhattan. I want it to be mine."

"But those women make you crazy!" exclaimed Lori. "Except for Mrs. C, of course."

"Not all of them. If it were my salon then I could pick and choose my clients." He plucked a garlic clove from the basket on the counter and started to peel away what he called the paper. Lori had taught him a few things in the kitchen. Actually, more than a few things. Mark felt he could actually dare to say that he could now cook.

"You really love it, don't you?" she said softly. "Doing hair."

"Yes. It's been my curse really."

Lori knew he had a stock broker father, came from a Republican family who lived in Briarcliff Manor in Westchester County about thirty miles from New York City. "Briarcliff Manor! Oh, for heaven's s sake! What is this—someplace John Cheever made up?" She teased him when he told her. How he laughed since the Cheevers were his parents' neighbors.

"Curse?"

"Oh, you know. I was supposed to get the MBA at Wharton and I dropped out one semester before graduation and my father will never get over it. Never."

"You never told me that," she murmured. She filled the pot with water for pasta, turned off the faucet.

"Well, that's what I did. After all the hoopla of getting in, I dropped out. But much worse, the stuff of massive strokes, was *coming out*. When I do something I really do something. The same week of dropping out, I pulled the coming out."

"Your mother is on your side, isn't she? More or less?" Lori tossed salt into the water.

"Sometimes more, sometimes less." Mark was concentrating on chopping the garlic. The knife was making little twak noises on the cutting board. "I think she hides talking on the phone with me." He scraped the garlic into the frying pan where the butter was melting. "Why couldn't I just be a leper or a terrorist, for God's sake? Something more acceptable than a fag?"

When this happened, when he got started on this, Lori talked him through it. She knew he suffered and she knew what to say. She knew when to listen and when it was veering into self-pity. She knew precisely when to tell him to snap out of it. Tonight, she said, "What about a movie later? I just got *The Crying Game* from Netflix," and he burst out laughing.

CORAL GABLES

The sun was setting over Biscayne Bay in a blaze of orange and yellow. The clouds were like whipped crème hundreds of feet high hovering over the ocean. A tropical Turner. Annie stood on her balcony combing out her wet hair, thinking, good for me. Even if he's married, I'm glad I am doing this. I'm having dinner with someone who isn't paying for the pleasure of my company. I have so little time off, she decided, that it's time for me to do something not related to real estate, not related to Imperial. Well, okay, not related to Imperial.

It wasn't a date, it was a time to talk about condos and money laundering. Or movies and books. He was very attractive with wonderful taste in clothes and very much in love with his wife. Annie didn't care. That was perfect, actually. She really wanted to talk and talk and talk and to be with someone she was not going to go to bed with. What a relief, she marveled. To not have to take off my clothes until I get home.

Their table was up a flight of stairs from the main floor of the French brasserie in Coral Gables. "A terrific change for me," she smiled as they sat down.

"Where do your swains usually take you?" he grinned. They both found the word *swain* absurdly funny. "As in swain flu?" she countered and he laughed. "Now, be serious! You're blonde and delicious. You must train the swain." He ordered a bottle of wine. "Is swain plural?" She giggled. He said, "I don't know. Do you have a main swain? Let's make it plural. Train the swain. Keep them *all* under control."

Annie tossed her pashmina over her bare shoulders and thought, I like this man. He's playful.

"What just went through your mind?"

Ordinarily, she would have hated the question and lied but this time she answered. "I suddenly thought this man is playful. What fun. Most American men aren't at all."

"And most American women don't know how to flirt. If they do, they have certainly decided not to."

The wine was poured, the banter only interrupted by a waiter reciting the specials. The mussels came and went; the red snapper arrived. Annie spoke French when she asked for another slice of lemon and Intriago suddenly said, "I want to know about you. Why did you come to Miami?"

"You really want to know? It could be very dark." Her blonde pixie spike haircut and her big blue eyes suddenly looked so innocent that he had to stifle a smile. "How dark? Think I can't take a little dark?"

"Bad love affair," she said nonchalantly, taking a sip of wine. "Baaaaad."

"And you fled the scene to start over?" He was being light but his sincerity was evident. Annie thought how long it had been since she'd told a man the truth about anything over dinner. Last night she'd told the Saudi that her mother was a princess in exile from Sweden and that nearly everyone in the family had been executed at the end of World War II. He had believed her.

So now Annie took a deep breath. "I went to the University of Wisconsin, majored in French. I wanted to be a writer and pictured myself on the Left Bank in a café scribbling in notebooks, drinking wine all day. The University itself is pretty liberal but I wanted something *more* liberal, very different, wanted to be far away from my family, from the winters." She looked past him, thinking. From my grandfather. From being hit, from the fear of being hit the next time. Don't think of him. Dead of a heart attack at seventy-two. "So, of course, I went to L.A., got myself an apartment and immediately fell into the whole California life. I dated all these men my own age—mostly screenwriters. You know, of course, that everyone in L.A. is writing a screenplay. Including me. I did it just like everybody else. If someone serves you coffee, they have this treatment in their apron pocket. When someone parks your car, he's got some typed pages stuck in his jeans waistband. It's wild." She paused. "I called them men but they were really boys. They were just like my dates in college but with less money and a tan." She smiled. "One step above or below all the actors waiting for the big break. I never decided if actors were more or less desirable."

Intriago took a sip of wine, listening.

"Everything is timing, isn't it? Just when I'd broken it off with about the fourth one of these unemployed screenplay writers, I swore off men."

"Completely? And forever?"

"Oh, yes, this was it. I'd had enough. Finito. Fini. I was on such an anti-man crusade that if I'd seen a convent on La Brea, I probably would have wrecked the car making a U-turn to get in." She sighed. "This is so predictable. Sure you don't want to talk about Iraq? The national debt?"

"It's not predictable to me." His voice was serious.

She took a sip of wine. "So, of course, at my lowest point, I met—or rather re-met this producer at a party. He was twenty-five years older, divorced again, from wife number four. On the prowl, on the loose. And of course, the more warnings I heard, the more I wanted to be with him." She shrugged her bare, golden shoulders in the yellow dress. "End of story." What she didn't say was that her best friend in L.A. had insisted it was a father fixation. It had really annoyed her so, of course, it stuck in her mind. Why did she say that? Just because he died when I was twelve? Or had he? If you say it enough times, does that make it true?

Annie decided years ago that it was easier to say her father died. The first time she thought it was bad luck to say, the second time she wondered what she would do if her father overheard and materialized before her. The third time she worried that it was true. But after the fourth time she said he died, Annie came to believe that he really had. Annie looked at the white damask tablecloth without speaking. Suddenly she could see his red truck parked in the driveway.

Intriago was silent, waiting. Finally he spoke. "You're not going to tell me what happened?"

"You are sophisticated. You figure it out." She was smiling ruefully.

"So he hurt you. Badly."

She shrugged and he could see the glint of tears in her eyes before she looked down at her lap. "I thought I loved him. Really loved him. Not like the little boy screenwriters. I thought I'd be his next wife and not just the good time girl between wives."

Intriago said nothing for a long moment. The din of the restaurant, the scraping of chairs, voices raised in conversation flowed around them. "Don't you dare feel used," he said in a stern voice. "I know what I'm talking about so pay close attention to me."

She looked up quickly, eyes wide in surprise.

"You weren't used. You had a good time. Do not feel he used you."

That's exactly what she had felt. Up till now.

Intriago went on. "You are too special to be used. And you weren't. You had fun with a man who likes to get married. He probably doesn't like to *be* married but he likes the weddings. The man is obviously lousy at the being married part." She stared at him then took a gulp of wine. Tears glittered in her eyes but didn't fall. "How long ago was this?"

"Two years or so," she said.

"How long did his last marriage last?"

She started to feel better. "A year and a half."

He looked at his watch. "Okay, it's now almost nine o'clock on the East Coast, and almost six in Los Angeles."

What was he getting at? She stared at him.

Intriago continued. "Wouldn't you rather be sitting here with me instead of in a lawyer's office in L.A.?"

She almost smiled. "Yes, I would."

He signaled the waiter and ordered a bottle of champagne. "Best you've got," he instructed then looked across the table at Annie again. "Might as well celebrate happy endings," he said. "Or fresh starts."

Annie blinked away the tears she suddenly saw as ridiculous and thought, I like this man.

It was the following Wednesday, another dinner in Coral Gables. Annie was thrilled to be picked up at home, at not having to drive and park and she loved his car.

"It's a 1983 Jag," said Carlito. The dashboard was shining, polished wood and the whorls looked like melted caramel and chocolate. Annie stroked it. "So smooth," she smiled. "And I love that it's cobalt blue. No other color would do. It suits you." Intriago looked pleased and passed a car on the causeway as if to emphasize the superior horsepower of his special car.

Intriago's wife was out of town. "Does she know about me?" asked Annie. "Is this really okay? Our having dinner together?"

"Yes," he said. "I told her all about you. We've got a daughter your age and she trusts me." He paused. "You will like her. We have a big Christmas party every year and you're on the list. It's time you two met."

They never saw him. Rafael Solito watched them enter the restaurant, watched them follow the maître d' to a banquette in back. "Pedro," he said, "Look who's here. Straight ahead in blue. Just sitting down. What a surprise. Tell me if she and that man with her are lovers or business partners."

A few minutes later, Pedro went to the men's room and walked by their table. "They are talking, drinking, but no, I don't think lovers," he said.

Rafael Solito did not like Alyssa being with Carlito Intriago. Intriago had been a federal prosecutor, he had worked closely with law enforcement. Was he a client? Or was Alyssa giving him information? It didn't matter. What mattered was that she was with him at all. Intriago was trouble.

The Colombians finished the meal and left the restaurant an hour later. Rafael climbed into the back seat of the black Mercedes 500SL as Chico, his driver, held the door open. Pedro got into the front seat. It was a big car fitted with bulletproof windows which was easy to have done in Miami. This was his 'dressy car,' whereas the big, black Escalade was for every day. The air was sweet outside but Rafael preferred the frigid breath of air-conditioning. The skyscrapers of downtown Miami rose majestically across the water outside the tinted windows; they glittered like towers of diamonds on the coastline which was often called the American Riviera.

Two hours later, Rafael could not sleep and thought a Montecristo cigar on the terrace would calm him. It did not. Neither did the last half of a bottle of Remy Martin. As the sky was becoming a soft gray backlit by the pink of sunrise, he went to his bedroom and, after gulping a handful of pills, slept.

ALBANY/MANHATTAN

Burton was on the line again. The third time this week. "Forget the formal investigations. We've got that covered from up here."

Gladly, thought Winters. "So you want the personal finances, the family, his father maybe?" He had the last of the bank records in an unopened envelope right in front of him.

"Exactly. Let's forget the political angle and go after the personal. I'll be in touch."

Winters hung up the phone. The personal. Good. He thought politics was about as exciting as flossing your teeth.

MANHATTAN

"Just do what I tell you!" he shouted. He was holding his briefcase about to ring for the elevator. Azura was clearing the breakfast dishes from the dining room beyond the front hall and could hear him but he didn't care. Usually he shouted on the other side of closed doors.

"Stanford, it isn't right to cancel at this late date and I simply won't do it. They asked us nearly two months ago and we accepted. It's black tie, it's a sit down dinner and—"

"I don't give a damn! I have to be in London and that's where I'm going to be!"

London? Claridge's? A little bell sounded in Brooke's head. London. Linked with Pliameri and sixty-two thousand dollars? "You have to be in London?" she repeated.

"Yes! I do! It's business and can't be changed!" He pushed the elevator button and said, under his breath, "Just go by yourself. Leave me out of it."

Brooke watched him. His face was red, he was enraged as he stepped into the elevator without so much as a nod or a "good morning" to Harry. She stood in the front hall for a long moment, thinking. I will go by myself but I won't leave you out of it. Something is going on and I will find out what it is.

She spent the next hour with a big white tablet. Brooke drew a line down the middle and labeled one side 'what I know' and the other side 'what I don't know.' The 'don't know' list was blank which actually made her laugh. What she knew was: S was wiring money every month from his account to HSBC to an account called Pliameri. Why was she linking this to London? There was no reason to as the HSBC branch was in New York City. A feeling. No. More than a feeling. The wires always went a week or a few days before the trip to London. Never after. That was the only pattern she could pick up from looking at her calendar because he kept his in his briefcase. She had not been able to get her hands on it. Brooke looked back at her date book and saw that every month for the past four, he had gone to London for two days and supposedly stayed at Claridge's. She found the number on the Internet and dialed. The invitation from the Blakeleys was in her hand. "Yes, I'm calling for Mr. Stanford Cortland to confirm his reservation on—" she looked at the date for the dinner. "The 14th of this month." She waited, listened. Impetuously, she asked, "Yes, and is that his usual room?"

"Mr. Cortland has reserved his usual suite for two nights. The Davies penthouse."

"Thank you so much."

She hung up the phone and suddenly felt very tired. He *was* having an affair. Stanford's miserly nature was a joke to their friends, to their sons. Clothes, cars, houses—he spent money on that but anything he decided was superfluous was unacceptable. Claridge's was acceptable but not the penthouse! She remembered their first trip together after they'd gotten married when he'd been asked if he wanted to take a larger room at the hotel. "No, thank you," he had said. "We'll be sleeping and won't know how big the room is."

So, the old bull won't be simply sleeping in his suite at Claridge's. And he won't be alone because all that square footage is to impress someone. She wrote a few more notes in the 'know' column and then as a last addition, wrote, carefully, in block letters: **STANFORD IS COMMITTING ADULTERY**. She walked to the window and stared out at the park eleven stories below for a long moment and then she made up her mind.

Mark arrived at noon to do her hair for the fund raiser at the Plaza that evening. Azura and a second maid set up lunch on a table in the room just off her dressing room which was a small sitting room with chintz sofas and yellow walls; pale blue sky was outside the windows.

As always, Mark was full of gossip about the salon which Brooke didn't relish the way he did but she was so fond of Mark that she enjoyed his enthusiasm. He and Lori, his downstairs neighbor, were close friends and they'd gone to see *Spamalot* on Broadway. He was going to the gym again plus he'd been happy to read that drinking a few glasses of wine every day meant one would live longer than any self-righteous teetotaler. "Let's toast those experts!" he said. It was a cheerful running commentary to Brooke, a restful sort of background music to the thoughts of Stanford spinning through her mind.

After the blowout, she looked in the mirror in silence; Mark wondered if something were wrong. "I've decided to ask Stanford for a divorce," she said quietly.

Mark tried to hide his sense of elation but couldn't quite do it. "Good for you! Good for you!"

Brooke put down the hand mirror and said, "But first, there is something I have to do."

Twenty minutes later, Mark knew her plan and had agreed to help her. "Let's put him through hell!" he chortled.

Brooke almost smiled, suddenly feeling a bit stronger. "Hell would be nice," she said, "but let's at least make sure his every waking hour is lived in a state of total panic."

BROOKLYN

Lori was very quiet when regaled with the news that evening. Mark was jubilant, highly excited and didn't notice. "We're going to punish him! The monster! The cheating bastard!" He splashed wine into their glasses and walked back and forth between the living room couch and the kitchen, talking nonstop. "Do you want to order pizza? I'm sort of in the mood. And do you still have any of those brownies we bought yesterday? Typical dinner for healthy New Yorkers, right?"

He was on the phone giving the address, specifying pepperoni on one, black olives on the other. "You don't want bread sticks, do you?" he called out to her. "Overkill," she called back. She was losing weight just being with Mark and knew it was time to buy jeans at least two sizes smaller.

Lori heard him hang up and start taking plates out of the cupboard. I'll just listen, she told herself. I won't say anything. I'm just a witness, a bystander. She took a sip of wine and clarified that to 'innocent bystander' but didn't believe it.

BOSTON

On Friday morning, Catherine arranged her bureau drawers meticulously. She shook out and refolded her already perfectly folded scarves. Separated her underwear by color. All was in order before she began but she felt she had to do something before leaving the house and she couldn't concentrate on the newspapers, didn't want to deal with Angie about the washing machine repair man or dinner menus. Her desk was immaculate as always. Her laptop was off, the lid closed. She went to her closet and decided two pairs of shoes should be taken to the shoemaker. At eleven, she began to dress with care. Turquoise sweater over the new aqua underwear, winter-white wool trousers, high boots, long gray cashmere coat. The hat, of course, and the dark glasses.

She felt that today would be the last time she would ever see Brad Baker. He had waited, had decided how to play it and this afternoon he would go at her with both barrels. He wanted Cate. The sophisticated and lovely young woman who had once been a cherub in his lap called Cathy Ann. He, with no children, at age forty-one, wanted his daughter.

Catherine could not let this happen, could not think of any way that this would turn out well for Cate, for Holtie or for her, so she would do all in her power to not let him ever find Cate. She told herself that he could not find her, not ever. She had a new last name, actually a new first name, had been legally adopted by Holtie and lived in New York. She was a grown woman with a stepfather she loved. The only father she'd ever really known and the best father anyone could wish for. Even if Brad promised to never tell her how he'd found her, it would come out. Maybe in ten years but it wouldn't be a secret forever. The afternoons in the Grand Plaza. The ad. The money. Catherine cringed. Nothing could ever persuade her to let Brad near Cate. She would lose Holtie, probably Cate, too, if they ever found out. Holtie had been an answered prayer to a struggling single mother in Ohio, disowned by her family. He had saved her life, both their lives actually. He had stepped in whereas Brad had stepped out. Left the scene, no forwarding address, no money. And if he hadn't really died, he might as well have. Holtie *was* Cate's father.

Catherine's father had physically existed but been distant, silent, a nonentity. Her mother had been the screamer. The only time he'd raised his voice was when he told her to pack a suitcase and leave. She remembered his shouting at her, calling her a tramp and a disgrace. He'd stood in the doorway of her room as she stared at her bulletin board with all those thumb-tacked photographs from high school. Absurdly, she'd wanted to take it with her. She had never seen either of her parents again and it was only on that hokey holiday, Father's Day, that she wondered if he were alive.

Cate was lucky, decided Catherine. She was adamant, would not be swayed. Brad Baker was not going to intrude. She left the house as usual, walked four blocks, got into a cab and fifteen minutes later was ascending in the elevator.

Her little watch said twelve noon exactly as she raised her gloved hand to knock. The same footsteps on the same marble floor—it all rushed back at her. That same excitement of every meeting.

He opened the door and smiled. She noticed a tiny cut under his ear and imagined that he had been nervous shaving that morning. Maybe nervous about seeing her, having this discussion. He didn't kiss her, didn't take her in his arms but motioned for her to come in and then, still not speaking, took her coat and expertly opened a bottle of champagne. Catherine sat on the white sofa where she usually sat and watched him turn the cork, heard the 'sigh' of the air being released, and told herself not to drink too much, not to relax too much. Be careful, she thought.

"It's good to see you," he said as he handed her the flute. His tone was serious. The bubbles were golden in the sunlight streaming in the tall floor-to-ceiling windows. He sat beside her then seemed to change his mind and moved to the other side of the glass and chrome coffee table to sit on the other white sofa.

"To us," he said and they both lifted their glasses and sipped.

Silence.

Catherine was thinking, here it comes. He's going to demand that I allow him to see her and I'm going to have to stand up to him. I must be strong. Now he wants to be a father! I'll ask where he was when I had no money to buy food, when I worked at the A&P for minimum wage at the check-out. Where was he when *our* child was sick and I had to borrow money from the neighbor for a doctor? Where was he when I was so desperate I remember adding water to the milk in her bottle? Where was he when I waited for the second bus every morning in winter darkness? Where was he when our daughter was still Cathy Ann and cried out for Poppy when she waked from a bad dream? I have plenty of questions, she decided. And plenty to say. She took another sip. I'm ready for him.

His voice crashed through her thoughts. "I want you back."

SOUTH BEACH

"Annie!" Intriago grinned. "What a surprise!"

They kissed cheeks back and forth, genuinely happy to see each other. "Lucky you, lucky me!"

Annie's spiky blonde hair gave her the look of a sprite; this evening her freckles showed under the light makeup. Pink lipstick matched the short fuchsia silk dress and the four-inch heels.

The reception at the Delano was for investors in real estate; Intriago was on his way out after meeting an old friend for a drink. They agreed that Annie would work the room and he would meet her at the bar in an hour. "Unless, of course, I am about to sell a twenty million dollar property," said Annie.

"Cut me in and all is forgiven."

"Finder's fee always honored," she said to his back as he disappeared into the crowd of men in pastel sports jackets and women wearing ornate jewelry floating on bronzed cleavage. The air was heavy with perfume.

An hour later, they sat at the bar, both a bit tired but not tired enough to end the evening. "A last mojito?" Carlito asked and she nodded.

When the drinks were placed before them, he said, "Annie, my little bird, what's wrong?"

Her smile was quick, nervous. "How well you read me." She lowered her voice. "Someone has been coming into my apartment. They've—"

"Who?" Carlito demanded. "Are you sure?"

She glanced at the bartender and instantly Carlito slipped off his stool, grabbed both glasses and said, "Come on. A table."

When they were settled across from each other, he asked, "Are you positive?"

"Yes. I am pretty careful about organizing my life because, in college, I was a mess." She thought it was a reaction to her perfectionism in high school. "I lost keys, my wallet would always be in the wrong purse. A disaster. So I did a one-eighty and now I know where every document, every piece of jewelry is. I have twenty-five pairs of underpants. My shoes are lined up like somebody's in the military. Most of all, I am meticulous about my desk. All personal documents are in one drawer. My checkbook is in a certain drawer with bank statements. Everything is at right angles, pages paper-clipped, files labeled. I alphabetize my bills on the 5th of every month."

"Christ," said Carlito. "That is terrifying."

She took a sip of the mojito. "So believe me when I say I know someone has been going through my things." Blonde eyebrows were raised. "I know."

"Have you called the police?"

Annie shook her head.

"Have you talked to security at your condo?"

She shook her head again, staring down into her drink.

"What is it? You can tell me. Come on. You're in trouble and I'm here. Open up, yellow bird." He put one hand on her slender, tan arm and waited. "So you know who it is, is that it?"

They sat in silence. She stared past him, those blue eyes focusing on nothing. He moved his hand away and waited. "This is really, really hard," she began. He didn't say anything. "Well, you know the Miami market has been pretty dismal." She gulped air. "I make some money on the side." She took a big swallow of the rum drink and plunged into what she considered a confession. "I work for an escort service. It pays well and so far, it's been very lucrative. It's been okay." She looked at his face with tears in her eyes. Suddenly she thought that maybe it wasn't okay. She had never imagined having to tell anyone she admired and respected about it. About taking off her clothes and fucking strangers.

"Annie! It is okay." He put his arm around her immediately. "It's fine."

"You don't think I'm horrible? That I'm a—whore?" she whispered dabbing at her eyes.

Carlito Intriago laughed. "No!" He handed her his white handkerchief. "I've been around, you know. I'm not twelve years old."

"I don't know if I feel better or worse that you know," she said. "The fact is that it's saved me. It's the reason I'm still here. My commissions this past year would not support me for a week." She bit her lip. "I keep wondering who."

"So you do think it might be someone you know? A client?"

She nodded. "It's just a feeling with nothing to back it up. I have no enemies. None that I know of. I mean, Marta, my boss at Mira, isn't crazy about me but she's been quite reasonable in tossing me listings lately." She shook her head. "There's no one in my life that I can imagine being curious enough to go through my stuff."

"You don't have to tell me but who, usually, are your clients?"

"I get businessmen down here who want a dinner or sometimes a whole night. They can be from Chicago or Texas or Phoenix or anywhere. The rest are nearly all South American. Some Eurotrash. Once in awhile a Saudi. Those are super wealthy and it's usually a night and lots of times it's two of us. They might talk their girlfriend into joining us or they'll fly in another girl."

There were ten girls in Miami but Caroline had been the other girl nearly every time since she'd been with Imperial before the others had been available. Plus, the clients liked her so she was usually the one for a threesome even if meant her coming down from New York.

They talked softly for awhile, finished their drinks. Carlito walked her to her car and waited until she was in the Mini Cooper, had clicked on the air-conditioning. "Seat belt," he reminded her through the open window. "I don't want to lose you, Annie. Be careful and call me on my cell anytime. Whenever. No matter what time it is."

He walked to his vintage Jaguar through the warm Florida night feeling troubled. Intriago was well aware that Miami was full of bad guys with evil on their minds.

LONDON—THE CALEDONIAN CLUB

The tall Scotsman in a kilt nodded and opened the door for her. Matthew had been the doorman at the Caledonian Club forever and was just as much a part of the atmosphere as the plaid carpeting or the animal heads mounted on the walls. The building had once been a very grand private house in London; it sat on Halkin Street just across from Belgrave Square.

"Darling!" said her husband, standing up and walking towards her. He was wearing a dinner jacket and holding a flute of champagne. "You look smashing!" He kissed her quickly on the lips.

"It must be this afternoon's walk in the park. It was drizzling and I loved it."

"Bet the monster canine did, too," he said. "Let's sit in here," he said leading her into a tremendous sitting room off the main lobby. The ceiling was very high and the long windows let in the last of the daylight and a glimpse of early spring leaves from the square. The floor moved slightly under them as this had been the ballroom which had been structured to give under the dancers' feet. "To keep them dancing til dawn," she'd been told the first time she'd been in the club. They sat down on one of the couches and she crossed her long bare legs which were still tan from a week in the Bahamas. "You look awfully, awfully, frightfully smashing yourself!" she teased him. Her accent was American. She put her hand on his sleeve and he put his hand on her knee.

"Let's celebrate something," he said. "Anything. Being with you. Let me get you a bit of this." He caught the eye of a waiter in plaid trousers who stood over them immediately.

"Just club soda," she said. "I don't want to get sleepy."

He looked at her, thinking: this is new. Then he said, "Tell me what we're seeing tonight. I haven't the vaguest idea what we're in for. I only know it's opening night and that it's dinner afterwards with the Grevilles."

She sat beside him in the darkened theatre and with a wave of emotion, suddenly thought how much she loved him. She hated the test results, hated the very idea of any tests at all but after three years of marriage it had seemed sensible to find out. At first, she insisted there had been a mistake. She seduced him every chance she could but sometimes saw the sadness in his eyes. With a man, it was all tied up with ego, with his feelings of virility and strength. It occurred to her at least once a day how much she loved him and she always felt renewed and pleased and fortunate. All new emotions for her, emotions that being with him had nourished. She turned very slightly to look at his straight nose, his handsome profile in the dark. I'd do anything to make him happy, she thought. Yes. She told herself to put it out of her mind, to not think of it now. My husband—such *a good man*. As if sensing her affection, he reached over and took her hand in his.

BROOKLYN

Lori had been on the phone for nearly an hour, having no luck. "I need at least three of you so if anything changes and you can come, text me or call me that minute!" She hung up with Karen.

She hated to do it but texted Bree asking her to call. Minutes later, her cell rang. "What's the problem?" came the calm voice from New Jersey.

"Erik von Haffen wants three or four girls for a party on his yacht in Southampton next Saturday night and—"

"We've got at least twenty girls in the city," said Bree. "They can't *all* be busy."

"The thing is: they all know him."

"Oh. That is a problem," said Bree. She was staring at her computer screen, flipping through the pages of the Imperial Club website quickly.

Erik von Haffen was the spoiled brat bachelor son of Donna von Haffen whose name was everywhere. She was to women's beach wear what Vera Wang was to wedding dresses. "He gives all these parties in his loft downtown so I guess everyone's slept with him already." Lori saw his name in magazines, in *The New York Post*, at least every other week.

"Have you called anyone who's not from New York? Anyone who's new? What about Karen?" Bree was staring at her photo on the screen.

"Busy. And I tried to get Sabrina but she's out of town for the next two weeks. Maya is having foot surgery, Simone is at Canyon Ranch. Savannah is booked. Caroline is booked."

"Okay. If you are sure there is nobody here in town for him, call him back and say that you have three girls in Miami who will be just what he wants. He'll okay the fare and the overnights. Alyssa is dependable. Get her. Try Madison and Donatella. If he wants more than three, tell him you'll do your best and see if Noelle or Guinivere in Boston can come down for the weekend. Do a deal for the three for Miami first. Get them locked in to do it. Two nights, plane fare, two hundred each for transfers. Maybe his helicopter can pick them up at Laguardia or downtown and get them out to Long Island." She stopped. "He may even have a guest in Miami flying up in a private plane. Be sure and ask."

Lori was taking notes with little clicks on her computer. She already had air fares for next Friday morning from Miami to LaGuardia on the screen.

"And Lori, before you call him back make sure you have the three in Miami. Or three from somewhere. Don't call him back without being able to offer the girls for sure. You know how these men hate details and call backs."

"Got it! Thanks, Bree." Lori was already writing down fares and schedules.

"Text me if you have any problems and I'll help you. We don't want to lose a good client." They said goodbye and hung up.

Five seconds later, Lori was saying, "Alyssa? Hi, it's Lori."

MANHATTAN

They decided a park bench was the safest place to talk. They'd used the 78th Street entrance at noon and were settled. Mark wondered if that squirrel was wearing a wire. He kept getting really close and he was staring at Mrs. C more intently than seemed reasonable.

"If we knew what Pliameri was and what the sixty thousand dollars—sixty-*two* thousand dollars was for, we could use that against him. To really scare the pants off him," Mark was saying, still watching the squirrel.

"Scare the pants off him?" said Brooke.

"Sorry, Mrs. C," he said quickly. "I just think that the more details we know, absolutely know, and can let him know we know then the more frightened he'll be."

Mark had looked for Pliameri on the Internet and, just like Brooke, had only come up with a few people on Facebook. All seemed to be teenagers or a minute older.

"I may be wrong but my instinct is that Pliameri and that money—since I don't actually know what it's for—are linked to London and those days he goes there. It has to be, doesn't it? But no one would pay that much for sex," Brooke stopped. "Would they?"

"No. It's crazy. Never," agreed Mark. He and Lori had never talked about the fees that Imperial charged but all those thousands of dollars? It was impossible. Then he had a terrible thought: what if it was some kind of really kinky sex? Like snuff sex when they killed people. No! He literally blinked the awful thought away and spoke again. "Could he be investing in a company called Pliameri? Could it be as simple and obvious as that and London and Claridge's have nothing to do with it?"

"Then why can't either one of us find Pliameri? It's just not anywhere and I can even 'Google' myself."

"Okay, then let's get him with what we know and maybe Pliameri will explain itself. But a penthouse suite at Claridge's every month should be enough. Should we start with getting a fake e-mail account and sending him a little note?"

"He doesn't really use the Internet much," Brooke was saying. "His secretaries do, his associates do but he's still a phone person, still writes letters to everybody."

"So if we go after him via e-mail then he'll have to ask for help and do we want that?"

"No. I want him to suffer alone. I don't want him to call in anyone to try to stop us or catch us." She hesitated. Would he hire a private detective? She didn't think he ever had. "I think we should do this in an old-fashioned way that he can handle on his own and that way he'll be the only person we have to fool." Stanford always thought he knew best. He was the expert in every little thing. He actually criticized the way she buttoned a jacket from the bottom button up. Every time. For thirty-five years. "Yes," she reiterated. "Let's make sure he thinks he can do it on his own. I don't want him to hire a detective." She hesitated. "Plus, he would be very reluctant to confide in anyone about this certain transgression. Even a stranger. Even someone he was paying to help him. Because," she smiled in triumph. "He would be furious at the idea of making a mistake and admitting that he'd been caught!"

Mark grinned. "I love it love it love it!" He was distracted by the Sabrett cart twenty feet away. "Hey, Mrs. C, we need sustenance for plotting. My treat. Mustard, sauerkraut? Both? Diet Coke? Diet Pepsi?"

In minutes, they were passing napkins back and forth and eating in contented silence. Brooke had taken off her tan suede gloves and her perfectly manicured nails with scarlet polish flashed brightly in the sun. Mark was thinking how lucky he was to even know a woman so graceful, so refined. Even the act of eating a hot dog on a park bench was imbued with elegance.

Brooke Cortland was thinking that nothing tasted so good as a hot dog, eaten in a park the size of Monaco with a good friend who made her laugh, who was loyal.

"So we skip the high tech and go old fashioned. I'm thinking movies of the thirties and forties. All that film noir," said Mark. "Paper. We use paper and notes printed on a printer at some Internet café or at some Kinko's on the West Side."

The West Side was another country to those who worked or lived on the East Side.

Brooke nodded. "And we have to wear gloves all the time." Suddenly she laughed. "But the money? How will we get the money? All I can think of is Hitchcock and lockers in bus stations."

"I don't think they have them in Manhattan anymore. Not at Grand Central or Penn Station or Port Authority. Not after 9/11."

Neither said anything for a few minutes and then Mark said, "Spies would use some contraption in the park that looked like a rock but opened up with a waterproof compartment in it."

Brooke laughed at the idea of Stanford, in one of his banker pinstriped suits, bending over trying to open a fake rock then attempting to stuff a shopping bag of bills into it. It was a cartoon worthy of the New Yorker.

They kept talking, kept trying out possible scenarios. "Simplicity," said Brooke.

"You're right, Mrs. C," agreed Mark. "We have to streamline this caper and watch our backs."

She looked at him and laughed happily then threw the last of her hot dog bun to the waiting squirrel.

BROOKLYN

That evening with Lori, Mark kept saying that he wished they had proof. He'd gone crazy looking for Pliameri and had come up with nothing. "Mrs. C is so funny plotting this! I've never seen her laugh so much. She's feeling so good getting him back. I've heard him actually yelling at her on the phone. Sometimes she holds it away from her ear he's so loud! He is a shit, a total bastard."

Mark was sautéing garlic in a frying pan as Lori made a salad. The water for the pasta was boiling. Lori was quiet but Mark didn't appear to notice. He was too busy trying out different ideas of how to send threatening notes and how to get the money delivered. "The money means nothing to her so I guess she will be taken care of in the divorce settlement," Mark was saying as he poured in the penne. "The money sounds wonderful to me but that's not the point, is it?" He went on, not waiting for an answer. "It's given her a sense of power after years, after decades of being bullied and shouted at." He put the lid on the big pot and Lori immediately took it off. It was one of about three running disagreements. He shrugged and continued. "It's making her feel strong and I love seeing that. Mrs. C is a good woman." He paused and amended. "A great woman."

Lori nodded, reached for the whisk and started mixing olive oil and lemon juice for the salad dressing. She wished Mark would talk about something else. He was opening one cabinet after another looking for something and really getting on her nerves. "If we knew what this Pliameri thing was and could find out what the sixty-two grand is for, *that* would give us real clout! That would give us a home run with this give-him-what-he's-got-coming-to-him plan! That would *really* level the bastard!"

The next evening, starting at eight, Lori was downstairs alone in her own apartment and her cell phone was "Pink Panther-ing all over the place," she would tell Becky. There were more bookings than usual and more than the usual "how is it going?" call backs. Noelle had texted her from a ladies room in Boston. "Horror show. Still at dinner. Dandruff, unibrow, hands like sandpaper. What do?" Lori texted back. "Eat v. slowly, be charming. Run the clock out. 1 hr. left."

Law & Order was on mute; she was missing the whole setup which was the first few minutes when the murder took place or the body was discovered. She knew she'd see it in reruns at some point in her life but this was a rather gloomy consolation. Lori fluffed up her pillows and reached for her cell again.

"Hi, Savannah. It's ten o'clock and he booked for three hours. Does he want another hour with you?" She waited. "Okay, get dressed, say 'ciao.'"

"Hi, Miranda. It's ten o'clock and his four hours are up. Does he want to book another hour? Okay, I'll hold on." She reached for the Diet Coke on her bedside table and waited then listened. "Good. I'll call you at eleven."

"Karen, it's Lori. Everything okay? His time is up. Ask him if he wants another hour or not. I'll hold." She took a sip of soda and stared at the laptop. "Great. You know how to handle it. I'll call you at midnight. Any problem, call me back."

Lori tapped the new hours into her computer then pushed it off to the side and leaned back on her pillows.

Mark was usually so with it! A suite at Claridge's—the penthouse suite for Chrissake— meant seduction and sex and adultery and it usually required a female person. Why couldn't he see that the sixty-two thousand was for *the girl*? And that Pliameri was linked to *the girl*?

Lori didn't know whether to keep listening to him agonize over proof or to just tell him. Bree and Jake would never know. Or would they? Who would Stanford Cortland blame? Who would he come after? Or could he come after anybody after Mark and Mrs. C worked him over?

PARIS

She thought about it incessantly. It was daring, it was unfathomably stupid but she couldn't stop thinking about it. What do I want? she said to herself looking in the mirror. She brushed her hair, put on pink lipstick then frowned.

She thought of last weekend in Gstaad with the banker from Zurich. She thought of the weekend before that in Cannes, high over the water, high over the port, with the Italian producer in his splendid villa. He was flirtatious, easy to please, rather juvenile. Last summer he had invited her for the Bastille Day fireworks. She and about a hundred guests, all tanned and attractive, had actually watched the fireworks *from above*. "We are special," joked an American film star. "We don't have to crane our necks but can simply gaze."

Mario had made a fortune making science fiction movies and loved spending it on fast cars, on race horses and on her. She decided she could sell the four diamond bracelets and the emerald ring and that would tide her over for awhile. Mario would never notice and anyway, she wouldn't see him again. She suddenly thought of what Klaus had given her. One night during dessert after dinner at the Ritz. There'd been gray metallic paper like silver and black ribbons which had floated into the chocolate mousse and been fished out. She'd impulsively licked a sweet dollop from the bow to the Count's unmitigated delight. It was an evening bag that had belonged to the Duchess of Windsor; he'd bought it at auction that afternoon. Van Cleef and Arpels. She'd never carried it; it rested in a bottom bureau drawer in her bedroom along with her good jewelry. Which is what it was. No larger than a paperback book, Art Deco in design set with diamonds and rubies. Bound to be worth something, she decided.

What do I want? I know what I don't want. I don't want to sleep with anyone but George. That means the only income I will have is from the shop since no one is buying my paintings. That means I have to leave this flat. She turned and looked at the large living room lined with five pairs of French doors opening onto the narrow terrace that stretched the entire length of the apartment. She took her morning coffee there and sometimes, if she were not going out in the evening, sat with her feet on the black wrought iron railing and sipped a glass of Sancerre five floors about the chaos of Avenue Montmartre. It was a Haussman building, elegant and grand. One of those buildings that tourists photographed from across the street. The apartment was perfect for her. A second bedroom and bath and a large kitchen were off the long hallway. Each room was painted a different shade of yellow, from what she called baby chicken to Dijon mustard, and furnished with what Americans called country French. She would hate to leave here but, unless she kept working, she could not afford the rent.

Je suis folle. I'm out of my mind, she thought. Delirious. Très stupide. In between the lectures she gave herself, she thought of him. He makes me laugh. My heart seems to hurt a little bit when I'm with him. Not hurt exactly, but I am aware of something in my chest. I could look at his face forever. I love his ears. A little bit too big but flat to his head. That shy smile. I feel light, alive. He holds my chair, he takes my arm crossing the street, he holds my hand, he looks at me as if I am a goddess and yet, he makes love to me as if it's the last time he will ever make love in his life. He devours me, he *takes* me.

The contrast between the George who now met her at a restaurant in that baggy American Brooks Brothers suit and the George who tore off his clothes back at the hotel and then held her in his arms and absorbed her, overwhelmed her, was unlike anything she'd ever known.

BROOKLYN

"Okay," said Lori. "I can't keep it from you any longer. You're my best friend."

Mark faced her on the new sofa. White leather. He had succumbed to the photograph in *Architectural Digest* and it had been delivered only two days before.

"What?" he wailed. This was unlike her. *He* was the drama queen and Lori was solid. Her very DNA was laced with common sense.

"You still need proof of Mr. C's adultery? Or did you find out about Pliameri?" Her voice was full of hope. Maybe she wouldn't have to tell him, after all.

He stared at her. "No. Same dead end with Pliameri, please play me Mary, pimento, palmetto, pistachio, whatever."

She took a sip of white wine and thought, okay. This is it. No turning back. "I can tell you but you can't tell Mrs. C what I'm telling you. Or—wait a minute. You can't tell Mrs. C how you know. That I know. That I told you."

"Are you going to tell me something?" he demanded. "Or just hint for ten years that you might someday tell me something?"

She put the wine glass on the coffee table then leaned back again. "Do you promise not to ever tell Mrs. C that I was the one who told you what I'm going to tell you?"

Mark stood up. "Yes! Yes, I promise! Lori! Tell me!"

"Okay. Because I think I could be killed if this ever gets out. I mean—"

"The mob? Pliameri is Mafia?" Mark's voice was unnaturally high-pitched when he was alarmed. A panicked soprano.

"Sit down. You're making me more tense than I already am."

Mark sat, leaning forward on the new white couch. Mark waited. He stopped breathing so great was the anticipation.

"Okay, here goes. I know Mr. C. He doesn't know I know who he is but he calls Imperial every month and orders a girl to be with him at Claridge's. She's thirty-one thousand a night and he has her for two nights. That's sixty-two thousand."

Mark was aghast. His eyes widened, his mouth dropped open and he clutched his chest with splayed fingers. "I had no idea of the numbers. You never told me it was so much! I never thought—"

Lori was determined to get it all out now that she'd begun. "A few days before his trip or sometimes even a week before, he wires the sixty-two grand to Pliameri Consulting. The girl gets some, Bree and Jake get some and I get my ten percent cut, as you know."

"Wow. So Pliameri is Imperial!" The proof! The sixty-two thousand! Now he and Mrs. C had all they needed.

Lori suddenly grinned. It felt good to tell him. "I always suspected that Stanford Cortland was a shit. He's rude to me for no reason so I can't even imagine what he's like to a wife. He thinks he is very, very special and everyone else is nothing. So you and Mrs. C take him for all he's worth. With my blessing! Bring him down! Taunt him!" Lori was thinking of all the times he'd been imperious to her on the phone. "Torture him!"

Mark started to laugh, delighted at the revelation, delighted at her enthusiasm. "Don't get carried away," he said. "It's just a little blackmail!"

MANHATTAN

Brooke Haverford Cortland had always been a good sport. She'd been the last to complain about a disappointment, even at age six. A canceled movie, a rained-out horse show, that was that. Couldn't be helped. She would never mention it again. She was the first to slap a Band-Aid on a skinned knee but the last to burst into tears about it. It was a great asset when dealing with riding or sailing, with tennis, skiing, skeet shooting. Brooke could be laser-focused on what she was doing and was known as relentless but when the contest was over, it was over. She accepted the trophy or congratulated her rival with exactly the same grace. As a grown woman, she had not changed.

Beneath the good manners and being a good sport, was a strong character. Once she had made up her mind to do something, nothing could stop her.

I am so pleasant with him, so 'this is just fine' with him, she was thinking. Maybe it's a flaw, she thought as she put on the pearl button earrings. Then she thought of Mark, took them off and put them back in her jewelry box. She opened the top drawer. "These crazy coin chandelier ones are just for fun!" he'd said when he'd handed her the box. Now she put them on and nodded. They twinkled and glittered. Mark. How sweet of him. She didn't care if they cost five dollars or five hundred. How long had it been since Stanford had given her a present? She wondered if she should count the anniversary dinner every June.

Maybe if I'd been more demanding at the start of the marriage. They say that second wives are always treated better. Maybe if I'd been Stanford's second wife it would have been different. But no, she'd married the smooth, handsome bachelor with the reputation for bedding every young girl on the East Coast. And I was made to feel that *I* was the lucky one.

So instead of being in a position to demand, which wasn't in me, anyway, I was in a position of putting up with what he was like. With getting used to doing everything his way. Getting used to always having him get his way. She put on lipstick and stared at herself in the mirror. *That* is going to change, she smiled. Mark and I are going to change that. Very soon.

"Brooke! Come on!" he was shouting from the front hall. As usual. He never came near her dressing room. He simply shouted until she came to *him*.

She stood up and thought, okay, here goes. I will *not* change my clothes no matter what he says.

It was several minutes later when he reached for his sunglasses on the hall table that he actually looked at her. She wondered how long it would take. "You can't be serious!" he roared.

"I'm perfectly serious," she said. "Everyone wears jeans nowadays. I will, too."

"No, you won't!" he shouted at her. "What's wrong with those things you usually wear? Those trousers?" He seemed to look at her more carefully and then erupted again. "A T-shirt! Do you think that's appropriate? You're not seventeen, you know!"

"Stanford, we're going to be late." It was unseasonably warm for the end of February and the navy blazer, the jeans, the cowboy boots he had not yet noticed were what she was wearing. No matter what he said, how he bellowed. She stood her ground on the Aubusson rug as he went on and on asking her what she thought she was doing.

"I'm going to a casual lunch in Connecticut on a Saturday afternoon and I'm wearing jeans," she answered calmly.

Since he'd rung for the elevator before seeing her, neither had noticed that Bobby was standing, waiting. His white gloved hand held the door open.

Old Mr. C was snorting and bellowing and his face was bright red, he would tell Harry later. "The old goat finally got into the elevator behind Mrs. Cortland and I took them down and they got into the Mercedes."

Bobby was pleased. He never would have dared but he wanted to wink at her.

There was that rush of happiness as she looked down and admired the shoes. She must have them. Chanel. Quilted leather ballet flats with the little bow and the patent leather tip across the vamp. "They're perfect," she told the clerk. "What other colors do you have in my size?"

"Let's see. We have red, the black ones you have on, of course. Umm. There's creme, navy and camel."

Kelsey smiled. "I'll take every color in size seven."

"Terrific. I'll pack them for you and be right back." The clerk went into the stockroom and whispered to Stacy who stood on a little ladder, "She's back again!"

"How many pairs this time?"

"Only five at $685 a shot. She must be going on an austerity kick." They both giggled. Linda found the shoes she was looking for and went out to face her customer.

Half an hour later, Kelsey was home and the boxes were in the front hall. Actually, there was no real front hall for her door opened directly into the living room. She'd just put up a screen wallpapered in lime green and white flowers as a room divider and created a sort of space three feet square that she called a front hall.

After making herself a sandwich, feeding Tinker and watching the news, Kelsey stacked the shoe boxes from the Chanel boutique on top of another row of boxes. This was the twelfth vertical row that reached her shoulder height. The arrangement of framed botanical prints was now completely covered and it was a bit difficult to open and close the front door. Kelsey pushed the boxes in more tightly and thought, maybe I'm due for a bigger apartment.

PARIS

Véronique was thinking that this evening, spending the entire night with him for the first time, was the happiest of her life. They wakened at about two and started talking as if they were sitting across from one another at dinner. "But this is better," he said pulling her into his arms. She put her face against his chest and nestled closer. "We fit," she purred. "Tell me what you were like as a little girl," he whispered. She laughed. "No, I want to know," he insisted. "Were you shy or a show-off, a tomboy, a little hellion or perfectly behaved?"

"I think I was perfectly behaved but my two aunts would tell you differently. I went to live with them when my father died. My mother left France to go to England as a governess for a family and she left me and my two sisters with them. They were very strict, very careful with us. With our clothes, with our manners. But they were good to me." She paused. "We had fun. We baked cookies, we played cards, we made dolls' clothes, we each had a dog. Three dogs. They were adorable aunts."

He told her about growing up in northern California. "That sounds as foreign to me as New Guinea," she said.

The conversation she had dreaded materialized. "But why?" he asked. "You are so magnificent. Why are you selling yourself?"

"I was going to do it just once," she said, snuggling closer to him, her cheek against his smooth chest. She paused. "And you opened the door. It was you. And . . ." She stammered. "I called them the next day and said I can't do this anymore."

"So I was your first one?"

"Yes. And I was so frightened. And then you were not what I expected and I liked you but I still decided to never do it again and I told them that."

"Them? The Imperial Club?"

"Yes."

"And what did they say?" asked George staring into the darkness. He felt very cold inside even though he thought he could listen to her accent forever.

"They tried to talk me into going out again but I just couldn't. Then they called and they said it was you and asked would I be with you." She wriggled closer and put her leg over his. "So now they know that I will only be with you."

George felt a wave of relief and pulled her up to face him. "So I was the only one you ever . . . ?"

"Yes. Yes, George. The only one." She leaned towards him and kissed him so sweetly, so gently that he thought his heart would burst.

CNN NEWS

Tonight Richard Quest had Dick Murton as his guest. He introduced the heavyset man, suitably suited and tied, as "the founder of Mirage, one of the most successful hedge funds ever." The interview was pretty standard until Quest said, "Governor Teddy Cantor has been coming down pretty heavily on Wall Street. Hedge funds have been bearing the brunt. It's in the news every day. Any comment you'd like to make about the governor of New York?"

Murton seemed to come alive. His anger was visceral and quite visible. "I can't use those words on the air. But I can say that he destroyed people who were decent. He shredded reputations. He came in swinging with a machete, took no prisoners and devastated a lot of good men. He—"

"O-kay," said Quest. "We're outta time but I want to thank Dick Murton for being my guest. It's always lively when I bring up the Sheriff of Wall Street.

Goodnight!"

CHICAGO

Brad was sipping coffee at his desk. He saw *The Wall Street Journal* headline and felt sick. It seemed to scream at him: QUIRE INSIDER TRADING INVESTIGATION UNDERWAY. "The Securities and Exchange Commission has launched an investigation into the holdings of . . ."

The article went on and on. Of course, Taylor Enterprises International was named as having purchased Quire, but, so far, he had not seen his name in print.

For Brad, the reality of it had begun the day before. His administrative assistant had opened his private office door and peered in, looking apprehensive. "Mr. Baker, there is a Mr. Souther from the Securities and Exchange Commission who would like to speak with you."

It had gone well. Or well enough, Brad thought later. He said the investigation was underway and was a matter of routine when so much stock was in the hands of one individual and had been purchased within weeks of an acquisition. "All routine," he had said as he thanked him and turned to go.

Brad picked up the phone and called his CFO, Tom. "What the hell happened?" he nearly shouted. "Do you know anything about this?"

Everyone at Quire was being questioned, everyone at Taylor Enterprises and all the lawyers, too. No one Brad knew knew anything.

The next day, Tom called Brad and said, "I heard from Randall that somebody bought a hundred thousand dollars worth of shares just a few weeks ago. It was that Wednesday that we were still negotiating with Biggs and Thompson. It was right smack dab in the middle of hammering down the details of the sale."

Brad swore. "So who the hell bought the shares?" he demanded.

"Nobody knows. Except the SEC and the FBI, at this point. And the U.S. attorney's office. At least nobody I'm talking to knows."

"We'll all know pretty soon because they're going to be like a pack of dogs on the stockholder and then they'll follow every path back to somebody. Somebody who talked." Brad pulled at his tie, stood up, sat down, listened.

"Okay. Call me if you hear anything and I'll do the same. No, no e-mail. Just the phone. No. Maybe you should just stop by my office or I'll come to you." He ruffled his hair and sighed again then stood up. "Dammit, Tom. I am so tense I think I'm going to get out of here, go to the club and play squash until I can't walk, can't stand up, can't think." He listened, he laughed and the two men hung up the phone.

BOSTON

It was just ten minutes after Holtie had left for the office. Angie was clearing the breakfast table when the doorbell rang so Catherine went to the door and was surprised to see two men in suits with briefcases and grim expressions. "Good morning, Mrs. Burroughs," said one. "I am Special Agent Gainey and this is Special Agent O'Donnell. FBI. May we come in?"

Wordlessly, Catherine opened the door, motioned them into the living room and told them to sit down. "Would you like a cup of coffee?"

As one they answered, "No, no thanks."

"My husband is at his office if you—what is this about?" she asked when she was seated across the coffee table from them.

"You are Catherine Burroughs, correct?" She nodded, put her hands together in her lap, telling herself to breathe. They want *me*. So, it was over. They know. Imperial. It was the stupid mail box idiot who reported me. I bet he opened an envelope, got suspicious and resealed it. Then he made a call. Now is when I say I want a lawyer but on *Law & Order* that always makes the person look guilty.

"Mrs. Burroughs? Are you listening? Do you understand what I'm saying?" asked Special Agent O'Donnell.

"Sorry. I'm . . . go ahead," she nodded.

The two men looked at each other and then repeated something about Quire stock.

Catherine was so relieved that she became her charming self. She was delighted to talk about *stock*. She had told no one. "Yes! Oh, isn't it amazing? It just went way up two weeks ago. I saw it on the Internet that night. The closing number was phenomenal!" Her face was alight. "I couldn't believe it. I bought it and I thought, why don't I just see what happens?" She went on, oblivious to the expressions on the men's faces. "I've never bought stock before. I wanted to surprise my husband. I wanted to see it go up and . . . as you know . . . it really did!"

They confirmed that her stockbroker was one Douglas L. Allen, asked her how she knew of the stock, why she had purchased it.

Catherine was awash with relief. She told them the same thing she'd told Doug. To her surprise, that wasn't enough. "The restaurant?" She tried to think of a restaurant she'd had lunch in the past month. "It was that little Italian place on Newberry Street. I was alone which was probably why I was listening. Well, why I overheard." She went there often and they could check. The waiters knew her. The manager knew her. Would they actually bother to check?

She didn't understand what was the matter. What were they getting at? "No, I didn't pay with a credit card. I always use cash for things like that." Since I have so much cash I could start burning it in the fireplace and wouldn't miss it, went through her mind.

A few more questions and they were on their feet and thanking her. "We will be back, Mrs. Burroughs. This is an ongoing investigation. We are working with the S.E.C. on ascertaining exactly—" When he saw the blank look on her face, Gainey explained, "Securities and Exchange Commission." Catherine nodded vaguely, "Oh, yes, of course."

Minutes later, as they walked to the car, O'Donnell grinned and shook his head. Gainey looked at him as he unlocked the driver's side. "Could anyone be that clueless? Could anyone be that lucky and buy stock that would shoot up overnight? On her first time in the market? She might as well have used a Ouija board or thrown darts at the financial section of the *Globe*. I mean could anyone be that dumb and that lucky?"

It was in the news day after day if one read *The Wall Street Journal*, if one listened to the financial news on CNN or CNBC. Quire and what some called Cantor's war on Wall Street. But the name Catherine Burroughs had not yet become public and though Special Agents Gainey and O'Donnell had come again to ask her questions, she had not said a word to Holtie.

STATEN ISLAND

"What?" said Becky. She leaned back in the desk chair and stared up at the ceiling she had painted black. It was a mistake, she decided. "Well, what did you do?" She unzipped one of her boots and tried to pull her foot out. It was really tight. She would not wear these socks again with these boots. She listened. "Are you telling me that he started blowing up balloons? That he filled up the room with *balloons*?" She started laughing. "Well, did you bounce around on them the way he asked?"

She listened, smiling. "Savannah, I'm learning all the time." She raised her eyebrows in disbelief. "He told you that there is a group of people who get turned on by balloons?" Becky laughed again and finally got her left boot off, wriggling her toes. "And they call themselves *Looners*?"

"I'm trying to picture this," she said. "You and this naked man are in a room at the Waldorf with about fifty balloons and he has this machine going blowing them up and you are drinking champagne and he is—"

She stopped to listen and then burst out laughing. "I guess that's why he has to pay. I mean, can you really imagine a girlfriend being asked to sit on a balloon and bounce up and down while he takes care of himself?"

Becky was silent, listening and then heard the call waiting beep. "Savannah, I have to go. If he comes to New York again, I'll give him to you. Now that we know!" She laughed and clicked to disconnect. Changing gears, her voice was smooth and deep. "Imperial Club V.I.P."

MANHATTAN/ALBANY

Winters called the cell phone, the only number he was allowed to use even though he had discovered two others connected to Burton. At last, he thought, something seriously interesting about this case. It was answered on the second ring. "Mr. Burton, it's Winters. I went into his personal bank accounts and discovered that he is spending thousands of dollars a month." He tipped back in his chair. "It's personal. But there's no paper trail. No checks, no credit cards. It's cash withdrawals and it doesn't make sense." He was thinking it was time to bill Burton again. When it was over, nobody wanted to pay. "Yeah, I'll get back to you. I think I've definitely got something."

BOSTON

That money is such a problem, thought Catherine as she brushed her hair and prepared to go downstairs and have a drink before dinner. She'd just stuffed another forty thousand in a brown envelope and put it in a shoebox on the top shelf of her walk-in closet. The Texan she'd spent the afternoon with always gave her twenty thousand in cash for the four hours. Plus three thousand as a tip. He liked to deal in cash. She'd have to meet with Bree and Jake next week for their cut and for what would go to the booker. "These damn envelopes are everywhere," said Catherine under her breath as she dabbed on L'Air du Temps.

As they watched the news together, she realized she had to tell Holtie. Something. She was not sure what.

"Darling," she began during an ad for something she called 'unspeakable' which made Holtie roar with laughter. Viagra. Cyalis. "Ohmygod," she cried out every evening and grabbed the remote and pushed 'mute.' "I have to tell you something," she began. "I bought some stock. I thought it might go up. I thought it would be a surprise for you actually."

Holtie smiled. "Good. Good for you." He paused. "What did you buy?"

"Well, that's the thing," she said. "The stock I bought seems to be a stock people are worried about."

He laughed. "Did it plunge to two cents a share within hours?"

"No, it didn't. It—"

Holtie was in the mood to tease her. "You bought Quire. You're the person the SEC is questioning." He sipped his martini, amused at the absurdity of the thought.

"Yes, that's what I did. Except I don't know anything about the SEC. It's the FBI people who keep coming back."

"What?"

Holtie's face registered shock. Catherine had never seen him look at her this way before.

She told him exactly what she'd told the FBI. "I was sitting in La Mela and I heard these two well-dressed women talking about something called Quire. I kept thinking 'choir' as in music but one of them spelled it and I just tucked it away in my subconscious, I guess. Then I went to see Doug—"

"You dealt with Doug?" He seemed outraged and she didn't understand why.

"Well, yes, because he's the only stockbroker I feel I really know and he's your

151

cous—"

"Yes, he's my cousin and yes, he's crooked as a snake!"

"Well, I never knew that," said Catherine evenly. Would this help her or make things worse?

"Dinner is ready, Mrs. Burroughs," said Flora from the doorway of the library.

They ate in silence and then, getting ready for bed, he started in again. "You're worse than the FBI!" she shouted at him, slamming the bathroom door.

They spent the night in the same bed, not touching, facing outward away from each other. They never fought. They might bicker and Holtie would leave the room or retreat to an armchair and pretend to read. Then Catherine would come over and kiss the top of his head and he'd pull her to him, usually into his lap, and it would be over. But tonight was not like that. Nothing like this had ever happened before. Both were wide-eyed nearly all night long; back to back they stared into the darkness in quite separate misery.

Holtie had one of the country's best lawyers on tap. After a brief phone conversation, he agreed to come to Boston the next day from Los Angeles. "He's coming to the house at two," Holtie told her. Told me, she thought. Didn't ask me. Told me.

Catherine told Lori she was unavailable for the next week. "No, I'm okay, but I have . . . uh . . ." She didn't want to say family matters because she didn't want Lori to know she had a family. "I have things to take care of. Why don't I call you when I'm free again?"

This gap was fine. She didn't want to see Brad again until she knew what to say to him. Catherine had made her way out of the suite, into the elevator, out of the hotel, out to a taxi and home in a state of disbelief. She heard his voice again and again in her head: *I want you back*. When the shock had worn off, amazement had taken its place. Coupled with a fizzy sense of excitement. Brad Taylor Baker, who had dazzled her at sixteen, the father of her child, wanted her. Wants me *back*. She couldn't get him out of her mind until the FBI had come barging into her life.

So now, she thought, I am giving up my lucrative afternoons in lieu of being hammered by those 'special' agents or being interrogated by Holtie who must have learned his tactics from an old movie about Nazis.

Catherine dressed with care. A Chanel suit of gray and a pearl choker and gray and red pumps she always felt good in. Probably the way Marie Antoinette felt on her way to the guillotine. She stared at herself in the mirror and remembered thinking, as a girl, that her mother could tell that she'd lost her virginity. Silly. She told herself that no one could possibly see anything in her face that could connect her to all those illicit afternoons.

Holtie came home for lunch, they ate lentil soup and roast beef sandwiches in silence and now it was precisely two and the doorbell was ringing.

"Catherine, this is Frank," Holtie said in the front hall. She nodded, he nodded. "I appreciate this very much. Guess you took the red eye. Come on in. Let's go in to my study." He glanced at Catherine and said, "Maybe you'd better ask Flora and Angie not to disturb us."

When she came back, the two men were seated on the two facing brown leather couches both waiting for her. There was no fire in the fireplace but the room was warm, filled with sunlight through the leaded windows, the atmosphere inviting. The walls were lined with shelves holding Holtie's first editions.

"So let's have it," said Frank. "Start at the beginning." He was of medium height, with a full head of white hair and tortoiseshell framed glasses. They dominated his rather square-shaped face which looked ruddy from wind or sun. He appeared strong and solid and reminded Catherine of Spencer Tracy. His pinstriped suit was identical to Holtie's and his shoes were Lobb, Catherine could tell. He crossed his legs and propped the blank yellow legal pad on one thigh.

"First, I had a call from Doug who said he was mailing me a questionnaire and to fill it out and send it back to him," Catherine began. "I did that."

"Doug is . . . ?"

"Doug Allen, the stockbroker. He's my second cousin and I don't much care for him," said Holtie. He sounded grumpy about it because he was grumpy about it.

Frank looked at him and then back at Catherine and said, "Questionnaire is standard, nothing unusual. Go on."

"Then the doorbell rang at about nine a few mornings later and two men from the FBI said they wanted to ask me a few questions." Her husband and Frank were both staring at her intently. "I asked them to come in and we sat in the living room. I think they were here for ten minutes."

153

"Do you have their names, did they give you their cards?"

"Special Agent Gainey and Special Agent O'Donnell," she said. "They are with the Boston office."

"What did they ask you?" Frank wrote down their names.

"They asked me to confirm my name and asked if Doug were my stockbroker and if I'd bought stock from him."

"Go on," said Frank.

"I said yes, yes, and yes, I had bought stock."

"Then they asked me what stock holdings I had and I told them I only had one stock called Quire." She sighed. "It seemed rather silly. They knew all the answers before they asked me, before they even came to the house."

"I am sure they did," said Frank. "What else did they ask you?"

"They asked me what I knew about Quire and I told them I knew that it had gone way way up and wasn't it amazing!"

Frank couldn't keep himself from smiling. Holtie looked at him and sighed. Catherine could be undeniably adorable. Even now, she was beautiful, feminine, entirely without guile and delighted with what she'd done! But what the hell had she gotten herself into?

When Frank had finished his questions and had flipped all the pages of the legal pad back to the first page and was staring at it, deep in thought, Holtie broke the silence. "What happens next?"

Catherine crossed her ankles and both men were aware of her long, silky, blonde legs. And both men were faintly annoyed with themselves for being aware.

"Let me explain how this sort of inquiry works. There are a few government entities involved here. You have FINRA, the SEC, the FBI, and the U.S. attorney's office here in Boston. FINRA stands for Financial Industry Regulating Authority. They monitor trading. They look at all the activity of accounts and when a stock leaps in value to, let's say, four times what it was worth the day before, then their computers will kick out a report. That's probably how this started. Your purchase, Catherine, was just a few weeks, actually a few days before the purchase of the company. Bingo! The Quire stock jumped and the FINRA computer saw it, saw when you bought it, what you paid. Now, it may have picked up on four other people who bought shares recently and had the same jump in value after the sale."

"So I'm not the only person of interest," said Catherine with a bit of relief in her voice.

Frank looked at her and Holtie explained, with one raised eyebrow, *"Law & Order."*

"You might not be. FINRA will then notify the U.S. attorney about this. Here in Boston. The company is here, the stocks were bought here. The U.S. attorney will have an assistant U.S. attorney take on the case."

The case? Catherine didn't like being a case. She told herself to keep her hands folded in her lap and to breathe deeply.

"The assistant U.S. attorney will be dealing with the SEC and the FBI. The three entities will coordinate the investigation and the interviews. They want to make sure everything is done, nothing overlooked, nothing duplicated."

"So the SEC and the FBI report to the U.S. attorney's office?" asked Holtie.

"Right."

Holtie was thinking he was sure he had a friend there. He must. He'd go through his address book later.

"What are they actually accusing me of?" asked Catherine.

"They will try to prove that you knew about the sale of Quire to another company and sought to profit from that knowledge. Insider trading."

She sighed. "Like Martha Stewart?"

"Well, that was what seized everyone's attention but she actually went to prison for lying to the FBI." Frank did not look at her. He was going to have to meet with her without John. Maybe she'd open up and he could help her. He was carefully placing the cap on his fountain pen and trying to sound casual.

"One thing we didn't cover," he said. "How much stock in Quire did you actually purchase? How much money did you give to Doug Allen?"

Catherine thought, Holtie had never asked that last night. He had gone around in circles with everything else twenty times but never asked that. She had to answer. "A hundred thousand dollars."

Silence in the room. The three of them stood up and Frank looked at her and said, "I think that you and I should talk again. Why don't I go back to my hotel, make some calls and then come back?"

Holtie nodded. He felt numb. One hundred thousand dollars! Where could she possibly have gotten that kind of money!

"Why don't you come for dinner, Frank? And we'll talk right before or right after. I know you must be very tired." Catherine had slipped into the role of hostess effortlessly. It was practiced but sincere, gracious. "Actually, why don't you stay here? We have a guest room waiting for you and you can use the phone, the fax, Internet, whatever you need."

"Thank you. It's tempting but I think I'll leave you two alone and come back for dinner. I'm already unpacked and they know me at the Ritz Carlton."

Catherine left them and went to tell Flora and Angie they would be three and to set another place. When Catherine came back into the front hall, conscious of her heels click click clicking on the marble floor, Holtie was waiting for her.

CHICAGO

"Mr. Baker, Special Agents O'Donnell and Gainey are here to see you," said Megan.

Brad nodded, smoothed his tie, stood up. "Show them in. Thanks."

The two men came in wearing identical khaki raincoats, black shoes, and the same weary expressions. "I want to know how this happened as much as you do," he said, after they'd sat down at one end of his office. All three men ignored the sofa and took straight-backed chairs. A Steuben sculpture of a leaping dolphin was beside today's Wall Street Journal on the coffee table between them. The living room furniture arrangement was meant to connote informality, even intimacy, but today it was not doing that. "Maybe I want to know more than you do," he added.

"Mr. Baker, we won't take up more of your time than necessary so we'll get right to it," said Gainey. Megan materialized and Brad asked if the men wanted coffee or tea. They refused and Brad thanked her and told her to close the door, to hold all his calls.

O'Donnell leapt in. "You travel quite a bit."

Brad nodded. "Too much, I'm afraid. I think it's finished a couple of fairly good marriages." The two Special Agents smiled, very slightly.

"Do you go to Boston?" asked Gainey.

"Yes, I do. Probably . . ." he hesitated, thinking. "Maybe once a week for the past few months."

"And where do you stay when you're there?"

"Always the same hotel. The Grand Plaza."

"How many nights?" asked O'Donnell.

"Two. Sometimes one. I don't think I've ever had to be there longer. Meetings and negotiations are pretty intense but usually are one day or one morning." He suddenly thought they might ask why he left the suite at 6 pm instead of noon.

"We've subpoenaed your itinerary for the past year and notice that you usually check out at about six o'clock on the second or third day. Isn't that unusual?"

"Not really. They know me there and they know I like to catch an evening flight back to Chicago."

There was a brief silence. Gainey and O'Donnell knew he was telling the truth. Everything he said was documented. They had the room service receipts and assumed from the expensive champagne that he was not eating and drinking with a business client but with a woman. "Do you want to tell us who you entertain in the suite?" asked Gainey. He and O'Donnell had decided it had no relevance but thought they'd be remiss not to ask.

Brad Baker laughed. "She actually entertains *me*. A very beautiful woman. But no, I don't want to tell you her name." He shrugged. "But I can assure you that my time with her is not spent discussing business. She is all pleasure."

The men nodded, decided to move on. They knew his background. Divorced and often seen with women half his age at the best restaurants. His broad shoulders, his build, his movements were those of an athlete. He was a man who kept in shape, who was well-tailored, didn't mind spending a few hundred dollars on a silk tie. Later, Gainey would tell O'Donnell he thought she was a call girl but O'Donnell would insist she was married.

"Do you know a Mrs. John Burroughs? Catherine Burroughs?" asked Special Agent O'Donnell.

He shook his head. "I've heard of John Burroughs. The publisher. Everybody knows who he is. Plus, he's well known as a philanthropist. The art world or the opera. Is that the man you're asking about?"

"We're actually asking if you know his wife, Catherine."

"No, never met either one of them." Now I know, he thought. She must have bought the stock. She's the one they're trying to connect with Taylor Enterprises. He stopped. "Unless it was in a receiving line at a wedding reception or he and I were on some board together years ago. That is always possible but no, I don't know them."

"She lives in Boston," said Gainey.

He shrugged. "So do a few million other people."

They thanked him and were gone. Across the thick tan carpet, through the heavy glass doors and into the oak-paneled elevator, they did not even look at each other. Only outside, and in the car, did they speak. "I think he's an honest man," said Gainey.

"You say that about somebody every five or six years."

"Yeah, like clockwork," retorted Gainey.

They checked in to the Chicago office and then were driven to O'Hare and flew back to Boston. The two men were in total agreement: Boston was where the stock had been purchased and Boston was where it would all blow up.

Brad sat down behind his desk and began to answer the e-mails that had accumulated during the past fifteen minutes. Sometimes he felt he was being eaten alive by minutiae. Only this wasn't minutiae. The F.B. I., the investigation—it would culminate in someone going to prison. He leaned back in his chair and closed his eyes. He could see Kitty's face. If only she were in Chicago, he thought. If only I could meet her for lunch, if only I could hear her voice. He picked up his cell and punched in the number. "Hi, there, it's Mr. B," he said. "I can't get to Boston this week or even next. Is there any way to reach Claudia?" He knew he sounded very nearly desperate. He was filled with longing. He wanted comfort as much as anything else. "Just to talk to her?"

It was impossible, of course. Becky was firm. He snapped his cell phone closed and put it on his desk. Then it hit him. Brad Taylor Baker felt as if he were drowning. He closed his eyes and put his palms over his face. My God. Kitty! She was Catherine Burroughs. He had never ever called her Catherine. She'd been Kitty all through school. No one had ever called her Catherine. She lives in Boston and she is married to John Holt Burroughs, the publisher. *Married*. That revelation was as shocking as the realization that Kitty had bought the stock. He stood up and walked to the window. Which means she heard about it from *me*. I'm the guy Gainey and O'Donnell are trying to find. And Kitty is married. Married! He'd thought it was possible that first afternoon then put it out of his mind as very unlikely. Then, because of the way they were together, he decided it was impossible and never considered it again.

Brad did what he'd done only once before. He grabbed his suit jacket, strode past Megan at her desk and told her he would be unavailable for the rest of the day. "He looked absolutely white," Megan would say to the receptionist as they washed their hands in the ladies room.

Brad drove home, changed into jeans and opened a bottle of very good Cabernet. His apartment overlooked Lake Michigan which sparkled in the sun. It shouldn't, he thought, taking a big swallow of wine. The sky should be black with clouds scudding back and forth at top speed. This is a day to get very drunk, quietly, all by myself. He'd left the office and done this only once before, with the television newscasts on in the background. Today, he thought, is my own personal 9/11.

O'Donnell and Gainey were to continue with interviews, were sent back again and again to talk to the same subjects. No one imagined they'd establish a rapport with anyone; it was to ensure that nothing was missed and to observe reactions.

A week later, they were in Brad Baker's office again.

"We are interested in a stock transaction made in Boston just two weeks before the company sale went through. Catherine Burroughs," said Gainey. "Ever met her?"

Brad shook his head. "Never heard of her." He paused. "Except you asked me about her before."

"She purchased one hundred thousand dollars of Quire stock on the 24th of last month," explained O'Donnell.

Gainey watched Brad Baker's face intently.

"Why did she do that? Is there any link you've found between her and anyone at Quire, anyone who works for me?" Brad seemed willing to be helpful.

"You don't know this woman?" insisted O'Donnell.

"No." His voice was level, he appeared to be telling the truth, they would agree later. Brad told himself he did not know the woman married to John Holt Burroughs. He knew *his* Kitty but did not know anyone named Catherine. This Catherine had an existence entirely separate from afternoons in bed with champagne, an existence that had nothing to do with being seventeen and feverish lovemaking in the back of his car.

Gainey and O'Donnell thanked him for his time, said they would contact him again and left the offices of Taylor Enterprises International. Silent as they waited for the elevator, silent as they rode down and silent until they were in the car, they looked at each other and both started to talk at once. "He's the one," said O'Donnell. "I can feel it in my gut."

"But how?" insisted Gainey.

"We have to keep digging. There has to be a link."

PARIS

George Forrester had never experienced such happiness. The walks on cobblestone streets with linked arms, stopping in a bistro for a glass of wine, the long dinners when they were the last to leave the restaurant filled him with joy. All with a woman he could not get enough of. She was the sun, the moon, the stars. Her radiance changed his world. Her smile made him feel that he had become another person. Véronique soothed him and she excited him.

He couldn't wait to get her into bed and when he woke up beside her he wanted to spend the day with her. For George, it was a cycle of wanting to see her face, hear her laugh, to please her and then to finally be inside her, to take her, to have her, to hold her as closely as their flesh would allow.

Tonight they made love slowly and languidly. Véronique felt herself float away under his hands, his mouth. They slept on their sides with him inside of her and then waked before dawn and began to talk again in soft voices. "Sometimes . . . sometimes," she began and then stopped.

"Go on. Tell me."

"Sometimes I wish you weren't so far away."

"I'm not," he said and held her in his arms very tightly until they fell asleep once more.

LONDON

Gabrielle lay under him as he panted over her. He seemed heavier the second time and he always insisted on a second time that first night as if to prove to himself that he could actually do it. For her this was the working part as it took him so long to actually come. She stared up at the ceiling, felt the sheet under her fingertips and moved back and forth. Back and forth, back and forth. Thank God, I'm not married to him, she thought. Thank God, I'm being paid. Plus I need this. Look at it that way. Maybe this will be the time. Back and forth. Rutting was an apt word. It has to happen soon, she thought. Oh, please, don't go limp so we have to start over. Back and forth. She could feel the perspiration on his chest and turned her head on the pillow to avoid his hot breath. Back and forth. She told herself to do multiplication tables, to think of something else. Back and forth. The tube stops. Baron's Court. Earl's Court. Back and forth. Gloucester Road. Knightsbridge. Back and forth. Hyde Park Corner. Green Park. "Aaaaaaaaah!" he shouted in triumph. Gabrielle sighed with relief as he rolled off her. Mr. Brown had come at Piccadilly Circus.

BOSTON

Catherine Burroughs was never again questioned without a lawyer. Frank Latham couldn't abandon his heavy schedule and relocate to the East Coast, not even for John Holt Burroughs, so he named an associate in Boston to take on the case. He was a Yalie, a graduate of Harvard Law, younger than Frank Latham, competent and very bright. And mesmerized by Mrs. Burroughs. William E. Middleton III had trouble not staring at her when she entered the room or sat across from him, and he believed every word she said.

Catherine would ask herself a hundred times a day, why are they so obsessed with the money? She had suddenly remembered while brushing her teeth that morning that she'd completely forgotten to put the fifty thousand in the joint checking account.

The money she'd told Holtie she'd inherited from Aunt Lillian. I would have gotten in trouble for *that*! That silly Patriot thing. Those bloodhounds would get a copy of the will and know I lied so thank goodness I forgot all about it! I bet Holtie has, too.

She sighed. But the Quire money just won't go away. Nobody, except Bill, believes I could have saved it. Why don't they believe me? No one has ever questioned my word before. Not in my whole life! Why do they act as if I'm lying? I've never lied before and suddenly now I am a liar. Frank didn't believe me, Gainey and O'Donnell wore those poker faces that are a dead giveaway for not believing me even as Bill was telling them I saved it. Holtie is just pretending to believe me. Probably because he wants to think I actually did save it.

Every single one of the men thought her remarkably unrattled by the investigation. Of course, they had no idea that she was actually relieved and felt that she'd made a narrow escape.

One chilly spring afternoon, Catherine took a walk to the middle of Longfellow Bridge and dropped the mail box key into the Charles. She watched it fall through the air rather slowly; the metal give a little wink as it disappeared in the dark water. Then she took the throwaway phone from her pocketbook, looked behind her to see if anyone would see, and gave it a good throw. That's why they call it that, she thought, pulling her gray cashmere coat around her more tightly then turning back towards home.

When all this blows over, she could decide what to do about Brad. She thought about him every day and every day she resisted Googling him. She felt she knew all she needed to. He was divorced and in love with her all over again. This mess with the stock was amazing timing. I am finished with Imperial and he can never find me whereas he's probably in the Chicago phone book. I'm safe, she told herself that evening as she brushed her hair before going to bed. It's all up to me. I have the power to see him again or not.

She turned off the dressing room light and walked into the master bedroom where Holtie sat in bed reading. He never wore a pajama top and his chest was still tan from summer, very smooth; his shoulders were muscular. Holtie smiled when he saw her and put the book on the bedside table. Then he flipped the covers aside and held his arms open for her.

MANHATTAN/ALBANY

Burton could barely breathe. He had never in his life imagined anything like this. Winters kept talking. He had the dates, the times, the places. "I've got photos of him wearing a baseball cap and dark glasses walking into the Waldorf. Middle of the afternoon. Five. No. Six times." Burton was taking notes. His fingers seemed to be sweating. He didn't want to interrupt but listened. This was like a good dream. "He always registers using the same name."

"What name?" Burton's voice was hoarse with emotion.

"John Wolf."

"Good work, Winters. Send me a bill."

The men hung up. Burton leaned back in his desk chair and took a deep breath. "You fucker. The nets are closing."

BOSTON

"They want to meet with us again," Bill was saying. "Tomorrow morning. Ten o'clock."

Catherine rolled her eyes and sighed. "When is this going to be over?"

"When they are satisfied that you did nothing wrong."

Catherine had actually convinced herself that she had done nothing wrong. She was now sure that she *had* overheard two women talking at lunch. "Has anyone ever heard of the word 'coincidence?' she asked.

He smiled and reached for the file. They had finished lunch and were sitting in the living room preparing for yet another round with Gainey and O'Donnell.

"I have a list of all employees at Quire and at Taylor Enterprises International. I'll start reading. It's hundreds of names but tell me if you know anyone. No, tell me if any name is familiar. If you have, ever in your life, even heard the name, stop me."

Bill Middleton began to read. He started with the Board of Directors, then went on to legal counsel and kept reading, turning pages. Catherine stared at the painting over the mantle of a 12 Metre under full sail in a stiff wind.

"Nobody," she said.

"Okay, let's move on to Taylor Enterprises International." He opened a large folder and flipped to the first page. "Brad T. Baker, Thomas—"

"What did you say?" she interrupted.

"Brad T. Baker, Thomas R. Braxton," he stopped, staring at her.

Catherine felt faint, her head was spinning. "Okay," she said then instantly regretted speaking.

"Baker? Is he someone you've heard of? He's the head of Taylor Enterprises. His middle name is Taylor."

She nodded but she wanted to scream, I know his middle name but I never connected him with Taylor Enterprises in *The Wall Street Journal*! I know everything about him including what it feels like to have him come inside me. I know him. In the Biblical sense, in every sense there is. She stood up and said, "Excuse me for a minute. I have to tell Angie something about dinner. Be right back."

Bill was astonished. He watched her leave the room quickly, with her impeccable posture, her light step, her slender figure in the perfectly cut tan trousers.

Catherine didn't go through the hall and the dining room to the kitchen but went up the stairs two at a time and into her bedroom. She closed the door and stood staring at herself in the 18th century mirror from Italy which hung over her bureau. They'll find out, she said in a whisper. What if they are asking Brad the same questions? What if he tells them everything? I'll lose Holtie. I'll lose Cate. I'll lose everything. She sat on the bed and stared across the big, pale blue room. Think! She screamed inside.

Tell the minimum, she decided as she walked down the stairs and back into the living room. Only what they can find out. Only what's on paper. But is it on paper?

"Bill, I have to tell you something," she began. "It's incredible. I can't believe it because it can't possibly be the same person!" She sat down across from him and leaned forward, fixing her beautiful wide-set, violet eyes on his face. "I am in shock. This cannot be happening!"

William E. Middleton III was stunned. He thought later that he had never been so surprised in his life. Certainly not in his law career which, admittedly, was not a long one. It was like the proverbial two-by-four over the head. They were still sitting there when Holtie came home from the office earlier than usual. He didn't stop in the hall when he heard their voices but walked into the living room and wordlessly sank into a chair between them. "I'll tell him," she said.

"Tell me what?" He put his briefcase on the floor.

"Bill was reading out all the names of anyone with Quire and anyone with Taylor Enterprises." She stopped. She forced herself to decide what was true, what had to be said. Nothing more would she say. "Holtie, you know that I was married when I was sixteen." He nodded. "Well, I was married to Brad Baker and he is the head of Ba—I mean Taylor Enterprises."

Holtie seemed to slump in the chair, as if limp with this revelation. "But how—"

Catherine drew upon how she'd felt in the suite facing Brad and summoned that emotion. "I thought he was dead. All this time!" Catherine's eyes filled with tears. "I was told he was killed in a car accident. Years ago. After our marriage was annulled. After everything was over." She dabbed at her face with Kleenex. "Cate was about three years old so I hadn't seen him for at least a year and a half. How could he not be dead?" She stopped, faced Bill. "How old is this Brad Baker? Maybe it's not the same man!"

Bill flipped open the folder again. "Date of birth. Don't see it but he's forty, maybe forty-two, I think I read somewhere."

Holtie had not said a word. He did remember that when he met her, Catherine had told him the marriage was annulled and that her former husband had died in an accident soon after. That had happened. So how could he be alive? Now he spoke very carefully. "But if you haven't seen him in all this time and, of course, you haven't if you thought he was dead then . . ."

Suddenly Catherine burst into tears. She was crying for all sorts of reasons. Crying because things were becoming very dangerous, crying because she was tired of answering questions, tired of having everyone silently accuse her.

Holtie was astonished. This was entirely out of character for his Catherine, the wife who never cried, who never complained, who sailed through life with grace, looking straight ahead with shoulders back. Holtie went over to where she sat on the chintz covered sofa and took her in his arms. Catherine, in floods of tears, was saying, "Everything just keeps getting worse!"

Bill excused himself and went to the front hall where he telephoned Los Angeles. "Frank, Bill Middleton. Call me back the minute you get this. We have to go over a few things before I meet with the Feds tomorrow morning." He started to hang up and then added to his message. "You aren't going to believe it when I tell you."

At that moment, across town, O'Donnell stood over a fax machine as it purred out the page he wanted. He grabbed it, stared in disbelief. "Holy shit! Holy mother-fucking shit!" said O'Donnell striding towards Gainey's desk. Gainey who never swore, looked up and calmly said, "Don't hold back on account of me."

"I told you! I fucking told you!" O'Donnell slammed the paper on the desk, right on top of what his partner was reading. "Look at this! Our little Beacon Hill princess was *married* to Brad Taylor Baker!"

"Jesus Christ!" erupted Gainey, surprising even himself as he stared at the photocopy of the marriage license.

"They had a kid together!" Cathy Ann Baker's birth certificate was slammed down on top of the marriage license. Gainey stared at it in awe. "Jesus Christ!" he repeated. "This case is the gift that keeps on giving."

Bill Middleton called the Burroughs house at eight the next morning and Holtie answered. "Mr. Burroughs, it's Bill Middleton. Good morning. Sorry to call you so early but Special Agent O'Donnell just postponed our ten o'clock meeting. I'll let you know when they reschedule." Both men hung up wondering the same thing: what next?

MIAMI

"Oh, ugh," said Annie to herself in the mirror in the ladies room. She washed her hands then plucked a little cloth towel from the silver tray on the marble countertop. "That cigar." She took a deep breath of air-conditioning and knew she had to go back, out to the deck where smoking was allowed. She kept moving her chair to get upwind but the breeze kept changing. This businessman from St. Louis was hell bent on polluting the entire Eastern seaboard with that one cigar. A Cuban cigar. He was so proud to tell her. And he was proud of his watch. She complimented him just because he'd caught her staring at it too long. "Titanium baseplate with bridges of aluminum lithium," he said. He described the bezel, the winding barrel teeth and told her the price. "Five hundred and twenty-five thousand," he bragged and then stuck the big cigar in his mouth again. Maybe, she thought, the cigar is not entirely a bad thing if it keeps him from talking so much.

"Oh, God, three more hours," moaned Annie as she dug in her purse for a lipstick. This boring, arrogant man collects watches when he's not smoking expensive cigars. "Cubans," she said aloud and the woman at the next sink, who was probably Cuban, turned to look at her. "Just losing my mind," said Annie cheerfully and left the ladies room with a big smile.

MANHATTAN

It had almost stopped hurting. It hurt to realize that she'd been betrayed, that she'd been loyal for thirty-five years in the face of the most searing disloyalty. It hurt to think of how foolish her husband thought she was. It hurt to be thought a ninny. She could hear the sneering way he said it. "What a ninny," he'd often declared this woman or that one to be after a dinner party with too much small talk. The pain subsided into an ache and then went away very nearly entirely as she and Mark plotted what she thought of as retaliation. She was not being a good sport this time. "You make me flat-out giggle," Brooke told him once. "Maybe that means more than anything right now." She went on with her life in the big apartment on Fifth Avenue, arranging dinners, running the household, being Mrs. Stanford Cortland, being her old self.

Pretending to be her old self. She looked in the mirror one morning and realized that she was becoming someone new. Stanford was the only one not to notice. Brooke stared at her new haircut, the bright lipstick, the new tomato red sweater that showed off her slenderness and said softly, "The Big S has no idea who I am or how difficult I can be."

She had not said a word to a lawyer or to Stanford. The Big S was what Lori and Mark called him. When Brooke looked puzzled, Mark had reluctantly elaborated. "The Big Shit. We hate him. Lori and I really hate what he did to you." He stared at her solemnly and then, to his great surprise, Brooke crowed with laughter. Then *she* started referring to him as the Big S, too. It was doubly amusing to her because Stanford had never allowed anyone to ever give him a nickname. Stan was out of the question and though a St. Paul's classmate had once called him Corty it was the first and last time.

Brooke had not met Lori but if she was Mark's best friend and he trusted her then she did, too. To be the booker for something called the Imperial Club! To finally know what Pliameri was! To be provided with all the proof she needed to go after Sta—the Big S, she amended and smiled. Why, *that* was extraordinary!

Brooke and Mark kept meeting in the park. They were careful to not sit on the same bench every time but were always a short walk from a Sabrett cart. Vengeance was being carefully plotted one hot dog at a time.

Today they worked on the drop. It would be in a rather public place but with enough people around for them or one of them to blend into the crowd. A mailbox was out of the question as he could hire someone to watch it and wait for them to come and they'd be caught. "What about Grand Central?" They ruled it out. "It should be dusk or dark so that he can't get a good look at us," said Mark. "Then you're thinking it should be outside, in the street somewhere?" asked Brooke.

After going back and forth suggesting and rejecting all sorts of landmarks from the Statue of Liberty to Grant's tomb, they decided on Central Park. "Let's make him walk into the park. I mean let's make it far enough in so that he has to be on foot, and so that we can watch him make the approach," said Brooke.

"And so that we can make sure he is alone," put in Mark. "Plus we'll have to watch him leave so that we can pick it up soon after that so that nobody else sees him leave it, gets curious and picks it up before we can."

Brooke sighed. She thought every minute of his being nearby multiplied the chances of being caught. "I don't like it but you're right."

"We'll have to give him a definite time. And there are plenty of trees to stand behind especially if we know which park entrance he'll take," said Mark.

"Got it!" exclaimed Brooke. "What about the Alice in Wonderland statue?"

They left their conference bench to take a look. Perfect. Stanford Cortland would be directed to the Alice statue which was on the east side of the park near 74th Street. The envelope with five hundred thousand dollars in it would be placed under the left knee of the Mad Hatter. "Envelope? How big? How big does it have to be?" they asked each other.

The time was discussed. "At seven o'clock, there won't be any kids around. We'll have to be here from six on, just to make sure we don't miss him." Mark was feeling good about this. Very, very nervous but good, he told himself.

"But don't forget, he won't want us to miss him. He won't like leaving that money for anyone else to find so he will do what we tell him." She savored that phrase 'will do what we tell him.'

"Right," said Mark. "That's an awful lot of money. Do you think it's too much to ask?"

Brooke looked at him. "When he can spend $62,000 in two nights plus the airfare and the cost of the suite at Claridge's every month . . ." She stopped. His usual suite, she had researched, cost over six thousand pounds a night or over nine thousand dollars. In our entire marriage, she thought, we've never stayed in a suite. An emotion entirely foreign suddenly infused her very being. Revenge. She felt angry and she felt strong. It came out of her mouth without warning. The first time in her life. "Fuck it!" she exploded. Mark told Lori later that he nearly fainted. Brooke was adamant and enthusiastic. "Let's ask for a million!"

"I don't know why you are asking me about him." Cate Burroughs sat, with hands folded in her lap, behind her desk at Christeby's. She shared the office with Bettina who had left quickly when faced with the two FBI agents. "He died."

"How old were you?" asked Special Agent Gainey. A carbon copy of her beautiful mother, he was thinking. She had the same nearly black hair, the oval face, those eyes. Maybe not quite as beautiful but I wouldn't kick her outta bed, he thought.

"I must have been two or three years old." She thought she remembered riding on his shoulders in the backyard, a vanilla ice cream cone, not much else. "Maybe I was two years old." She stopped, pushed her hair back from her face with one hand. "I know about Mother. That she's being questioned by the FBI Does this have anything to do with the stock she bought?" How could it possibly be related, she was wondering.

"Yes," said O'Donnell. He didn't know what to do which was unlike him. He'd told plenty of people that their fathers, mothers, sons, daughters, husbands, wives, whoever, had died. He'd never had to tell anyone that their father had *not* died.

"Ms. Burroughs, thank you for your time. We may have more questions," said Special Agent Gainey.

The minute the door closed, she put her head down on her desk and nearly groaned with relief. Then she sat up straight and opened her mouth and screamed silently. When they'd introduced themselves and asked to speak with her alone, Imperial Club had flashed into her mind. In hot pink neon. Flashing like a sign in Times Square. The end. She was going to stop doing it. She would tell Lori something. Tell Becky something. Tell them not to call her anymore. My God, the FBI.

She grabbed her cell phone and punched in the number. "Mother! What is happening?"

It was so easy, they marveled. They picked a pay phone in Harlem and Mark, who was a natural mimic, telephoned Stanford on the landline on Fifth Avenue. All he said was, "I know you misbehave at Claridge's every single month and—"

"Who the hell are you?" shouted Stanford James Cortland.

"Listen carefully. The price for silence is a million dollars. Leave the cash in hundred dollar bills—"

"Don't tell me what to do! Who is this?" he shouted again.

Mark never faltered. Mrs. C had prepared him well. "Tomorrow night, seven o'clock. Enter Central Park at 74th Street and go to the Alice in Wonderland statue. Leave the shopping bag with the bills under the left knee of the Mad Hatter and walk away. Tomorrow. Seven p.m." He was firm. "Come alone, leave the shopping bag and leave."

There was silence. "A million dollars in cash or I talk about those nights in London."

"Who the hell are you?" It was a shout of rage and anguish. "Who—"

Mark replaced the receiver thinking he wanted to wash his hands. New York pay phones. Ugh.

Mrs. C was standing beside him, fists clenched, hands together under her chin.

He turned to her. "How did I sound?"

"You sounded a hundred percent Cockney. It was eery and it was great!" Then she demanded, "But did he say anything? Did he say 'no' and tell you to go to hell?"

"He shouted at me but I can tell he's scared." Mark was excited, breathless, felt as if he'd run a mile. "Let's get outta here." He flagged a cab and, in seconds, they were in the backseat. The two of them laughed maniacally for an entire thirty blocks as the driver sped downtown hitting all the green lights.

SPRING, 2008

If things seem under control, you are just not going fast enough.
—Mario Andretti

They were naked, sleeping deeply, with legs and arms entwined. Bree's head was under Jake's chin, her dark hair splayed across his chest. The bedroom was very large, with a tray ceiling; a large chandelier hung over the king-size bed with the massive carved teak headboard. Bree's desk was to the left by the door to the enormous green marble bathroom. She kept it very neat, with only her computer out. Check books were in the drawers along with bank statements, address books, CDs. All she needed was in the laptop.

Jake's desk was in another room they called the office. His desk was awash in papers. Dozens of vegetarian recipes printed out from the Internet were under a stone paperweight Buddha. The paperbacks stacked in a pile on the floor beside the desk touted spiritual enlightenment, personal improvement, the love of humanity, and the joy of tofu.

The apartment was silent except for the tick of a clock in the kitchen and dark except for the living room with its reflected panorama of Manhattan. But even the city's lights were dim in those hours between club closings and street cleaning.

Crash! There was loud banging on the door. The front door. Shouting! Men's voices. Bree sat up, eyes still closed, groggy; Jake rolled over and out of bed, dazed. The bedroom was pitch-black the way he liked it. He stumbled towards a chair to grab his undershorts as Bree mumbled, "What? What is it?" A dozen men came charging into the room with drawn guns, shouting to get up, to put her arms over her head.

Lights went on. Someone threw a bathrobe at her and she struggled into it, tying the sash, fumbling, with fingers that were clumsy, wouldn't move properly. She could hear her heart beat above the yelling men. They were wearing gray bulletproof vests over dark clothes. The backs were stenciled in block letters: FBI. They were unplugging her laptop, going through drawers, pulling them out and turning them upside down. Book shelves were raked clean and the books were shaken as if their pages might hold papers or documents. Someone was in the walk-in closet and she could hear hangers and clothes being tossed around.

A woman dressed like one of the men pushed her into the bathroom and stood in the doorway staring at her. "Get dressed!" she ordered. Bree shivered, literally shook with fear, as she tried to pull on jeans, thinking I should wear underpants but where are they? They were in the bedroom bureau with all those men in the way. "Can I brush my teeth?" she asked and the woman barked, "Hurry!" Minutes later, handcuffs were snapped in place and it was then that she realized that Jake was gone. He'd been taken away. Bree was disoriented and terrified.

STATEN ISLAND/ BROOKLYN

On that Monday morning in March, Becky was doing the all-nighter. She called Lori at six-thirty and told her to get rid of the phone. Immediately. "Like now!" The Pink Panther theme was to never sound again. Lori reached for her landline and called Mark who said he was on his way. She unlocked her front door then she went into the kitchen and took a hammer to the cell phone. Or tried to. It kept shooting off the counter. Absurdly, she thought of a sea lion trying to open a clam on a rock. Some nature documentary she'd watched in the middle of the night. Finally she put it between two cookbooks and started pounding. Becky told her, during that last frantic call, that she was going to throw her cell phone out the kitchen window into the air shaft the minute they hung up.

Both Becky and Lori were so crazed with panic that the idea of removing the SIM card never occurred to either one of them.

Mark stood there in his undershorts, watching her swing the hammer, looking alarmed. Suddenly he sprang into action. "Your computer! Is it on your bed?" He hurried into the bedroom, put the laptop on the desk and sat down.

His watch said quarter to seven and the arrest was on the local news already. He went into the directory and began. Some of the names were obvious. Click. Copy. Click. Delete. Then he heard the *Today Show* theme song whining from the kitchen. "Name the files," he shouted. "Tell me which ones are Imperial Club."

She ran in, barefoot. "All of them are! I only use that computer for that!" She stood behind him, making little whimpering noises until he told her to leave the bedroom. He was entirely focused on the screen. Kept clicking, clicking, clicking. Copy. Move cursor. Copy. Move cursor. Copy. Then delete. Delete. Delete.

"An escort service called The Imperial Club V.I.P. may serve as New York Governor Teddy Cantor's Waterloo . . ." Matt Lauer was droning. Mark pushed the button and waited for the CD to eject then grabbed it from its little holder. He hurried into the living room where Lori stood by the window like a statue. "I erased everything but the FBI can probably recover files. I'm going upstairs. I wiped my prints off the laptop and off your desk." Lori couldn't say a word. She appeared frozen, in shock. He looked into her face. "Should I stay with you? I will. Do you want me to stay with you?" She blinked as if waking from a dream and shook her head. "Get out of here. Now go!"

"It's going to be okay. Tell them whatever they want to know. It's okay. It's okay! Don't talk to anyone on your landline. Just answer their questions. They won't blame you for erasing your hard drive and they can get it back anyway. It's going to be fine." He looked at her. "Breathe! Breathe!" he urged and she inhaled as if a doctor were standing over her with a stethoscope.

Mark put his palm to her face gently and stared into her eyes. "I will come down tonight. It's going to be okay."

He raced through the living room and out the door then ran up the stairs to his apartment and locked the door behind him. He slipped the disk between *Vanity Fair* January 2003 and *Vanity Fair* February 2003.

The 'whoop whoop whoop' of the siren sounded approximately four seconds later. He looked out the window and counted six men jumping out of the three cars and wondered if it were really going to be okay.

MANHATTAN

Bree would always call this the incident. She kept asking for Jake and no one would answer her. The men had put her in handcuffs, gotten her into the elevator, hurried her through the lobby, then they'd pushed her into a black car doing that head push you always saw on the news. Mug shots, fingerprints, the process of being arrested. She wanted a hairbrush, she wanted underpants and she wanted to go home. There had been hours and hours of questioning and bail set at half a million dollars which meant jail for twelve days. The newspaper headlines were blazingly awful; she told her mother and then her father that there'd been a mistake. Worst of all was being separated from Jake.

The incident brought a governor down, a presidential hopeful. The media screamed that it had destroyed his marriage and his career. That was all known, all in the news, but there were the aftershocks no one could have predicted and a cast of characters in the wings waiting for them.

KEY BISCAYNE

Monday evening, Annie had the television on as she got out of the shower and paraded back and forth from the bathroom, getting dressed, putting on makeup. It was a reception at the Raleigh and she had to look great, had to hand out her business cards as if the world were coming to an end. CNN was on but it was only background; she wasn't paying attention until she sat down to rub hand lotion on her legs. The newscaster was saying, "Before dawn today in New York, three women and one man were arrested for running a prostitution ring called The Imperial Club..."

MANHATTAN

Cate was with Jason for dinner and missed the evening news entirely. He'd heard it from someone at the office and told her all about it over pasta at Elio's. She heard her voice as it were not her voice at all, saying, "Thirty thousand a night! That's incredible!"

It was news in London, Paris, Geneva and Rome for anyone hearing CNN or having a late dinner, coming out of the opera or the theatre. CNN had the story first and then every network had it. Monday night all across Europe, Asia and South America, in New York City, Boston, Miami and Los Angeles, there were fifty attractive women and at least eight hundred wealthy men having trouble falling asleep in their respective time zones. An international epidemic of insomnia.

The newspaper headlines assaulted anyone who'd missed the Monday newscasts. On Tuesday, it was the lead story for *The New York Times*, *The New York Post*, and *The Daily News*. There were two big stories that were too late to have made yesterday's papers.

One was the details of the arrests in the early morning raid which closed down the high-end prostitution ring called the Imperial Club V.I.P.. The other story was that the Democratic New York State governor, who had been considered a viable candidate for president, possibly the first Jewish president, had been identified as the heavy spending Imperial Club's Client Number 8. One tabloid headline called him The Love Guv. No one knew yet exactly how much money had been involved. He was said to be planning to ride out the storm but various Democratic Party leaders were pushing him to resign. Republicans were in a state of what a talking head called, "Raging, ecstatic euphoria." Wall Street was joyful; all on the trading floor of the New York Stock Exchange had burst into applause and loud cheering when the news was known. Teddy Cantor, after all, was seen by many as self-righteous and arrogant. Nicknamed The Sheriff of Wall Street, he'd pledged to rein in the hedge funds, make them accountable. His campaign platform had emphasized he would bring "morality" back to government.

The Sun trumpeted:

Federal prosecutors say they have broken up a high-end international prostitution ring that ran a thriving business in New York. Prosecutors yesterday charged one man and three women with running the prostitution service, which advertised itself on the Internet as Imperial Club V.I.P.. The Web site described Imperial Club as the "elite recreation venue and private club for those accustomed to excellence."

Court documents unsealed yesterday said the Imperial Club involved 50 prostitutes who billed between $1,000 and $5,000 an hour. Several phone numbers associated with Imperial Club has been under surveillance by the FBI which intercepted more than 10,000 telephone calls and text messages during the investigation, according to court documents.

A criminal complaint charges Ivan Kuznetsov, 62, with running the prostitution ring. He was arrested yesterday morning along with a 23-year-old former college student, Chantal Silver. Prosecutors say Ms. Silver managed the day to day running of the Imperial Club. They lived together in an apartment in New Jersey. Agents found over $980,000 in cash at the apartment, an assistant U.S. attorney said in U.S. District Court in Manhattan yesterday.

The Imperial Club had prostitutes in New York, Miami, Los Angeles, London and Paris and would send them to meet men anywhere in the world, the complaint alleges.

Authorities arrested two other women, Lori Stevens and Rebecca Sullivan, whom prosecutors described as booking agents in charge of setting up meetings between clients and prostitutes.

The defendants are charged with conspiring to violate federal anti-prostitution laws. Mr. Kuznetsov and Ms. Silver are also charged with money laundering.

The defendants did not enter any plea in U.S. District Court yesterday. Prosecutors are said to be undecided whether Governor Cantor will be charged with any crime.

Stanford Cortland muttered, "Jesus Christ," and put *The New York Times* in his briefcase. If Brooke ever finds out about this! Jesus Christ!

Brad Baker put down *The Chicago Tribune* and sighed deeply. "God Almighty," he said under his breath and took another bite of toast.

The Cowboy from Houston heard it on his car radio and yelped, "Holy shit! Holy fuckin' mashed potato!"

George Forrester's first reaction was what about Véronique? He put down the morning paper and stared into space across the green dining room, past his wife who weighed eighty pounds. Sylvia played with a solitary corn flake that floated in two ounces of milk. She was sitting at the table which is a triumph, he thought, even if she is in a wheelchair. It was nearly eight o'clock and, as usual, the sheets were being changed in her bedroom in the wing of the house that had been taken over with medical equipment and nurses.

George's thoughts were far away. His interludes with Véronique were the best times of his life but that was over. It had been over since that last morning. They'd said goodbye and she had meant forever. What had he done wrong? What had changed? George thought he knew why poets and composers wrote about heartaches because his was aching. At least it was a pain in the vicinity of his heart, deep in his chest, and not unlike what he remembered feeling when he was homesick that first summer at sleep-away camp. He couldn't talk himself out of it; he felt empty, alone and sad. Homesick, he thought. This is exactly what it's like. In her arms, I was home.

Carlito Intriago saw it in *The Miami Herald* and immediately punched in Annie's number. She didn't answer and suddenly he thought maybe he shouldn't leave a message. She had never told him she worked for Imperial so maybe she didn't. He flipped the phone closed and thought, oh, little girl from Wisconsin, please be alright.

I was in Philadelphia and I saw it on the news, again and again, and every time, I though, wow! What a story, what characters! It was risk and money and sex and secrets. It was too fabulous. You couldn't make it up. If I weren't so busy being a private detective, I'd dive right in and have Cordelia Blake start writing a really juicy novel.

Governor Cantor was seen wearing a baseball cap and a sheepish expression getting out of a taxi on Fifth Avenue in front of his father's apartment building. The evening news gave it a few seconds as Charlie Gibson said that the governor had still not made any statement to the press. "There have been numerous calls, from both Democrats and Republicans, for him to resign."

ALBANY /MANHATTAN

Winters was watching the news when his cell phone rang. It was Joe Burton and he was cackling with glee. He'd been drinking. "That arrogant mother-fucker! We got him, Winters! Looks like we weren't the only ones after him. The FBI was right there, too! Everybody hated him and now everybody's celebratin' . . ." he slurred.

The last invoice had been paid and Winters was finished with the case.

Burton's language was colorful; ice cubes clinked in a glass. Winters tore the cellophane wrapper off a package of cough drops and crushed it in his fist. "Can't hear you," he said. "Too much static." He clicked the phone closed.

On Wednesday, March 12th, the news conference was live on every TV channel then the clips were shown over and over again. The tall, ruggedly handsome governor of New York stood in front of a bouquet of microphones looking beaten. There, at his side, wearing a pastel blue suit and a string of pearls, was his slender, brunette wife staring into space towards him but beyond him, focusing on nothing. "I owe the people of the great state of New York an apology," he intoned in that way he had of stopping for applause at every phrase. There was no applause today. "I have betrayed your trust and am unworthy to serve as your governor. But most of all, I have abused the trust of my wife, Sharon, and of my family. I am truly sorry for what has transpired in the past two years and I intend to atone for my behavior. I ask to be forgiven for my bad judgment." He stopped, biting his lip and looked down. Sharon appeared frozen, standing ramrod straight beside him.

"Stand by your man," sang Mark as he extended his glass and Lori poured the wine. She looked drawn even though the arrest, the handcuffs, the shock had been the day before yesterday. Mark and Lori had an unspoken commitment to watch the 6:30 national news together. Unless he was with Mrs. C. A close up of Sharon was on the big screen. "Look at her. Just *look* at her!" erupted Lori putting down the bottle. "Looks like she just heard her whole family was killed in a fire."

The governor appeared tired, defeated. It was, after all, a concession speech. "I wish to make it clear that the money used in these transactions was mine, not public funds..." The sound of cameras clicking threatened to drown out his words.

"Look at him! Look at that guy! Stupid! Threw his career away!" Stanford Cortland was standing at the bar in the Yale Club. There were women members but tonight there happened to be no female in the room. Everyone was now silent, a coterie in shades of gray. They were bankers and lawyers in their pinstriped suits, staring up at the screen, drinks in hand. Many of the men had known Teddy Cantor as far back as Exeter. The minute the camera switched away from him to a commentator, someone muttered, "Asshole!"

"Not for doing it," said someone else. "Those girls must have been hot. Thirty grand a night!"

Another man chimed in, "He's an asshole for getting caught, Garson!"

Several of the men laughed and then began to joke about what a hooker could possibly *do* to make it worth that much money."

Gabrielle, naked and smiling, legs spread on the huge bed, leapt into Stanford Cortland's mind. He downed his vodka martini and realized he would never be able to see her again. Maybe it was all for the best. She was worth sixty-two thousand every month but he hadn't counted on that last million. He signaled the bartender for another drink and told himself to stop thinking about leaving all that money under that goddamn statue. It made him sick to think of it. He hadn't told anyone. There hadn't been time to do anything but get the money and obey the directions. He knew that Bill Frankel would want the police involved which meant that the whole mess would probably be leaked to the press. Everything the NYPD did seemed to show up on the front page of *The New York Post* or *The Daily News* the next day. At the very least, he'd be an item on Page Six. If he were lucky, it would be a blind item but it would be there all the same. Stanford gulped the second drink wondering what he would do if he were ever contacted again. More demands for more money! A fucking nightmare. Jesus Christ. Forget it, he told himself, I'll deal with it if it happens again but it may not. Maybe the blackmailer has gone down in flames right along with the Imperial Club in the last twenty-four hours.

Someone called his name and he turned to face Bill Frankel. "I hope you're not on any client list," he quipped.

"Client list?" said Stanford trying to sound light.

"Just kidding! No one's mentioned finding it yet but they are tracking all the bank records." Bill nodded at the bartender. "Scotch, any kind, and a splash of soda. A few rocks." When he turned back to Stanford the older man was staring into his glass. He looked quite pale.

OMAHA, NEBRASKA

George Forrester told himself he didn't want to know anymore but he couldn't resist. It was the second page today. After all, this was Omaha. He kept reading.

> The Imperial Club had prostitutes in New York, Miami, Los Angeles, London and Paris and would send them to meet men anywhere in the world, the complaint alleges. Authorities arrested two other women, Lori Stevens of Brooklyn, NY, and Rebecca Sullivan of Staten Island, NY, whom prosecutors described as booking agents in charge of setting up meetings between clients and prostitutes.

Lori Stevens! It can't be! It's a common name. But she does live in Brooklyn. He'd called her last Christmas. His thoughts raced. Did I ever speak to her on the phone to make a booking? Should I call her and ask if there is anything I can do? What if she recognizes my voice?

His cell phone rang and he jumped. "Yes, George Forrester." He listened. "Right. Thanks. Noon tomorrow. My office." He snapped the phone closed and thought, Lori Stevens!

BROOKLYN

Every channel was pushing the story. Lori plopped down on the couch beside Mark as Charlie Gibson turned to George Stephanopoulos for an opinion. "The Republicans were calling for impeachment. He really had no choice but to step down."

All she could think of was her personal drama. Racing around between the kitchen and the bedroom literally trembling with fright. That ridiculous hammering of the phone which had been found and confiscated minutes later. All the men swarming into her apartment, the trip downtown in the back of a police car with a metal grill between the back seat and the front. A cage. Right away she'd been put in a cage. Perhaps most horrible of all, were the handcuffs. She had been released at noon. Her lawyer had told her he would take care of everything. "If you cooperate, you won't get jail time. I'm ninety percent sure of that."

Stephanopoulos was droning on. Lori took a gulp of wine and thought, what about the other ten percent?

MANHATTAN

Kelsey stood in her bedroom, mesmerized as Governor Cantor was shown with his wife beside him. CNN and CNBC had played the clip all afternoon and now it was evening and still being replayed. "Thank the Lord," she breathed, "I never slept with him."

Later that evening, at dinner, Thierry, a French lawyer she was dating, went on and on about the scandal and joked about how it would have played out with a French politician. Kelsey made appropriate comments, wondered if anyone would question her and then wondered if she should start dating an American lawyer.

Brooke stared at the television screen in her dressing room and then turned back to the mirror and applied eye liner. Carefully, taking her time, as Mark had taught her to do. Stanford was meeting her at the Met for the opening of the new Greek antiquities wing at seven-thirty. She didn't know where he was now but he was usually on time. Brooke watched CNN's replay as the governor ended his statement and the swarm of reporters surrounded him like a pack of dogs about to be fed.

She walked across the room to the closet, pushed open the sliding doors and stared. I think I have too many clothes, she thought. Grasping one padded hanger after another, she finally chose the pink silk dress.

"Are you still involved with prostitutes?" shouted a reporter on television. Vaguely, as she decided to wear the pear-shaped diamond ring, Brooke wondered if Stanford were watching the same newscast somewhere. She felt quite dispassionate about it. Had he been to whores their whole marriage? To others before the Imperial Club? It was still amazing to think about him with someone in London. A whore. The broadcasters were calling them prostitutes but what really was the difference?

She reached for the diamond earrings and then smiled in the mirror. Brooke thought of hiding behind a tree and watching her husband creep towards the big statue. His head was on a swivel, Mark said later. He was looking in all directions frantically, behind big sunglasses, but he couldn't see them. Afterwards, Brooke followed him, from tree to tree, and confirmed that he had left the park and was waiting to cross Fifth Avenue. Mark, on speed dial, answered immediately. "Gone?" he'd whispered and she'd said, "Coast is clear," feeling quite giddy. Then Mark, dressed as a woman, complete with black wig, head scarf and an old raincoat, had retrieved the bag.

Though the two wanted to go somewhere and count the money and celebrate, they decided that they should not be seen together right then, that Mark should take the money to his apartment. "All here!" was the message on her cell phone an hour later.

Brooke applied blush to her cheekbones and wondered what sort of mood the Big S would be in. Suddenly she realized she didn't care. She gave a last look and turned out the mirror lights. I suppose I might have broken the law, thought Brooke, but if it's taking money from my own husband, maybe it isn't. She laughed softly. What fun.

BOSTON

"Amazing," said Holtie as he sipped his scotch in the living room. The big, flat screen TV was usually hidden behind the painting over the mantle but every evening at six o'clock, Holtie pushed the button that exposed it. The clip of Governor Cantor was being shown yet again. "Catherine, can you believe this?" he said as she entered the room and sat down beside him. "Teddy Cantor! The man had enemies twelve-deep waiting to bring him down and he knew they were after him! And still he kept dealing with the escorts! It boggles the mind. And no matter how much the politicians in Albany hated him and were after him, I don't think anyone ever imagined they'd uncover a prostitution ring!" He sipped his drink and changed his tone. "He's a Democrat in New York. He'll be out and Lloyd will replace him. Business as usual. Wait and see. I know I'm right."

Catherine leaned towards the television as if to absorb every word and then sat back on the couch without speaking. She felt weak.

"Thirty thousand a night! I love it!" Holtie was shaking his head and smiling. "This is much better than Hugh Grant getting caught with that street prostitute for what—what was it? Fifty dollars?" He laughed. "If you're going to do it, do it right! Make it worth it!"

Worth it? Five thousand dollars an hour. Had it been? Catherine wondered what sort of bookkeeping Becky and Lori and Bree did. Would anyone ever connect her with Claudia? They couldn't. She'd been very careful.

No e-mails. Just the one from the public Internet place when she'd answered the ad. Then the one from Bree she'd picked up a few days later to tell her to go to the Copley Plaza for the interview. But that e-mail no longer existed and she had not used any name. If anyone tried to find her using Bree's computer they would be led to an Internet café next to the Simmons College campus. Period. The end. No checks, nothing on paper. Only cash and the throwaway had been thrown away. Nobody would dredge the Charles for a trakfone. The post office box would expire and, according to her calculations, there was nothing in it now and would never be again. If there were one last envelope, it would be addressed to Jane Sweeney and the thug was welcome to it. He'd be delighted to keep the money and there was a slim chance he'd ever tell anyone, let alone call the police. No more awful trips there. Suddenly she wondered if there had been a surveillance camera and then discounted it as that dump was so shabby, so run down and whoever heard of anyone robbing a mail box place? Even if there had been a surveillance camera and even if that slimy character called the police, Catherine was certain she could not be identified. At best, she'd be a woman in a raincoat, wearing dark glasses with a hat pulled way down. No eyes, no hair color, not much for anyone to recognize.

"Now we turn to Iraq. A car bombing today in a Baghdad market—" Catherine was barely listening. Maybe something would happen to distract those bloodhounds Gainey and O'Donnell away from the Quire stock mess. She was beginning to feel safe again. She moved closer to Holtie and he smiled and put his arm around her. He seemed to have begun to believe that she had saved the money and that everything was this amazing coincidence. Catherine had started to believe it herself.

BROOKLYN

It was a week after the takedown of the Imperial Club and Mark was on his cell to Brooke, laughing. The black wig was on the white leather sofa and the raincoat had been tossed on the kitchen stool. Lori came in the front door which was always unlocked and yelped when she saw the wig then put her hand over her mouth.

Mark waved at her to come in. "We did it, Mrs. C! I just counted and it's all there and dye didn't explode in my face like bank robbery money and it's not one hundred dollar bill on top of newspapers cut to size. It's all there!" Lori closed the door and walked across the living room. A Bloomingdale's Big Brown Bag shopping bag was on the floor beside the couch; Lori peeked in and gasped.

"But don't you think I should hand it over to you?" He was quiet and then said, "Okay. I'm coming to do your hair tomorrow at noon. Yes." He listened. "I'll take a cab. Nobody will rob me in the back of a cab." He listened. "So he hasn't come back yet? It's probably good that you won't see him tonight. Try not to scream with happiness when you have breakfast with him. No gloating over the shredded wheat." Laughter. "Ciao!"

He clicked closed the phone, dashed across the room and grabbed Lori by the shoulders and shook her. "We did it! Again! Home free!" he exulted. "The more Mrs C thought about what he's done, the madder she got so this time we asked for *three* million! We decided that the demise of the Imperial Club must have him in a state of nonstop tachycardia and the Big S left the cash with the Mad Hatter just like we told him to!"

"My God!" Lori exploded. "You and Mrs. C are out of your minds! You have gone entirely insane!" She stared at him, wide-eyed and repeated slowly. "En-Tire-Ly-In-Sane. You have to stop doing this! Now! Did it ever occur to you two that blackmail is *against the law?*

Mark laughed. "And being the hooker booker for Imperial Club is perfectly okay?"

Lori's face fell. "Point taken. But," she picked up the black wig and held it in front of her at arm's length with distaste. "Get rid of this thing. I thought it was a dead animal when I came in. And by the way, the security is a little lax around here. You might want to lock the door once in awhile just because you've got three million dollars sitting in a paper bag."

Mark grinning, pirouetted through the living room and clicked the four locks closed, one by one. Then he snarled, in an atrocious imitation of an Italian gangster, "Hey-a-, baby, I'm a gonna make-a you an offer you can't-a refuse. How about penne alla vodka and a whole lotta vino bianco?"

JUNE and JULY, 2008

*Whoever said money can't buy happiness
simply didn't know where to go shopping.*
—Bo Derek

PHILADELPHIA

"What are you after? You haven't told me." I listened. It seemed it was one of those dive-in-and-see-what-you-find assignments. "You'll have the retainer agreement before the end of the day. Before the end of my day," I amended. He was twelve hours ahead. "Thanks, Mr. Lo. I'll get back to you once I've located the subject and made contact."

I hung up and shouted, "Wow! Wow! Wow!" and the dogs came running up the stairs with a great clattering of paws and jingle of collars and then bounded into my office assaulting me under my desk. "Sherlock! Vidocq! What do you think, boys?" I asked, pushing back my chair and bending down to pet them. "I am going to interview the madam of the Imperial Club V.I.P. and I'm going to be paid for it!"

The scandal screamed 'novel.' It was a beach read, a my-flight-has-been-delayed-three-hours-but-I-don't-care book. I had devoured everything about the story, stared at every grainy photograph of Bree a.k.a. Chantal behind big sunglasses after the arrest and wondered what she was like, who she really was.

I'd done that money laundering case in Taiwan three years ago but hadn't heard a word from Mr. Lo or his associates since and now—suddenly—I would work for them again. Delighted didn't cover it. I was over-the-moon excited. Of course, I had absolutely no idea how I would get the madam to meet with me or talk to me but I knew that I'd probably figure it out so I asked for a retainer and was hired.

The young woman was outrageously difficult to track down. Her mother had married again but her new name was a mystery. My data base people can track cell phones but, as expected, every one was out of service. Her father was supposedly living a few miles outside of a small town in a rural area. I decided to go there and ring his doorbell. One day I took a train to Manhattan and then a second train north of the city. Arriving at the little station, I grabbed a cab and gave the driver the address. Simple. I thought. I then endured two hours of being driven up and down back roads bordered by pastures with cows in the distance. My cab driver had no dispatcher, no map, no GPS and apparently no instinct for direction whatsoever so I finally called the local police who said they'd never heard of the road but the desk sergeant was sure the Fire Department would know. The Fire Department didn't know but thought Joe's Auto Repair might know.

Thirty minutes later, the dazed driver and I found it. We drove up a steep hill to a rather grand modern house built on the edge of dense woods. I noted the motorcycle in the garage. The front door was opened by a man in his fifties with gray hair and in two minutes he had agreed to ask his daughter to call me.

Euphoric over this tiny triumph of actually finding a link to Chantal Silver after weeks of dead ends and disconnected cell phones, I started the trip back to New York City and then back to Philadelphia.

I didn't think she'd call me. She was being hounded nonstop by all manner of journalists. From *The New York Times* to *The National Enquirer* and *People* magazine, everyone wanted an interview, everyone lusted to know what the handsome, powerful Governor Cantor was like in bed and who else might be in Bree's computerized little black book.

But she did call and she did agree to meet on a Saturday afternoon.

MANHATTAN—THE WALDORF ASTORIA

I thought the setting was the stuff of old movies. The hotel was located at 301 Park Avenue though no one needed to know the address. The Waldorf was the Waldorf and even a taxi driver from Uzbekistan knew where it was and what it represented.

One could imagine Cary Grant striding up to the concierge desk in an impeccably tailored gray suit and asking for the key to his suite. The flower arrangements were lavish, fragrant, impossibly splendid; the chandeliers sparkled overhead as big as Mini Coopers. Underfoot, the Art Deco-patterned carpets muted the sound of the guests and the staff crisscrossing the lobby which seemed the size of a football field.

So this was Bree. This is the madam, I thought, as I watched her sit down and arrange a black leather handbag over the back of her chair. Chanel. Expensive. She was very thin, five feet two inches tall, with fine features and perfect teeth. Her eyes looked black but later I would see that they were brown with flecks of green. Her smile was rare that first hour but absolutely dazzling. She was dressed entirely in black and was wearing a black leather jacket even on this warm, summer day. No makeup. Pale, very pale.

The wine came. We drank sauvignon blanc at a tiny table just a bit away from the main lobby. It was a good place to talk, the waiters didn't hover and three p.m. was an off hour. No one was sitting within fifteen feet or within earshot which was all I cared about.

Initially very wary, she began to relax. We were both astonished to be meeting another Charlie as it was Chantal's nickname, too. I said, "I'm going to find it difficult to call you Charlie so I'll call you Chantal," and that was fine. I would look back and don't think she ever called me Charlie either. Both of us had lived in Coral Gables at the same time. Chantal had been at the University of Miami fairly strung out on drugs while I'd been a few miles away in my penthouse starting Green Star Investigations. There was no hiding that. I had debated flying in under another name and then decided to brazen it out. There I was on my own website as a P.I. The Internet. Terrific *and* disastrous in the world of private detectivery.

So I told Chantal that I had been a private detective but wanted to focus on being a writer again. And then, as often happens when I'm undercover, I began to believe my own story. I suck myself right into the lies. I have created the little scene and I'm the main character. I believe what I'm saying and on a certain level, I can relax. This doesn't mean I'm not hyper-vigilant every minute and very much in control of every detail. No conflicting stories, no jagged time lines. But once I decide who I'm going to be, I smile internally and start to enjoy being that person.

After the first twenty minutes, something clicked and Chantal appeared to actually want to talk to me. A magazine piece or newspaper article was out of the question but a novel was appealing. "It will only appear far in the future and you can always deny anything or everything. There'll be a disclaimer saying it's a work of fiction," I promised.

The young madam soon opened up like a college roommate. She barely touched the wine so it wasn't the effect of alcohol.

"So Jake would have counted it in the car, with his knees apart, tossing the bills on the floor as we waited for one of the girls to show and by the time we got home we were finished with business and could just eat, watch a movie, whatever," said Chantal.

"Did you have a safe? Where did you or he put all those envelopes?"

She erupted in laughter. "In the closet."

"Was there a safe in the closet?"

"No! Just in the closet! He tossed it in the closet unless he left it on his desk. His desk was a mess and when I'd see that he had about twenty thousand dollars sitting out then I'd take the money and just toss it in the closet."

"First National Closet?"

Chantal yelped with laughter and the bartender some distance away turned to look at us. Sometimes she seemed like a giddy teenager and I would be reminded that she had just turned twenty-four. "We didn't really care about the money."

"Didn't care about the money?"

The afternoon wore on.

"I have to ask. What makes a girl worth $ 31,000 a night?"

Chantal smiled. It was a little cat smile of pleasure. "Nothing." I waited. "The men liked the idea of paying it. It made *them* feel special. It's that simple. Period."

We covered a lot of territory that first session. So much money, but there was always the element of risk. I felt chilled when Chantal leaned across the table and said, "When the door opens you have one second to think 'is he crazy?' And then you take a step forward and you think, 'am I going to get out of this hotel room alive?'"

The madam would be sentenced in December. Jake had not been given bail; his Israeli passport had convinced the judge that he was a flight risk and he'd gone directly to jail. Chantal was hoping to persuade the court that she should not receive prison time. "I have a job, a real job as an administrative assistant, and I am tutoring a third-grader named Brianne. I do volunteer work at a soup kitchen once a week and I'm going to school. My grades are the same. Always 4.0."

The girl was bright but not bright enough to not be where she was now.

"When is the sentencing?"

"It's December first which is a Monday."

Of course, it would be probation or a suspended sentence. Of course. Anything else was unthinkable. She didn't use the word 'prison' but talked about 'going away.' We were both aware that 'going away' was a possibility.

Another round of wine, more talk and then we were saying goodbye on Park Avenue. Chantal, in black knee-high boots and a miniskirt, turned to walk downtown as a Waldorf doorman opened the door of a taxi and waved me in. "Penn Station, please," I told the driver. Amtrak. All the way back to Philadelphia I made notes and thought of Chantal. I think it went so well between us just because she couldn't talk that way to anyone else.

PARIS

She decided to take charge.

The little jewelry shop was doing enough business to merit the rent she paid and she didn't mind being there, talking to people who wandered in to look, sometimes to ask about an Art Nouveau piece in the window. However, without the escort money her apartment was far too expensive to keep. She sat with a notebook and scrawled expenses in one column and income in the other. I will give myself two months, she decided. I don't want to pay more than two more months of rent from my savings which is enough time for something to happen, for something to change.

That weekend she took every canvas from the second bedroom she used as a studio into the middle of the living room. One by one they were dusted and photographed. Sally, her neighbor, helped her with the website and by Sunday afternoon every painting had a title and was posted. On Monday, she had cards printed with her name, Diane Montague, and 'artist' underneath. She held one card in her hand, read it again and again, and ran her fingers over the raised type; she was thrilled. The website and the address of her shop were at the bottom. There had always been business cards for the shop, of course, but this card was different. She was proclaiming to the world, in print, that she was, in fact, an artist.

On Tuesday, she spent all morning moving displays and glass cases in the shop. The heaviest one looked impossible to budge until she managed to lift a corner and push the edge of a towel underneath. Then she could push it a few feet without scratching the floor. At the end of the day she had her favorite paintings hanging on the back wall of the shop. Her entire body ached in the tub that night. On Wednesday, she put all thirty paintings on the front walls. Her best landscape she put in the window. On Thursday, a man from Lyon bought it.

She was elated. But, she thought, it's as if I am two people. The other person I am is suffering. Where is he? Will I ever see him again? Did I do the wrong thing that last morning? Why hasn't he called?

She told herself that she had dared to do something that she would have hated herself for *not* doing. Now he understood that I want only him, that there was no more calling the Imperial Club. The timing of the arrests just a week later had been a shock but it was lucky that he now had a way to reach her. So why didn't he? Had he decided it was too risky and that he only wanted to deal with the Imperial Club? Does he have some kind of arrangement with them that I don't know about? But that doesn't matter because Jake and Bree in New York are no more. Lori and Becky are no more. They might even go to prison. Was he so frightened after the arrests that he decided to never see me again and to be faithful to his marriage? She knew nothing of his wife, not a name or how long they had been married. Nothing. He did tell her that he had no children and he seemed a little sad saying it.

She could not get him out of her mind and her thinking led her only in circles. In the bathtub that evening with a glass of wine she meant to toast herself and selling the painting but she could only think of George. She said aloud, "George! George! George! Call me!" She added more hot water to the tub, determined not to cry.

CORAL GABLES

"The idea is to see my friend who's getting married in two months and I haven't been to New York in ages," she was telling Marta. A perfect time as Simon would be away on business for the week so she and Amber could be on their own. Annie stood on one leg and then the other in front of her boss's big, cluttered desk.

"Take a few days off. Absolutely," said the older woman. She didn't smile. No smiling in the office these days. That would have been too much to expect, thought Annie, but her voice was fine. "Annie," Marta added and the young woman stopped in mid-stride and turned back to her. Shit. Almost a clean getaway. Annie held her breath. "If you don't have anything pending and you're having a good time then stay for a week or ten days from one weekend through the next weekend."

"Really?"

"Really," repeated Marta. She finally looked up from the computer and very nearly smiled. "Have a good time."

MANHATTAN

"I feel so free," she said. "I want to look in a hundred store windows, stare at everybody and everything and tomorrow I'll go to the Met and to MOMA."

"Glad you're independent," said Amber putting papers into a folder. "And so sorry I can't play hooky with you. But I'll be home by seven."

They conferred over the keys and left the apartment together. It was a perfect day, thought Annie, waving goodbye as Amber hailed a cab. She started walking west towards Lexington, got all the way to Bloomingdale's and then decided she'd head uptown again. She headed east to York.

York seemed to be lined with apartment buildings rather than shops and Annie felt a pang of disappointment until she saw that she was in front of Christeby's. An auction of Boteros was scheduled in two days and today was the preview. In minutes she was inside the world's fourth oldest auction house. She sensed a cool, serene respectability. A uniformed guard pointed her in the right direction and, practically on tiptoe, Annie entered the vast space with a sense of awe. Lots of Miami collectors focused on Latin American painters and sculptors but she'd never seen so many Boteros in one room. She looked up at the bold colors, round, sturdy bodies, plump faces and thought of Juanita who gave her pedicures in Coral Gables. She looked exactly like a Botero and so did her husband and their daughter. As a woman passed her, walking quickly,

Annie turned and saw that a piece of paper had fallen in her wake. "Excuse me," she said, catching up to her. The woman stopped and turned. Annie breathed, "Caroline?"

They had lunch in a rather dark Italian restaurant, sitting in a booth in back. "We can talk here," said Cate.

After the initial 'what are you doing in New York' and 'what do you do at Christeby's' questions were answered, all barriers were down and they realized that, at last, they could talk freely.

"I don't know what to do," said Annie snapping bread sticks in half nervously. "I came up here to get away from the feeling of being followed and for awhile this morning I felt wonderful—" She looked around at the empty tables. "But I still have that feeling."

"If only we could get in touch with Bree," said Cate. "She would know how to handle this. She would at least have an idea of whether it's connected to a client or not."

The pasta primavera arrived and they were silent until the waiter walked away.

"Isn't it all incredible?" Annie blinked. "I mean the governor of New York!"

"I'm waiting for the next explosion."

"What do you mean?"

"I mean I'm the one who was supposed to get on the train and go to Washington and meet him at the Mayflower. At the last minute, I couldn't go so Bree sent that other girl."

"Ohmygod," said Annie. "That was supposed to be *you?*" She was breathless. "What's her name—something French? Renée? Monique? No. Renée. She's everywhere giving all those interviews! And she's so cheesy! Really cheap!" Annie was overwhelmed. "But you had been to the Mayflower with him?"

"Lots of times. He was my most regular regular."

Annie was stunned. "Is it true about the socks?" she demanded.

"No! He always took them off. That's ridiculous to keep reporting that."

Annie had a hundred questions. "Do you think anyone will find out it's you? What about your job? Can you be connected to Bree, Jake, the Imperial Club?"

She shrugged. "I don't know. Becky is talking her head off to the FBI so she won't have to go to prison. At least that's what I read. Lori? I don't know. But I bet she's out of her mind terrified. I know I am. I think I'm on the books as Caroline but the checks to compensate for the credit card transactions were all made out to Cate Burroughs."

"I have a friend in Miami who always says 'follow the money.'"

Cate wanted to change the subject. She worried about the bank records, all those checks and being found out every waking minute. Plus there were at least a hundred e-mails to and from Lori, Becky and Bree. She'd deleted them then consulted someone about erasing her hard drive. He'd asked for a thousand dollars and she'd started to write him the check but suddenly thought, what *am I doing*? She didn't want to leave her laptop behind in his grubby little studio apartment and have him copy her hard drive and use it against her. She'd hurriedly zipped the little case, said she'd think about it and rushed out of the Tenth Avenue fourth-floor walk-up.

The idea of being caught gnawed at her. It was a dull pain, a slight headache that wouldn't go away. It started the moment she groggily reached to shut off the alarm clock at seven a.m. and only ended when she finally succumbed to a fitful sleep hours after going to bed. Her thoughts surrounded her like a cold gray fog and were with her every waking moment. She saw the fear on her face when she brushed her teeth in the morning and in the ladies room at work when she put on lipstick. Cate was beginning to wonder when she would be arrested and not if. She forced herself to smile. "Tell me about him."

"Oh, he's just a friend. He's older and he's very sophisticated and he's also married. The first Ecuadorian I've ever met. It's not romantic. He's made it very clear that he loves his wife and somehow that makes it even better. I can talk to him about anything."

"We all need friends." Cate looked at Annie across the table. She was lightly tanned and her hair was platinum and stuck up like Tweety Bird feathers; her earrings were tiny mother-of-pearl seashells. "I'm so glad to see you. You have no idea. There is no one in the world I can talk to." Cate hesitated. "It's as if I've been playing a game and suddenly somebody changed all the rules and I'm losing."

Silence was between them like a third person at the table. Annie remembered those giggling sessions with the girl she knew as Caroline. The striking brunette that made men gulp at first glance. That dark shining hair, those eyes a shade of blue she had never seen before and the body of a *Sports Illustrated* swimsuit cover. Good times. Taking showers, talking about clothes and shoes and getting dressed for those dinners. Champagne bottles being opened with a whoosh! The sha-wunk noise of the ice in those big buckets on stands, the flowers on the table, the men and their expensive suits. The cufflinks twinkling as they moved their hands and told a story or reached for a wine glass. The two of them had been a great team making the client laugh, taking turns flirting with him. She remembered faking the orgasms during the oral sex as this or that South American watched. There was a way to lean your head so you never touched but the men could not see, never knew. The girls agreed that timing was really important. "Don't start moaning before I've even gotten on my knees!" Caroline had commanded in a whisper as they were undressing each other in a make-believe state of breathless passion. Neither one of them understood why men got so turned on by two women when it was all they could do not to burst out laughing. That had been Caroline then but here and now, in the dim light of a lamp fashioned from a Chianti bottle, Cate looked very tired.

"I think it'll be okay. Jake is in pretty deep but Bree might get out of this. As for us, we didn't kill anybody and Jake always said we were just a dating service."

Cate smiled at how ridiculous that sounded but it was kind of nice, actually refreshing that Alyssa was so naïve. As the plates were being taken away, she looked at her watch then put a twenty dollar bill and a five on the table. "This should cover half. I have to get back."

Annie said, "Oh, don't you miss the money? I do."

"I miss the money but not the risk."

"Hey, it was 18 carat, diamond-studded risk."

Cate shook her head. "I see it as shiny and platinum. Even though I was smiling, it was metallic and cold-in-the pit-of-my-stomach platinum. Every single time I waited for a stranger to open the door."

"Platinum risk," said Annie. "I guess it was that. For Governor Cantor, for all of us." She put her credit card on the table and said, "Give me your number and I'll give you mine. Can't hurt now, can it? And by the way, my real name is most definitely *not* Alyssa." She paused. "I'm Annie. Just plain Annie."

PHILADELPHIA

"Surveillance seminar?" I had to laugh.. "Oh, puh-leeze! What are they going to do, go around checking on our posture in parked cars? Yeah, yeah, yeah, Mickey." I was drawing triangles in green ink on the back of an envelope. "Go and take notes for me. I have better things to do than Jersey on a Saturday hearing an ex-cop talk about the finer points of cocker spaniel duty."

Mickey, a P.I. pal in New York, went on about it, how it might be a good thing to see who was there, how it could be good for networking which we both hated. He wasn't interested in networking. He just wanted the latest gossip, wanted me to find out who showed up. That was the whole thing. Curiosity in a detective? Off the charts.

Mickey went on trying to talk me into doing something *he* didn't want to do until I said, "I am devastated to inform you that I can't possibly go. I'll be getting a pedicure." Mickey snorted, he hated any feminine details like that. I grinned and we hung up on each other.

I flipped open the top file in front of me which was yet another capital case. It was nearly five o'clock on a Friday afternoon. My work starts early so when I can turn off the computer before six and leave the office I always feel a sense of triumph. At that hour, I like to pour myself a glass of wine and sit in the library on the second floor. Painted a pinkish terracotta color by my Dutch friend, Frans, the large room glows in daylight or candlelight. Three walls are floor-to-ceiling shelves. All my Graham Greenes are by a window next to the Faulkners and the Tennessee Williams. My Egyptology books are above the biographies of Oscar Wilde. Between two of the windows are all my true crime books: *Murder Machine*, *The Evil Empire*, crime in Victorian London, femmes fatales, several books on the Kimeses, smuggling, art theft, gunrunning, money laundering, the history of the Mafia, biographies of Sam Giancana, John Gotti, Big Paulie, everybody who's been bad. My novels fill another wall of shelves.

There is a black marble fireplace on the fourth wall and several prints hang over the mantle. A chandelier in the form of a very large wrought iron lantern from Spain presides over the scene.

I was on the second floor landing when the phone rang. Holding a stemmed glass, I hurried into the library. "Ciao, bella!" The English-accented voice was welcome. "I almost spilled my vino!" I complained as I put the glass on the coffee table and sat down.

"What else are your doing? Besides drinking alone?" Rowena didn't wait for an answer but launched into a diatribe about Berlusconi's latest exploit.

Rowena will call just before going to bed and sometimes chat for an entire hour between five and six my time. She is English, has been married to Dick forever and lives in a Roman palazzo with perpetual plumbing problems. Dick writes books on philosophy that few people read but they keep getting published anyway and Rowena manages a local newspaper for expatriates. It runs ads for everything from apartments to used vacuum cleaners, from job openings to language lessons to free kittens.

"Berlusconi could only exist in Italia! Can he be impeached?" I asked. "What do they do with these characters in Italy nowadays? Maybe they should go back to doing what they did to really rotten emperors."

"Oh, darling, that would be so easy. They just killed them. Think of Caesar leaving the Senate. Et tu, Brutus and all that."

"Did you say You Tube, Brutus?" I asked and we both laughed.

She hated Berlusconi with a passion. "I fantasize that we could try a drop of poison in his cappuccino or something lethal and powdered put into the Parmesan. That absolute last plate of pasta..."

We chatted for a few minutes and then Rowena commanded, "Don't hang up!" and there was the sound of footsteps running down the marble hallway I knew so well. "Back!" came Rowena's voice about forty-five seconds later. "Had to get some wine!"

"Oh, good! Don't let me drink alone. It could be dangerous. Remember growing up and hearing about housewives drinking at the ironing board, in secret, and how they were on the road to alcoholism, degradation and disgrace? All because one should never drink alone. Remember that?"

"Darling! I most definitely do not remember that as I didn't grow up in a suffocating southern Presbyterian household the way you did."

We chattered on, laughing, talking about the past, chatting about nothing in particular and I thought how much I love my friends.

OMAHA, NEBRASKA

George Forrester walked through the big, white living room sock-footed which his wife hated him to do, and then padded into the kitchen. The chef was off for three days at his brother's wedding in Chicago so he and the nurses were on their own. Terrific to have a chef, he thought, because if I waited for Sylvia to cook I would starve. Right along with her.

She'd told him she was a great cook before they married but that was just another misrepresentation. Yes. Absolutely Cordon Bleu, if you count adding water to a can of Campbell's soup.

Absentmindedly, he opened the refrigerator, bent down and peered inside. He sighed, closed the door and walked back into the living room. The remote was on the big, glass coffee table; he grabbed it, punched 'power.' Minutes passed before George realized that the television was on 'mute.' He clicked it off then stood up and pulled his wallet out of his back pocket. The stiff card was folded as it was larger than an American business card. He smoothed it flat and stared at it for the fiftieth time. DIANE and the Paris exchange and a phone number were written in blue ink with a fountain pen.

As they were saying goodbye, he had been kissing her and she had pulled away and said, "I've decided. There is no more Véronique. Here." She'd put the white card in his hand. "Call this number. Whenever you want." Her dark hair was loose around her face. How he loved pulling the old-fashioned hair pins out of her chignon and having the shining waves fall to below her shoulders. Her light brown eyes were unblinking, staring into his. "I miss you already," she said softly. She had kissed him one last time and was gone. He could still hear the click of the door closing behind her, could see the rumpled sheets of the bed, and imagined that he could still smell her perfume.

THE WALDORF ASTORIA

Chantal said she didn't mind if I took notes but it was difficult because she demanded my total attention. It was unblinking eye contact and it was damned tiring.

"The first thing I want to know is how you feel about Governor Cantor."

She smiled wanly. "He is the reason the house of cards collapsed. Imperial Club was collateral damage."

"I agree. He had political enemies and they were relentless. But he made big mistakes. His own banker was suspicious of him when he wanted to send wire transfers under another name."

"We always had problems with John Wolf. That's what he called himself. Money problems. He wouldn't use a credit card or wire transfers so he would take cash to the post office and buy money orders. And then he'd mail the money order and then he'd call and say has it come, did you get it? And maybe the mail was late or it hadn't come and he'd be really stressed about it."

It seemed faintly ridiculous to me. The governor in line at the post office buying a money order.

"But I was firm. I was not going to let Becky or Lori send him a girl without the money."

Our waiter put the two glasses of wine down and retreated.

I looked at Chantal across the table. Bree was gone forever but the Ivan Kuznetsov on the news was Jake and remained Jake. She always called him that because it was the way he had introduced himself at the start. "I was attracted to him right away," she said.

"How did you meet him?"

"I was in New York for the summer after my freshman year. I was eighteen, going to the University of Miami, and I was in a pizza parlor thinking I should get a waitress job. Somebody had left *The Daily News* on the table. I flipped through it and saw this ad for 'University Educated Girls Wanted as Models.' I called the number on my cell phone and this man said we should meet and asked me where I was and I told him. He said to go to the corner of

23rd and Eighth so I did. He waved at me to get into this white van."

"I got in. There was an Asian woman in the front seat and they asked me how old I was, a few questions."

"What were you thinking?"

She shrugged in the black leather jacket. "I wanted to make some money. I was bored. Summer school was just three courses and it was easy."

I am well aware of how accelerated summer classes are. Six chapters covered in one lecture. "Easy? I know you're a good student and that your prep school was good but—"

"Very easy," she said. "I get school. I know how to get As."

I nodded. "Okay. What happened next?"

"They drove me to an apartment on West 25th Street and Jake took me up to the fifth floor. It was a one-bedroom apartment. Very clean, new. He told me to wait there so I sat in the living room and about half an hour later, he came back with this Japanese guy. He was good-looking, in his thirties. I went into the bedroom with him and afterwards he left. I came out and there was Jake with another man. So I went into the bedroom with him. There were a couple of other girls there later and we sat and talked in the living room, we ordered take-out, and joked around. Jake would leave and then come in with another man and someone would go into the bedroom with him. At some point, someone made a room divider and then someone was doing it on the sofa." She looked a bit pained. "I never did it on the sofa."

"So Jake and these men were coming and going and you were there with two other girls?"

She paused to think. "There were five of us girls at most. Anyway, I woke up four days later with thousands of dollars and went back to the dorm."

"Did someone drug you?"

She laughed. "No! We were all on drugs. Coke, marijuana, mostly coke. That's why it was so easy and I had no idea all those days had passed." She added, "It was Chinese take-out and drugs and pizza and telling jokes and waiting around for Jake to come back. The next thing I knew I woke up with hundred dollar bills all over the bed."

"How much were you charging?"

"I don't know." She shook her head. "Later it would be half for Jake, half for the girl. All I knew at first was that I was making so much money and that it was much better than being a waitress. "

"Did you know that's what the ad meant?"

"They told me it was a dating service."

"And then, suddenly you were in the bedroom and it was okay? Didn't it bother you? Were you frightened taking off your clothes, alone in a room with a strange man?"

She shrugged. "It wasn't hard to do but I think the drugs made it easier."

"Did you realize what you were doing?"

"I was on Valium and not in a great position to make decisions."

I stared at her. Sometimes she looked about twelve. I halfway expected a waiter to come over, card her and whisk the wine away. "How did you get started with drugs?"

"My roommate at University of Miami asked me if I wanted a Percocet. The first day. I didn't even know what it was. But I found out."

"So, after four days, you went back to the dorm, back to your classes at N.Y.U. When did you see Jake again?"

"Maybe a week later, I called him and he came, with the Asian woman, and picked me up. We drove all the way to Queens and he let me off in front of this hotel. A crummy hotel. I was supposed to pick up the room key and go up to the room and wait. I went up but it was creepy. I left. He lost a lot of money on me because the man came and I was gone. Jake was a little bit mad but then he would call and say, 'Can you work today?' And I would go. Then sometimes the men would ask for me."

"Was the Asian woman doing this, too?"

"No. She was older and I think he'd married her so she could stay in the country. They were never in love. Later I found out that it was her idea, that they started the business together."

I hated interrupting her so I let her go off on tangents.

"I told you how I was attracted to him right away so I was curious about the Asian woman. Jake had been married for years to a woman he really loved. They came to the U.S. and lived in New Jersey. She died and I think that he was very lonely and he started going online and he met the Asian woman. It was her idea to start the business." She took a sip of wine. "But he wanted to make it more upscale. He told me once that he was running a hot dog stand and he wanted to own a five-star restaurant." She stopped. "He wanted better girls, better clients, repeat clients and to charge more. But first of all, he had to get better girls and that's where the ad I saw came into it."

"Did you go to other hotels?"

"I did it when I wanted money, when I was bored. I went to a few hotels and we used that apartment he owned on 25th Street. That was okay. I never went to that awful hotel in Queens again."

Chantal explained that when September came she went back to Miami for her sophomore year. She had a boyfriend but she still thought about Jake. "Then the next summer, I was back in New York and I called the cell phone number and the Asian woman answered and said that she and Jake weren't together anymore. She told me to call another number. He asked me if I would come and see him in New Jersey. I took the ferry to Weehawken. I'd never done that before. I didn't even know there was a ferry to Weehawken."

I looked at her young face and saw real excitement over taking the ferry across the Hudson. Her face had been blank when she'd described having sex with strange men.

"It was a great apartment overlooking the river. An awesome view."

"Did you sleep with him then?"

She nodded. "I was always really attracted to him." I waited. There was a pause and then Chantal said, "Afterwards, he tried to pay me."

I was silently horrified, took a sip of wine hoping my face showed no reaction. "What did you do? What did you say?"

"I wouldn't take the money. I told him to just give me more clients."

MANHATTAN/ KEY BISCAYNE

"Annie? It's Cate." The voice was strained and very soft as if she were afraid of being overheard. "Can you talk?"

"Hi! Sure I can talk! How are you?" Annie kicked off high-heeled sling backs and sank into a pale blue living room chair.

"Not great. I wish you were still in New York. I wish we could meet and drink wine. I wish—" Her voice had a desperate edge to it.

"Cate! What's wrong?"

"I think what's been happening to you has started happening to me."

"Where are you? What are you talking about?"

"I'm in New York. In my apartment."

Annie ruffled her hair nervously. She had exactly one hour to shower, change her clothes and show up to show a condo on Brickell. "Tell me what's happened," she said though she was afraid she knew.

"Someone has been following me. A man. I saw him at the newsstand on Third Avenue yesterday and again when I went out to lunch. He's young, thin, Hispanic. I did not see him today but I have the feeling he is around. It's horrible." She stopped. "And what's worse is that someone was in my apartment. Last night when I came home I knew immediately. It was as if the

203

very air was disturbed. Nothing like a bureau drawer turned upside down or things moved but it was more of a feeling. A very strong feeling that someone had been here." She pulled the tortoiseshell hair band out of her dark hair and laid it on the coffee table. "Nothing was taken but someone got in past the doorman and got out again." She remembered the ice-cold sensation that had gripped her as she stood in the open doorway with her keys in her hand. It was as if she could *smell* the intruder.

Annie reminded herself of Intriago when she asked, "Did you call the police?"

"No," Cate said. "And you know why."

"So you think it's a client? Has to do with a client?" Annie stared out the balcony doors at the sweep of blue water and listened. "I wish we could find Bree."

"Well, we can't find Bree," said Cate. "Every journalist in New York wants to find her and I keep looking for a little teaser on Page Six of *The Post* saying she was spotted in Soho or she was seen having dinner with someone and there's nothing. She's in seclusion somewhere."

"Maybe Wyoming."

"Not Wyoming," said Cate. "She probably can't leave New York. Or New Jersey."

"Well, let's forget about Bree." Annie paused. "I guess Lori and Becky are out of the picture, too."

"They either tossed their cell phones or the FBI has them so I don't think we want to call them up and say 'hello.'"

"Actually," said Annie. "We don't know where they were, even what state they were talking to us from." She frowned. "Bad grammar but you get it."

"Stress brings on bad grammar," stated Cate. She sighed. "Do you think this is someone we have in common?"

"Seems logical to me. We have a lot in common to anyone who knows about Imperial Club. Bree, Jake, Becky, Lori." She kept thinking: if only we could find Bree.

"Then there are the clients," Cate said. "How many threesomes did we have?"

"I think the first one was over a year ago. Was it the Fontainebleau?"

They talked, they tried to remember. "I was never flown to New York; you always came down here," said Annie.

Half an hour later, they hung up and Annie raced into the shower. In minutes, she had pulled on a white cotton dress, grabbed her big tan leather bag which served as both briefcase and purse and was slamming the door. She put on lipstick and mascara at the traffic lights and was only five minutes late. Roiling through her mind was the mantra: if only we could only find Bree.

KISS THE RISK

MANHATTAN

Cate sat in her living room and thanked God for Annie. The only person in the world she could tell about this. She remembered always being happy to see her, to think she was the other woman. They were so good at the theatrics of the phony passion and had laughed so much. Nothing remotely romantic about any of it, not at any point in the evening, thought Cate. The two of them had agreed that, even after dinner and mojitos or Cristal, the getting undressed in the suite in front of the client, the lacy underwear coming off as they prepared for their 'act' always felt like changing for ninth grade gym class.

Thank God for Annie, thought Cate again. It never crossed her mind that Annie might be the reason these things were happening to her.

PHILADELPHIA

A hot day. Humidity like Mississippi without a breath of a breeze. I'm on the third floor in my office with a little revolving fan under the desk blasting at my bare legs. Wearing minimal clothes. Short khaki shorts and a white T-shirt. And earrings, always earrings. My aerie is painted chocolate brown with all the molding and the deep window frames painted a crisp, high gloss white. It's like being inside a Hostess cupcake. From my desk I can stare out the two large windows and see the top of my neighbor Betty's tree and blue sky. Between the windows hang framed illustrations of Moriarty looking evil and of Holmes in a London railway station. Beneath the illustration of the great detective with his suitcase was written, 'The beginning of another adventure.'

Behind me on the wall is an enormous black and white poster of the Vito Genovese crime family which was a Christmas present from Mickey. It was a roster of who was in jail for what, their FBI or NYPD numbers, and their nicknames. Tony Cheese, Four Cents, Frankie the Bug. If they were dead there was a big X over the face. Beside the poster is a signed photograph of my first boss, Vinny Parco. He'd written 'to Charlie, my best student' in one corner in black Magic Marker. Beside this is a framed newspaper photograph of Lucky Luciano being arrested in 1936. Five New York City detectives, all in trench coats and fedoras, were taking him into custody; Luciano was dressed identically. My private detective license for the Commonwealth of Pennsylvania hangs at eye-level beside my license for the State of Florida.

I paid my dues as a female entering a macho profession fourteen years ago. It was tough, sometimes demeaning, often surprising. I started at eight dollars an hour in New York City, endured the dirty jokes, the sexist comments and

205

stuck it out. The physical demands meant all-nighters in parked cars and stakeouts; there were tails on foot in the snow or in hundred degree weather. A complaint about conditions never crossed my lips. I was never, as a woman, going to be the weak link.

Moving from one firm to the next, I gradually made more money per hour, alongside a different class of male. I went from hanging around with men who read comic books to men whose firms were occasionally mentioned in *The Wall Street Journal*. My partners on stakeouts wore cowboy boots, jeans and flak jackets. Later I'd sit in board rooms with lawyers and ex-Company types who wore wingtips and suits that cost double my rent. By 'Company' I mean THE Company, the CIA.

No one ever treated me with kid gloves, but at last they stopped testing me and finally I was told they respected me. Now, in Philadelphia, with my own firm, I take on my own cases and specialize in criminal work. I flipped open the police report on top of the nearest file. My newest client had been arrested for rape; bail was impossible so I would visit him in prison tomorrow to hear his side of the story. Another man in orange.

The familiar ringing of Skype. I grabbed the headphones, put the cursor on the little green telephone logo and pushed 'answer.' "Charlie? Are you there?" It was Call Me Jack as usual at noon. Europe was six hours ahead and he had to call before he went home. Maybe. Wherever home was. Home to her. Whoever she was. If there were a wife or lover or dog or cat though Jack didn't seem to be the sort of man with a cat. Then again maybe he was calling *from* home and lived with a pet gecko.

"Hi, Jack," I answered, fumbling for my notebook. My place mark was an Oreo from yesterday. I licked my index finger and blotted up a few black crumbs. Sometimes I worried about ants in the office but not enough to change my habits.

"So how did it go?"

"Very well. She seems to trust me. Or else she is the most open person I've ever met with someone she doesn't trust." Or she could be lying. That was always possible but then why bother to waste all this time? Why not just *not* meet with me? The subject had nothing to gain by lying. Well, maybe lunch.

"How long did you talk?"

"About two hours. I don't want her to ever get tired. She could easily go on but I don't want to have her leave me feeling anything but up. I don't want her to ever not want to meet the next time."

"Good." He asked a few more questions as I stared at the calling number on the screen. It was infuriating that I could not trace it, could not know his identity. With his nearly maniacal penchant for secrecy, it had most likely been created just for Skype, just for me. The country code was 41 which was Switzerland. The city code was 22 which was Geneva. But was he really calling from there?

Ordinarily, I would not have taken a case without knowing more about the client but the Hong Kong firm I knew and trusted. Mr. Lo had been the middle man at the start. Now it was just me and this mysterious client on Skype.

"What next?"

"Next Saturday if she can. She's very busy being very good. She'll text and let me know. She has a job, volunteer work, exams and generally a lot on her plate."

"I must say I'm astounded that you've come so far. It was so damn difficult to even find her and now she's actually meeting with you and talking." His voice was a rich baritone. Was it an English accent? The other day I'd thought it might be Scottish. It was a curious mix somehow. I thought of Sean Connery and then Rex Harrison and frowned in frustration. Maybe he was a German who'd been to Gordonstoun or Eton. Could be anyone, any nationality, calling from anywhere and faking the accent. As I stared at the screen, he disconnected with that bloomp! noise that sounded like a plug being pulled out of a bathtub.

PARIS

George Forrester was staying at the George V this trip. He had never been back to the Plaza Athénée again and actually avoided Paris when he could. Tonight he was eating alone at a restaurant he'd seen reviewed; he was thinking of the early morning flight out of Charles de Gaulle. It had gone well that day; the corporate headquarters in Paris had committed to using his software in every branch office and there were forty-five of them which made it very lucrative for Forrester Tech.

He ordered escargot in French, unaware of his waiter's disappointment. The young man had recited a litany of special starters and besides, the fat snails came from China. George could only think how pleased Véronique would have been to hear him. The pain of that last morning hadn't gone away and sometimes he thought it hadn't lessened either. Time healing all wounds was certainly a joke.

George thought, if I weren't a man, I'd be close to tears most of the time. But if she thought that I was nothing but a man with money to pay her and that she was interchangeable with another woman then how could I ever feel anything towards her again? Obviously, my feelings overcame all common sense for me to have imagined she felt the same. I was blinded by my own need for her. She was an actress, that was all. Maybe she has ten men who feel the same way about her as I do. Did, he corrected himself.

What an actress. He remembered the evening they had to leave the restaurant and had ended up outside on the sidewalk, literally holding onto each other for support. Both had been crying with laughter. Later, with ice cream cones, walking along the Seine, she had suddenly exploded with laughter again. "You did not pay for zee champagne!" Her accent, her laugh, her giggle like a little girl's. He missed her and he hated himself for falling so hard for someone who was nothing but a very good actress.

PHILADELPHIA TO MANHATTAN

I stared out the window as the train swept past a New Jersey landscape of salvage yards. Twisted metal, rusting refrigerators and old tires. On time. It was just past one o'clock and the meeting was at two-thirty. Be careful, I reminded myself. Don't make judgments, don't express anything but curiosity and interest.

Chantal Silver had gone to a good prep school; it was expensive and excellent scholastically. She'd been second in her class, been headed for any college she wanted. Her father was a rather attractive man in his fifties, a successful businessman, divorced, living in a beautiful house way up on a hill only an hour or so from New York City if you knew how to find it. Her mother was happily remarried, living in Connecticut. "My best friend," Chantal insisted.

What could propel this exceptionally bright, articulate young woman into a life of prostitution? Was it just a one-word answer? Jake? No. Even if she wasn't turning tricks herself at the end, she was organizing and masterminding the whole setup. Prostitution might not be considered a crime in certain circumstances but I can't understand how the person I am beginning to know could be so jaded about the sex act. My mind flashed back to marriage proposals, to romantic walks on beaches, to black tie dinner dances, to being kissed under a full moon. I've just been in love too many times. Maybe that's it. I've never taken off my clothes and not meant it.

Chantal's response was matter of fact. "If a man is stupid enough to want to pay me for it, then sure. It's money. Let him pay me. I'll take his money."

It sounded like something Jazz would say. Rowena's daughter. Jazz had once been what she called 'an escort.' Maybe she still was.

I closed my eyes and wondered how much a man would pay to spend the night with me. I wakened at Penn Station, left the train, swiftly made my way through the crowds, up the escalator and hurried out to Eighth Avenue to find a cab.

THE WALDORF ASTORIA

"Let me get this straight. Even though you were sleeping with Jake, he was sending you out?"

Chantal nodded. "I wanted the money." She could not be more direct about it. "My father gave me an allowance at school but he always had a problem with drugs and I think that's why he never gave me any extra money. He thought I'd spend it on drugs." She shrugged. "And he was right. So I had to get my own money for drugs and having Jake send me out was the way to do it."

"But you said that being on Valium and coke was the reason you could have sex that first time?"

"That was part of it. It made it pretty easy actually. I was functioning, I was still making good grades but—"

"But you wanted money for the drugs and it didn't matter how you got it?"

Chantal stared at me as if it were all so basic. "Exactly. Sleeping with them was not a big thing and the money just poured in. I spent it all on drugs so I never had any extra and when Jake would call, I would always say yes."

"Condoms? Did you always make them wear a condom?"

"Yes. I think I did. Sometimes I was a bit out of it. But with Imperial Club, absolutely. If a client put up a fuss it was up to the girl to decide but the girl could leave."

Well, that's a relief. "So, at this point, that second summer, the summer after your sophomore year, it was just you and Jake? The Asian woman was gone and it was just you and him?"

"Yes."

"Was he sleeping with the girls? I mean you were sleeping with him and with other men, too, but what about Jake?"

"He would sleep with some of them sometimes but that stopped." She smiled. "I remember once, right in the beginning, he told me that someone had asked him if I were his girlfriend and that he'd said yes. I was thrilled because there were all these beautiful girls around. But he stopped with the others and we were together."

I was thinking that it was so junior high school, so twisted, so entirely zany. Jake was older than her father and sending her out to sleep with strangers and she was thrilled to be called his girlfriend.

Chantal continued. "We started talking about making it a better business. I wrote better ads and we put them in better places. Like *The New York Review of Books*, *The New York Observer*. I put together a website that we used to attract girls and I wrote up an application so that they could fill it out, send it in. The application would decide whether or not we met with them."

"What kind of background does Jake have? Is he an educated person?"

"He is brilliant about some things and—" She erupted with laughter. "And not so bright about others. Like keeping the money in the closet!"

I laughed and took a sip of wine. "Where is he from? There was something in the paper about not giving him bail because he has an Israeli passport."

Chantal's face was alight. She had fine bones, a flawless complexion, and that toothpaste-ad-perfect smile. Breathlessly, she spoke of Jake. Her lawyer had forced her to show the court the tattoo that read 'Property of Jake' to illustrate the older man's grip on the young girl. It was placed way below the top of her thong. "He was born in Russia. Incredibly poor. His father worked in a factory and they used some kind of chemical there and he went insane after years of being exposed to it. His mother died soon after that." She took a sip of wine. "Jake fell in love and married this woman and they came to New York, lived in New Jersey. She had cancer. During one of her remissions Jake got interested in holistic medicine, in being a vegetarian." She took a breath. "He became a CPA or maybe he already was one and someone introduced him to somebody else and before he knew it he was hired to take care of money for the KGB in New York."

"What?!"

Chantal laughed. "I know! It sounds crazy but it's true! What's even crazier is that someone who could hide money for the KGB would not do the same thing for himself." She looked pained. "And instead he would just toss it in the closet."

I lifted my hand for the waiter. The bartender in the distance caught my eye and nodded. "The KGB?" I repeated in a low voice. "Are you sure about that?"

"Why would he say it if it weren't true?"

I didn't answer. Sometimes Chantal appeared so naïve that it was hard to grasp who she was, all she'd done in her short life.

Chantal continued. "So his wife died. Somehow the KGB stopped using him, he was lonely and got on the Internet. I think that's how he met the Asian woman."

"Any children?"

"A son. Almost as old as my father."

"How old is Jake?" I'd read he was sixty-five but wanted Chantal to actually tell me.

She grinned, shrugged as if she couldn't quite believe it herself. "He's older than my father." I waited. "It doesn't matter to me. It never mattered to me. He is careful about what he eats and I thought he was in his forties. I know that after we started living together, I noticed things. There was that time we were at Kennedy flying to London and he was so nervous about my seeing his passport. But I didn't care. I was going to spend the rest of his life with him." This was a statement of fact to her. "There was another time when I saw something black on his hands and I realized that he was dyeing his hair." She stopped. "But I don't care!"

The waiter put down two glasses of wine and took the empty glasses away.

"When did you start living with him? You went back to Miami for sophomore year, then back to New York for the summer, then back down there for junior year."

"I went back to school at the end of that summer but I was in a mess with drugs." She paused, remembering. "Jake and I were flying back and forth, New York to Miami all the time that fall, every weekend. My grades had fallen and my father was upset with me. It was October. Then Jake came down and said, 'you are coming back to New Jersey to live with me.' That was that. I did."

"What did your parents think of Jake?"

"Nothing. They didn't know about Jake and I didn't tell them I'd dropped out of school until months later." She took a swallow of wine.

"So what was it like living with him? Did he care you were on drugs?"

"He was cool with it. In the beginning. He is completely against drugs but he'd see me doing coke in the front seat of the car and wouldn't say anything. When I lived with him, it changed. I was always awake. It was the drugs. I was excited and tense. We were trying to get the business off the ground and he was doing a lot of the work. I'd done the website but we had to meet the girls, do interviews. I was out of it. I wanted to score drugs all the time. I was in bad shape. One day, he sat me down and said 'Look, I didn't sign on to take care of an invalid. Either you help me with the business or we call it quits.' It shocked me."

She stared into her glass. "That gave me my opening. I must have been relatively lucid at that moment. I said, 'When I left Miami, you said we were going to do this fifty-fifty.' He asked if that was what I wanted and I said yes."

"I knew I had to kick drugs. It was hell. I would be clean for a week and then I'd call my old roommate in Miami and have her overnight FEDEX every prescription drug that could possibly be abused. So that would arrive the next day and I'd run to answer the door or go out and take a walk and pick it up. Or I'd find a UPS store near where we were going to have an early dinner and in the middle of it, I'd excuse myself to go to the ladies room, sneak out of the restaurant, run down the street, get the package, tear it open, jam everything into my purse and then run back and sit down at the table literally sweating."

Her face showed how painful it was to remember. "Jake was hiding drugs from me in the apartment and when I freaked out he would give me something." She tried to explain. "You know when you first get high and then you keep wanting that high again and you keep taking drugs and you just feel bad?"

I didn't know and I didn't answer and Chantal went on. "But he got me clean. He stopped smoking. And other things started to change. Once the phone rang in the apartment and Jake answered it. It was an old client who asked if I were available. I was sitting right next to him. Jake said, 'I'll check,' and turned to me. 'Do you want to do it?' he asked and I said no. "

"Did you want to do it?" I leaned forward.

"Yes, but I knew I had to say no. I wanted to do it. For the money."

More Imperial Club fallout in the press. Supposedly the governor had spent over $ 80,000 on prostitutes. Was it public money? asked the pundits. Was it his own? His family was quite wealthy. His wife had been an attorney, he had been one, too, of course. Sixteen years of marriage later and who knew what money was whose and now one could only guess what services it had purchased. There would be an investigation by an independent committee formed immediately.

PHILADELPHIA

"How is the novel coming?" she'd asked when we were saying goodbye. I had stifled a wince and answered, "Really well. I'm mapping it out, getting lots of ideas." I turned off the hot water. For the money, went through my mind as I leaned back in the bubble bath.

Money. Chantal wanted money for drugs. She was living with a man who took care of her, had a father who still gave her an allowance and thought she was spending her days in class at the University of Miami. Instead of living with a man older than he was, running an escort service in New Jersey. I cupped a mountain of bubbles, admired the glint of rainbows and then blew it apart. For the money. And I'm doing this case for the money and I don't know who Call Me Jack is and he has not given me the reason for hiring me. It's no longer a sin of omission. He's hiding something. I can't seem to find out what it is or why he is or who he is but I'm dealing with him for the money.

Deep down, I know it isn't the money but I wanted to find a way to relate to Chantal. How far would I go for money? There's that old joke about the Englishman asking a woman to sleep with him for a hundred pounds. She was angry, offended. He offered a hundred thousand pounds and she hesitated then agreed. He then lowered the price back to a hundred pounds and she retorted, "What do you think I am, a whore?" He answered, "We've established what you are and now we are just deciding the price."

This case for Call Me Jack wasn't about the wire transfers going into Wachovia. Not at all. I lusted for the thrill of the chase. I laughed, all by myself, in my bubble bath. This detective would have taken the case for free.

AUGUST, 2008

Love is the answer but while you are waiting for the answer sex raises some pretty good questions.

—Woody Allen

PARIS

George Forrester hated Paris. Everything beautiful in the City of Light made him think of Véronique. A plate put before him with a flourish, the sparkle of light in a glass of white wine, someone laughing, a woman with long legs wearing a short black skirt—there was no escaping her.

So it was with dread on this Tuesday morning in August that he stood in line for a taxi at Charles de Gaulle. "Hey, Omaha!" called someone behind him. George turned and saw Barry Richardson grinning four people away in line. "Hey, Omaha, want to share a cab?" The two of them tossed suitcases in the trunk and then poured themselves into the back seat of a Peugeot. "What are you doing here?" asked Barry. "How long are you here for?"

Barry was from New York City; they'd met at a conference in L.A. the previous year and had a dinner together. George liked Barry, even looked up to him a bit for he saw in him an East Coast sophistication that he felt he himself did not possess. Barry, for his part, was impressed at how someone as laid back as George had parlayed his computer business into an international success. The Midwesterner seemed to make money without the least bit of effort. "I don't know anybody in Paris right now. In the summer, they all run away," Barry was saying. "I'm going to take it easy for a few hours but how about a late lunch?"

George hesitated. He felt very gloomy about even being in Paris, didn't know if his dark mood would manifest itself with another person. Maybe it would be better to be morose on his own.

"Come on! Let's have a long four o'clock lunch, pretend it's dinner. That's what I do and then I stay up till nine or ten and crash. The next day I wake up with all the Parisians. It's the only way to skip jet lag."

Four hours later, showered and changed they met at Chez Bernard and, in a nearly empty dining room, had a stupendous meal. Two bottles of wine and brandy afterwards. Barry was gregarious and talked about his ten-year-old in Little League, the spring trip to the Caribbean, breaking ground for their new house in Bedford, the architect they'd hired being arrested for having child pornography on his computer. George was an appreciative listener, relieved to not have to think.

"How is Sybil?" asked Barry.

"Sylvia," corrected George. "She's left me."

"Oh, I'm sorry to hear that." Barry blinked.

"Don't be." The words hung in the air and George then felt a little sorry for Barry. He took a sip of brandy. "I am actually relieved. She filed for divorce last month claiming I am not 'sympathetic enough.'"

Barry didn't know what to say.

"Ever heard of anorexia nervosa?" asked George.

"I thought teenage girls got it." Barry sat up straighter in his chair.

"It started after the miscarriage, according to one of her psychiatrists. Distorted body image, self-esteem issues, depression." He took another sip of brandy feeling a curious relief to be saying things out loud. "It has been our whole marriage—twelve years. So now she has gone back to live with her parents." He shook his head. "I am sad for her but I don't think I could have done anything more." He stared down into his snifter. "She has become like a child somehow. She told the doctors and then me that she doesn't want to be married, that she wants to go home to live with her mother."

"Psychiatrist?"

"Absolutely. In just the past year, a parade of shrinks, counselors, therapists, psychologists, nutrition specialists, dietitians. Sometimes I sit in with the psychiatrists and I'm asked about *my* relationship with food. The clinics. The Mayo. The live-in nurses. The driver. She can't drive a car anymore, she can barely walk. She's in bed or in a wheelchair. The specialists in Los Angeles. The doctor from London who was supposed to be brilliant. I pulled all the strings possible to get him to admit her to his clinic. She was too frail to be on a commercial flight so I leased a jet." He remembered the private ambulance, the attendants in white uniforms, the wheelchair going up the ramp. The tiny figure wrapped in blue blankets. "But I suppose it was a success of sorts because she did gain four pounds in one month. Then she begged to come home, stopped eating again, the same . . ." He couldn't finish the sentence. George suddenly felt exhausted.

Barry lifted his hand for another round of brandy and their waiter hurried over with the bottle. George held out his snifter like a child for more milk. "Sometimes divorce is a *good* thing," Barry said quietly. He had no idea what to say. George lifted his glass. "To divorce," he said. Barry repeated, "To divorce," and sipped.

The two men sat in silence as the first people for dinner arrived. "I'm selling the house, moving to San Francisco," blurted George. He had just decided he could not go back to the huge place in Omaha. It was as if his litany of the past years, spoken aloud, had made him realize how untenable it was. He would never live in Omaha again.

"Good. Do it! San Francisco will suit you. You lived there before, didn't you? How did you ever end up in Omaha anyway?"

"Sylvia grew up in Nebraska."

Barry absorbed this and said, "San Francisco. Good idea."

They paid l'addition and the pourboire, overtipping outrageously, and stood up. "Let's take a walk," urged Barry.

It was a very warm summer evening and the Parisians were on their way home from work. "The holidays so the city is comparatively empty," said Barry. "This store might be closed until September." He turned off rue St. Antoine to a narrow side street. The shop windows on rue St. Paul glittered with jewelry, paintings, men's haberdashery, lingerie, stationery. Barry stopped in front of one. "Oh, it's closed," he said. "There was an Art Nouveau pin that I wanted to buy for Tina the last time I was here but the store was closed and I had to leave for the airport at eight the next morning. I wonder if somebody bought it or if it's just not in the window anymore."

George put up his hand to block the reflection and saw earrings, cuff links, bracelets, and necklaces all laid out on black velvet. Above them, dominating the tableau, was a painting of the ocean. A pale blue wave curled towards shore, frozen forever at its apex, below a sun that seemed to smile on the summer day below. "Nice painting," said George. "Really like that. Could look at that every morning."

"Never been in this place," mused Barry. "Bad timing." They turned away. "It's number twenty rue St. Paul. I'm going to come back tomorrow. I have meetings until noon and then I'm going to come back."

"I have meetings until two and then I'm off to Frankfurt but back in Paris in two weeks." George felt a bit disappointed about the painting.

The men walked for another thirty minutes and then deemed themselves sufficiently tired to retreat to their hotels. Barry was at the Plaza Athénée and George was at the George Cinq.

George slept deeply that night and wakened feeling very good until he remembered how it was to waken with Véronique. He tried to put her out of his mind. He thought of the painting and wished he had time to go back and buy it. The first possession for his San Francisco life.

San Francisco. A new start in a place I used to love. Maybe I'm shaking her. Maybe some little switch in me has turned and I'm over her. Reason has prevailed. The radiant, sweet, tender, funny Véronique is out of my life and I accept that.

A few hours later at Charles de Gaulle, after the chaos of check-in and security, he was in the Duty Free shop buying Cognac. When he opened his wallet to pull out his credit card, the folded white card that said 'Diane' fell to the floor. As the clerk offered him a pen to sign the receipt, George saw the card beside his left shoe and decided not to pick it up. It's a sign, he thought, scrawling his signature. "Merci."

He walked out into the crowded terminal telling himself he believed in omens. Her fingerprints were on that card and now there was absolutely nothing to link him to her. And I'm leaving Paris, the scene of the crime. The card stays in Paris, Véronique stays in Paris. Over, he decided. He looked at his boarding pass and thought that soon this feeling in my chest will go away. I have lots to do. Deal with the divorce, the settlement, the house and a new place on the other side of the country. He stood under a Departure screen looking for his Lufthansa flight and the gate announcement. Over, he said to himself very definitely. "Excuse me, sir." It was the clerk from Duty Free. He looked at her in surprise. "You dropped this." She handed him the folded white card. "I thought it might be important."

PHILADELPHIA

I slipped the DVD into the red envelope to mail back to Netflix. The movie, *The Girlfriend Experience*, was a glossy look at a young girl in New York City who slept with men for money and had a boyfriend who accepted that reality. They lived in a loft downtown and looked as if they'd stepped out of an ad for Ralph Lauren. Chantal told me that 'the girlfriend experience' was just the opposite of what I thought it was. She said, "When they ask for the girlfriend experience I always worried. It's not anything but sex."

I had looked at her long and hard and wondered why she was lying.

Now I stared across the library at nothing, deep in thought, worrying that I might be giving Call me Jack information that he was using against someone else. Was Call Me Jack in the business of blackmail? Who was he anyway?

What did he want? And why did he always ask if Chantal had mentioned any names? For the hundredth time, I wondered if Call Me Jack had been a client. Could he be *waiting* to be blackmailed? Could he have done unspeakable things to a girl and be afraid that she would talk about it? Were there fetishes too bizarre or grotesque to imagine?

If the blackmailer can link one of the girls to the Imperial Club, that's all the information he or she needs but these girls are no longer bringing in the big bucks. Call Me Jack is paying me big money so he has money. A client is blackmail-worthy but the girls are not.

Sherlock and Vidocq came to join me and curled at my feet. "Hey, who's wearing a watch?" They wagged their tails with delight. "I swear that you guys must know how to tell time." I reached for the remote and clicked on the television. The three of us always convened for the 6:30 news.

My scream wakened me. I sat up in bed, blinking, disoriented. The room was in semi-darkness but I could see that the street lights on Columbia Avenue were still on. The clock said half past four. I sank back among the pillows and wondered why I bothered with a queen-size bed if I were destined to be alone in it.

Pieces of the dream came back. Little torn edges I tried to align. I had been wearing the headphones for Skype, not at my desk, but walking down a dark, deserted street. Call Me Jack's voice was going on and on, asking for names and I was giving him dozens of names. Adele, Audrey, Elizabeth, Carol, Betty, Linda, Lucy, Susan, Jennifer, Rhonda, Rita, Pamela, Alice, on and on. Names that meant nothing to me. I stepped in something wet on the pavement and the dark landscape became vivid daylight and I could see bright red blood on my shoe. A few drops on the vamp of my silver ballet slipper. I realized I was standing in a pool of blood. Chantal appeared, holding a menu, asking, how is the novel coming? And then I saw that there was blood on her arm, and covering her clothes and Chantal kept saying, how is the novel coming? That was when I started to scream.

MANHATTAN

Lori was on the subway going into Manhattan for the day, for a day of shopping which was as foreign to her as an expedition through Patagonia. It had been years and it was time. Mark is good-looking to die for and I owe him this, she told herself. Since the demise of the Imperial Club, she had been able to have a normal sleeping schedule and she and Mark had been seeing movies, going to plays. They both loved the theatre whether it was Broadway or a performance in a Brooklyn church basement.

Lori clutched the metal bar over her head as the train rattled towards Manhattan. I want to look better, she decided. I want to look really good. He'd mentioned cutting her hair months ago and when she'd groaned he had not brought it up again. I should let him, she thought.

Lori left Bergdorf's an hour later, stunned that she could pull on size-eight trousers and easily zip them. An hour and a half later she was leaving Bloomingdale's.

At four-thirty she was back in Brooklyn, in her apartment with shopping bags scattered all over her bed. At six-twenty she was in new white jeans and a red T-shirt, amazed at how good she felt and quite ready to go upstairs at half past six to watch the news.

PHILADELPHIA

I'd been at my desk since before daylight. Couldn't sleep. Too many cases needing attention. I'd lost myself in crime scene photos so completely that the Skype ring actually made me jump. I grabbed the earphones, put the cursor on the little green telephone logo and gasped, "Here!"

Call Me Jack laughed. "Were you miles away?"

"Far away mentally. Drowning in pre-trial stuff."

"So, what happened with the contract?"

"She made a few changes but we've both signed."

"Give me a brief update on what it says now."

"We agree that her name will not be used in the novel or in promoting it. It's not to be based on a true story. Technically not. There will be a disclaimer. I'm giving her one and a half percent of the profits. If that sounds skimpy, I explained to her that a novel can easily take a year to write and that I'll be doing that all alone in a room. It's ditch digging."

"She signed? We're off and running?"

"We will be once I pay her the five grand."

"It'll be in your Wachovia account tomorrow."

"I know that you want to know about publicity. She told me that she's met with an agent but she didn't like the ghost writer they brought in so that's off."

"Off forever?"

"Afraid it might mean a parade of candidates for her to vet."

"So it's possible it'll happen?" His voice conveyed that he was unhappy with this news.

"Possible. The bright side of this is that she turned down a TV producer and two documentary film makers. She sees no point in being interviewed. She is a very bright young woman." I stopped. "And she keeps asking me how the novel is coming."

Silence from across the ocean. He could be calling from Stockholm, Cairo, across town, anywhere. "Don't you think it's time you told me the real reason for all this?"

"Just keep talking to her. You're doing brilliantly." He sounded so English at that point. "Find out all you can about how they did it, who was involved. Everything."

"I don't understand why—unless you are a client—and that's fine if you were—but if I'm clued in to what you're after then I—"

"You're delivering what I want. I'm happy with your work. Call you next week."

Bloooomp went the disconnect. I yanked off the earphones and stared out the window at the dawn sky. He's not leveling with me. Why the hell not?

I suddenly felt off-balance. Chilled. I rubbed my bare arms. I never think about danger, about being afraid. Not when I was wired to do undercover for the FBI or working for OCID in New York. That stands for the Organized Crime Intelligence Division of the NYPD. Not when I was sent alone into a Chinatown warehouse to deal with the Born to Kill gang. People always ask and I always say the same thing: if I worried about it then I wouldn't do what I do. If I were afraid then I *couldn't* do what I do. Danger is an ugly word.

The sky was fading from gray to that summer white which meant another scorcher of a day. Vidocq and Sherlock had to be fed. I reached for my espadrilles under the desk and then decided barefoot was better. Barefoot was reality, I decided. Danger was imagination.

PARIS

George thought of that seascape again and decided he would go back and see if it were still for sale. Two weeks had gone by, he worried, but maybe it was still there.

At half past twelve he took a cab to rue St. Paul, paid the driver and got out to walk. A taxi was parked in front of number twenty. When he pushed open the door, a bell tinkled and made him smile. It was so old fashioned, so quaint. Pink roses in a Lalique vase scented the air. "George!" came the delighted shout. "What a surprise!"

"Barry! Did you find the—what was it? The pin for Tina?"

"Yes! Take a look." He picked it up from the counter and held it out. "It's 1885, made in Paris. Of course."

George looked from the Art Nouveau flower pin to the woman behind the counter and froze. "What do you think?" Barry was demanding.

George stammered, "Magnificent." He didn't think he could breathe. What was she doing here? Her hair was twisted up and off her neck and the thick bangs above her brown eyes were as he remembered but she was wearing street clothes. Some kind of light cotton dress. Blue. Her slender bare arms were tanned, her face was flushed.

"I weel wrap eet for you. Az a geeft. Un moment." Véronique turned and disappeared behind a maroon velvet curtain.

Barry explained that he was off to the airport. "My cab is outside. The flight was supposed to be this morning but it's delayed. Finally I've found this store open."

George nodded and murmured as he moved around the shop like a man in a trance. His vision blurred, he had no voice, he felt dazed, dizzy and was actually afraid he might fall into one of the glass cases. Then Barry was shaking his hand, saying goodbye and he was alone, staring at the painting which had been moved out of the window.

"George."

He turned to face her. His beautiful Véronique.

"Ow are you?" It was her heavy French accent that had always made him want to smile.

"Why are you here? Why are you talking to me?"

"Why didn't you call me? I guess you nev-air wanted to see me again."

"Véronique!" he blurted. "How could you say that?"

"You nev–air called."

"You said goodbye and you gave me the name of someone else. Why would I ever want to be with someone else?" His voice was anguished, not his own.

She turned, plucked a white card from the counter and handed it to him. It was engraved: DIANE MONTAGUE, Art Nouveau Jewelry and Art, 20 rue St. Paul. He stared at it for a long moment as she watched. Oh, George, she thought. You didn't understand. You gave me your true name and you thought . . . "I am Diane. When I decided that I only wanted to be with you, Véronique was no more."

She stood before him, quite still, waiting, wondering if he had caught her mistake. "Will you have dinner with me?" he whispered as she stepped into his arms.

PHILADELPHIA

"So everyone was protected from knowing anyone else?"

"Yes," I spoke into the microphone mouthpiece. He insisted I use the annoying headphones so that his voice would not be heard on speaker. As if Vidocq and Sherlock would sell out to *The Philadelphia Inquirer*. "It was actually very clever. Chantal and Jake knew everything but no one else did. The FBI is questioning the girls but no one will be able to tell them much. Below Jake and Bree was a booker, actually two bookers since they needed the phone answered twenty-four hours a day. These bookers could be anywhere. A farmhouse in Vermont, a bedsit in London or anywhere."

"All the phone lines, the phone numbers were forwarded then?"

"Exactly. As simple as call forwarding. The ad in London had a local code so any client there thought the service was right there. The ad in Paris, in New York, in Miami were each with the appropriate area code."

That was it; he had no questions. "Are you ready?" I asked.

At first, there had been nothing in writing but now I typed up the report, waited for his Skype call and then sent the file. Never allowed to let them 'hang' in the air as he put it, never allowed to send them in advance of his call. No e-mail, no landline, no cell phone. "File sent," I said.

"Received," he said. The light on my screen stopped blinking. "Thanks. I'll call you in a few days."

"I see her for lunch today. My train is at eleven."

There was the blooop! noise which always made me imagine a line falling through clouds and splashing into the Atlantic. East of Newfoundland.

THE WALDORF ASTORIA

Chantal was already sitting at the table when I arrived. The last table in Peacock Alley, farthest away from people. The silver, the goblets and the flowers, all very civilized a setting to discuss a subject so base: sex for sale. "How are you?" she smiled as I slid into the banquette. "How's the novel coming?"

"I feel good about it." Truth was I felt rotten about it.

Chantal began to talk. She'd gotten a letter from Jake that morning. "He is so upbeat and he is encouraging *me* to be strong! You'd never imagine that he was the one suffering. The one in prison."

I am actually being paid to talk to someone who loves to talk. Sure, I have my squeamish moments since I am lying to a person I actually like but the detective in me couldn't think how I was hurting Chantal. The client was the problem here.

Call Me Jack can't just keep throwing money at this and Skyping me or can he? He didn't appear to be leading up to clueing me in. I'd felt so uneasy this morning and here I am now having a nice lunch with Chantal who, obviously, badly needs to talk about Jake. The next time he Skypes, he'll tell me. Or he'll make a mistake. It'll be clear what he is up to and I can decide whether to go on or to quit the case.

Wine came and I lifted my glass. "To you. You're having an amazing life."

Chantal raised her perfect, arched black eyebrows. She was always impeccably groomed. "Maybe it's been a bit too amazing." We both sipped and put the glasses down.

Time to dive in. "I can't imagine taking off my clothes in front of a strange man, all alone in a room, on his turf." I hesitated. "That I was going to let him do what he liked. Were you ever afraid?"

"One time Jake sent me to an apartment. There was no doorman. It was a loft downtown. Very arty. I was thinking that a painter must live there or someone in the art world. But no doorman bothered me." She sipped the wine. "I was going up in the elevator when suddenly my head cleared and I thought what am I doing? What am I doing here? I was on drugs a lot of the time but knew enough to do what I had to do." She stared straight at me, remembering. "I knocked on the door and this man opened it and he was wearing a bathrobe." She stopped. "The thing was—his nose was bleeding."

I betrayed no reaction. Waited. Chantal took another sip of wine and said, "I know what you want to know. Yes, I went in and yes, I did what I had come to do. And I left with the money."

Later, as the train pulled out of Penn Station, nausea swept over me. He'd obviously been so far into the nose candy that he was bleeding. Disgusting. These lunches were seldom like that. Most of the time I came away thinking maybe it's not such a big thing. But right now I think, oh, how absolutely horrible to have a strange man touch you with his hands, his mouth and to be counting the minutes until it's over. Chantal didn't seem to think that way. The other girls must not think that. I looked out the train window and thought, I guess I would get through it if I had to and then, afterwards, I would wonder who I was.

THE METROLINER—BOSTON TO NEW YORK

He noticed her right away. She got on at New Haven, made her way down the aisle looking for an empty seat then sat directly across from him in the grouping of four. The tight little figure in jeans, the red cowboy boots, the delicate profile, the boyish haircut. He uncrossed his legs to give her more room and watched her deposit a canvas shoulder bag in the empty seat beside her. Then she dug through it for a notebook, found a pen and began to write industriously. She never looked at him which was intriguing. He was used to women looking at him.

By the time they'd stopped at Stamford, he'd introduced himself. "Ned Bartlett. And you are?" He had a terrific, confident smile.

"Kelsey Ritter," she said in her husky voice. The train started to move again. "Going to New York?"

"That was the last station before Harlem so we don't have a choice."

She didn't respond and started to turn back to her notebook but he couldn't resist. "What went through your mind just then? I mean, it's not anything I usually ask but—" he hesitated, hating to appear rude. "Don't answer if you don't want to. Ignore me. Go back to your work."

Her olive complexion went slightly pink. "I was actually wondering when I'm going to get up the nerve to get off the train in Harlem. I've never been there."

This isn't like me, he thought. Not at all. He got off first then turned, took her bag and grabbed her hand as she came down the metal steps. Once on the platform, together they looked up at the big sign that said 125th Street and then at each other. Neither one of them knew where to go or what to see so they just walked. Past brownstones, past pawn shops, past the ubiquitous Duane Reade, and they stared at everyone as if they'd arrived in another country. The restaurant was packed but they were given a table and they ate sweet potatoes, fried chicken, chitlins and catfish. "We don't have food like this in Cincinnati," Kelsey grinned as she picked up a slice of corn bread.

"We don't eat like this is Boston either. It's just codfish day after day," he said.

She told him about her doctorate at Yale and he asked all the right questions about the art world. Cate, Cate, Cate went through his mind. But, I've made progress, he told himself. Sometimes I don't think of her for an entire day. Lifting his arm, he motioned the waiter for another pitcher of beer. Talk was easy, she was a bit of a flirt, but someone who looked directly at him when he talked. She seemed to drink in his every word.

"So you're a stuffy banker," she teased.

"Trying not to be. It's actually pretty exciting to deal with futures. That's my field. Cocoa, coffee, tin, gold, pretty much anything that grows or comes out of the ground. It's predicting weather patterns, political instability and what the market will be like in the next year or two."

"So it could be a strike at a gold mine or a hurricane that decimates a crop?"

"You got it. It's as simple as that," he said. He thought she was smart. And cute. And he wanted to take her to bed. He looked at his watch. "It's midnight. Let's get a cab." He paid and grabbed her amazingly heavy bag again and in seconds they were in the back of a taxi heading downtown. He took her face in his hands and softly kissed her. "Stay with me," he breathed into her neck.

Suddenly he didn't want to let her go. "Stay with me."

The suite at the Carlyle was waiting. The lights were on and the bed was turned down. After all, he was Edward Horton Bartlett II and he was expected.

They wakened before daylight and slowly made love again, without the urgency of the night before. Kelsey cried out when she came and he groaned like a man in pain. That's how it began.

PHILADELPHIA

Call Me Jack's calls were just as frequent, usually before a meeting with Chantal and just after but they had changed in tone. He seemed more tense. He mentioned getting all the information possible before the first of December. It was months away. When I asked why, he'd been a bit gruff and said something cryptic about 'a turning point.' What was going to happen on that day? Or after? December first was the sentencing of Chantal. Was he afraid that she would make a statement in court or as the sentencing drew closer implicating him? A last minute plea bargain? Was there any reason the authorities might use her to get to him? Was it a personal deadline when he decided that he would not spend any more money on this because he wasn't getting the information he wanted?

I looked at the kitchen clock; he'd be on Skype in half an hour. Or maybe not. These days I never knew when he'd call. The beagles were out in back and no one was barking to be let in. I got the Marmite out of the cupboard, grabbed a Coke Zero out of the fridge and perched on the tall wooden stool. The television news was on, the usual last night's North Philadelphia shootings as a prelude to the *Today Show* at seven. The apple green kitchen was gray and restful in the early morning shadows and I moved around without turning on the lights.

I shook out the front page of *The New York Times* and placed it flat on the counter, using it as a plate while I spread Marmite on a slice of rye bread. Couldn't concentrate on the casualties in Iraq or read about Mayor Bloomberg's bike lanes. Was Call Me Jack a client? Worried about exposure? Was he married? Was he a politician like Cantor? Maybe he was with the U.N. calling from Geneva using that number I can't trace. Why is he so interested in how the operation worked? Could *he* be law enforcement? But no, that was ridiculous. No law enforcement agency would pay an independent contractor the kind of money I'm having put into my account every month. The wire transfer was no clue to Call Me Jack's identity as it always originated from the firm in Hong Kong. They knew who Call Me Jack was but obviously think I don't need to know. Could it be safer for me not to know?

Was there something he wanted from Chantal? What? Chantal was probably not telling the Feebs about the client with the nosebleed but she'd listed all the accounts, they had her computer and all the phone records. She told me that faced with prison, sitting in a horrible room with no windows, in handcuffs, that she'd told them everything. I want to believe that.

If law enforcement knew everything he wasn't law enforcement. Back to my initial theory: a client afraid of exposure. The money trail? Had he used money he didn't have, money that didn't belong to him for sex? Was that why he wanted to know how the Imperial Club worked? Maybe he wanted to know how much time he had before it all caught up with him.

Meanwhile, he pays my set fee. Before the third of the month, every month, the thousands for that month are in my checking account.

I thought of Chantal telling me that Jake had taken her to the bank one morning when she was still on drugs. All the documents were ready and all she had to do was sign. "It didn't look good later," she said. "Everything was in my name."

I had to ask. "Did you ever think he was using you?"

She answered quickly. "Oh, yes! And he used to say I think you're using *me*." I remembered her direct stare across the table at me. "It was all a test of love."

"What exactly?" I asked.

"All of it. Everything. It was all a test of love."

STAR ISLAND, MIAMI

Pedro and Chico were drinking Corona beer together in the room off the big kitchen. It had minimal furniture, a bathroom, and a refrigerator and was where Chico showered, changed in and out of his chauffeur uniform, started and ended the day.

Pedro lived in the main house and slept next to Rafael Solito's master bedroom. The main house had twelve bedrooms, twelve and a half baths and had been purchased with eighteen million dollars cash in 1994. There was a pool, tennis courts, a gym, a gazebo, a ballroom Solito had no use for and a private dock with deep water access. This was a very convenient feature for any visitors who preferred not to arrive via the one bridge from the causeway.

Drivers on this causeway en route to Miami Beach might see the small sign that announced the turn to the island and some of them might know that Madonna, Sylvester Stallone, and Rosie O'Donnell had once had houses there. Al Capone had spent his last days on Star Island, slowly losing his mind in the final stages of syphilis.

It was pricey property to begin with and then Rafael Solito had spent a second fortune on the most sophisticated security system money could buy. He never felt entirely safe but, as he told Pedro, "I can feel better."

Chico and Pedro got along whereas Pedro had not been unhappy to see the previous driver leave. He'd been lucky to be fired and to walk away for Señor Solito was not known to possess a forgiving nature.

This afternoon Pedro was cleaning one of his handguns with a soft rag and Chico was scratching lottery tickets with a bowie knife. He had about twenty of the colored cards on the table before him. "The boss is too nervous," said the driver.

"Si. He is very jumpy. He saw the girl with Intriago and he cannot sleep, he worries all the time." Pedro heard him walking around the house at night so it meant that he couldn't sleep either. "I see nothing, I hear nothing, and I tell him but he does not change his mind. He is sure this is trouble," said Pedro shaking his head.

Chico took a swig of beer, swallowed then declared, "A whore you like is always trouble."

MANHATTAN

Kelsey stared at herself in the mirror and thought, not bad. The new red dress fit her like a glove. All those sit-ups do pay off, she thought as she closed the clasp on the silver bracelet. "What do you think, Tinky?" She reached to pat the little white dog sitting on her pillow. "This one okay? It's dinner with Ned." The bed was littered with what she had decided not to wear. Kelsey was always exhausted by the time she left the apartment because she worried so much about what she looked like, about picking the right clothes. And she had so much to choose from. She would become frantic as she pulled this blouse and that dress off hangers and opened and banged closed her bureau drawers. Miraculously she was never late but she took at least one grueling hour to prepare herself between a shower and going out the front door. "These silver earrings, Tinky?" The dog tilted his head to the side as if deciding.

Kelsey opened the closet doors and stared. The shoe boxes were stacked in rows six boxes high right up to the hems of her skirts, right up to her hanging trousers. What shoes to wear? Oh, God, oh, God, what shoes? Only one thing calmed Kelsey but the fix was fleeting and expensive. Shopping.

PHILADELPHIA

"Hey, Sherlock! Vidocq! Where are you, boys?" The two beagles came down the stairs at a precariously high speed and into my arms as I crouched beside the front door. They were all over me trying to be first to have the leash clipped on to their collar. Then it was outside and down the steps with a great jangling and much confusion of paws.

The sun was bright on my face and I thought, the dogs save me. From a bit too much solitude. They were euphoric when I turned my key in the lock and always greeted me as if I'd returned from a round-the-world adventure. They were quiet companions when I read or worked in my office. We all three liked making popcorn in the late afternoon. The minute I reached for my sunglasses and walked towards the kitchen, they knew. I am old-fashioned about popcorn and my method involves hot and often spitting oil. If I had welder's goggles I would wear them.

I feel new to Philadelphia even though it's been two years. Miami was two years ago, for three years. Mornings of waking up and wondering if we'd had Christmas yet. It was day after day of wearing the same clothes. The reason for coming to Miami—that money laundering case—was the best thing about my life there. Selling my Coral Gables penthouse meant I could buy this rather large house in Philadelphia. Twelve rooms. But now I wonder why I'd made such a commitment. Commitment is not a word I use often.

I have lived in New York City, Beverly Hills, Miami, Toronto, Ottawa, London, Rome, Porto Ercole, and Geneva and, in every city, I had friends. Just not here. I adore my immediate neighbors but that's it. Maybe it's my work.

Maybe it's me. But the house is wonderful. I loved painting walls my colors, buying rugs, making each room my own. Steve the Junk Man, which is what he calls himself, haunts the Main Line estate sales and brings back furniture, paintings, books, and chandeliers which are sold by a cheerful, smiling James from a garage on Third Street. I found the place on my bike and often ride over there just to chat with James, to get away from my desk. My purchases are delivered for free by the two men with much hilarity especially when something enormous has to go up to the third floor.

Everything I'd had in storage for years was now with me. There were seashells from Capri, Monty the stuffed albino cobra from Delhi, and backgammon boards from Egypt. All that was good. But the house symbolizes stability and that's not a word I like. It was coming to symbolize isolation, too.

My good friend, Lucia, tells me New York is where I belong and yes, I've always been happy there. Lucia is in Europe until the new year which is good for it would be so easy to have dinner with her and spend the night on her living room couch after a session with Chantal. And far too tempting to say what I was working on. I wouldn't, of course, but it was easier that it was only e-mail between us right now. I answered at least fifteen personal e-mails a day; my friends were *not* in Philadelphia. Mickey and Winters, the detectives I like working for best are in New York. Even my dentist and Mara who waxes my legs are in New York. No one understands the Philadelphia situation. For me, it is work and this big house. Art gallery openings, lectures at the library and not much else. Lucia doesn't understand why I don't come back to Manhattan and Rowena doesn't understand why I don't come back to Rome. Friends, conversation, excitement. I need them. House as albatross.

The dogs dragged me along in the park, tails wagging, noses to the ground. A new book out claimed that beagles have over 300 million receptors for smell and that humans possess a mere 6 million. No wonder they are more enthusiastic about life than I am.

Maybe I feel fatigued because I've been immersed in four big trials and didn't go away this summer. It's already August. Maybe it's as simple as that. Unclipping their leashes, I let the dogs race me home on Columbia Avenue. Laughing, I ran up the steps and turned the key in the big blue front door and we all three clattered in, out of breath and exhilarated.

CORAL GABLES

Annie answered all her e-mails and then stood up and told Raquel at the next desk that she had to get some air. Maria, sitting one desk farther away, gave her an odd look. No one in Miami did anything like that. Why would anyone leave an air-conditioned office on such a strange mission?

Annie walked to the corner on Ponce de Leon Boulevard and stopped. It was hot, perspiration was starting to trickle down under her arms in the sleeveless striped dress. I'd better go back, she thought. The hair on her neck was damp. She wanted to put things in order, to calmly prioritize. I have the closing at two o'clock. I will compartmentalize. I will not think of last night until I can really think of it, until I can devote time to it. I will not let it torture me now. Not now. I've worked too hard for this deal and God knows, deals are few these days. Miami in 2008 is not the Miami of 2005. Someone in my apartment has nothing to do with my life until I can get home, lock the door and pour myself a glass of wine and decide what to do.

With renewed resolve, she strode back to the office, smiled at Maria, picked up her phone, punched in a number and said, "Mr. Hernandez! Good morning. It's Anne Larsson. I wanted to confirm our appointment for the closing. Commerce Bank at two. Yes." She listened. "Twelfth floor. See you there. And congratulations!" She hung up. Then she looked at her watch, asked Maria and Raquel if they were ready for lunch and picked up the phone again to order chef salads and iced tea.

The day was long but at eight o'clock, Annie was home, wearing shorts and a tank top, barefoot. She glanced around at the white furniture, her paintings. The apartment had been photographed for *Southern Style* magazine only the month before and all was pristine, perfect. The front door lock had been changed two days ago but still, last night, someone had come in again. Annie sat down on the couch, her bare legs a golden tan, her toenails bright coral. She stared out at the water for a long while without moving and then she started to cry.

ROME/PHILADELPHIA

Rowena was on the phone. There was a leak in her kitchen, under the sink, and all she could do was put a huge pot there to catch the drops. "Can you imagine that Cesare, my plumber, is unavailable because he is sailing on the Costa Smeralda?"

I laughed. "You're paying him too much! Unless he is outrageously good-looking and is the lover of some principessa on the side."

"You might be right because he is fiendishly handsome. Maybe he is the illegitimate heir to Fiat and no one is telling me. And I can't get him to come in the autumn because he goes grouse shooting in Scotland!" Rowena was very exasperated.

"Does he have a brother in New York? Too much to hope that he has a twin in Philadelphia."

"Mi dispiace, caro! Don't you wish we could rent men like Cesare? Just for a weekend. The way men do it with really fabulous women?"

I frowned. Didn't want Rowena to start thinking. "Well, we actually could rent them. Escorts, gigolos. We could."

Rowena asked, "I keep meaning to ask you. Have you been following the Imperial Club fiasco? At first, it was the front page of *The Herald Tribune* and then it was in *Il Messaggero* and *Corriere della Sera*. There are rumors that there were girls in Rome." She laughed. "The Romans love fantasizing about who might have, who would have, who possibly . . ." I held my breath. Didn't want to talk about it. Rowena went on. "It was when? In the spring? But everybody's still talking about it. Every week there's a new bombshell. I think that the whole world saw the press conference when he apologized."

"Who? Governor Cantor?"

"Yes. It was broadcast on CNN, of course, but it was on the Italian news, too. His wife aged about thirty years during that one press conference. They keep replaying it, having talking heads talk about it. On and on. Another American woman forgives her flawed husband."

"Hillary Clinton stood by her man, last year it was Governor McGreevy and his wife and now Sharon. And the wives are so bright, so good-looking. Not a one of them dull or dowdy. They're all achievers in their own right."

"I always think . . . always wonder . . ." began Rowena.

"Don't torture yourself." I knew where this was headed and felt helpless to derail it.

"I keep thinking that—"

"Stop. Rowena, stop! Have a glass of vino and . . ."

"Oh! I have to hang up! The pot is overflowing!" There was a shriek from Italy and a dial tone.

I replaced the receiver and reached for the wine glass. Sherlock padded in and jumped into my lap. He was getting huge and it was awkward. It would have been self-indulgent to tell Rowena about the case but how I wanted the release, the relief. I know I can't tell anyone. I didn't pick up the phone to call friends these days. E-mails were safer. I took a sip of wine lifting my glass over the beagle's head and thought it was too bad the conversation had taken that turn with Rowena. Sherlock gazed at me with big brown eyes. "Well, Rowena brought it up," I said defensively. His tail moved one swing in reply. Guess she cannot stop wondering. She would always be the girl's mother no matter how many years go by. "I wonder if Rowena will ever see Jazz again," I said aloud. Jazz was often on my mind these days. So now I know two of them, I thought. Chantal and Jazz.

The phone rang and I reached for it at precisely the same moment that Sherlock decided to spring for the door to greet Vidocq. "John, hi," I began as the dogs started to wrestle on the slick hall floor. They rolled back and forth nipping each other and mock growling, tails wagging. One of these days one of them was going to tumble right down the stairs. Or both of them end over end. I tried to ignore the dogs. John Bertram, a court-appointed attorney I did work for, was asking if I could interview a last witness for the shooting case. "We go to trial in three days," he said.

A capital case. I hate the death penalty cases. I took notes thinking, oh, piece of cake. Witness lives in North Philadelphia in a horrifyingly dangerous neighborhood and John was saying, "He may not want to cooperate." I frowned but didn't say anything. "Watch out. I don't have to tell you that." He hesitated. "Last year just one street over somebody shot at me. Broad daylight."

"Didn't like your tie?"

He laughed then became somber again. "Listen. It's drug dealers and low lifes. Dirt poor except for the dealers."

"I get it. They shot at you so now you send me."

"Correct."

"I've only been here two years but will somebody please tell me why they call this place the City of Brotherly Love? I mean, is this even civilization?"

There was a sigh from his office downtown near City Hall. "Welcome to

Philadelphia, Charlie."

We hung up and I flipped my notebook closed as Sherlock clambered into my lap and settled himself heavily, clumsily, missing his footing. When he was still, I looked into his handsome face and asked him, "Why do I get the easy ones?"

HYANNIS PORT, CAPE COD

Catherine was standing on the deck overlooking the ocean, admiring the breakers of cobalt blue. Terracotta pots of white geraniums lined the railing; seagulls were squawking overhead, the sky was going orange striated with yellow then pink. A long white linen shirt flapped around her thighs over the wet bathing suit; she was barefoot and felt aglow with a sense of well being.

"Technically, the last real Saturday of the summer," said Holtie putting his arms around her waist from behind and resting his face in her wet hair. Monday was Labor Day.

"Water's always warmest now," she said. "Takes all that sun all summer long."

"You would know, my little fish." Holtie sailed, was not much of a swimmer. Catherine was the one who got herself past the breakers and spent half an hour doing her graceful breast stroke, her Australian crawl.

They stood in silence until the sun dropped into the sea and the air took on the coolness of evening. "Wine?" he asked moving away from her. She nodded and they went into the house through the sliding glass doors. "Quick shower," she said. "Be out in a flash." Then she added, "Holtie, make me a vodka with tonic instead, would you? There are limes on the table in the breakfast room. In the basket."

"Anything you want, you got it," he sang mimicking Roy Orbison, making her smile.

In the bedroom, she stripped off her suit and, naked, suddenly sat down at the foot of the double bed. It had been another spectacular day; her skin felt alive with the salt, her body had been buffeted by waves, her muscles felt strong. "Please," she whispered. "Don't let me lose Holtie. Don't let me lose Cate. Don't let me lose these moments." She looked down at her tan hand, at her wedding ring. "Please, god of the sea, god of the sky, my protector," she said softly.

Ten minutes later, on this September evening, out of the shower, wearing white slacks and a lavender T-shirt, she looked into the mirror as she put on lipstick, brushed her hair and spritzed on perfume. Brad, she thought, loves this perfume. Fleetingly, she wondered where he was on this Saturday night and then she thought, a bit defiantly, Holtie loves this perfume, too. She turned out the light and left the bedroom.

AUTUMN, 2008

Dare to be naïve.
—Buckminster Fuller

"She could talk about Jake forever," I told Call Me Jack. "She's obsessed with him. It's Jake Jake Jake but I wanted to get the details about money this time." I looked at my notes. "If a client wanted to extend his time for an hour or more then the girl would take his credit card, put it on the paper, rub a quarter over it and have him sign on the spot."

"What about a man having such a good time he wants her to spend the night?"

"Not happening unless he has a suitcase of cash beside the bed. There was that ten grand limit on a credit card." I paused. "Chantal is very tough and said if the girl decides to stay and the man does not pay then she's responsible for the $31,000." I continued. "She told me something extraordinary. The clients were asked to sign papers Jake prepared that said that prostitution was illegal and that anyone participating in it would be immediately terminated as a client and that the escort would be fired."

"What? And they signed this paper? In front of the girl? In the hotel room?"

There was a quick laugh from wherever and I laughed, too. I pictured a bald man, pot-bellied, entirely naked except for reading glasses, being offered a pen by a beautiful naked girl. "Plus when the booker called the client the next day to ask if everything had been satisfactory, they were not allowed to mention sex." I was smiling. "Chantal said that Jake was sure there would never be a problem if they pretended it was just a dating service."

As innocent as a movie and ice cream afterwards.

Another short laugh from wherever. "Did she tell you about the offshore banks?"

"There weren't any. It sounds ridiculous but all the money was in the U.S. in banks or on the floor of the closet."

"You're joking!"

"No. I checked newspaper articles again today and several of them refer to Jake or Ivan as 'a tax specialist.' Plus, she told me he was actually working for the KGB as an accountant which is—"

"A bit dodgy, yes, of course," he interrupted.

Funny, I thought. Did he already know about the KGB? Or does he not *want* to know about it? I went on without hesitating. "She said Jake never got around to putting anything offshore. His desk was a mess. Chantal seems to have been the organizer. I know her lawyer says she was so much younger and that Jake completely dominated her but in ways that just isn't true." I added, "When the judge was sentencing him, he said that one reason he was giving him no less than thirty months was because he was four decades older than Chantal and he'd met her when she was only eighteen. The judge called Chantal a victim." I stopped. "She was and yet she wasn't."

"Explain."

"He told her prostitution was legal in England. And she believed him."

A laugh came over the line.

"That's naïve. But she took control, put up a terrific website, raised the quality of the girls hired, made sure the money was paid. She was a victim but he needed her. She ran it."

"I can see that. Let's go back to the money."

"There were a dozen New York City bank accounts all in her name; the wires went to Pliameri Consulting. Law enforcement reportedly found nearly a million dollars in a garbage bag in the closet." I paused. "My biggest question about money is why a man would pay that much. Chantal says it makes them feel good to know they *can*."

I wondered how much longer he would want me to meet with her.

"You're doing brilliantly. Lunch on Saturday?" He sounded Australian today.

"Absolutely. Talk to you afterwards."

Blooooooop! went the connection. I looked at my watch and saw that it was 12:29. I raced down the stairs, two at a time, to the library, flipped on the television and sank into one of the coral silk chairs as the familiar theme song began. Vidocq and Sherlock came racing in with collars jangling then arranged themselves at my feet. Exactly half past twelve and just in time for us all to watch *The Young and the Restless*.

MANHATTAN

Cate stood at her bureau putting on gold earrings. Suddenly tears sprang into her eyes. Dammit! Don't be a baby! Especially not when you've just put on mascara. It's a new day. The locksmith is coming at noon. I'll be here, I'll have new keys and I'll feel safe again.

Standing in the hall, on the threshold of the living room, her eyes flickered to *Architectural Digest* on the coffee table, the novel she kept meaning to start reading, the yellow roses from Dirk in the silver pitcher, the Ming on the mantle, her laptop on her desk in the corner. Cate suddenly had the oddest sensation of standing in a stranger's apartment. It was as if nothing in the room belonged to her.

She pulled on a blue linen jacket over the sleeveless dress and gave herself a last look in the mirror in the front hall. "I'm okay," she said aloud, grabbed her keys, her pocketbook, her briefcase. She left the apartment, closed the door firmly behind her then locked the first and the second lock. In the hall, she reached for the knob again, turned it and pushed. Just to make sure. "I'm okay," she repeated.

Cate was much more than okay, thought the new doorman as she hurried past with a quick nod and the slightest breeze of Chance perfume. At five foot eleven, a brunette with those amazing blue eyes and an alabaster complexion, he couldn't believe she wasn't a super model. He'd have to ask Bailey about her when he came on at four. He watched her walk quickly towards Fifth Avenue, thinking how sweet it was to see such great legs so early in the day.

"Dammit, dammit, dammit," she swore out loud. Oh, god. Oh, god. She paced back and forth in her living room. The one-bedroom apartment was more jammed with clothes, boxes, shopping bags than ever even though she was paying $215 a month for a storage bin way up in Harlem.

Kelsey was talking to herself. "I refuse to be a panicked person, I refuse to imagine the worst." Her beloved Tinker had died the week before and she ached with missing him. Her eyes often filled with tears. She had always talked to him and he'd understood; he'd been a calming influence. She'd wept over Mr. Beluga a whole Sunday afternoon with the little poodle in her lap. Technically, Tinker hadn't died of old age even though he was fourteen; she'd had to have the vet "put him down" but she couldn't allow herself to think about that. She went weak with guilt whenever she thought of that last day and preferred to lie to herself and say he died on his own.

"Think! Think!" she said firmly. She was biting her thumb. She'd really thought it was all over, that she was in the clear. So many months had passed but only yesterday she'd read that the investigation was "ongoing." What an awful word!

"If only I could find Bree! I don't know if Jake would help since he pretended we weren't even doing what we were doing but—"

The doorbell rang. Kelsey froze. The doorman hadn't buzzed to say anyone was coming up. Could it be? Maybe they didn't have to buzz. Maybe there was some kind of federal law that excused them. She felt sick with fear and literally held her breath.

"Ms. Ritter! It's Max, the super!"

With one hazel eye glued to the peephole, she exhaled and unlocked the door.

"Sorry to bother you but we've got a leak up in 9B and I thought I'd better take a look and make sure you're okay down here."

Kelsey nodded. "Sure. Come on in."

He walked past her quickly, tool belt clanking, and into the kitchen, gazed up, then said, "Looks okay. Sorry to bother you."

She thanked him and locked the door, all three locks, behind him. Her heart was still pounding. She resumed her panic just where she'd left off. If only I could find Bree. She'd tell me what to do, what to say.

It was the following Friday morning that the doorman buzzed to say that there were two FBI agents on the way up to see her.

THE WALDORF ASTORIA

It was another Saturday at the Waldorf at 'our' table at Sir Harry's Bar. The bartender could see us from a great distance and a waiter took a long time to get to us. It was perfect. "I'll have a glass of sauvignon blanc," I said and Chantal ordered an appletini.

Initially it was yet another monologue on the brilliance of Jake. Chantal's mother blamed everything that had happened on Jake but her father had grown to like him. "Before the incident, my dad had started going out with somebody my age. Actually younger!" She laughed. "And so Jake and I would have dinner with them and my father started to like Jake."

"Quite a quartet," I said. "What was she like?"

"She was stupid. She would text all through dinner."

I had to laugh. "You're the one studying psychology so don't you think it's cause for comment that you're dating someone older than your father and he's with someone younger than you?"

"I've always been attracted to older men." Her tone changed. "I blame my dad for a lot of this."

How easy this was. It had stopped being an interview with a focus long ago. There had never really been a focus. More like dragging a net across ten acres of grass and seeing what had been snagged later. "Why do you say that?" I asked. "How old were you when they got a divorce?"

"I was twelve." Her thoughts were scattered. "He used to give me way too much information. Once we were talking on the phone and he said he hadn't slept all night. He's usually not alone but I don't want to hear about it! Plus he drinks about a pint of Amaretto every night before bed."

What provoked this? I took a sip of the white wine and was quiet.

"He's in his fifties and he's going through his adolescence." She lifted her glass. "I like someone strong. Jake is strong." Chantal took a gulp of her drink. She was upset, emotional. "My dad hires escorts. But not Imperial Club. Really crummy ones, cheap ones." Her voice was scornful. "He's such a Jew."

I was very still. This constant comparing of her father and her lover. Their age, their habits, their role with her. She is bright enough to intellectually see it, even if she doesn't want to acknowledge it. Chantal went on talking about Jake. She called him brilliant.

"Chantal, you're studying psychology, surely you see—"

She interrupted. "Of course, I see it all the time but that doesn't stop me from feeling it."

"Tell me," I insisted.

"I feel it a lot and it does have to do with my father. What I'm doing, all that's happened. It's all my father."

"Tell me what you mean."

"I know that one time, in the beginning, I was a little bit high but I still knew what I was doing." She paused. "I came here, to the Waldorf, went up in the elevator and down the hall. I checked the room number twice and as I was standing there I had this very weird feeling of 'why am I doing this?' A man opened the door before I could knock and I was surprised. I looked at him and said, 'I thought you were my father.'"

Chantal's dark eyes were staring at me as I concentrated on remaining expressionless. "It wasn't a cool thing to say. We went through with it and I was paid but it didn't go very well."

BOSTON

Sometimes he wouldn't see her for two weeks, sometimes he'd see her twice in one week. Always in New York. Always dinner and then the Carlyle. It depended on his business meetings. "I've never dated anybody from the Midwest," he told Eric after one of their weekly squash games. "There is something very wholesome about her." He wiped his face with a towel. "I like it. It seems clean and honest and straightforward to me."

"Come to Boston," he insisted on the phone that night. "We'll have the whole weekend. I want you to meet some of my friends."

Kelsey said yes and it was planned but she had to be somewhere first on Friday. She was vague; it was something about seeing someone in downtown Boston before she came to him. She said she'd call him at seven-thirty on Friday night and she'd be at his apartment by eight at the latest.

Ned had loosened his tie, taken off his suit jacket. He was in his living room standing by the window. "Kelsey," he said aloud. "You didn't telephone and it's half past eight and where are you?" He called her cell and got voice mail. Then he punched in the number of the restaurant. "I have a reservation for Bartlett at eight-thirty and I wonder if I could move that up to nine." He listened. It was Friday night and the place was obviously packed. "I understand. Right. Another time."

The maid had come that day and all was in place. It was a very elegant bachelor apartment with Oriental rugs, good paintings and contemporary furniture but he thought of it as temporary. Ned was a house person; he required a mud room and a pantry, a basement for ski equipment, a garage, a garden. Deciding all was in order, he sank onto the brown leather couch and watched ten minutes of news on CNN then he grabbed his laptop and started looking at the market. It had closed way up.

The doorbell rang at ten o'clock. He was on his third scotch on the rocks and not overly happy to see her when he opened the door. "Hi," he said taking her suitcase, barely looking at her. There was a second large suitcase beside her. He bent down and grabbed that one in the other hand and took them over the threshold and into the apartment. She stood in the hall looking uncertain. "I . . . I never know what to wear," she said when she saw him glance at the second suitcase. "I know I'm late. I can't tell you how sorry I am." She was dressed so differently from the Kelsey he knew. Very high heels, a low-necked black silk dress and chandelier earrings. It made him think of a cocktail party and not a Friday night dinner in Boston. He'd assumed she was meeting with one of her professors.

"Come on in. I'll fix you a drink and then we can make a plan." He pushed the knot of his tie in place and told himself to relax. He didn't lean down to kiss her. An hour later they were having grilled swordfish at a little neighborhood bistro and laughing about something but it wasn't the same.

It was past midnight, after lovemaking, but he couldn't sleep. She never explained, he thought, why she was late or dressed that way. She'd taken off the earrings and pulled a sweater over her dress but he kept seeing her as she'd stood in the doorway. He carefully eased himself off the bed, grabbed his boxers from the floor, pulled them on in the hall and went into the living room. They'd both drunk more than usual and she'd giggled a lot in the elevator which had annoyed him. One of her suitcases was open by the coffee table; she'd been looking for her toothbrush and it was still open, the contents in disarray.

Ned sank onto the couch and stared into space. She'd been impressed by his paintings. His grandfather's, he confessed. Three by Maurice Prendergast, an Edward Hopper and three Winslow Homers. There were framed Homer sketches lining the hallway. The view was spectacular, too. Boston from the twentieth floor was a grid of lights and traffic glowing softly, moving silently below.

Get over it, he said. You like her. This is one little blip. So what if she went to a party without me. I don't own her. She'll tell me tomorrow what happened. She's here. Tomorrow is a walk through town, lunch at the club, maybe a movie, the drinks party, introducing her to Eric and Cynthia, dinner. He uncrossed his legs and started to stand up when something caught his eye. He could see frilly underthings but it was not that, it was something else. The glint of metal. He walked over and bent down to really look.

Under the handcuffs mixed in with her panties were the dildos, the lubricants, the strange toys, the condoms. He didn't want to touch them but stared. He flipped the suitcase top closed. *New York* magazine was stuffed in the outside pocket. Evidently she'd emptied her mailbox as she was leaving her building to catch the train. Then Edward Horton Bartlett II did something he could not have ever imagined doing. A bit drunk, in the middle of the night, after pawing through her suitcase, he held the two small white envelopes up to the light and then he opened them. No tearing required, the flaps were barely closed. Maybe the justification was as childish as "if she can do that then I can do this." Suddenly she was not Kelsey, she was a stranger. She was a stranger he had trusted and made love to and now he felt burned and betrayed. And he felt naïve. Maybe that was the worst.

He had no idea what he would discover. In some ways, seeing the numbers in print was as jolting to him as the sex toys. She owed Bloomingdale's $76,430. The American Express card showed the interest due on the 19th of this month as $3,512. He closed his eyes not wanting to see the balance owed and carefully folded the sheet and put it back into its envelope. The Bloomingdale's envelope wouldn't cooperate but the glue in his desk drawer took care of it. The magazine and the rest of the mail were carefully pushed back into the outside pocket of the suitcase.

At four o'clock he took a sleeping pill and washed it down with scotch, swigging it straight out of the bottle. His mind raced. His heart was beating way too fast, he felt sick. He slept.

When he wakened on the couch, he was cold and unsure where he was. He opened his eyes and saw that the desk lamp was still on though it was daylight. He stared up at the cove ceiling and the taupe walls and then saw his favorite Prendergast with all the bright American flags. His eyes focused on the clock on the mantle. Eleven-thirty! He sat bolt upright, trying to clear his head. Then he remembered. He stood up and saw a tremendous empty space where the suitcases had been. He strode down the hall and into the bedroom. The bed was unmade and empty.

He looked in the bathroom for any trace of her, avoiding his own face in the mirror. Ned returned to the living room and turned out the lamp. It was like a dream, he thought. Aloud, he said, "Thank God, she's gone."

PHILADELPHIA

"Sometimes it's just basic stuff and other times, like yesterday, she will actually name names." I adjusted the headphones to a better angle. Was there a catch in

248

his voice when he asked me what names she'd given me?

"She said that the Duke of Westbridge was a client she really liked. He was the only person she got in touch with after her arrest. By e-mail. She did mention girls. There's an Australian named Adrienne. There's someone at Christeby's called Caroline. A very sharp real estate agent in Miami called Alyssa. There are four girls in London, twenty in New York. One in Paris named Véronique. There was a Japanese student from N.Y.U. and an Argentine student at Hunter who also worked as a bartender. All in all there are about fifty girls."

"Did she name the girls in London?"

So, I thought, what happens in London is what you are after. "No. I was surprised she gave me any names at all. It was more as if she suddenly felt the need to tell me about this one or that one. One girl was given a hundred thousand dollars and a Ferrari by an Italian count, another given an incredible emerald ring by an Arab. Apparently, it was usually tips in cash and the tips she did not know about. That girl, Renée, who was caught with Governor Cantor was strictly 'B' team material, according to Chantal. When she met with her for the initial interview, she said no but it was Jake who said let's take her on. Chantal claimed she was 'bottom heavy' and not attractive enough. Now this last choice has become the face of the Imperial Club." I stopped to look at my notes. "Sometimes the governor liked having several girls, one hour at a time, maybe three in one day."

"What?"

"Chantal didn't call him a sex addict but he would have one girl after another and virtually no conversation with them. There was one who was a little different. He was fond of someone named Caroline and requested her most often but was caught with Renée. Caroline was the one he sometimes wanted for the whole night. She was the one who usually went down to Washington to be with him. Evidently, he liked to talk to her."

"Does she ever—did you ever ask her about the clients?"

Maybe this is it. "Over half the clients were Jewish. Nearly all married. Spending half of their lives on business trips, in airports."

"Do you understand why the girls do this? Has she explained it to you so that it makes sense?" His voice was tight; he was emotional. He cleared his throat.

"She says it's nothing but money. The girls have not been sexually abused as children, they aren't rape victims. None of them hate men. As a matter of fact, she claims they love men or they wouldn't be able to do this." I waited for him to say something and when he didn't, I continued. "By the way, I disagree. Every book I've read, every memoir, every prostitute has a major father problem." Jazz flashed into my mind. Wow. Hadn't made that connection before. "Usually he's absent. The parents are divorced or he walked out or he died. Chantal is different; her father might be too present in her life." I was thinking, yes, but not every woman with a bad father experience becomes a prostitute. Otherwise, I'd be naked in some hotel room right this minute. "I do not think it's only the money. Maybe for the streetwalker or the cokehead hooker who charges twenty dollars for a blow job but not for these girls."

I glanced at the stack of books across the room on the bookcase under the Sherlock Holmes print. *Hos, Hookers, Call Girls and Rent Boys. Diary of a Married Call Girl. Secrets of a Hollywood Super Madam. Unzipped. Indecent. The Price. Callgirl. The Manhattan Madam.*

"If it's only the money then they wouldn't be as well educated as she claims they are," he countered.

"There is one who is getting her doctorate at Yale. I'd say that's well educated. But she's working part time at an art gallery downtown and can barely pay her rent."

He was quiet. "Are any of them doing it for drugs? For drug money?"

"No. She says not. She says a man can pay two hundred dollars for someone on drugs. Imperial Club couldn't charge those prices and have the girls all coked up."

"Right." He began again. "Are any of them financially just fine and doing it for kicks or for some reason we don't know?"

"Good question. Chantal claims they all have other lives and are just as afraid of being discovered as the clients are. Plus, she seems proud to have prosperous clients. Hold on, let me find this quote in my notes. Here is what Chantal said. 'You have to understand. Sometimes I felt honored to be with these men. I mean, their haircuts cost more than my education.'"

"Hmm. Are any of the girls married?"

"There is one widow from Munich. Gorgeous. And there is another who might have been married or still is. She dropped out and then came back just a few months before the arrests."

Silence from Geneva. Or from wherever.

"Where was the married one? London?"

This is a big clue. This is the second time he's asked about London today.

"She didn't say where."

"Why would a girl stop? Why do you think?"

"Marriage might stop her. A husband."

"What else?" he pressed.

"Well, some of the girls didn't like it. They quit. The other thing was if they were dropped by the Imperial Club. Because of complaints. "

"What sort of complaints?"

"The biggest complaint made by clients is that the girl is too professional. Fake breasts, too long fingernails but mostly too businesslike. Men don't want that. They really want the fantasy that this luscious girl wants to spend the evening with them, wants to go to bed with them."

"Amazing," came the deep voice from far away. "So, it was really the men who were the romantics, who clung to the illusion that this might be attraction and affection? And it was the girls who—"

"Wanted the cash."

"Got it," he said softly.

"But not always," I said. "What about Cantor?"

Bloooooop! went the Skype connection drowning out my last words.

I pulled off the headphones and wondered why he had sounded so sad about the men wanting the fantasy. Or was he sad about the girls wanting the money? For some reason Call Me Jack didn't want to hear that. But what the hell *did* he want to hear?

MANHATTAN

Kelsey was crossing Fifth Avenue intent on getting to Saks to buy shoes she'd seen advertised that morning in *The New York Times*. They had four-inch heels and a tiny ankle strap. Suede. Six hundred fifty dollars a pair and she planned to buy all three colors if they had her size. Suddenly she heard the squeal of brakes and felt herself thrown into the air.

"Kelsey! It's your mother! Can you hear me?"

She opened her eyes then closed them again.

"It's the medication. Don't worry. A broken arm, three broken ribs," said Dr. Flynn. "And a slight concussion. She's going to be fine."

Janet Ritter and Bruce had flown in from Ohio within hours of the accident. Kelsey's doorman took their bags and got them a taxi to rush them to the hospital where they paced the hallway outside her room until allowed in. Late that night, the super unlocked Kelsey's apartment which is where the Ritters would stay, at least until Kelsey could come home and take care of herself. She and Bruce were both mystified by all the clothes and the towers of shoe boxes.

When Kelsey awakened the following day her mother and brother were at her bedside. "Someone from the emergency room called me. It was that 'in case of accident' card you had in your wallet. Thank goodness," her mother said. "And thank goodness, you're going to be alright." A pretty woman, she wore her uniform of navy pantsuit with white ruffled blouse and had her omnipresent needlepoint in her lap. The house in Cincinnati overflowed with pillows. Kelsey hated them. She detested reading things like "Home is Where the Heart Is" and wished her mother would stitch things like "If you can't say anything nice then sit next to me." Impossible, but at least she had stopped the Bible verses.

Bruce grinned. "I hear you bounced," he joked. Kelsey screwed up her face, holding her sides with her one good arm across her torso. "Don't make me laugh!" she begged. "You don't know what broken ribs feel like until you want to laugh."

Kelsey came home on Friday, a bit shaky, and very shocked to realize that her mother and brother were actually *in* her apartment. She'd never had guests there and she'd let the cleaning woman go six months before.

Kelsey's mother slept on the foldout couch in the living room; her brother went to a hotel after spending half the night in a chair and three hours on the carpet. There was no hiding the stuffed closets, the canyon of shoe boxes, the garment bags hanging from the shower rod in the bathroom, the clothes still in shopping bags crammed under the bed or the piles of credit card bills.

Her mother had questions, her brother was quiet, not looking at her. Her explanations were ridiculous. "What is this?" she shouted at them." Some kind of intervention? Is Dr. Phil going to pop out of a closet with a camera crew?" She slammed her bedroom door with her good arm and didn't come out for nearly two hours. Mid-afternoon she walked into the living room where her mother was reading a magazine and Bruce sat in front of the TV. Boxes and shopping bags covered all the chairs and most of the sofa. Kelsey looked around and seemed to suddenly realize the situation. She moved a glossy white shopping bag out of the way then sat down on the floor and cried.

Bruce worked for three days cataloging shoes alone and, in five days, had put everything for sale on eBay. He opened up a PayPal account; the money started to arrive, the apartment began to empty. Kelsey gasped when her younger brother handed her a check for five thousand dollars to pay off some of the credit card balance with the highest interest. "You're my sister," he said. "It's an early Christmas present."

Janet Ritter was also a take-charge personality and managed, against all odds, to locate a therapist in Manhattan who would come to the apartment on Mondays and Wednesdays at four in the afternoon.

"This one is called Associazione Fitil Onlus. In Africa," said Jessica, handing Brooke Cortland the file. "I didn't print out the entire website but go on www.fitil.org if it interests you enough to want to know more. It's there at the top of the first page."

"Thanks." She liked having an assistant, wondered why she hadn't hired someone years ago. Probably because Stanford would have called her lazy, he would have labeled it self-indulgent. Jessica would have been worth the row, she thought. Very bright, a sociology major, she seems almost intuitive about what I want and how I like things to be done. Working part-time to pay for courses at Hunter College.

Brooke flipped open the file, at least the fortieth one this week, adjusted her tortoiseshell reading glasses and began to read. A minute later, she put the pages down and turned to her computer. Fifteen minutes after that she was on Skype facing Bettie Petith, the president and one of the founders. She was American, with white hair and the rosy, wind-burned complexion of someone who loves the outdoors, who was probably happy on a sailboat. Brooke's first impression of her image on the screen was one of enormous vitality and strength.

After introducing herself, Brooke asked, "Is it convenient to talk to me? Is this a good time?"

"Absolutely," was the quick response. "Nothing I like more than talking about Fitil Onlus. I could talk about it for days on end."

Brooke smiled at her enthusiasm and picked up her pen, preparing to take notes. "I like the strong emphasis on education. Tell me the basics and then maybe I'll know enough to ask questions."

Bettie began, "Every year it's three girls and two boys from their village primary schools—four different villages—who are sent to the middle school in Niou."

"Niou? What is that? And why more girls than boys?"

"Niou is a town. More girls than boys because, apart from the obvious wish to help them get ahead, it also avoids early forced marriages." She continued. "This is called Adopt-A-Student. We also have a literacy program for adults."

"In what language? Burkina Faso's official language is French, isn't it?" Brooke hoped she was right.

"Yes. French is used in all the schools but there are sixty-five languages in the country. Our area is Mossi which is the largest ethnic group and they speak Mooré so the literacy classes are taught in Mooré."

"So it's reading and writing."

"It's not just reading and writing. It's also fundamental math but also learning by doing projects."

"What sort of projects?"

"Let's see." Bettie hesitated, gazing into space. "A group might raise pigs for sale. They might choose a water project or a health project. They are becoming empowered to improve their lives." She paused. "Mrs. Cortland, we are—"

"Call me Brooke. Please."

"Yes, and I'm Bettie. Glad that's out of the way." Both women smiled at their computer screens. "We're starting a three-year pilot project of sports for girls in the primary schools."

"Which sports?"

"Volleyball and football. Soccer to Americans." Bettie paused to lift a dog of dubious provenance into her lap. "Gypsy," she said by way of introduction and then continued. "We are thrilled at the response. Now lots of NGOs, sports authorities and even some nuns want to join the program. They are throwing around words like 'revolutionary.'"

The women kept talking. Brooke asked questions, Bettie answered. Brooke was thinking, I'll get a tutor. I am sure I remember a smattering of French from Rosemary Hall. They talked for over an hour about the possibilities for the future, about the differences education could make to a person, to a family, to a society. One woman sat at her Louis Quinze desk in her Fifth Avenue apartment and the other sat at her kitchen table on via Cartari in Rome.

Jessica, going through the mail on the other side of the room, watched Mrs. Cortland's face. Her eyes were bright, her voice was alive with enthusiasm. Jessica smiled to herself. I'm watching someone change their life.

BOSTON

Catherine heard Bill Middleton's voice coming from the study. He'd flown in from Oklahoma City late the night before and would catch a flight to L.A. tomorrow morning. So for this one full day he was going over documents and wanted to close the case. "Search warrant?" he was saying. She froze in the hall outside. A search warrant for what? For the whole house? For my closet with all my fat brown envelopes? I could get them out of the house but where will I take them? To Sunswept? I could put them in the trunk of my car but would there be a search warrant for the car? For every place in my life? She listened. "There is no reason for a judge to order a search warrant," Bill was saying. They probably want my laptop went through her mind. They can have it, she thought. Nothing on it to link me to anything. I looked up E-trading once. That's it. But the envelopes! I can't let anyone ever find the envelopes. She felt ill.

The young lawyer sitting at Holtie's desk was being firm. Catherine stepped into the room and put the cup and saucer on the blotter. He looked up at her and went on in a calm voice. "This has dragged on for months. My client has cooperated fully, in every way, with you and the authorities and there is no reason to continue any investigation of her. She will not be meeting with you again unless a valid reason for questioning is presented to me." He put down the receiver and reached for his coffee. Catherine wondered, for the hundredth time, if this meant the bad dream was really over.

Bill Middleton told her and Holtie that evening at dinner that he thought so. The next day, just before the cab came to take him to the airport, they were alone and Catherine decided to risk it. He was the only person in the world she could ever ask. "I have one more question," she said. Bill looked up from stuffing papers into his briefcase which rested on the table in the front hall. "Between you and me, I've saved more than the hundred thousand." He blinked. "It's all cash," she added in a whisper.

Bill gave her a long look and said, "Race track, Mrs. Burroughs?" When she didn't answer he realized she wanted an answer. He spoke very softly, conspiratorially. "Look, if no one can prove you broke the law obtaining the money then I think you're in the clear. Watch how you spend it. Don't wave flags in front of the IRS."

At that moment, there was a honk outside, he snapped closed the briefcase, raised his head and then stood very still as if deciding what to do next. He stared into her eyes, very aware of her perfume, and for a split second, she was afraid he was going to kiss her. She knew he had a crush on her and also knew it had given her a distinct advantage: her every little lie had been believed. He had always been on her side. Catherine impetuously threw her arms around him and kissed his cheek which pleased him no end. "You have been my knight, my prince, my champion!" she said stepping back. "Thank you for everything."

The young lawyer positively glowed as he strode out the front door to the waiting cab.

The week before Thanksgiving, Douglas L. Allen went before Judge Joseph Heller to be sentenced. Charged with criminal negligence under the Patriot Act, he stood beside his lawyer, hearing his heart beat in his ears. His suit felt stiff and strange like cardboard, his collar seemed too tight and he resisted the urge to wipe the perspiration from his upper lip. The stockbroker felt close to fainting with fear. He saw the judge's mouth move but couldn't make out the words. The gavel came down and it was over. A suspended sentence. Emily rushed into his arms then he shook hands with his lawyer, wondering if he should apologize for his sweaty palm. With false braggadocio, he said, "Let's all go somewhere fabulously expensive and have a huge lunch."

PHILADELPHIA

I was downtown on Filbert Street in court for two long days, with fingers crossed I would not be asked to testify. Private detectives never want to take the stand.

Now in my office again, I was going over the notes of the last lunch for the report to Call Me Jack. Chantal had been all over the map from the revelation that she had no idea what phone sex was to her personal preferences. "I'd rather have sex with a stranger. No hang-ups, no background to it. No waking up with him the next morning." As our plates were being put down, she said, "I like them small so I can get them into my mouth." I thought our waiter was going to pass out.

Some girls were unreasonable. "One girl was $5,500 an hour and was asked to do a week in France. She wanted to fly first class and when she pushed for that, the client called it off. Stupid."

There were girls who were difficult. "I can deal with difficult," stated Chantal. "If a model hasn't eaten in four days she can be difficult. Give her a piece of bread and she's okay."

I smiled remembering another description. "A Barbie doll. Her emotional development had ended at age five."

Silicone. Absolutely no silicone. A sign of a pro in the adult industry.

I flipped my notebook back to my notes of two weeks ago, three weeks ago; there were things I hadn't relayed to Call Me Jack. I'd asked what the girls took with them to a hotel. Sex toys and lubricants. Everyone in New York went to Fantasy World on Amsterdam and 77th Street.

Yes, I thought as I typed away. Definitely better to write this down and not have to say it on Skype. Toys. Sex. Money. Ego. I reached down to scratch Sherlock behind the ears. Ego. Chantal described men who would call from a five-star hotel and say, 'Can I see somebody at two? I have a meeting at four.' He can walk in to the board room and think 'you'll never guess what I was doing an hour ago.' Chantal described the behavior as a coping mechanism to deal with a stale marriage, a boring wife. Sometimes the girl would spend days in a luxurious hotel, going to the spa while the client went to business meetings.

I kept typing. I'd asked about fetishes. Had any girl arrived to find the client in bed with a llama? Chantal had exploded in giggles. "No! No llamas! We didn't get many fetishes."

What about Governor Cantor? What would Chantal say to Sharon Cantor? "I'd say if he hadn't come to us he'd have gone somewhere else."

So what did she think of marriage? Of having children? "Never want to have children." She was definite. "Jake asked me to marry him," she said, obviously happy at the thought. "He gave me a huge diamond ring on Valentine's Day of 2004."

"Were you going to marry him?" I'd asked.

Chantal shook her head. "It would have screwed up my health insurance. I'm still on my dad's."

I had laughed and asked where the ring was. Typing in her answer, I laughed again. "After I got bail, I was so angry about the incident that I threw it out the window of a taxi going up Third Avenue."

Chantal had been terrified that she and Jake would be arrested. "I felt I was cheating at the game of life. There was so much money and it was so easy but I worried that at some point it would explode." She described hearing a noise in the apartment while she was taking a shower and how she imagined men running in with drawn guns.

I looked at the scrawled notes in the margin of my notebook. "Why didn't you stop? You had all that money! And you were starting to feel afraid! Why didn't you stop?"

Chantal had smiled faintly as she stared off into the distance. "Because there was always a more beautiful girl and always a richer client."

DECEMBER, 2008

Sex is one of the nine reasons for reincarnation.
The other eight are unimportant.
—Henry Miller

I didn't want her to see me. The courtroom was crowded with the reporters packed into the two rows allotted to them; they all leaned forward in an effort to hear. I recognized three from the Irene Silverman murder trial.

On TV, you hear every word but it's not like that in real life. So when I'm not a part of a case, not sitting in front, all I can do is try to see what's happening and smell the scene. This courtroom smelled like freshly-sharpened pencils and wet wool.

Chantal stood up for the sentencing. Her lawyer reached for her hand but she pulled away and stood alone, quite separate from him. A study in black, of course. All five feet two of her, her cap of dark hair flipped under, her face white as milk, her shoulders narrow in the black jacket. I could hear nothing. The gavel banged. People were standing up, putting on coats, reaching for scarves; the reporters were rushing out to file the story.

The next time we met, it was over. Or maybe it was just beginning to be the end. The Friday after the Monday. Chantal described how shocked she'd been in the courtroom, to have the judge hand down a six-month sentence. The judge declared that he could understand being on drugs for two years but not for four years. He called her a victim but perhaps because of the high profile of the case had to give her prison time. "I did charity work, I got straight As in school . . ." Her voice faltered. Now she would be counting the weeks, days and hours until June first when she had to report to Danbury Federal Correctional Facility.

I watched her face and decided not to tell her that I'd been there.

Now, at the Waldorf, on this Friday afternoon, I listened to her talk about Jake. The omnipresent, omnipotent Jake. I thought of her in front of the judge and breaking the law and going to prison and I sipped my wine and thought how terribly, terribly sorry I was for her.

Kelsey was reminded of Ned whenever she took the train. That Saturday morning when she waked without him, she felt a dart of worry. It was stupid to have left her suitcase open like that but they'd both had so much to drink. When she walked into the living room, saw him asleep, saw the closed suitcase—she knew. Kelsey told herself he was too conservative for her, very rigid in his approach to life. Harlem. She saw how hard he was trying that first day. He wanted a certain kind of female and only wanted her for marriage. That's not me. Not now. Maybe not ever. Nine men out of ten would have come into the bedroom and asked to play with some of those toys, would have been turned on. Yes, of course, they would have, she thought. She only blamed herself for scheduling the Boston client for six o'clock.

THE WALDORF ASTORIA

The deadline of December first had come and gone and there had been no communication from Call Me Jack though the wire arrived at Wachovia as usual. I kept inviting Chantal to lunch but we no longer talked about Imperial.

It was unspoken but we both knew I had plenty enough material for the novel. The novel I was not writing.

Today, even from a distance, she looked tired but when she saw me at our far table in Peacock Alley, she smiled. We ordered wine. "Listen, I know it's horrible. You're twenty-four years old and it's going to be one forty-eighth of your life but this time next year it will be over. You'll be *starting over*."

"I'll be home for Thanksgiving," she quipped.

"You'll have your life back," I said and I meant it.

"All I want is to get my master's and my doctorate and be a psychologist. That's all."

The wine came and we ordered. The food came and Chantal ate two bites and talked about Jake. His letters filled her with hope. She adored him, she admired him. I had heard all this before. "I'm talking to Jake's lawyer to find out when we can write, when we can see each other. I love him and I'll wait years. The judge gave him thirty months, you know. Doesn't matter how long it takes. We are supposed to be together."

Chantal's face was aglow, her voice changed when she said his name. I looked at her and wondered if the madam would marry her pimp. "Tell me about your life together. I know you were busy running the business but did you two go to movies, do any sports, what did you read, is he a good cook? Did you have friends over for dinner? How was your life together?"

"Sometimes we'd have dinner with one of the girls. Nobody else because we couldn't tell anyone else what we were doing. Vegetarian restaurants but usually it was Chinese take-out. Jake reads a lot of self-help books, books on philosophy. He's a genius."

"What did you do together?"

Chantal burst out laughing and rolled her eyes impishly. I shook my head. I'd heard all about Jake's bedroom prowess. "Hey, other than that."

"We played chess. We played chess while we were waiting for men to show up, that first summer in the apartment downtown. And while we were waiting for someone in the bedroom to finish. And then later in the apartment in New Jersey."

The glamour, the excitement! Running an international multi-million dollar prostitution ring and it was a game of chess for fun? Thousands in cash tossed into a closet and eating vegetarian take-out? I could see that Chantal liked expensive handbags but that was it. No Maserati, no diamonds, no champagne, no excess.

She stopped, stared into space and I could read her mind. "Danbury can't be that bad," I told her. "You're going to where Martha Stewart wanted to go."

"Martha's first-choice prison. I'll remember that." Chantal stared down at her salad. She looked so small to me, so young, so fragile.

On the sidewalk later, saying goodbye, I impetuously threw my arms around her. She shrugged away like a cat. We had never touched before. I don't think we had ever shaken hands.

STAR ISLAND

Late one afternoon Rafael Solito called Pedro into the living room. It was filled with antique furniture and the tall windows were covered in heavy damask curtains so it was dark and seemed crowded. The chairs, the tables, they are all so big, thought Pedro, with plenty of gold and red velvet. One of the maids had told him that everything was very old, very expensive and had all come from Spain.

"I went in again and there is nothing," Pedro was saying in Spanish. "I put all in place again, very carefully." He wondered if it were important to describe something that had confused him. "One odd thing."

"Si?"

"She has one drawer in her bureau that is some kind of collection."

"What kind?"

"It is the bottom drawer and inside are all these little things. Some cuff links, some studs like you wear in your dress shirt."

"So, maybe she is going to give the cuff links to a man for a present."

"No. It's not like that," said Pedro. "It's just one stud, one cufflink. Nothing matches." He stopped. "It's as if she is collecting souvenirs from men. One at a time, of no use to anyone. Like one button, one collar stay. Many white collar stays; most of these things are little. Muy pequeño."

Rafael Solito frowned. "Strange. She is just a whore, who knows what she is thinking." He laughed. "Or if she ever thinks at all!" But, he thought, she was the best whore money could buy. He liked paying a lot for her. It made her more valued *if* he could ever value a whore. Then he resumed his worrying. "But she sees Intriago, she talks to him. It is not good." He was well aware that Intriago had been successful in putting several high profile drug dealers behind bars. People he knew had crossed swords with the federal prosecutor and things had not gone well for them. "Not good," he repeated. Solito put his cigar down in the heavy silver ashtray which was shaped like a scallop shell.

Pedro did not smoke; he worked out, cared about his body. His boss's cigars offended him. He thought they looked like dog turds and smelled nearly as bad.

"What about that other girl—Caroline—in New York?"

"Chico's friend in Spanish Harlem is watching her. He found nothing in her apartment except lots of cash."

Rafael was alarmed. "He didn't take it, did he? No robbery, nothing like that!"

Pedro shook his head. "No, he says he did not. We are paying him enough so that he is not tempted." Plus, thought the bodyguard, he knows he could be killed for disobeying an order.

"You have Alyssa's apartment number?"

Pedro nodded and handed him a yellow piece of paper. He had bought several tablets in different colors at Staples and liked any excuse to use them. Pedro could barely write but loved little notebooks, stationery, felt-tipped pens. Once he had spent an hour just walking the aisles of a fancy paper store in Miami while waiting for his boss. Rafael reached for his cell phone and punched in the first four numbers. Then he looked at his watch and hung up. "She will be at the real estate office," he said. "Remind me to call her tonight."

STAR ISLAND/KEY BISCAYNE

"Hello," said Annie. She listened. "Señor Blanco, yes, hello. " She was surprised, then alarmed. Her heart was beating fast. "How did you get this number?"

He laughed. "I no want to lose you," he said. "I would mees you too much."

Annie had never spoken to him on the phone. Everything had always been set up by Lori or Becky. The Imperial Club was no more. How could he be calling?

"Please don't be afraid. I see you drive into the building garage in your leetle yellow car yesterday. I ask the doorman your name."

"Oh," she said.

Señor Blanco seemed harmless. He was overweight, a teddy bear sort of man from Venezuela; he had told her and Caroline that he was in the sugar business and had five children with three wives. "Never enough women!" he always laughed. "Never too many! And never enough!" He usually drank too much and preferred watching her and Caroline's acrobatics to any physical activity of his own. The two women would then take turns taking care of him. It was always an easy all-nighter.

"Dinner?" he asked.

Annie didn't know what to say. She'd thought all this was over but this call changed everything. No booker, no splitting the fee. It would be an entire thirty-one thousand. She had read that the FBI planned to talk to some of the escorts but no one had contacted her and maybe no one ever would. Annie imagined that maybe it was all happening in New York and that no one really cared about Miami.

"Come on, Alyssa," he urged. "I mees you. We have a nice dinner in South Beach. I weel have the thirty-one thousand in a new Louis Vuitton handbag for you. Maybe you must give Imperial something before but this time it weel be just for you."

Annie was silent, listening to him go on. She was undecided but definitely tempted. "Pretty please with sugar on it," he said in his heavy Spanish accent which made her laugh.

"Okay," she said. "Let's have dinner."

Rafael Solito snapped his phone closed and looked at Pedro who was across the room pretending not to have heard his boss say 'pretty please with sugar on it.' "I am going to ask her. About Intriago. I am going to fuck her and then ask her. She will tell me the truth," he stated. "After dinner, after I feel good."

PHILADELPHIA

I grabbed the headphones. At last! First call from Call Me Jack since before Thanksgiving. "I want to break it off. The investigation, I mean. Let's stop this now."

"What's happened?"

"Nothing happened."

"Something has happened," I said.

He laughed. A real laugh. Very different from the little coughs of humor he'd expressed before. There was barking in the background. A big dog, "Jack! Stop! I'm coming!" he shouted.

"So you have all the information you want? Are you going to tell me what you were after?"

"I don't want to know any more. Put together a final bill and I'll Skype you tomorrow for it."

"Great." I tried to sound glad. Another case closed, another client happy or at least satisfied, but no answers for me. This drives me crazy as a detective. It's like being yanked out of a movie during the last five minutes.

Blooooomp! went the disconnect.

MANHATTAN

It was a bitter cold winter day, gray, windy, with a wind chill factor nobody wanted to know. Mark and Brooke had a late lunch at Nosidam and were on Fifth walking slowly back to the apartment. The Big S had moved out. Today Azura was there with the contractor and the new interior decorator. The four million dollars of blackmail money was in Brooke's bedroom safe which was hidden behind a painting by Mary Cassatt.

All had gone so well but, as was their habit, they headed into the park to talk freely with no chance of being overheard. Their breath came out in little white puffs as they settled themselves on the nearest bench.

"So it's final in April?" he asked.

She nodded. "I can have the apartment and my settlement is ridiculous . . ."

"Ridiculous?" gasped Mark. "Did he—"

"Oh, no, not what you're thinking! Ridiculously big. Best of all, there is nothing to dispute as it was a post-nup agreement signed years ago. No one could argue with the bank statements and evidently Stanford confessed to his lawyer." She paused. "The Big S won't have to start shopping at WalMart but he has to feel a little bit pinched. He is no longer one of America's 25 Richest men!" She laughed. "And that alone will infuriate him forever!" She smiled with delight. "It was all over in half an hour. I was relieved that he did not have to be there and he didn't come. Best of all, maybe the high point of the entire exercise was his lawyer, whom I've known for years, walking me to the elevator afterwards. Bill Frankel put his arm around me and said he wanted me to know that he thought I'd earned the settlement."

Mark grinned. "I think so, too."

The two of them were silent. It was very cold and getting dark but neither felt like breaking the spell. Brooke remembered the second chance and taking Stanford back. He had been so wonderful for about two weeks and then all had returned to what was normal in their life together: his criticism, his outbursts, his selfishness, those petty grievances he seemed to nurture.

Mark was thinking of all those revenge conferences on benches in the park. He was waiting for her to speak again. She was changing her life. He remembered the day she had cried in the chair in the salon. That had been the beginning of his new life. And of a great friendship.

"I don't need all that money. My sons are all doing well, my grandchildren will be taken care of and I was thinking that I want to do something good with some of it. I've picked an organization in Africa. I want to be involved." She paused. "You know when you educate a girl then you help her have a healthy baby, instill in her the value of education for her children. She may change her husband's ideas about women and she will certainly have sons who respect women. Of course, I believe in educating everybody but I think for girls in Africa it might have long-range, very valuable effects. On the next generations."

"I admire you so much. I don't have the words to tell you," said Mark.

Brooke smiled. "Wait till I've done something good to admire me. I'm just getting started. I have this amazing feeling that I'm about to fly." She adjusted her scarf more tightly against the cold. "Actually, on January fifteenth I will be flying to Ouagadougou."

Mark's face showed such surprise that she had to laugh at him. "It's only about four hours from Paris."

"I'm stunned," he gasped. He could see his breath.

"But I'm also thinking that I want to invest in a business. Here. In New York."

"What kind of business?"

"A salon. An excellent hairdresser with a spa in the same building." Mark stared at her as she went on. "Something that you would own, that would be yours to run as you saw fit."

"Oh, Mrs. C!" Mark was wide-eyed.

"You and Lori seem to be best friends and though I've never met her she must be a good person if you like her and she's been out of work since last March." She paused. "Maybe she could be in on the organization of it."

"She's amazing at handling people and a whiz with numbers. She actually did my tax returns." He stopped. "Lori is like the sister I never had." Suddenly, without warning, Mark's eyes started to water. "Because of the cold," he gasped, pulling a white handkerchief out of his pocket.

"That four million dollars is yours."

"Ohmygod, ohmygod," he breathed.

"You deserve it. I couldn't have done it without you. Could not have gotten through the past twelve months without you. It was about this time a year ago that the Big S was wiring money to see his whore in London. I didn't know it until February and if I had known it would not have been the same to know it all by myself."

Mark thought it was unreal, a dream. "Mrs. C, are you sure you want to give me all that money?" he blurted.

She nodded. "Absolutely. The money is yours but we must pretend that it's my investment. You can't just turn up with four million dollars in cash nowadays." She stopped. "We'll meet with my accountant and my lawyer to sort out how I can give it to you and the tax situation and make up a business plan with a location in mind. What do you think about Fifth Avenue or do you think Madison is better? Midtown or uptown? Downtown maybe? What clientele do you want to attract? There's the meatpacking district and Soho.

Where would you like to be?"

They sat there talking until the park lights came on, showing through the bare branches of the trees, and then they walked out to Fifth and headed uptown. Mark embraced her on the sidewalk. This is not my glamorous Rosalind Russell aunt, he decided, but this is my fairy godmother who is making what I've fantasized about for years actually happen.

"Oh, another thing," Brooke said when they stepped apart, both of them a little emotional. "I think you might want to move to Manhattan. I know you've always wanted to and now's the moment. Maybe an apartment near the spa. Or maybe it's more your thing to buy a loft. It's a good time to buy, prices have dropped. You can use the entire four million for that since I'll be investing, really investing other money, in the spa."

As he told Lori an hour later, "I just stood there on the sidewalk on Fifth Avenue crying like a fool."

Lori said, "Yes, you are a fool. My favorite fool in the whole world. My favorite pasta fool, my favorite 'let's watch *Casablanca* again' fool and my favorite blackmailer, by far. I can't believe how much I'm going to miss you."

"You aren't going to miss me! I think we should *both* move to Manhattan. Haven't I always said we didn't belong in Brooklyn? With the drop in real estate prices, maybe we can get apartments on the same floor and save lots of elevator time. Or a really big two bedroom."

Lori was speechless and then, ever practical, she voiced the looming possible negative of such a move. Something she often considered: a third person. Would she be jealous? Would they all get along? "What if you fall in love with somebody? And you want him to move in? It could happen!"

Mark said, "What if you decided to get married?" She made a face but he was insistent. "It could happen! Especially now with the new haircut I gave you!"

Lori actually blushed. She barely recognized herself in the mirror lately. In one year she had been transformed. The haircut was jagged bangs and lots of layers that made her eyes look enormous; Mark had talked her into blondish streaks. She who had eaten all night in the past was now thirty pounds lighter and even walked differently.

They poured two glasses of wine and sat on the couch outlining possibilities. Mark was euphoric and Lori was saying that they should be very careful. Suddenly he said, "Stop!" and she went silent, staring at him. "You are the closest thing to a sister I've ever had in my life. We'll have papers drawn up in case we have a fight over whether or not to put a lid on the pasta but I vote we go full speed ahead and buy whatever we want."

She stared at him, his brown eyes alight with excitement. "I've never had a brother so I guess you're it."

Mark nodded. "Okay. Settled. Why don't we get two lofts on top of each other with a circular stairway cut in between. Or a giant, humongous penthouse and sit around on the terrace every Sunday . . ."

STAR ISLAND

It was nearly one o'clock in the morning when Pedro went to get his jacket out of the Mercedes and that is when he saw the fingerprints on the driver's door. They were not fingerprints, he realized, but smudges that been left by someone wearing a glove. Even in the dimness of the garage, they were apparent. Three tiny scratch marks were on the lock and four smudges marred the pristine sheen of black metal. Chico loved that car and wiped it down religiously after every outing; Pedro had never seen a speck of dust on it. It was still locked but someone had tried to open that door and been interrupted.

In minutes, Pedro had thirty of his men surrounding the house looking through the foliage for any sign of an intruder. The alarms had been evaded, obviously. All the bright outdoor lights were turned on, transforming the three acres into an eerie day for night landscape. The men cast big, black shadows as they moved silently, quickly, across the lawn, through the trees and down to the docks with guns drawn. Pedro stood on the pier for a moment smelling the brine and listening to the water, black as ink, lap at the pilings. He turned to stare back at the house which resembled a Spanish castle; it was lit so brightly that he could have counted the red barrel tiles on the roof.

Rafael Solito did not come out and ask what was happening so Pedro decided he would not disturb him. Maybe he had actually fallen asleep. Maybe tonight, he thought, Señor Solito will sleep.

KEY BISCAYNE/MANHATTAN

"I don't see any reason not to," Cate was saying. She'd kicked off her heels and had her feet up on the couch in her Manhattan living room. "And it is a lot of money."

Annie was sitting on the Mexican tile floor wearing only a white lace thong; she leaned forward to touch up a chipped toenail with hot pink polish. The landline was on speaker. "I agree with you. He asked me two weeks ahead which has given me too much time to think about it. Remember when it was Lori or Becky and 'are you free tonight?'"

"Yes. Wish I were there actually. It would get my mind off things. I go to work and look over my shoulder about forty times a day. I wonder if he knows where I work because I know he knows where I live." She paused. "Bettina at the office keeps asking me what's wrong and I keep wondering if I should tell her that someone is going into my apartment and I know I can't tell her because then I'll have to tell her about Imperial."

Annie put the tiny brush back in the bottle and screwed it closed. "No. Don't tell her. This is going to blow over."

"It has to," said Cate. "I'm so tense I can't sleep. I just lie there in the dark with all my muscles clenched. I look like hell and I keep trying to guess what anyone would want from us. And how they keep getting in here past the doormen! Nothing makes sense. I have money in my apartment and they haven't taken it. I've moved it out now and put it in my office but why didn't they take it? If it's blackmail, then why don't they make contact and ask for something?"

"I think I am going to ask Intriago to try to find Bree. I will call him on Monday."

"Oh, that would be great! That's the best news I've had in ages!"

"Don't celebrate yet. You were the one who told me it was impossible. But Intriago is on our side." Annie was now smearing hand lotion on her legs and then on her arms.

"I feel better. I really do." Cate's voice had changed. "Where are you going? What are you wearing? Are you meeting Blanco somewhere?"

"He knows my real name, where I live so he is picking me up. There is a new Italian restaurant called Da Francesca in South Beach. I think it's on Lincoln Road. I'm dying to go there because it was photographed and written up in *The Miami Herald* last week. It's amazing he got a reservation on a Saturday." She stopped. "It would be like old times if you were here. I think I'm wearing that white sheath dress you've seen before. With the gold thing on the belt. You once called me virginal, remember?"

Cate laughed. The sound was unfamiliar to her. When had she last thought anything warranted a real laugh? "Yes, I remember! Let's lose any adjective starting with 'virgin.'"

"Yeah. Think we're past that. Say, do you remember the Panamanian Maniac and that time he kept wanting to play horsey?"

Cate giggled. "And he was so upset when neither of us had a riding crop and we were taking turns hitting him in the rear with the rolled-up *Time* magazine?"

"And what about that Frenchman from Martinique who just wanted to watch us dance naked?"

Cate burst into laughter, putting one arm across her stomach, holding her sides. "And he had all those Strauss waltzes on a CD and you kept saying you knew how to waltz and we kept tripping all over each other because we couldn't decide who should lead . . ."

Annie burst in, "But what about the time you were supposed to be doing unspeakably lustful things to me and when I gave one of my Academy Award-winning moans of pleasure, you got the hiccups?"

BROOKLYN

Mark and Lori had been in a state of manic euphoria over the myriad of possibilities for the spa but now all their enthusiasm was focused on a five-story Beaux Arts mansion between Fifth Avenue and Madison on East 65th Street. They saw it the first day and they knew it was right. Brooke loved the high ceilings, the marble fireplaces. Lori and Mark were stunned at all the space and couldn't wait to renovate the roof terrace.

It was Saturday afternoon. "Okay," Mark was saying. "We'll be there. I can't wait. And I'll tell Lori." He snapped the cell closed. "Mrs. C, I mean Brooke, has organized an architect and a contractor to go through the house with us on Wednesday morning."

"It's really happening," said Lori from her perch on the kitchen stool. "It's like a dream. Like the best dream I've ever had."

"My feet aren't touching the ground yet." Mark was in the living room pulling *Vanity Fair* magazines out of the bookshelves. The night before Lori had stared at him and repeated, "It's all online," about six times and he had finally decided to part with his beloved collection.

Lori stood up, grabbed her keys from the kitchen counter. *The New York Post* was beside the toaster. "So you saw this?" she said. "Page Six?"

"Haven't read it yet." He was already lost in his world of *Vanity Fair*.

Lori thumbed the paper open and began to read aloud. "The soon-to-be-divorced billionaire let's call SC was spotted at Le Cirque for lunch with a dishy blonde young enough to be his granddaughter. Kayluh, yes, that how it's spelled, is on leave from teaching her Zumba class in Montreal."

"Are you kidding me?" shouted Mark. "Zumba class! Are you kidding me?"

"Kayluh rhymes with duh," said Lori. "The Big S. An old fool." She shook her head, put down the paper and said, "Now for important stuff. The spa is moving forward but I'm not going to be happy commuting from Brooklyn. I'll call Sandra and see if she has anything we might like." She looked at Mark, head down, totally lost in his magazines again. "I'm pruning my clothes today." Everything before her summer shopping trip was too big for her. "Monday it's the Salvation Army. I'll get a cab so if you want me to take anything let me know."

"Right." He didn't even hear her. Mark was on the floor engrossed in an interview of a rich Argentine polo player who'd married six women and murdered at least one of them. Lori raised her eyebrows, shook her head and left the apartment.

An hour later, he was pulling a new armful of the fat, heavy magazines off a shelf when something fell to the floor. A CD. Silver, unlabeled. He'd forgotten all about it. That nightmare morning, the sirens, Lori white as death and nearly catatonic with fear.

Mark held it in his hand and thought how light it was. All those names, e-mails, and phone numbers and it weighs as much as a postcard. My days as a blackmailer are behind me, he said to himself and put it on the coffee table. For the next two hours he immersed himself in the magazines, re-reading articles, thumbing through photograph spreads. He decided not to give the magazines away. The spa should have a very cool library, there was plenty of room for one and these would be perfect there. It would also be an excuse to subscribe to every single fashion magazine that existed. Starting with French and Italian

Vogue. Everything.

The little silver disk was on the coffee table all afternoon. Lori came up to watch the news and when she walked into the kitchen to get glasses, he quickly propped it on the shelf out of sight behind the clock and told himself he'd deal with it tomorrow.

STAR ISLAND

The evening air was like velvet and the slight breeze was heavily scented, very sweet with the gardenias that grew beside the driveway. Pedro and Chico were in front of the house by the Escalade. It was a big, powerful looking SUV with bulletproof windows like the Mercedes. Pedro had persuaded Señor Solito to take it tonight. He felt it was less conspicuous than the luxury German car. Actually Pedro didn't want him to go out at all. "He says he's going. He needs to relax."

Chico shrugged and took a drag on his cigarette. "The boss is the boss."

The two men spoke Spanish softly, afraid of being overheard, even outside.

"Tonight is completely different. We are going to pick her up at Key Biscayne, take them to the restaurant. After dinner, he is going to the Delano. I have booked two rooms side by side. Miguel and I will be outside in the hall taking turns watching and Pablo will remain in the lobby."

"You want me to drive you from the restaurant to the hotel, si?"

"No." Pedro frowned. He had such a bad feeling about leaving the house tonight. "I don't want him to walk around South Beach but he says the crowds make it safe. So he and she will walk and I'll be behind him and Miguel and Pablo will be in front. Miguel and Pablo are coming at ten o'clock, and will be at the restaurant when we leave." He shook his head. "I don't like it, Chico."

Chico put his hand on Pedro's shoulder so he could balance on one leg as he stubbed out his cigarette on the sole of his shoe. He put the butt in his black uniform pants pocket and said, "El jefe es el jefe." The boss is the boss.

Rafael Solito had never seen Alyssa in such a vibrant mood. She smiled at everything, touched his arm affectionately and seemed sincerely happy to see him. It was good to get out of the house, he thought. Later, she will tell me what Intriago is to her, why she sees him. Maybe he is nothing. If Intriago were the problem then I would be served papers, arrested. So maybe my bad feelings do not have anything to do with Intriago. And Alyssa? Freckles, that funny almost white hair, short and sticking straight up, and that smile that made you want to give her a kitten to hold. She looked so innocent; his mother would say she looked a little bit like Doris Day. Photos of the actress from old movie magazines were Scotch-taped all over her house in Colombia. But his mother said that about any blonde with short hair and any blonde with longer hair looked just like Marilyn Monroe. Rafael glanced at Alyssa again. She was just a whore but, he often said to himself, she was the best that money could buy and even though she was a whore, he had to admit he could not dislike her. And Pedro had found nothing in her apartment. Not in any of the four times. He looked at the girl, smiling in profile, and thought he would not send Pedro there again.

Solito did not want to think of someone trying to get into the Mercedes. Someone had actually evaded security and had gotten that close to his house, to his bedroom. To plant explosives? It shocked him. Could Alyssa have anything to do with that? Why did he have such bad feelings? No, he told himself. Not now. Tonight is to have fun.

The Cadillac Escalade with the bulletproof windows sped across the MacArthur Causeway passing the Port of Miami on the right. The tremendous cruise ships docked there twinkled with lights; they looked like office buildings turned on their sides. The SUV passed Star Island on the left. Pedro and Chico were in the front seat speaking Spanish and salsa was playing on the radio as they raced over the water towards South Beach. The great expanse of Biscayne Bay shone dully under the full moon like a solid sheet of steel. Annie wished Cate were here. She'd call her tomorrow and give her the gories. "I talked to Caroline a few days ago," she told Rafael. "And we laughed so much my sides hurt. We were crying on the phone."

"Crying?" he said. "Poor baby!" He gave her tanned bare knee a squeeze.

"Crying in a good way," Annie tried to explain. "She says 'hello' and she wishes she were here."

It was yet another perfect Miami evening which meant that the sidewalks of Lincoln Road were crowded with tourists and the surrounding streets were clogged with cars. Chico turned to Pedro and said, "I can't do anything about the red lights." Pedro shook his head, his voice showed his tension. "I know. Just get us there."

A few minutes later, the Escalade pulled right up to the front of the restaurant, practically onto the sidewalk and then the door was opened and someone was helping Annie out. The doorway, draped in bougainvillea, was just six steps away. Annie's immediate impression was of lush purple flowers. She stepped down carefully in her gold sandals with the four-inch heels, leaning on Pedro's offered arm. Rafael was right behind her; she could smell his aftershave.

The bullets sounded like firecrackers and then the screaming started.

DELAFIELD, WISCONSIN

Ingrid Larsson was wakened at midnight Central Standard Time by someone at the front door. Kristin stood behind her mother, both of them in plaid bathrobes, groggy and a little frightened just because of the hour. Kristin turned on the porch light and could see, through the glass side panels, two uniformed policemen standing on the front steps.

Officer Nielson introduced himself as being with the Delafield Police Department and then said he had bad news. "Mrs. Larsson? The Miami Police Department contacted us. It seems that your daughter, Anne . . ."

Officer Blane broke in at that point. "Anne Larsson is your daughter?"

"Yes, yes, yes," blurted a second girl with nearly-white blonde hair.

"We're terribly sorry. She's been in an accident and she died a few hours ago."

The sisters sobbed and embraced each other. Ingrid Larsson was silent with one hand over her mouth as if she had stopped breathing. Within seconds, the two girls had retreated, clutching each other, stumbling like wounded birds, down the dark hallway to the kitchen. Mrs. Larsson murmured something vaguely, like someone lost in a dream, about making tea. The men closed the front door and shuffled down the front steps, feeling big-footed and clumsy, not knowing what else to do.

In the squad car, Blane said, "I guess they assumed a traffic accident. Do you think we should have told them she was shot?"

Nielson sighed and turned on the ignition. "They'll know soon enough."

At the kitchen table, Annie's mother stared glassy-eyed at the refrigerator door. It was crowded with photographs of her three tow-headed girls, laughing, skiing, blowing out birthday candles. She felt such a wave of cold, black grief that she wished she had died instead.

The next morning, *The Miami Herald* splashed the lead story in a bold banner headline across the front page.

Drug lord killed in South Beach bloodbath

Rafael Solito, Colombian kingpin of the Mega drug cartel, was shot to death last night in a hail of automatic weapons fire in front of a South Beach restaurant. Also killed was his companion, Anne Larsson of Key Biscayne. Solito's bodyguard and his driver both died immediately of gunshot wounds; their names were unavailable. No one else was injured.

Witnesses said they saw three men open fire in front of Da Francesca as the doors of Solito's Escalade SUV were opened. The gunmen escaped into the crowd.

Solito, known for his cunning and cruelty, owned an estate on Star Island and is said to have employed a small personal army. His fortune has been estimated at over ten billion dollars. A Louis Vuitton handbag was found in the vehicle containing $31,000.

Ms. Larsson, 27, grew up in Delafield, Wisconsin, but had lived on Key Biscayne for three years. She was a real estate broker with Mira Properties in Coral Gables.

Carlito Intriago felt like vomiting when he saw the paper. He drove to the beach, parked the Jag then marched along the sand, staring up at the sky, wanting to exhaust himself. An hour later he was physically spent; he'd yanked off his silk tie, his suit was damp with sweat. He drove home, too fast, showered and then tried to start his day all over again. He felt a terrible emptiness laced with guilt that he hadn't done enough, hadn't seen this coming, hadn't saved her. My God, that monster! Solito! How many times a day has he crossed my mind in the past two years? Oh, Annie, he thought, you were playing with fire.

The story was on the front page of *The New York Times* but below the fold so Cate didn't see it until she shook open the paper just before lunch. She sobbed at her desk until it was decided that Heather from 19th Century European Art would be the one to take her home in a cab and stay with her for the rest of the day.

Becky saw it in *The New York Post* and burst into tears. She knew it was Alyssa. Lori saw *The Daily News* then called Mark on his cell phone. "It's definitely her. Thirty-one thousand? That can't be a coincidence. Plus, there was a photograph in the paper and it's the same mouth. Her face on the website, all except for her mouth, was covered with a scarf." They both wondered if Solito had been a client and what name he had used. Of course, he would have paid in cash, no credit cards, no wires. Or had Alyssa given him a private number and gone out on her own? This is what Jake and Bree always worried about. His companion, the article called her. Thirty-one thousand dollars? Had Alyssa been free-lancing all along or just this one time?

COCONUT GROVE/PHILADELPHIA

I snapped up the phone, disturbing papers; a rogue Oreo fell off the northern edge of my desk. "Hey, favorite private detective!" came the voice from Coconut Grove.

I laughed. "Hey, yourself, favorite Ecuadorian money laundering expert. I can hear you smiling," I said.

"You have that effect on me. When are you coming to Paradise for dinner?"

"Watch out. I can be on a flight in an hour."

I could hear him closing a door. His voice dropped. "Charlie, we need to talk."

"Solito. I know. You didn't get your white whale. I'm sorry." I'd sent him the Manhattan property data and then put Solito out of my mind.

"That's not the worst of it. I knew the girl who was gunned down with him."

"Really?" I wondered whether to ask him about the thirty-one thousand dollars and decided not to. The number had jumped out at me from the newspaper article.

"Okay, changing gears. The governor, that international call girl mess. Know anything about it?"

Changing gears? Felt like the same subject to me. "Oh, my intriguing Intriago," I said with a lilt in my voice. "Which international call girl mess? I'm swimming in them."

He laughed. "I know you know."

"Then you also know I'm up to my eyebrows in non-disclosure agreements."

"Well, hell, you really do know! So clue me in."

"You think your charm and a few mojitos is all it would take?"

"Okay, okay. I've been put in my place. I have been suitably subdued."

"You? Subdued? Ha." I took off my left earring. "Is this money laundering?"

"Yes. Been hired by—hell, I can't tell you!"

"But the charges, the prosecution, the sentencing . . . it's all over. I don't get it."

"Hey, you know what they say: I'm up to my eyebrows in non-disclosure agreements."

"Touché." I stared out at Betty's tree. It was black branches against the white winter sky. It might get up to twenty degrees today. "What do you need? If I can tell you without compromising what I've done, I will."

"I want to find her. The madam."

"Oh, that's easy. Right now, until classes start again in January, she's living with her mother in Connecticut. I'll find the address and the landline and e-mail you. Can't give you her mobile or she'd know it came from me. You don't know me, you didn't get anything from me and by the way, be really, really nice to her."

He exhaled. "Christ. I sensed this was your sort of case and I was right."

"It's not what you think," I stated firmly.

"I don't know what I think so how could you know?"

"Well, it's not."

"Listen, Charlie. This isn't a simple little situation of dazzlingly gorgeous girls making a bit of extra money. It isn't just rich men, expensive hotel suites. This is huge. This is honey pot schemes and blackmail, espionage and people disappearing."

"Disappearing?" Girls who knew too much?

"They're keeping that part of it out of the press. But the possibilities of what could happen to girls, to clients . . . it's pretty much endless."

"Honey pot schemes? All I can think of is the Cold War. Those Western journalists in Eastern European hotel rooms with sexy Russian spies. Compromising positions. Those old cameras with the flashbulbs . . ."

"You've got the right idea. It's the same principle but the technology is a bit advanced. These are wealthy, powerful men doing things they don't want known. They run countries. It's not just money and prestige, it's politics."

"So nothing's changed."

"No. Not even the bad guys."

"What do you mean?

"I mean that I have evidence that the KGB is involved." He paused. "Actually running it."

My heart gave this sick little flutter but I didn't let on. "Oh, that's absurd. They went out of business years ago. That's why Putin struts around bare-chested being madly athletic all the time. He can't get used to—"

"Hey, Charlie. This is serious."

I didn't say anything. I hadn't really believed Chantal but I believed Intriago.

"Whatever you know, I hope it isn't too much. You're pretty good at what you do."

"Thanks." Intriago saying I was pretty good was anyone else praising me to the skies. I heard the little click click click of the beagles' toenails on the bare wooden floor. They sat down together under the window; Vidocq rested his head on Sherlock and both beagles closed their eyes.

"KGB, huh?" I tried to sound casual. "And I guess once you work for the KGB, you always work for the KGB. Once you're in, you can't get out." I wanted him to say it wasn't so. But he didn't.

"Ivan?" he said. When I didn't say anything, he asked, "Interested?"

"Maybe."

"Still in."

I was silent then I tried to sound casual. "Interesting."

"Very. Thanks for the tip about finding her." I heard him move in his chair. "But Charlie, I mean it. I'm serious. Be careful."

"Always am."

"And you're always invited to dinner in Miami."

"See you when I see you," I said and we both hung up.

That conversation started to bother me. Intriago hoped I didn't know too much? Christ. I knew what Ivan was like in bed. I'd bravely endured excruciating details as I gulped sauvignon blanc. Too much? Dildos was too much. Hearing about pubic hair styles described on the website was too much. Then I had the damn dream again. Blood everywhere. Dammit! The KGB! Men behaving badly, men with secrets. All those lunches with Chantal and I never felt anything but a sense of fun and curiosity. Could Call Me Jack know about the KGB? Maybe he was MI5. But no, British intelligence wouldn't be hiring a one-man firm like Green Star to get information or would they if there were no other way to get it?

Certainly no cloud hung over the hours with Chantal but Ivan was another story. If he felt that I knew too much, had misrepresented myself to get information, would he, would someone object? Would anyone want to know why? Would they think I was MI5? Or CIA? It wouldn't be the first time. Ivan would be out of prison in a few months, good behavior would shorten his sentence and Chantal had already told him about me and our interviews. How many times had she asked me, "How's the novel coming?" What if she wanted to read the manuscript? What if *he* insisted on reading it?

Those three little initials scared me. I never thought the CIA played fair but the KGB had an entirely different set of rules. Or no rules at all. Maybe I'd be pushed into a taxi and simply vanish. I had to lie to Chantal about writing a book to get her to talk. Should I say my agent hated it? Should I say my computer crashed and the entire manuscript had been eaten by the ether? Should I plead writer's block? Was any excuse at all believable? Chantal would be very disappointed that there was no book and I hated disappointing her. I genuinely liked her. Disappointing Chantal I could handle but what about disappointing Ivan? Or disappointing the KGB?

Damn! Oh, damn! I have three death penalty cases, a missing person to find, and that background check for the fiancée who cried on the phone for half an hour yesterday. I don't have time to write a book. I looked at the blank computer screen, thought of Chantal, thought of Ivan, thought of the KGB. I could see the blood on my silver ballet slippers.

No choice. I have to do it. I'll start in January and write like a maniac. All that time with her. All our liaisons. Most of them at the Waldorf talking about all those liaisons that had gone on upstairs. I thought of the governor striding through the lobby in a baseball cap and dark glasses.

I stared out the window. All the players in New York, Paris, London, Miami. The Duke of Westbridge, drug lords, press barons, little princes, big tycoons, high rollers, the most powerful politician in New York. Risk as aphrodisiac. Kiss the risk.

It all started with an eighteen-year-old in a pizza parlor, answering an ad, getting into a white van on a summer day on Eighth Avenue. Chantal, the lover of the Russian with sinister ties. Ivan couldn't have done it without her. She pushed the business to evolve from the hot dog stand to the five-star restaurant. Chantal Silver was the main character, the star on center stage, the ringmaster of all the girls with knowledge of all the men, and the banker for all that loot. The five-foot-two, twenty-four-year-old with the quick mind and the daddy problems. The KGB. If Intriago said Ivan was in, then he was in. Did Chantal know? She lived to please Ivan. Would it have mattered to her?

In all the hours of talking, Chantal never changed in any way. No regrets. No sudden self-awareness. She will always blame her father. Yes, she threw the diamond ring out the window of the taxi but except for that burst of anger, from the moment I met her until that last lunch, all she wanted was to please the Russian pimp she called Jake.

This is a story worthy of Danielle Steele or Jackie Collins. That's the way it ought to be written. No mention of bodily fluids. It'll be great lingerie and glitz. I'll use the right fees and I can weave in what Chantal told me but I will have the power to decide how it all plays out. The novelist always has more power than the private detective. I can punish a few bad guys and banish the hundred maybes that float around in my head like clouds.

BOSTON

"I want to feel safe again," Cate was saying, her voice ragged with tears. Her mother sat on the edge of her bed with her hand on her arm. It was Cate's childhood room with the pink roses on the wallpaper and her dolls still displayed on shelves.

"Safe? Safe from what?" Catherine asked again and again but Cate couldn't seem to answer, would always succumb to sobs. "I don't want to go back to New York. To that apartment. To Christeby's. I don't want any of it."

"Alright," said her mother. "Let's talk in the morning. About what you do want." Leaning down, she kissed her on the forehead and adjusted the covers then left the room and walked downstairs.

Holtie was reading in the living room. The fire was almost out, reduced to a few burning embers, the television was off, the house seemed unnaturally quiet. He put down the book and looked at Catherine.

"I know her friend was killed with that drug person in Miami but I don't know what that has to do with her. They were evidently close friends but . . ." she sat down on the sofa, thinking that Cate had never touched drugs. How could she possibly be connected? "She says she wants to be safe."

Holtie stood up and walked over to where Catherine sat. Standing over her, he put his hand on her shoulder. His voice was soft. "We all want to be safe. Come to bed, my darling."

ROME, ITALY

The little yellow Fiat taxi sped along the highway towards Rome with me in back, my suitcase digging into my leg on the floor beside me. I wanted a shower, fresh clothes, and to talk for hours.

The palazzo is right on Piazza di Spagna. Rowena and Dick's top floor apartment is up several flights of circular stone stairs which are killing the first time but not the second. Maybe it was because by the second time you have seen the view from the terrace and your legs have decided the vantage point is worth the climb. The front door on the street was open so that I didn't have to ring and could take my time. Top floor. I rang the doorbell, panting.

They greeted me with exclamations and embraces. Dick took my suitcase and Rowena led me to one of the guest rooms. "Do whatever you want. Take a shower, have lunch with us, take a nap until dinner, whatever you'd like."

"A shower and I'll be dressed and out in fifteen minutes."

Lunch was festive. A huge bouquet of sunflowers and goose feathers adorned the long trestle table. Rowena is the earth mother I wished I were. Plates of cheeses, olives, prosciutto with figs, breads, two kinds of pasta and tomatoes with buffalo mozzarella and basil were passed back and forth.

"Can't believe I talked you into this! At the last minute." Rowena is older than me, a very pretty woman with dark hair and gray eyes who seems to dress in layers of long skirts, sweaters and shawls. She floats through summer in gauzy caftans. She is English but because her first husband was American she and her daughter, Jazz, spent years in New York. We'd been introduced at a cocktail party the first year I'd been a detective and become friends immediately. I was always a little sorry we hadn't met years before when we'd overlapped in Italy.

"How could I resist? I have been in a state of euphoria since our last phone call." Dick poured more wine into my glass. "Those years here, all those thousands of times wandering through Piazza di Spagna, up and down the via del Corso."

Every time I arrived in Italy I felt joyful. It was nostalgia for being part of the foreign press corps years ago mixed with the delight of the familiar. Now I looked forward to two weeks in this place where the sky seemed a deeper blue than anywhere else.

"I love Rome at Christmas time because the Romans don't become crazed about presents, they don't lose their minds for months in advance the way some of the English and all the Americans do," mused Rowena as she cut another wedge of cheese.

"Let's not talk about losing our minds," said Dick in his dry way. We two women burst into laughter. He was Rowena's rudder and often joked she was insane but only barely managing on the "outside" because of his steadying influence.

After the table had been cleared, Rowena led me out to the terrace; we clutched our wine glasses from lunch. "It's still and always glorious," I proclaimed looking out at rooftops and churches and palm trees. Rome was a watercolor splashed with terracotta, rusts and all shades of yellow from mustard to palest sun color as this was the law. Strict zoning for the centro.

The via Condotti with its chic stores like Valentino and Fendi was one artery stretching below us, the Spanish Embassy was nearby. Piazza del Popolo was just down via Babuino; the Hotel Hassler and the Villa Borghese were behind us.

I was so glad for the invitation to come. The whole summer and fall had been given over to criminal trials, those lunches in New York, to being available for the next Skype call and now I wanted to stop thinking of anyone called Bree, of Chantal, of Jake in prison, of Call Me Jack. I would clear my mind of that case and all its characters. For awhile. Rome with Rowena was the perfect place for me to do that. And then, I would go back refreshed and write the novel.

Inevitably, as I knew it would, the conversation turned to Jazz. Rowena's only child, her only family other than Dick. My dearest friend always blamed herself for the rift, especially after a few glasses of wine. "Why did I have to scream and carry on like a witch?"

Okay, here we go. I'll say the same things I have always said and hope that Rowena will listen. Will hear me. Maybe this time will be different. I suddenly felt very tired from the time change and the wine was adding to the sense of fatigue. "Rowena! You reacted normally. You had just discovered that your beautiful, college-educated daughter was a high-priced call girl! How were you supposed to respond?"

Rowena actually moaned. "I just don't know! Maybe I should have asked her why and listened instead of having a fit!" She took a gulp of wine.

I had heard the story so many times before. I ached for Rowena but found it difficult to summon any sympathy for her daughter. Even after all those hours with Chantal telling me it was easy money and meant nothing. Jazz, with her history, fit the profile; she could have worked for Chantal and Jake. I knew she was making a fortune as a model but Jazz wanted still more, always more, and didn't care how she got it. Rowena didn't want to know that but it was a fact. All over again, Rowena told me how she stormed out. Four years ago.

We sat down on the stone bench side by side. I thought Jazz was one of those daughters born to a mother so different that it was difficult to reconcile they were related in any way, could even be friends. Jazz was selfish, self-serving, self-promoting, materialistic and had a downright mean streak. Rowena told me about her bullying younger girls at school. Though exquisitely beautiful, she could be a real shit. A monster. I'm not sure 'bitch' covers it. Whereas,

Rowena is a lover of all humanity, kind, generous and sensitive.

"Funny thing," she said. "I got an e-mail from Fiona Hamilton and I didn't even know she knew my e-mail. She wrote that she saw Jazz a few weeks ago. In Harrod's."

"Really? So she's living in London?"

"I don't know where she lives. They didn't speak. She was several aisles away in the Food Halls." The Food Halls, marble, grand, enormous, a cathedral of butchers, bakers, fishmongers, purveyors of the best, always clogged with shoppers. "Maybe she was on a trip. Maybe she lives there." Rowena took a swallow of wine and put her glass on the bench. "Maybe I'll never know."

Here we go again, I thought. I put down my wine glass and took both Rowena's hands in mine. She has the most lovely hands. "This can't go on forever." I was on automatic pilot. We'd said all the same things dozens of times. "She knows where you are. She has to decide to come back to you."

"What if she never does?" Rowena's face was etched with pain, her eyes shone with tears.

"Jazz will come back," I said, sounding more positive than I felt. Yes, maybe. Someday.

The two of us sat in silence as the golden Roman afternoon was folded into the navy blue of evening.

I thought it was more than the argument about the escort service. Maybe it went way back to Jazz blaming her mother for what happened to her father. That had been the big argument before. I didn't think it had ever gone away. It had never been resolved and certainly never forgotten.

As if reading my mind, Rowena broke the silence. "When I had to tell that little girl that her father died . . ." She shook her head. Jazz was eight years old. "A month after I asked him to leave the apartment because of the drinking."

"Look at me. Listen to me."

Rowena turned to face me in the fading light. Wine never helped Rowena when she started in on the Jazz saga. I was stern. "You had nothing to do with a horrible accident on the New Jersey Turnpike. What if Jazz had been in the car with him? Have you ever thought of that? What if she had died, too? What if she had ended up in a wheelchair?" My voice was loud, I felt angry and frustrated. This was the same discussion all over again. "You did nothing wrong by showing what you felt about your daughter becoming a prostitute!"

Rowena flinched but I didn't stop. "That's what she was. You said it to her and she, wanting your approval or maybe ashamed in the face of your obvious disapproval, stormed out." I shook my head. "But she can't blame you."

Rowena wiped tears away using both hands. "I know you're right. But it doesn't matter who's right or who's wrong anymore."

"I think she'll get in touch with you when she's done something she is sure you will approve of." I extended my glass towards the sky. It was a gesture partly facetious because I resented this spoiled, selfish, money-hungry girl who caused my sweet friend such pain. "Here's to Jazz. Wherever she is. Harrod's. Wherever."

Rowena lifted her glass and blinked as a tear slipped down her face.

BOSTON

Two psychiatrists were "no help at all," as Holtie put it. "Depression? Yes, I suppose so if you cry all the time," he shrugged in irritation. "How'd they come up with that?"

Cate did stop the full-scale crying but tears welled in her eyes several times a day and she carried Kleenex in the pocket of her jeans. She stayed home, would not even go for a walk, became "far too thin" as her mother put it, and read voraciously. At least a book a day. Boxes from Amazon arrived twice a week.

Two girls from college called and Heather and Bettina called from the auction house. She wouldn't go to the phone.

MANHATTAN

It felt like forever but Kelsey finally got the cast off. Her mother telephones nearly every day, sometimes quite early in the morning. "Yes, okay, I will think about it. Yes, it would be nice to be there for that weekend over New Year's. I'll have to make a reservation soon. I know, Mom." She was plucking her eyebrows at the kitchen table peering into a magnifying mirror. These calls are fine, Kelsey decided, as long as I can put her on speaker and be doing something else at the same time.

She takes cabs all over town to avoid walking past stores, reads no fashion magazines and Bloomingdale's, Bendel's and Bergdorf's are no longer in her life.

BOSTON

The Burroughs had an uncharacteristically quiet Christmas. "Ned telephoned," said Catherine at dinner the next evening. "He heard you were home from his mother who saw Faith Adams at the Gourmet Café. Wants to see you."

Cate was very pale, her cheek bones prominent in her thin face. "White as paper," Angie said to Flora in the kitchen as she put plates in the dish washer.

"He really wants to see you," repeated Catherine. When Cate didn't answer, Holtie asked, "Why don't you see him?"

"Okay."

It was as simple as that. The next afternoon, Ned arrived at the front door wearing a navy blue parka, his old tan corduroy trousers, his beat-up topsiders. He seemed to take up too much space in the front hall under the chandelier with his radiant good health, his broad shoulders, his big confident smile. Cate sat on the top step like a little girl watching him greet her mother. He looked up at her and called, "Hey, first mate, get down here! You want to go sailing? It's only forty degrees on the water but the wind's good. Can you handle that?"

Cate descended the stairs slowly, wearing a baggy gray sweater and jeans that had become at least one size too big. She hesitated on the bottom step and then, wordlessly, ran into his arms, sobbing violently.

Catherine left them, feeling helpless, thinking that the last time they'd seen each other Cate had given the ring back. She went into the kitchen to discuss a grocery list with Angie but kept waiting to hear the sound of the front door closing so that she could go back and comfort the daughter who had become a sad, strangely fearful waif. Someone she scarcely recognized.

Ten minutes later, the kitchen's swinging door was pushed open. It was Ned. "Mrs. Burroughs, we're going out in the Snipe. I've got foul weather gear in the car and we're off. I'll have her home in time for dinner."

Three days later, they were engaged. The wedding would be as soon as possible. It was a different ring, a different Cate. Ned was euphoric.

JANUARY, 2009

The secret of life is to appreciate the pleasure of being terribly, terribly deceived.
—Oscar Wilde

LAKE FOREST, ILLINOIS

Brad Taylor Baker knew people were talking about him, about what he was doing but he didn't give a damn. His thinking was that she was an adult and could make up her own mind. "It's just that I'm my dad's daughter," she had grinned at their first dinner.

And now, he thought, my old college roommate is about to become my father-in-law. It's hardly incestuous. It's just a little age thing.

On this Saturday afternoon, Brad was at his new house in Lake Forest crouched on the living room hearth building a fire. Reaching for an old newspaper to crush and put under the kindling, he saw that it was the Sunday *Boston Globe*.

The paper had come to the Chicago office for a while when he was making so many business trips to the East Coast and now it was being forwarded to the house. He'd speak to Megan about canceling it. It was last weekend's paper. Shaking it out, Brad saw the front page of the Weddings section and felt a jolt of recognition. He didn't have to read a word to know it was his daughter. Brad stared at the oval face, the cloud of dark hair and experienced something close to pain in his chest.

"Darling," came the voice from the front hall. "Do you want to have an early dinner in there beside the fire?"

He turned to look at her as she came into the room; she was petite, slender, with black hair and blue eyes, even features. Her name was Carlene but he had nicknamed her Kitty. "Terrific idea," he answered then he wadded up the page, stuffed it under the logs and lit the match.

MANHATTAN

Kelsey received her History of Art doctorate from Yale. She thinks she might like to teach but there is no rush to decide. Karen, who cried all one Sunday afternoon over Mr. Beluga, has her own website charging $3,500 an hour. She uses the PayPal account her brother set up. Most of the money goes straight to Visa but some of it pays for the psychiatrist.

SAN FRANCISCO

George Forrester and Diane Montague were married last October in Aix-en-Provence. Her sisters and her aunts were invited to the wedding, of course, and

George decided to take a chance and invite his cousin. Lori couldn't come but she sent a pair of elegant silver candlesticks. The Forresters are now living in a suite at the Fairmont Hotel until they find just the right house. They want to be settled in San Francisco before the baby comes though they plan to keep Diane's apartment in Paris as a pied-à-terre. George is taking French lessons.

MANHATTAN

Sharon Cantor did not become a guest on *Oprah*, did not talk to Larry King, did not write a book describing the agony of being a political wife, and she did not divorce her husband. There were no interviews, no salacious details, no news at all from her and soon the mocking 'she stood by her man' snipes stopped. It was announced that former New York State Governor Teddy Cantor had signed a contract with CNN; he would appear five evenings a week as co-host of a political talk show with a Pulitzer prize-winning female journalist.

NIOU, BURKINA FASO

Brooke sat on a very low, rickety little stool in the back of the classroom. Her knees were under her chin; there was mud on her jeans and her sneakers were soaked. Her rear hurt from being bounced around in the truck.

Thirty-three little African children shouted what seemed to be numbers at the teacher who stood in front of the room beside a chalkboard. They were loud and enthusiastic and when any one of them turned to look at Brooke, she would smile and they would giggle.

Bettie crouched down then sat on the earth floor beside her. "Ça va bien?"

"Oh, yes," said Brooke. "Très, très bien." She could not remember being this happy for a long time.

MANHATTAN

Mark and Lori left Brooklyn the first week of January and moved into a very large, modern penthouse on 66th Street and Third Avenue, a short walk from the spa. It would be temporary until the renovations were done; they were still looking for their perfect living situation.

On this evening, from the kitchen, Mark proposed a toast to Brooke. "She'll be there for another two months."

"I know you miss her," called Lori from where she sat on the living room floor opening boxes. "But think of what she's doing and of what adventures she's having."

Pop! went the champagne cork. Mark rushed in handing her the flute which was overflowing and they both laughed. "To Brooke," said Lori. "To a woman as fantastic and special as you always said she was."

Mark raised his glass, suddenly feeling nearly overcome with emotion. "To a generous woman with a beautiful heart who might just change the world with kindness."

KEY BISCAYNE

Annie's funeral was at the family's Lutheran church and the burial was next to her grandparents. After New Year's, Kristin flew to Miami to pack up her sister's apartment. Mira Properties would handle the sale and put the condo on the market the first of February.

Kristin found the little collection, just as Pedro had. She emptied the drawer on the bed and picked up the onyx cuff link, examined the diamond stud for a dress shirt, scooped up the collar stays and the gold tie clip shaped like an arrow, and stared at them. Some bad feeling made her bring the black garbage bag from the kitchen and toss every little item into it. Then she began work on the closets. She cried folding her sister's clothes and putting them in boxes and she cried when she saw the framed photograph of herself on the little desk in the den. That night she cried in her sister's bed.

The next morning she realized she'd done nothing in the kitchen and opened cabinets and tossed cans of tuna in a cardboard box. There wasn't much. She'd leave it. The refrigerator was nearly empty but the cigar box with the money in it was in the freezer behind a pint of Häagen-Dazs peppermint ice cream. Under it, nearly hidden in the frost were the sandwich bags filled with more cash. Kristin sat on the Mexican tile floor and counted seventy-one thousand dollars. All in hundreds, tightly pinched in rubber bands. When she had finished counting, she said out loud, "Please, don't ever let me know where this came from. Please," she said, in a whisper to no one. "Don't let me ever know."

The bills were divided into bundles and put in the side pockets of her carry-on suitcase. The six boxes of clothes, photographs, jewelry and shoes would be sent to Delafield via UPS by Marta later in the week. The furniture and the modern paintings would be part of the condo sale. Now, Annie's car. It would have to be so sold. Maybe one of the realtors would take care of that.

The little car was downstairs sitting in its assigned parking place. Kristin saw the yellow Mini Cooper and decided that it was more like her sister than the apartment or anything in it. She would drive it back to Wisconsin. The super of the condo took the spare set of keys from the wall board in the garage office and walked over to her. "We keep them for emergencies," he explained. Kristin thanked him. She could be her sister's twin, he thought. Awful what happened to her. He wondered if she were in the same business.

Kristin opened the trunk which was now empty. She slammed it closed and got into the driver's seat. The car started immediately. She checked the gas gauge and turned off the ignition. The super watched her, in her short dress, get out of the car. "Do I owe you anything for keeping it here?"

"Not a cent," he said. "It's part of the deal when you have a condo."

"Oh, that's so nice," she smiled. He felt good about not asking her for money when he could have. But maybe things shake out even, he thought. Me and Carmen are having a lotta fun with all the toys and crèmes I found in the bag I took from the trunk.

BOSTON

Catherine did not ask Holtie for advice. She googled and read all she could about capital gains and taxes. Half of the Quire stock she sold before the end of December so that it would count as income for 2008 and today she had given the order to sell the rest. Bill had told her she had every right to and to declare the profit and move on with her life. Fine. She didn't want to ever think of it again. She went online then tapped in the symbol for Quire and saw that it had increased by another twenty-one dollars a share since the mammoth leap that had initially triggered the drama. There was still all that money stuffed in brown envelopes in her drawers, in her hatboxes, jammed behind the chest in her dressing room which was too heavy for the maid to move when she cleaned.

She and Holtie would never worry about money again.

Catherine's diamond and sapphire engagement ring sparkled as she closed the laptop. All those afternoons she had taken it off and left it in her jewelry box. Brad's face flashed into her mind, his grin. The white suite of light and glass and chrome. Those FBI bulldogs and Bill Middleton. The Cowboy from Houston with the huge belt buckle. It was over. She was safe. She stared out the window and whispered, "Thank you, god of the sky, god of the clouds. Thank you. Oh, thank you."

ROME

That first week of January, Rome returned to normal. The centro seemed to be exhaling after the excitement of Christmas. My Italian was coming back to me and I felt content; Philadelphia didn't exist. Rowena and I had been out all afternoon. It was the bakery, the wine shop, the best place for that special cheese, the butcher shop with the incredible prosciutto, and Campo dei Fiori for everything else.

As we panted up the final flight of stairs, with bags hanging from all four wrists, we heard laughter. Pushing open the apartment door which was never locked, Rowena gasped.

"Mother?" A tall, slender, very lovely brunette was standing by the fireplace.

Rowena dropped the bread; the wine bottles clanked on the stone floor as she rushed to take her daughter in her arms. Then she pulled away and stared at her as if confirming the reality. "This is Lawrence," said Jazz. "I married an Aussie. An awesome Aussie," she grinned at the figure beside her.

Rowena then embraced a strikingly good-looking man in a tweed sports jacket, who smiled widely. "Heard a lot about you," he said with a note of innuendo. Rowena laughed and teased back. "An Australian? With a slight Scottish accent? Who dreamt you up?"

The voice. At that moment, I knew. Call Me Jack was standing ten feet away. All these overlapping circles. Jazz. A madam named Bree. Skype, the phone calls from Rowena, those lunches with Chantal talking endlessly about Jake and the Imperial Club and it all adds up to this: Jazz and Call Me Jack and me here in Rome. All of us with our secrets in the same room. Call Me Jack's money actually paid for my ticket to be face to face with him at last.

"Charlie! Been such a long time!" said Jazz smoothly. "How are you?" That lazy, slow, seductive smile. We kissed on each cheek. She was wearing a brown velvet empire dress and chocolate brown knee-high boots. Her hazel eyes seemed larger than anyone else's; the wide, clear forehead, the widow's peak and the thick mane of shining hair all set her apart. Much later, one would notice that she had her mother's elegant, long-fingered hands. "Charlie meet Lawrence. Lawrence, meet Charlie McCall, one of Mother's best friends in the whole world."

I had to give him credit. He was unblinking, suave, charming. "Never met a glamorous Charlie before."

"And I've never met an Australian with a Scottish accent," I countered.

"Scottish grandparents," he explained. "I lived with them until I was twelve and some of that brogue stuck with me. Lucky for me, Jazz claims to actually like it."

"Vino!" said Dick. "Lawrence, help me do the honors. Glasses in the cabinet. Nope. Other side of the fireplace."

"Mother," said Jazz taking her hand and leading her towards one of the guest rooms. She put one finger to her lips. "I think he's sleeping."

Rowena came out a moment later and grabbed my arm. "A little boy! Jazz had a little boy! He's adorable, he's perfect, he's . . ." Her face crumpled and she started to cry.

I pushed her into the kitchen and handed her a paper napkin. Rowena blew her nose; her face was pink and splotchy with tears but she was smiling. There was laughter from the living room. Rowena said softy, "Thanks for listening to me say all the same things all these years."

"We're even. You're endured my love affairs."

Jazz appeared in the doorway and wordlessly put her arms around her mother. Another burst of masculine laughter from the living room. I left the kitchen to join the men, to set the table for dinner.

That night in bed, I lay awake in the dark. Dear Rowena. She'd suffered so much over Jazz. The prodigal Jazz was back. She was no longer the scatter-brained model who hooked on the side but a wife and mother. She would always be self-centered and a bit ruthless but she was back. With a husband who doesn't entirely trust her. Which isn't a bad thing. However, they seem entirely besotted with each other, as Rowena would say.

He hired me right after the arrests, the explosion of the club. Jazz would have been pregnant. That December deadline. The due date. And he was suspicious it wasn't his? Suspicious that Jazz might have gone back to her old life? Had she ever left it? What, if anything, had she told him? Maybe he was on the edge of leaving her and December was his personal deadline. Maybe somehow he knew he couldn't be the father but then he saw the baby and didn't care. Maybe he thinks the baby looks just like him and that isn't it at all. Maybe I've got it all wrong. Maybe Jazz left her old life when she married him. What if he was a client and that's how they met? Maybe she stopped sleeping with strangers and he didn't. Maybe he was waiting to be blackmailed. Maybe he thought Jazz would leave him if he didn't pay and she found out. Maybe when it didn't happen by December, he decided it wasn't going to happen at all. Maybe . . .

I fluffed my pillow and pulled the duvet up to my chin. This is so typical of my life as a detective: I will never know the whole story. I fell asleep with the window open and piano music coming from somewhere across the piazza.

THE END